Two Worlds, Two Loves...

From the moment she saw Chris caressing another woman in the bed they shared, Gillian knew she had to escape. She could no longer live with him, and didn't want the child she had conceived by him.

So she left San Francisco to live and work in New York. Soon she had begun an exciting career—and a delicious romance with Gordon, a gentle and mature man who was devoted to her. Her problems all seemed solved.

But the rich passion of a genuine love is not so easily forgotten....

DANIELLE STEEL

GOING HOME

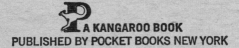

A KANGAROO BOOK
PUBLISHED BY POCKET BOOKS NEW YORK

Distributed in Canada by PaperJacks Ltd., a Licensee
of the trademarks of Simon & Schuster, a division of
Gulf+Western Corporation.

Another *Original* publication of POCKET BOOKS

The quotation appearing on page vii is taken from Sonnet XLVIII of "Fatal Interview" by Edna St. Vincent Millay. *Collected Poems*, Harper & Row, Publishers, Inc. Copyright 1931, © 1958 by Edna St. Vincent Millay and Norma Millay Ellis. Reprinted here by permission.

POCKET BOOKS, a Simon & Schuster division of
GULF & WESTERN CORPORATION
1230 Avenue of the Americas, New York, N.Y. 10020
In Canada distributed by PaperJacks Ltd.,
330 Steelcase Road, Markham, Ontario.

ISBN: 0-671-82770-7

First Pocket Books printing October, 1973

Trademarks registered in the United States and other countries.

Printed in Canada.

To the endless list of people who have meant so very much to me, and this book. I address you alphabetically, because there is no order to how I needed you. I loved and needed you all.

Kate Reed Cains
John Mack Carter
Sidney M. Ehrman
Charles Flowers
Franklin K. Gray
Edward Kessler Jr.
Timmie Scott Mason
Inez Nutzman
Mary Evans Richie
John Schulein-Steel
Kuniko Schulein-Steel
Fred R. Smith
Norma Stone
Phyllis Westberg

and especially to Clo and Beatie, for putting up with it all.

Now by the path I climbed, I journey back.
The oaks have grown; I have been long away,
Taking with me your memory and your lack,
I now descend into a milder day.

—Edna St. Vincent Millay

GOING
HOME

1

It was a gloriously sunny day and the call from Carson Advertising came at nine-fifteen. The stylist was sick and they needed someone to assist with a shooting up the coast. Was I free? Would I do it? And how much? I was, I would, and the price was right. One hundred and twenty dollars for the day, plus expenses. After working as a stylist in New York, I had been lucky in California. They were impressed, and they paid well. And it was easy work. All I needed was a job or two a week and, added to my alimony, Samantha and I could live well. Sometimes there was no work for a few weeks, but we made out anyway, and we were happy.

We had left New York one grizzly, rainy day, like pioneers off to another world. I was twenty-eight, she was almost five, and I think we were both scared. Brave New World. And off we went. To San Francisco, where we knew no one, but it was pretty and it was worth a try. So we were trying.

We'd been there for a little less than three months the day that Carson called me for the job on the coast. We lived in a tiny flat in the Marina, with a peaceful view of the bay and Sausalito in the distance. We could look out the window and see the sailboat masts just out front, as the boats bobbed around tied up at the Yacht Club dock. And on sunny afternoons when I wasn't working, I could take Sam down to the tiny strip of beach, and I'd lie there while she raced up and down the sand and then up the steps onto the grass. It was still snowing in New York while we were lying on the beach. We had done the right thing, and we'd come to a lovely place. We were happy there. We were alone and still very green at being pioneers, but everything was going to be okay. I'd look at my daughter, all brown and healthy, and I'd look at myself in the mirror in the mornings, and I'd know we had been right. I looked ten years younger, and at last I was alive. Gillian Forrester had been reborn at twenty-eight, in a city that spread itself over a series of beautiful hills, next to the mountains, and within breathing distance of the sea. San Francisco.

I looked out the window at Mount Tamalpais in the distance that morning, and then at my watch. It was nine-thirty, and the truck from Carson was due at ten. The crew was driving out together, except for the people from the film company who were shooting the commercial. They had their own truck. And probably their own ideas. I wondered briefly what they were going to think of having me to "help" them. Probably not much. The advertising agencies always liked to have an extra hand, but cameramen and the like never thought much of the idea. Thus far, it had been kind of "Who's she? . . . What? . . . A stylist? . . . Man, you've gotta be kidding . . . From New York? . . . Oh, Christ . . ." Yeah, but what the hell. I was getting paid for the job, and they didn't have to like me. As long as the agencies liked my work and kept calling.

The school bus had already picked up Sam, and I had just enough time to shower and climb into a pair of ancient jeans, a denim shirt, and my safari jacket. It was always hard to tell about the weather. It was early April, and it might be cold if the shooting got late. And sooner or later the fog would roll in. I dug my feet into an old pair of riding boots, put my hair in a knot on top of my head. And I was all set. A quick call to a neighbor who would wait for Sam to pile off the school bus at noon and keep her till I got home, and I was all ready for Carson Advertising.

We were to shoot a cigarette commercial on some cliffs overlooking the sea, north of Bolinas. And they were using four models, some horses, and a fair amount of props. It was going to be one of those healthy looking ads with the deceptive air of nonchalance and fresh air. Fresh air there would be, but nonchalance relatively little. Hence the need for me. I would spend the day making sure the models looked right, setting out the picnic, making sure the two female models didn't sit on the horses the wrong way round, and no one fell off the cliffs. Fairly easy work for a hundred and twenty dollars, and it might be fun.

A horn honked outside at exactly ten o'clock, and I sped out the door with my "magic bag" over my arm. Band-aids, aspirin, tranquilizers, hair spray, a variety of makeups, a note book, a collection of pens and pencils, safety pins, clothespins, and a book. The book was an anthology of short stories I never got to read at shootings. But it gave me a nice illusion of "one of these days."

As I hopped down the three steps outside our flat I saw a dark green pickup truck and a military-looking jeep out front. The truck was filled to the gills with equipment and props; there were two sleepy-looking girls in the back with sweaters pulled up to their chins and scarves over their heads. They looked like the Bobbsey Twins. Our female models. Sitting in front were two frighteningly virile-looking guys, also in turtle neck sweaters, with carefully kept ear-length hair and strong jaw lines. Their whole look told me that they were gay, and I knew that they were the male half of our modeling team for the day. All set. At least they'd shown up for the shooting. But I had stopped worrying about things like that. In San Francisco, people show. It's not like New York. They don't get as much work, so when they get a call, they show. The male beauty queen seated nearest the window waved, and the man in the driver's seat slid out and came toward me with a smile. He was small and sturdy-looking with jet black hair and bushy eyebrows, and I had met him at other shootings with Carson Advertising. He was their chief art director, and a hell of a nice guy. His name was Joe Tramino.

"Hi, Gillian. How've you been? I'm glad you could make it."

"So am I. Looks like a nice day for the shooting. Are the guys in the jeep with you too?" We stood on the sidewalk and he rolled his eyes in semi-Neapolitan style.

"You bet your ass. Those are the account guys. Three of them. This commercial is for our biggest account. I'll introduce you." He strode over on his short legs and one of the men in the jeep rolled down the window. "This is our stylist, Gillian Forrester. Gill . . . John Ackley, Hank Todd, Mike Willis." They all nodded, smiled, and shook hands with me, without looking particularly interested. They had a fifty-thousand-dollar commercial to get out for an important client. And that was all they cared about. Making charm with the stylist wasn't what they had in mind.

"You wanna ride with them or with us? It's gonna be crowded either way." Joe shrugged his shoulders and watched me for a minute, wondering what I would decide. I could tell that he liked me and thought I was a "good looking broad." I was a little taller than he, and my complexion was as fair as his was dark. That was probably what fascinated him. My brown hair and blue eyes had never seemed like such a big deal to me, but he seemed to like the combination, and I could tell he liked my ass.

"I'll ride with the crew, Joe. No sweat. . . . Nice to meet you, gentlemen. We'll see you there." I looked at Joe as we walked away from the jeep, and broke into a laugh. "Surprised? What do you think I am? A snob?" I gave him a friendly shove and then hopped in the back seat of the truck with the girls. One of them was asleep and the other was reading a magazine; the boys up front were talking "shop." According to them, men's fashion was going all to hell. I saw Joe roll his eyes and give me a wry grin in the rearview mirror and then we were off. He slid the gear into drive, let out the brake, and stomped on the accelerator, and we sped around the jeep and off toward Lombard Street, which would get us onto the Golden Gate Bridge.

"Jesus Christ, Joe, you drive like a goddam Italian." I was hanging on to the front seat so as not to squash the girl sleeping next to me.

"I make love like an Italian too."

"I'll bet."

"What's the point of betting? Try me sometime. . . . Try it . . . you'll like it."

"Yeah, sure." I smiled back, and then sank into my own thoughts as we approached the Golden Gate Bridge which never failed to have an effect on me. A feeling of overwhelming power and beauty would sweep over me, and I'd raise my eyes to dizzying heights, like a child, feeling pleased with the effect. The deep orange color of its spires stood out in the blue sky, and its sweeping lines reminded me of kite strings.

"Whatcha looking at, New York?" Joe had seen the slow smile spread over my face, and I leaned against the window and looked upward.

"I'm looking at your bridge, Joe, just like a hick."

"Come on, I'll give you a better view than that." He leaned backward in the seat, turned a handle in the ceiling of the car, and slid a panel back. It was a sun roof, and by opening it the view had improved still further. The Golden Gate Bridge stood over our heads in the sunlight, and the fresh Northern California air whipped our faces.

"Wow . . . this is neat. Can I stand up?" The opening looked just big enough.

"Sure. Don't step on the girls though. And look out for the cops. They'll give me a ticket." I saw him watching my behind again as I gently placed my feet between the two sleeping girls and disappeared through the roof. He was some Italian. And that was some bridge! It was hard to breathe, standing unprotected in the wind, and my hair started to whip around my head. And up above was . . . it. My bridge. And my mountains and my sea. And off in the distance behind us, the city. My California. It was stupendous.

I felt Joe tug at my jacket as we approached the end of it, and I came back in and sat down.

"Happy now?"

"Yeah."

"All you Easterners are nuts." But he looked pleased

with what I'd done. There was a nice atmosphere in the car, everyone was minding his own business, we were all going to work, and no one was feeling hassled. It was a far cry from what I'd experienced working in New York, first at an ad agency and later at a decorating magazine. Everything was different in California.

"Who's shooting the commercial? Shazzam or Barclay?" I had learned that Shazzam was the "in" new group that did most of the really with-it movie production in town and Barclay was the most established production house around.

"Neither one. That's why all the account guys came along. They're tearing their hair out. I'm using a new house. They're young, but they're good. They're not even a house, really, just a team. A crazy young guy and his crew. They look like lazy, good for nothing freaks, but they've really got it. And their bid was terrific. I think you'll like them, they're easy to work with." I nodded, wondering if they'd like me. "Freaks" don't usually like stylists from New York, even if I didn't look like one anymore.

We were past Sausalito and Mill Valley by then and already on the winding mountain road toward Stinson Beach. It was lined with immense trees, and the smell of eucalyptus was everywhere. And it was beginning to feel more like a day in the country than a job.

The models were all awake by then and everyone was in a good mood. We started down the other side of the mountain and the view was breathtaking. Great splashes of panorama would appear, the mountains would drop down to cliffs at unexpected moments and the sea roared up to meet them with a great gush of spray. Everything was lush green and soft brown and bright blue. God's country.

We came down the mountain singing songs and then drove on past Bolinas up the coast to a place I didn't know. But it was more of the same. More mountains, more sea, more cliffs, and more splendor. And I was glad I'd come.

"You look like a kid at a birthday party, Gill."

"Oh shut up, you blasé dago. That's the way I feel about this place."

"It sure as hell ain't New York."

"Thank God."

"Is that so?" He grinned at me again and pulled the car off the road onto a dirt track which led across some hills, high above the coastline.

"Where the hell is this place?" The models were craning their necks but there was nothing to see. We were miles from civilization. There was still no sign of a waiting film crew.

"You'll see in a minute. It took the camera boys three weeks to scout this place. It's fantastic. Belongs to some old lady who lives in Hawaii and hasn't been here in years. She rented it to us for the day."

We came to a bend in the road then and swooped down toward a plateau lodged between the hills and the cliffs. The sea was hurling itself at the shore with greater force than I'd seen at Big Sur, and there were trees sticking out along the cliffs like giant flags. Huge boulders stood in the water below and the spray sprang up from them so high that it seemed as though it could have watered the trees. Maybe it did.

I saw the jeep then and wondered how they got there before we did, especially the way Joe drove, but there they were, parked alongside a horse trailer, an old car, and a dilapidated truck with a lot of hippies crawling all over it. We hopped out of the pickup truck and the various groups merged into one as everyone prepared to do their bit and get the show on the road.

The account men from the Carson agency stood slightly aside in a nervous little clique and began to look over their notes. The models jumped back into the pickup and started doing their faces and hair. They left me with Joe and a bunch of rag-tag looking boys who looked like they had run away from home the day before.

I watched them unload their heavy equipment as though it were weightless and saw Joe standing near the cab of the truck with a tall, blond boy. He had a strong, muscular body, a full head of shaggy hair, strangely wide-set eyes, and an incredible smile that exploded two deeply entrenched dimples. And I saw that he was watching me.

"Gill, come here a minute," Joe called out to me with a wave and I wandered toward them wondering which of the crew this boy was. He looked younger than the others and seemed to have less to do. "Gillian Forrester, Chris Matthews. He runs this madhouse."

"Hi." The smile widened and I saw that he had beautiful teeth. His eyes were of a soft green color. He didn't hold out a hand to shake, or seem particularly interested in who I was. He just stood there, nodded at me, seemed to keep an eye on his troops, and went on talking to Joe. It made me feel a little out of place.

"Hey . . . where you going?" Chris asked. I had decided to go back and check up on my models.

"I thought you two were busy. I'll be back."

"Wait a sec, I'll come with you. I want to see what I'm shooting." He left Joe and strode along the hillside with me, kicking through the weeds in his boots and looking up at the sky. He had all the mannerisms of a young boy.

The models introduced themselves and I was pleased to see them looking about right. They were pros and it was nice not to have to start from scratch with them. I had been on a shooting the week before with a bunch of kids who hardly knew how to comb their hair.

Chris stood aside from the group after a moment and then shook his head. "Joe!" His shout rang down the hill and caught Joe's attention instantly. The kid had a hell of a voice. He beckoned to Joe and I could see there was a problem but I didn't want to intrude. It was obviously between him and Joe.

"Okay. What's up?" The little Italian huffed and puffed as he got there and he didn't look happy. He sensed that there was trouble and that was all he needed, with the account boys sitting on his neck.

"We've got a problem. And it's going to throw the budget out of shape. You've got five models. We only needed four." Chris looked unhappy about the excess and Joe looked baffled.

"We do?" He cast a glance into the truck and shook his head. "No, we don't, you jerk. What'sa matter? You can't count? One, two, three, four." He pointed to them one by one, and he was right. Four.

"Five." Chris shook his head and pointed again. And Joe and I both burst into laughter as he did. He was pointing at me.

"Four. Relax. I'm the stylist. I thought you knew." Joe gave him a friendly shove. Chris burst into a laugh himself and the dimples came to life. Then he shook his head.

"Christ, you should've told me. What the hell do I know? All I do is take pretty pictures. I wouldn't mind taking some of you sometime either." He faced me with a long appraising look.

"Flattery will get you nowhere, Mr. Matthews."

"No. But it'll get me a friendly stylist. Get your ass in gear, lady. I start shooting in five minutes. And if your models aren't ready, you know what happens?" He was looking at me in a fierce, unfriendly way, and I suddenly decided that I wasn't so far from New York after all. They're all the same. I shook my head in answer to his question and waited for him to threaten to fire me. "If they're not ready, it's simple. We all quit and get stoned. You think I want to bust my ass working all day? No way." He shook his head and threw up his hands with a gentle look as Joe and I started to laugh again, and then Joe tried to put on a serious face. He could see that the men in the jeep were watching us.

"Listen, you lazy bastard. Stop threatening my fancy stylist. And get off your ass. Move it out." He gave a military sounding yell, and Chris ran back down the hill. We were finally about to start.

The horses were led toward us, the models were in full uniform, and the camera equipment was all set. Some of Chris's men lit a blazing campfire and I went to check out the food to make sure it looked right for the "picnic" we were shooting. The food was all cemented into place and heavily lacquered so as to look right, and it seemed fine to me. I spread it on the ground, loosened a scarf around the neck of one of the boys, calmed down the female models' hair, put a little more rouge on the second man, and moved back. I'd be busier later in the shooting when things started to look rumpled.

I watched Chris with amusement as we got under way. He joked with everyone, shot from a variety of strange positions, and heckled the models. He had everyone in hysterics at the end of half an hour and the account men looked alternately thunderous and panic-stricken. At one point he disappeared down the side of the cliff, and with a clutch of fear in the pit of my stomach I assumed we had lost our photographer. Joe and I raced to the edge to see what had happened, fear in our eyes. As we leaned over, Joe bellowed Chris's name toward the water, but there was no answer and there was nothing to see. He had vanished. . . . Oh my God. . . .

"Chris . . ." Joe tried again, and the echoes seemed endless, but then I saw him.

"Shhhh . . . what'd you want to do? Scare the shit out of me? I'm having a smoke. Come on down." He was sitting on an indented and well hidden ledge, not six feet down from the top, straddling a sturdy looking bush and smoking a joint.

"You crazy sonofabitch, what the hell . . ." Joe was incensed, but visibly relieved. And I burst into nervous laughter. The guy was obviously nuts but he was so natural about everything he did that he was easily forgiven the outrages he perpetrated on the world.

"Is this our break?" I tried to seem as though I were not impressed, but I was. For a moment, I had been so sure that he was gone.

"Yeah. Sure. You smoke?" I nodded and then shook my head.

"Yes. But not on a job."

"And neither should you, you crazy bastard. Get the hell up here and come back to work. What am I going to tell the account guys?" Joe looked genuinely nervous.

"You really want to know what to tell them?" Chris looked pleased at the idea. "Tell them that they can . . ." Joe cut him off and looked apologetically at me.

"Come on, Chris . . . please . . ." By then I was in stitches again. The whole scene was so absurd. Joe and I were leaning down talking to an invisible bush off the side of a cliff, and our chief film genius for the day was enjoying a leisurely smoke of dope. We had already waved to the rest of the crew to let them know that everything was okay, but it must have looked ridiculous anyway.

"Okay, little Joe. I'm a-comin'. Up, up, and away." And with that, the long, lean, muscular body of Christopher Matthews sailed past us and landed back on the plateau. He took something out of his pocket and the next thing I knew there was a shrill whistling sound in the air. He had blown a little toy whistle and pulled a water pistol out of his pocket. "Come on, you guys, let's get this show on the road." He then proceeded to squirt everyone within range, including the account men from Carson, and he looked immensely pleased with himself. He was having a good time. "Places . . . action. . . ." A pair of sunglasses emerged from another pocket and he was busily playing director when I went back to set up the picnic again. One of the horses had walked across the set. It took me ten minutes to get everything back in place, and after that I sat back on the running board of Chris's truck to watch them shoot, feeling useless, but amused. It was the best shooting I'd been to in years.

"What do you think, Gill?" Joe collapsed next to me and lit a cigar.

"It's hard to tell. Either he's brilliant or he's a disaster. I'll reserve judgment till I see the film. He's nice to work with anyway. How old is he?" I figured he was about twenty-two and maybe fresh out of some new-wave film school.

"I'm not sure. Somewhere in his thirties, but nobody's told him yet. He acts like he's twelve. And man, I hope he does some good stuff for me today, or else I can forget my job, starting now." We both glanced over toward his col-

leagues and Joe shook his head. He was right, with the
show Chris was putting on his work was going to have to
be fantastic to justify the fooling around.

I watched in mild amazement as everyone went through
their paces though, and there didn't seem to be any problems. His men did precisely what he wanted, the models
were marvelously loose and unselfconscious, and things
were moving along. It was hard to tell exactly where
things were at, but it looked as though the shooting was almost over. And then suddenly I knew that, whether or not
the work was done, it was. Chris stopped dead for a brief
moment, looked around blindly at the crew, and then
began to reel to one side, clutching his heart. This time I
was sure he wasn't faking, he was sick. I wondered briefly
if it were an overdose of something as he slid to the
ground and lay there unconscious.

Joe and I arrived at his side within the same instant and
Joe gently turned him over. He had been lying face down
on the ground. And as we rolled him onto his back and I
reached for his pulse, his face broke into a vast, boyish
grin, and he giggled.

"Fooled ya, huh?" He was delighted. But not for long.
Joe pinned him to the ground and pointed toward something behind him while looking straight at me. And I knew
what he meant. The water bucket for the horses. I ran to
get it, emptied it a bit so I could carry it, and rushed back
to dump it on Chris. All of it. But he only laughed harder,
and then I was pinned to the ground and he was pulling
my hair, which had come undone.

With that, the agency men ran up to see what was going
on and Chris's men and the models joined in the fray.
It was a free-for-all. I heard Joe shout over the din
that we were all through shooting so not to worry, and
I went right on wrestling with Chris Matthews until I felt
Chris put something strange and pointed between my ribs.
I tried to see what it was.

"Don't move, Forrestal. Just get up and start walking."
His face and dialogue were straight out of a grade B Western.

"In the first place, the name's Forrester, and in the second place, just what exactly do you think you're doing?" I tried to sound unruffled and at the same time awesome, but didn't succeed.

"We're gonna ride, little lady. Just step lively . . . nice 'n easy. . . ." I knew the guy was nuts as I suddenly realized that he had a gun in my ribs. What the hell had Joe gotten me into for a hundred and twenty bucks? I wasn't working for him to get shot in the back for chrissake . . . what about Samantha? "Keep moving . . . that's it. . . ." He was walking gingerly at my side, and my eyes searched wildly for Joe in the tangle of arms and legs and water on the ground. They were still going at it. I saw that Chris was walking me toward the horses, and watched him deftly untie one from the back of their trailer with one hand while still keeping the gun on me, which I couldn't see.

"Come on, damn you. Cut it out. The fun's over." At least it was for me.

"Nope. It's just beginning." He spotted a megaphone lying near the trailer, dragged it closer with his foot, and then kicked it into the air so he could catch it, never loosening his hold on either the horse's reins or the gun. He seemed to know exactly what he was doing and punctuated most of his actions with his dazzling smile. To hell with his smile. I had had enough. "Bruno!" The sound of his voice boomed through the megaphone. "Pick me up at the Watson in Bolinas at eight." I saw an arm wave in the crowd and then felt the gun push harder into my flesh. What was the Watson? And why eight? It was only a little after one, and what the hell was he going to do to me? "Get up. You do know how to ride, don't you?" A momentary worried look crossed his face, like a little boy who's been given a cap gun with no caps in it.

"Yes, I can ride. But I don't think this is funny at all. I have a little girl and if you shoot me you're going to wreck a whole lot of lives." It was a dumb melodramatic thing to say, but it was all I could think of under the circumstances.

"I'll keep that in mind." He looked singularly unmoved

by my speech and I swung into the saddle, glad I'd worn
my boots, and wondering what was next. He hopped up
behind me, I felt the gun still in the same place, and burst
into a fresh wave of worry as he nudged the horse into a
fast trot and then a slow gallop. What if the gun went off
by mistake? What would happen then? The mountains
were rough terrain to ride over and the horse might stum-
ble, and then . . .

In less than a minute, we were out of sight of the plateau where we'd been shooting and we were faced with the
splendid range I'd admired on the drive over. But it was a
whole other thing to ride over the mountains and I didn't
give a damn if they were beautiful, I'd had it. Suddenly a
wave of fury swept over me at this insane boy-man who
was playing with my life. He was a snotty, pompous, care-
less, stupid hippie who thought he could do anything he
damn well pleased, from getting stoned on a job, to pretending he had died or fainted, to shooting me. . . . Well, he
was wrong. He couldn't shoot me at least. My body had
tensed into a steel beam and I swung around with every
intention of knocking him off the horse. But when I turned
around my attack was temporarily delayed by a squirt of
cold water in my face. The water pistol . . . that's what he
had been holding in my back all along.

"You lousy, rotten . . . ," I spluttered within two inches
of his face, trying to wipe the water out of my eyes, and
wanting to kill him. "You big shit . . . you . . . I thought . . ."

"Shut up." He squirted the pistol in my mouth this time,
and I choked on a burst of laughter. Christopher Matthews was something else.

The horse had come to a stop at some point during
Chris's watery attack on me, but I didn't notice until I had
wiped the water from my eyes and saw that we were
standing near another cliff again, with the Pacific stretching as far as we could see.

"Pretty, isn't it?" His face was peaceful and he looked
like a cowboy in repose. The mischievous child was momentarily gone. I nodded and looked out to sea, again
with that immense feeling of having found my way to

where I had been meant to be all my life. The hysterical feeling of riding over the mountains at gunpoint was gone, and I was watching a bird swoop slowly down toward the water and wondering what it would feel like to do that when Chris slowly turned my face toward his and kissed me. It was a long, tender, gentle kiss. Not the kiss of a lunatic juvenile. The kiss of a man.

When we pulled away from each other and I opened my eyes, I saw him smiling at me and looked pleased. "I like you, lady. What did you say your name was?"

"Oh, go to hell." I pulled the reins from his hands, exhorted him to hang on, and I took over the horse. That was one thing I could do well. I had been riding since I was five and it was a marvelous, heady feeling to be pounding over the mountains, not a house or a human being in sight, just a lovely, leggy horse under us and a beautiful man in the saddle behind me, however crazy he was.

"Okay, smartass. So you can ride. But do you know where you're going?" I had to giggle to myself as I realized that I didn't, and I shook my head in the wind, my hair whipping his face, but I didn't think he'd mind. His hair was almost as long as mine anyway.

"Where do you want to go?" As if I'd know how to get there. We were in his world and I was just a tourist. But a happy one.

"Bolinas. Head back toward that road down there, take the first right, without falling into the water, please. I can't swim."

"Bullshit." But I followed his instructions, walking the horse down the mountainside and then cantering along near the road in silence until I saw another road off to the right.

"That's it." He kicked the horse for me and I tried to slap him playfully but the water pistol was suddenly aimed at my ear again.

"You know what you are, Mr. Matthews?" I shouted into the wind. "You're a pain in the ass. And a bully."

"So I've been told. Hey, take this next right too, and

then a left." There were only one or two cars on the road, and I moved the horse onto it and took the appropriate turns. It was fun riding again, and I was beginning to like the nut with the shaggy hair and the water pistol. He had a nice grip on my waist and I could feel his thighs pressed into mine.

"Is this it?" We were in a nondescript-looking place, down on shore level, but there was nothing much to see but trees.

"Ride through those trees over there . . . you'll see." And I did. A long sandy strip of beach, the sea, and an inlet. And on the other side a still more beautiful beach which stretched for a couple of miles and then was stopped by the mountains again, dropping down to meet the sea. It was a splendid sight.

"Wow!"

"This is Bolinas and that's Stinson Beach. Can you swim?" He looked pleased at the expression on my face and he dismounted and held out his hands to catch me. I realized again how tall he was as I slipped to the ground next to him. I'm 5′7″ and he must have been at least 6′3″.

"Sure I can swim, but you can't. Remember?"

"Well, I'll learn." I watched what he was doing with sudden surprise and wondered just what he had in mind. He had pulled off his jacket and boots and was proceeding to remove his T-shirt. What next? His jeans? I wasn't quite sure what this was all about. "Whatcha looking at?"

"Let me ask first. What are you doing?" He stopped and looked at me for a long moment.

"I thought we'd swim the horse from here to the end of the land spit over there—it's an easy distance—and then we can ride on the beach. And swim, and stuff. Take off your clothes, I'll tie them to the saddle." Yeah . . . sure . . . and swim and stuff. Stuff, huh? . . . Oh well.

I tied up my hair again and then pulled off my own jacket and boots . . . and then my T-shirt, my jeans, and my pants. There was no one else on the beach. It was warm that April, yet on that side of the bay and on that Tuesday afternoon there was no one on the Bolinas Beach but us. Christopher Matthews and I stood facing each other beneath the mountains, stark naked and smiling peacefully, while the horse seemed to wonder what was next. And so did I. I wondered if Chris were going to leap at me and rape me, or squirt me with the water pistol again, or what. He was hard to predict. But he seemed matter-of-fact as he strapped my clothes to the saddle and led the horse toward the water. The three of us walked in, Chris showing nothing of the shock of the cold water, only slowly leading the horse into it and checking back over his shoulder to make sure I was okay. I was, but I was freezing my ass off and hated to show it. I dove under the water to see if that would feel better, and swam past him towards the opposite shore. It felt fabulous, and I smiled to myself as I surfaced and looked over my shoulder at Chris. Here I was in California, swimming from one beach to another with a horse and a crazy young filmmaker. Not bad, Mrs. Forrester, not bad at all.

We walked slowly up on the beach on the other side and Chris tied the horse to a long piece of drift wood. Again, there was no one on the beach but us. It looked like a movie and felt like a dream. He stretched out in the sun and closed his eyes, making no move toward me. He was doing what he wanted to do and I was free to do the same.

"Do you always run your shootings like this, Chris?" I was stretched out on the sand, with a respectable distance between us, my head was propped up and I was looking out to sea.

"Not always. Just most of the time. There's no point working if it's going to be a drag." Apparently he really believed that.

"Joe says you're good."

"Joe's got his head up his ass, but he's a nice guy. He's been giving me a lot of work."

"Me too. And I need it. He's nice to work for." We were roaming around comfortable subjects and it seemed a little funny to me to be making small talk about work as we lay naked in the sun.

"Where are you from, Gill? Back East?"

"Yes. New York, but I hate to admit it."

"That's a bad place. Bad for the head. I wouldn't go near it flying 40,000 feet above the ground."

"You're probably right. I've been here three months and I'm beginning to feel that way myself."

"Married?" It seemed a little late to ask, but maybe that was his style.

"No. Divorced. You?"

"Nope. Free as that bird over the water." He pointed to a gull drifting slowly downward in a lazily swooping arc. "It's a nice way to be."

"Lonely sometimes though. Isn't it for you?" He didn't look as though he'd suffered from much loneliness. He didn't have that sharp look about the eyes that one gets from trying to survive.

"I guess it's lonely sometimes, but . . . well, I work a lot. And I guess I don't think about being lonely." I envied him and wondered briefly if he was living with a girl, but I didn't want to ask. I didn't want to know. He was the first man I'd met in a long time who had guts and style and a sense of humor. "You look like a thinker. Are you?" He had rolled over on his stomach and was watching me with an amused grin.

"A thinker?" He nodded. I was stalling . . . yes . . . I was a thinker . . . what was wrong with that? "Yeah, I'm a thinker."

"And you read a lot." I nodded. "And you're lonely as hell." I nodded again, but what he was saying was beginning to bother me. It was as though he lived on the top of Mount Olympus and was looking down.

"And you talk too much." I stood up and looked at him for a second before walking toward the water and slipping into the waves. I liked him but I wanted to be alone for a bit. He seemed to stand very close and see a lot. And I suspected I could care about him. A lot. About what he thought, and what he was. I even liked how he looked. . . . Chris Matthews was what I'd been waiting for, but now that he'd arrived I was afraid.

A sudden splash in the water next to me caught me by

surprise and I turned quickly to see if I was being attacked by a local sea monster. But it was only Chris swimming by, and then turning back to swim at me again. He was really just a giant kid. I waited for him to dive at me from underwater, or try to dunk me, but he didn't, he just swam toward me and then kissed me as the waves swept by.

"Let's go back." He had a quiet look on his face as he said it and I was glad. I was getting tired of the games.

We swam toward the shore side by side and I started to walk toward where we had lain before, but he took me by the hand for a moment and looked at me.

"There's a nice cove back there. I'll show you." He kept my hand in his and walked me slowly around the point to a tiny cove nestled in the tall dune grass, like a secret garden. And suddenly I felt stronger and more desirable than I'd felt in years. I wanted him and he knew it and I knew he wanted me. . . . But it was too soon, I hardly knew him . . . it couldn't be right . . . it . . . I was scared.

"Chris . . . I . . ."

"Shhh . . . everything's going to be okay." He wrapped his arms around me as we stood in the tall grass with our feet dug into the sand, and then I felt my body swaying with his, until we lay in the sand, and I was his.

2

"Do you do this a lot, Chris?" The sun was still bright in the sky and we were still lying in his secret cove.

"What? Screw? . . . Yeah . . . I do this a lot."

"No, you smartass bastard. I mean like this. Here, in this cove. With someone you don't even know." I was serious. It had all seemed a little bit set up, the way he knew about the hidden cove and all.

"What do you mean? Hell, I know you. Your name is . . . uh . . . hang on just a sec and I'll get it . . . your name is . . ." He scratched his head with a feeble-minded look on his face and I felt like hitting him, but instead I laughed.

"Okay. I get the message. Mind my own business, right?"

"Maybe. I'll let you know when you bug me. New Yorkers just like to ask a lot of questions."

"Oh . . . is that so?" I looked mock pompous as I said it but I knew he was right. New Yorkers are nosier than Californians for some reason, probably because they're used to living in closer quarters with more people underfoot in a world of terrifying anonymity, so when they sink their teeth into someone for questioning they go all the way to the bone.

"Wanna go for a ride, Gill?"

"On the beach?" He nodded as he scrounged in the sand looking for shells. "I'd love it. But I'll ride behind you this time."

"Bareback okay with you?"

"Terrific."

"So are you, New York." His words were the barest whisper, and he leaned over and kissed me as he pulled me slowly to my feet. Everything he did had a sensual quality about it, as though he enjoyed life to the fullest, but as though what he liked best was making love. "Here . . . I found a present for you." He pressed something into my hand as we walked toward the horse, and I looked down to see what it was. With his sense of humor, I figured I'd be lucky if it wasn't a jelly fish he'd found on the beach. But it wasn't. It was a sand dollar. A strange fossil-like shell with imprints of a flower on either side. It was so delicate you could almost see through it, and it was lovely.

"Hey . . . it's beautiful, Chris, thanks." I reached up and kissed him on the neck and felt another stirring deep within me. I hadn't had a man since I'd come to California, for a while before even, and Chris was quite a man.

"Quit kissing me or I'll make love to you right here on the open beach."

"Don't make promises you don't intend to keep." I was teasing and he knew it, but he grabbed me by the arm, spun me around, and the next thing I knew we were lying on the beach making love again. And when we stopped we both broke into delighted chuckles.

"You're crazy. Do you know that, Mr. Matthews?"

"You forced me into it, so don't blame me."

"Bullshit. And if you're trying to make me feel guilty, forget it. I'm glad."

"So am I. Now . . . as I was saying, let's go for a ride." He unbuckled the saddle and put it down on the sand, stroking the horse's head and flanks with a knowing hand, and then he jumped gracefully onto the mare's back and held out a hand to me.

"Whatcha waiting for, Gill? Chicken?"

"No, something else. Happy. You're nice to look at." And so he was, sitting tall and proud astride the sandy-colored horse, his bronzed flesh standing out against her pale hide, and the grace of their two bodies making me think of poetry I'd read as a girl. Chris looked so beautiful.

"You're nice to look at too, now hop up." He gave me a hand and I slid up behind him, put my hands around his waist, and leaned into him as we sailed into the wind. It was the most marvelous feeling I could ever remember. Racing down the beach on a pale golden mare with a man I loved . . . loved? . . . Chris? . . . I hardly knew him. But it didn't matter, I was already in love with him. From that first day on.

We galloped up and down the beach until sunset and then took a last swim before reluctantly taking our leave.

"Do you want to swim the mare back to the other side?" I asked. I was a little worried, the tide was coming in, but he had seen it too.

"No, we'd better go by the road this time. It's less fun but it makes more sense."

"It does, huh? You're beginning to make me wonder if

you just swam her over so you could make me take my clothes off." I hadn't even thought of that at the time.

"Is that what you think?" He looked hurt and I was sorry I'd said it. "Well, you happen to be right." He let out a delighted laugh, and I stood watching him again. The giant boy who'd taken my heart at water-pistol point. Not bad.

"What's next on your agenda, Conceito Bandito? You leave me tied naked to a telephone pole till morning?" He would be capable of it.

"No. I feed you. How does that sound?"

"Intravenous or regular?"

"You're disgusting, Gillian. Regular, of course. The Watson House, the best Bolinas has to offer. Have you ever been there?"

"Nope."

"Wait and see." We got back on the horse and trotted slowly down the beach to the part that belonged to the state, then walked the horse slowly past the empty parking lot to the road. It was a fifteen-minute ride into Bolinas and we got there just as the sun was setting; it seemed as though the entire world were lit in red and gold.

We stopped in front of a small dilapidated Victorian house and tied up the horse as I looked around. There were a number of hippies wandering in and out of the house and a discreet sign said "The Watson House," but it offered no further information as to what it was.

"What is this place?"

"A restaurant, dopey. What did you think?"

"How do I know? Hey . . . by the way, I have to call my neighbor and tell her I'll be late. She's taking care of my little girl."

"That's okay. They have a phone inside." He swung slowly up the steps to the house and opened the screen door without knocking. It had the look of a private house belonging to a large family and certainly no suggestion of a restaurant about it. Vast quantities of laundry hung on a clothesline, and a strange assortment of bicycles and motorcycles stood outside, while two cats and a dog played in the grass. It had a friendly, homey look to it which appealed to me and seemed well-suited to Chris Matthews.

"Hi, gang. What's doing?" Chris walked straight into the kitchen and sniffed into a pot on a brilliantly clean, museum-piece stove. There were three girls in the kitchen and a man. The man wore his hair to his waist, tied neatly back with a leather thong. He was wearing what looked like a pajama top over his jeans, and it probably was, but what struck me most were the bright, kindly eyes that stood out above his beard. Without moving a single muscle in his face, his eyes seemed to smile and say a dozen welcoming things. The girls were all pretty, young, and simply dressed.

"Gillian, this is Bruce . . . Anna, Penny, and Beth. They live here." Bruce and the girls all said hi, and Chris shepherded me back to a little room decorated in cheerful Victoriana and Tiffany lamps.

"What is this place, Chris? It's neat."

"Isn't it? It's actually a hippie commune, but to support themselves they run a restaurant, and it's the best goddam food this side of the bay. You should try the escargots, they're terrific."

"I will." And I did, and they were. And so was the coq au vin, and the homemade bread, and the salad, and the mousse au chocolat and the tarte aux fraises. It was a royal repast. Chris had been right, the food was superb. But there was more to it than that. The friendliness of the place was endearing too. I had been right on the way in—it had the feeling of a home with many children in it. There were twenty-seven people living there at the time, and each one contributed his or her efforts to the restaurant. They drifted in and out as we sat there in the candlelight at one of the eight small tables. Everyone seemed to know Chris, and a few stopped and sat at our table for a few minutes before going into the kitchen, or back upstairs.

"Do you come here a lot?"

"Yes. Especially in the summer. I rent a small shack in Bolinas and sometimes I just come by to bullshit with the gang. Sometimes I come here to eat. But only on special occasions." He was teasing me gently, but he had a nice way of doing it. His smile lit up his face as he did, and his eyes said that he meant no harm. He was a gentle man.

"How old is your little girl?" He seemed only vaguely interested, but it was nice of him to ask.

"She'll be five next month. And she's something of a terror. Her main ambition in life is to become a cowboy. If she'd known we'd spent the day with a horse, and without her, she wouldn't speak to me for a week. I think she was under the impression that we came out here to be cowboys."

"Maybe we could take her riding sometime. Is she a brave kid?"

"Brave enough. She'd love it. I was her age when I started."

"I figured, but you don't know your ass from a hole in the ground when it comes to Western Saddle. I could see that too." I blushed faintly and wound myself up to say something insulting, but then broke into a laugh and threw up my hands in defeat.

"You're right."

We talked on for another hour or so, of nothing in particular, California mostly, and work, and why the simple life was better for both of us, when a group came in that looked vaguely familiar.

"Whatcha looking at?" Chris had noticed me looking at them.

"Nothing. I thought I knew those people, but I don't think I do." They were three hippies much like Chris and the ones in the house, and I think it was just the familiar type that had struck me.

"You know them?" He looked surprised.

"No. I just thought I did."

"Well let's find out. That's really funny." He signaled to them to come over to us and I began to wish I were dead.

"Chris . . . no . . . really . . . look, I . . ." But then I knew where I had seen them before. They were Chris's crew. He saw the recognition in my eyes and he and his boys started to laugh. They had heard the brief exchange and knew Chris was up to one of his tricks again.

"Oh you big, lousy bastard, Chris Matthews. . . . Hi, boys. Nice to see you again. How did the fight wind up? Did anyone drown the account guys from Carson?"

"No, they went back in the jeep almost as soon as you two left. And we spent the afternoon drinking wine with Joe and the models. They were paid for the day so we all figured what the hell. How was it with you?" They seemed to be addressing Chris more than me, and I let him carry the ball. He also wanted to know how they felt about the shooting and what they hoped they had gotten on film. Everyone seemed to feel it had gone well, and I was relieved for Joe Tramino from Carson. I would have hated to have him suffer for our craziness. Our? . . . Well, I had ridden off with Chris, and that was bad enough. They hadn't been expecting that from their "stylist from New York," but then again neither had I.

We paid the check at the Watson House then and the five of us ambled outside where Chris's truck, the car, and the horse trailer stood near our mare. It was nice to see her again. She reminded me of what had happened on the beach.

"I'll take the car. Thanks for dropping it off." They said goodnight and took charge of the horse as we hopped into Chris's somewhat dubious chariot. As Chris fought with the choke, I wasn't sure I was going to enjoy driving back over the winding mountain road in that, but maybe with Chris I would.

As it turned out, it was an easy drive. There was no fog that night, and the moon lit up the road with a lovely silver glow.

I sang old ballads that I had known as a child, and once in a while Chris joined in. We looked at each other in the moonlight, and kissed from time to time, and very little was said. We didn't need to. It was just nice to be there.

I saw the entrance to the freeway with regret and wished that there were a longer way home. I hated to see

all the people and cars again. I had liked our lonely mountain road . . . and our deserted beach.

"Where do you live, Gill?" We were already crossing
the bridge, and it was pretty to see the lights of Sausalito,
Tiburon, and Belvedere on one side of the bay and San
Francisco on the other. Usually the fog was in by sun-
down, so it was a rare sight.

"I live in the Marina. On Bay."

"Fine." He took the first turn off, I gave him the address, and we were home in a few minutes.

"This'll be fine, Chris. I have to pick up Sam next
door."

"Sam?" He raised an eyebrow and looked surprised.

"My little girl." He nodded, and I was pleased to think
he might have been jealous.

"Shall I wait, or will that screw up your scene?"

"No, that would be nice. I'll be right out." I rang my
neighbor's bell and went inside to scoop my half-sleeping
child off their couch. She was groggy but not in a deep
sleep yet. And I was surprised to realize that it was only
nine o'clock. I thanked the neighbors and went out to find
Chris sitting on our stoop. I put a finger to my lips and
handed him the key, so as not to wake Sam. She had already drifted back to sleep in my arms.

He looked at her for a moment and then nodded his
head in approval as he turned to open the door, and then
Sam's croaky four-and-a-half-year-old voice rang out in
the night.

"Who's he, Mommy?" I grinned and Chris laughed. He
had the door open and I set her down inside.

"This is Chris Matthews, Sam. And this is Samantha
. . . now, time for bed, young lady. I'll get your pajamas
and then you can have a glass of milk if you want."

"Okay." She sat in a chair and eyed Chris sleepily as he
sprawled on the couch, his long legs straight out in front of
him, his hair looking shaggier than ever after our day on
the beach. I got Sam's pajamas and was walking back toward the kitchen when I heard her ask Chris in a hoarse

whisper, "Are you a real cowboy?" There was hope in her voice, and I wondered what he would say.

"Yes, I am. Do you mind much?"

"Mind? No . . . no . . . I wanna be a cowboy too!" The tone was conspiratorial.

"You do? That's great. Maybe we could ride together sometime. But first do you know what you have to do?" I couldn't see her face but I could imagine her eyes opened wide, waiting to hear what he was going to say. "You have to drink a lot of milk, and go to sleep when your mom tells you. Then you get to be big and strong, and you'll be a really extra terrific cowboy."

"I have to do all that yucky stuff?" Sam sounded disgusted.

"Of course not. Only if you want to be a cowboy, silly."

"Oh . . . well . . okay . . ." I walked into the room with her glass of milk and was grateful for Chris's speech. For the first time she drank it in what looked like one gulp and headed for bed like a flash, with a last wave toward Chris and a mumbled, "Goodnight, Mister . . . Mister Crits . . . see you at a rodeo someday." I tucked her into bed, kissed her goodnight, and went back to find Chris looking pleased with himself.

"Thanks. That made things a lot easier for me."

"She's cute. I like her. She seems like a nice kid."

"Wait, you haven't seen her in her full glory. She was half-asleep. Next time she might try a new lasso trick on you and give you rope burn. She's something else." But I was pleased that he liked her.

"You're something else, too. And I'm not sure I'd trust you with a new rope trick either. You might try to strangle me. I really think you were trying to knock me off that horse today when you thought I had a gun on you. But I was waiting for you." He looked amused at the memory of it.

"Good thing for you that you were. I was planning to knock the bejesus out of you."

"Wanna try again?" He held out his arms to me as I stood across the room and I walked toward him with that feeling of having been reborn again. It had been so long since anyone had given a damn about me, or wanted me as a woman. And now I had someone who wanted me as a woman. Whether or not he gave a damn about me was something I'd find out in time.

3

The phone rang at nine-fifteen again on Wednesday morning, and I was torn between hoping it was Chris and wishing it would be another job. I needed the money.

"Hello?"

"Gillian? Joe."

"Oh. Hi. That was quite a shooting yesterday."

"Yeah. I just thought I'd call and check that you weren't pissed off at me for getting you into that madhouse scene. And I wanted to be sure he hadn't dropped you off a cliff or something." Pissed off? ? Wow!

"Nothing of the sort. I had a great time. That was the easiest hundred and twenty bucks I've ever made. He had me a little worried with the water pistol though."

"He did? I thought you knew."

"No, I didn't. And he almost got himself knocked off the horse as a result, but it all turned out okay." Yes . . . it did. . . .

"I'm glad. Say, listen, I called to ask you something. Are you free on Friday night?" Huh? Friday night? Shit, no job. A date. And I wanted to go out with Chris, not Joe. "It's the annual Art Directors' Ball, and it's a bit of a free-for-all, but I thought you might like it." Oh hell, why not?

"Sure, Joe. I'd love to." But what if Chris should call? What if . . .

"Great. Wear anything you want. Sort of far-out type stuff, nothing formal. We're having it in a warehouse downtown. Sounds a little crazy but it might be fun."

"It sounds terrific, Joe. And thanks for asking me."

"Prego, prego, Signorina. I'm delighted you can make it. I'll pick you up at eight. See you then. Bye, Gill."

"Bye." We hung up and I wondered if I'd done the right thing. Joe had never asked me out before and I didn't want to get into a heavy scene with someone who could give me work. It was bad policy. And Joe wasn't really my type . . . and what if Chris wanted to . . . oh shit. I figured he'd understand, and anyway I'd accepted, so why stew about it. I could talk it over with Chris. . . . I could have that is, if he had called.

As it turned out, the week ambled by without a call from Chris. Sam and I went to the beach, I painted the kitchen floor with red, white, and blue stripes and painted stars on the ceiling, I got a job from Freeman & Barton Advertising that took me all of two hours to do on Friday afternoon, and still no sign of Chris. I could have called him, but I didn't want to. He had left me early Wednesday morning with the first light of day and he had said he'd call. But he hadn't said when . . . next year maybe? Or maybe he was just playing it cool, but that didn't seem quite his style. Maybe he was just busy . . . making movies . . . but all work and no play wasn't Chris's style either, and I was getting very down about it by Friday evening when I fixed Sam's dinner.

"Why are you going out tonight, Mommy?"

"Because I thought it might be fun, and you'll be asleep, so you won't miss me at all." I tried to sound light-hearted for Sam's sake, but I was feeling lousy.

"Yes, I will. Am I having a sitter?" I nodded and pointed to her dinner she wasn't eating. "Maybe I'll tie the sitter to a chair and set the rope on fire. That's what Indians do. It's called being an Indian giver."

"No, being an Indian giver is giving something to someone and then taking it back." I thought of Chris and cringed within myself. "And you're not going to tie the babysitter to anything or I'll give you the spanking of your life when I come home. Is that clear?"

"Okay, Mommy." She sank into her milk with a look of boredom and despair and I went to my room to pick out something to wear for the Art Directors' Ball. He had said something far-out, so I dug around and came out with a flowery gypsy skirt I'd forgotten I owned and an orange halter top. I had a new pair of orange suede boots and a pair of gold loop earrings, and I knew that would do it . . . and maybe after a bath I'd feel more like me again.

I could hear Sam rummaging around in her room and at ten to eight I went in to check on her and announce bedtime.

"Okay, Sam. Put your stuff away and get your pajamas on. The sitter'll be here any minute."

"You look pretty, Mommy. Are you going out with Mister Crits?" My heart rose and sank almost simultaneously, and I shook my head. No, I wasn't going out with "Mister Crits," but I wished I were, and I suddenly began to wonder if Chris might be at the party.

The doorbell rang at eight and Joe Tramino and my babysitter walked in together.

"Hi, Sam's in her room. It's time for bed and I'm all ready to go. Hi, Joe. Goodnight, Barbara. Bye Sam." I blew a kiss toward her room and walked outside with Joe. I didn't want to get into any of Sam's editorials on the situation and I wanted to get the hell out. I was feeling restless.

"Christ, Gill, you look fantastic!" I could see in his eyes that he meant it and felt briefly guilty for being unenthused about the evening. Hell, maybe it would be fun.

"You look pretty good yourself, Mr. Tramino. Very snazzy." He was wearing tobacco-colored suede levis and a dark red turtleneck and it struck me that, side by side, we clashed terribly. But maybe that was just how I felt inside. We walked to his car parked at the curb and he helped me in. It seemed a little funny to be a girl to someone you had played "one of the boys" with, but that's all part of going out with someone you've worked with. It always seems a little funny to me.

"I thought we might stop for dinner somewhere on the way. Do you know Nicole's?"

"No, I'm a new girl in town, remember?"

"You'll like it. French food. It's terrific." He was trying so hard to please that it was painful. Poor Joe. I knew he was considered a prize catch at the agency. He wasn't beautiful, but he was thirty-six years old, had a good job with an impressive salary, a nice personality, and a good sense of humor. And he didn't turn me on. He hadn't before, but now it was worse. He wasn't Chris.

We joked with each other through dinner and I tried to keep a spirit of camaraderie in the conversation. But Joe was trying to turn the tables on me. He was plying me with a heavy red wine and we had one of the best tables in the house. He had chosen a really pretty little restaurant. It was decorated like a large summery tent at a garden party, the tables were covered in red and white checked cloths, and the room was ablaze with candles.

"Who's going to be at this party, Joe? Anyone I know?" I tried to make it sound like idle conversation, but it wasn't.

"Just the usual troops. The art directors from most of the agencies in town, a lot of models, some film guys, nothing special." But he was on to me. He knew I had meant Chris and he was waiting to see what I would say next.

"It sounds like a good group. There's a thing like that in New York every year, but it's so big you never really see anyone you know. Just a great thundering horde, like the rest of New York."

"It's different out here. Everything's smaller. San Francisco is a very small town. And everyone knows everyone else's business." What was this all about? "Like I know that if you fall for some people you could get hurt. I mean Chris, Gill." There, he'd said it.

"Oh?"

"Look, I wasn't matchmaking the other day. I was setting up a job. I even had another stylist lined up but she
got sick. Gill, he's a terrific guy and I'm crazy about him,
but he has no morals, he collects women, and he doesn't
give a damn about anyone but himself. He's a lot of fun.
But don't go falling in love with him. Maybe I'm way out
of line, but I thought I'd say it. And just so you don't get
your hopes up, he won't be there tonight. He hates these
kinds of parties. Look, the guy's a hippie. You're a nice
girl from New York, probably from a good family. And
you've had your troubles, you're divorced . . . don't mess
around with him." Wow . . . quite a speech.

"You haven't left me much to say, Joe. Of course I'm
not in love with him. I just met him last Tuesday, and I
haven't seen him since"—goddam it—"and I agree with
you, he's fun to work with but probably lousy to get involved with. But I'm a big girl and I can take care of myself. And I'm not involved. . . okay?" . . . Who says?

"I'll take your word for it. But I'll be sorry if I hear that
you two get into something serious with each other. I'd
feel guilty as all hell . . . and I'd probably crawl the walls
of my office in a frenzy of jealousy! Here's to you." He
toasted me with the last of the bottle of wine, and, as I
drained my glass, I silently wished that he would be having
that jealous fit before too long.

We left Nicole's then and drove downtown on Broadway, past the neon hysteria of the topless dance parlors,
and then turned onto Battery Street, near the entrance to
the Bay Bridge. It was a district that had once been a port,
and the shipping lines were still within a block or two.
They had put in landfill in the early 1900s and the area
had only recently become one of the more interesting parts
of town. A lot of the ad agencies were moving in there,
and the decorating business had taken over years ago. The
result was a series of dismal-looking warehouses inter-
spersed with well-designed new buildings with brick sides
and glass fronts.

Joe parked outside one of the warehouses and we went
inside. It was a hell of a scene. Miles and miles of shiny

mirrorlike Mylar had been hung from ceiling to floor and flashing strobe and neon lights made the room look as though it were about to explode. There was cellophane confetti all over the floor and an acid rock band dressed in silver lamé jeans and shirts was blasting their message through the building at an ear-shattering, heart-pounding pace. There was an ingeniously designed bar in one corner of the room. It looked like an iceberg, and the girl doling out the drinks was wearing a skirt made of plastic icicles, and no top. And in the center of the room and along the walls were the guests. And they were wearing just what Joe had suggested . . . really far-out stuff. Fuchsia satins, and green suedes, dresses that were frontless, or backless, or seemingly both, hair of all shapes, colors, and varieties. Boots by the truckload and blue jeans by the ton. It was a crazy scene and one that only the artistic community of any city could produce. No one else would dare. I almost felt like Little Bo Peep in my gypsy outfit, but I was glad I'd worn it. It gave me a chance to stare at everyone else in reasonable anonymity while still looking fairly with-it.

I noticed a group off to one side of the room staring up at the ceiling then, and Joe tugged at my arm.

"Take a look." And when I did, what I saw made me laugh. Suspended from the ceiling, about twelve feet off the floor, was a small but perfectly normal ice-skating rink, with a girl in an ice follies outfit quietly doing her number. She moved to her own slow, graceful beat, totally apart from the crazed sounds of the acid rock band. She was marvelous.

"Where the hell did they get her?"

"I don't know, but you haven't seen anything yet. Take a look over there." He pointed again and this time I saw a ballerina doing quiet spins in the corner, and every few minutes or so she went into a dead faint on the floor. Then she'd revive, pick herself up again, and do her pirouettes for a while before seeming to die on the floor again. She was even better to watch than the skater. And I began to look around the room myself for more oddities. As it turned out, there was only one, a gentleman who looked like a well-dressed, well-stuffed bank president, and who walked sedately around the room, speaking to no one, and blowing huge bubbles with what must have been a wad of bubble gum the size of my fist. They were terrific. And eventually, inquiries disclosed that they and the room's ingenious decor had come from an enterprising service organization called "Rent-a-Freak" run by a young San Francisco artist who thought it was a good idea. He was right, it was. And it made the party.

Joe and I lost and found each other several dozen times in the course of the evening. I met a few people I knew from other agencies, and danced with what seemed like an endless series of similar faces. They all looked the same, none of them looked like Chris, none of them was Chris. And Chris wasn't there. But I was, and in the end I had a good time.

We left a little after 3 a.m. The party was still in full swing, but we'd had enough. Joe took me to the Buena Vista for an Irish coffee and a pleasant view of the bay and Sausalito sparkling on the other side, and then we called it a night.

He pulled up in front of my house and I noticed with some dismay that all the lights were out. Which meant the babysitter had passed out. Nuts.

"Thanks, Joe, it was a really super evening. That was one of the best parties I've been to in years."

"And you're one of the best dates I've had in years. Could we make it again sometime?"

"Sure, Joe. And thanks." I pecked him lightly on the cheek, pointed my key in the lock and turned it quickly, and was relieved to see that Joe was on his way back to his car. No sweat. No hassle at the door. Peace.

I woke the babysitter and offered to call her a cab, but she said she had her own car, so she vanished only moments after Joe, and Sam and I were alone again in the quiet house.

Too quiet. The sitter had said the phone hadn't rung all night. No messages. Damn.

4

On Saturday morning the sun was up before we were, and Sam and I headed for the Marina Beach next to the Yacht Club for a little sun before lunch. We had a lengthy discussion on the sand about the merits of the life of a cowboy, and I described the party to her. She was impressed. A ballerina and a skater and a man who chewed bubblegum? Wow! That had to be some party! And I noticed with amusement that the newspaper said it was, in roughly the same terms as Sam.

At noon, we munched hot dogs and potato chips on the stone steps near the boats and threw bits of the rolls to the sea gulls who waited to be fed.

"Mommy, what are we going to do today?"

"Nothing much. Why?" I didn't have any plans, and I was a little tired from having only managed three hours sleep before Sam arrived to order her corn flakes. Sleeping Beauty I was not privileged to be.

"Let's go see some horses." . . . Christ . . . how about a game of football? . . . You're a girl, Sam. . . .

"Maybe we can go see the horses in Golden Gate Park." But I wasn't particularly enthused.

"That sounds like a nice idea to me." But the voice that spoke behind me wasn't Sam's. It was a man's voice. I turned to see, but I already knew. It was Chris.

"Hi, Gill. Hi, podner. Don't you girls ever stay home? I dropped by twice this week. No one home." I was feeling unglued.

"You did? Why didn't you leave a note?"

"I never thought of that. Anyway, I figured I'd catch up

with you sooner or later." Yeah, but it turned out to be later than sooner dammit. But who cared? He was back.

"It's nice to see you. How did our film turn out?"

"Great. Tramino's going to love us." Us? That was a nice touch. And I could see that he was genuinely pleased with the film. "But let's not talk about work. I take it you're going to see the horses in the park. Can I come?" Are you kidding? Of course you can come! After three days of not seeing him he could have come to the dentist with me if he'd wanted to. The three days felt like years.

"Will you come with us, Mister Crits, please?" She stretched out the please and my heart with it, and I nodded happily.

"Why don't you, Chris?"

"Thank you, ladies, I'd be delighted. But don't call me Mister Chris please, young lady. Or I'll call you Samantha. How would you like that?"

"Yerggghh." She made a face that illustrated the point and Chris and I laughed.

"That's what I thought. So you call me Chris. Just Chris. Okay?" She was about to burble into ecstatic speech but I shook my head and Chris raised an eyebrow. "No go, Gill? Come on, don't be so stuffy. Okay, how about Uncle Chris?" He seemed amused at the idea and I felt better. Sometimes my stiff childhood training stuck out in funny places.

"That's better." I gave my dowager's approval and all was well.

"Okay, Sam. Call me Uncle Chris. Sound okay to you?"

"I like that better. Uncle Crits. That's good." She nodded thoughtfully and then smiled and offered him the last of her potato chips.

"Thanks, Sam. How about a piggyback ride back to my truck?"

"Yes! Yes!" She hopped on his back and grabbed him around the neck and off we went. I carried the beach towels and a happy heart and we were on our way to a merry day.

We stopped at the house to feed Chris a tuna fish sandwich, send Samantha to the john, comb my hair, and collect a few odds and ends of gear, like Sam's teddy bear and a bottle of wine to take to the park. And then we loaded ourselves into the cab of Chris's truck and headed for the park. We found the horse paddock there and took rides on two rather tired brown horses. Sam rode with Chris and he told her a modified version of our riding on the beach the day of the shooting and swimming from one beach to the other with the horse. Sam thought it sounded wonderful. And on hearing it again so did I.

Then we went to the Japanese tea garden and munched strange little cookies and drank tea. And after that we lay on the grass in the botanical garden till five. Sam played with her teddy bear, Chris and I drank the bottle of wine, we played tag and hide and seek, and it was a glorious day. We hated to go home but it was getting cold.

"How would you like a home-cooked meal, Mr. Matthews? Pot luck."

"Can you cook?" He seemed to be weighing the invitation and I was momentarily reminded of Joe's warning. Maybe he had something else to do.

"I can sort of cook. But if you're going to be picky you can go to hell."

"Thanks a lot. I'd rather eat at your house than do that. If that's the choice, I'll come to dinner." He nodded his head sagely and Sam let out a delighted whoop which said everything I felt.

We picked up some groceries at the supermarket, and Chris gave Sam her bath when we got home while I made spaghetti and meat sauce and a giant salad.

Chris and Sam came out of the bathroom hand in hand. She looked terribly pleased about something and I figured maybe they'd faked the bath. But what the hell? No one ever died of a little dirt.

"Hey, Gill . . . you've got a problem with the dinner." He was speaking to me in an undertone and I wondered what was wrong.

"What is it?"

"There are worms in the meat sauce . . . but don't tell Sam."

"Worms? Where?" I practically screamed the words. Worms? Never mind upsetting Sam, the very idea made me feel sick.

He nodded his head again, reached into the bowl with a fork, and came up with a long slithering piece of spaghetti. "Take a look at that. That's the biggest worm I've ever seen."

"Oh you ass. That's a spaghetti." As if he didn't know.

"It is? No kidding?" The boyish smile happened all over his face as he said it, and I could have hit him with my frying pan.

"Worms my ass. Now, everybody, let's eat dinner."

"Gillian!" His face froze into a look that reminded me of my father and cracked me up. The three of us sat down at the table. And chaos reigned for the duration of the meal, until Sam went to bed and the dishes were done.

It was a far cry from the evening I'd spent at the crazy Art Directors' Ball the night before with Joe. It was a happy time for all three of us. And Joe Tramino's warning be damned. There was nothing wrong with Chris Matthews. He had his own style, he liked to play jokes and indulge in pranks, he had an enchanting childish side that made me think he was more Sam's friend than mine, but he was a good man, and I could only see happy days ahead.

"Can I take you two to the beach tomorrow?" He was sprawled out on the couch, drinking wine and waiting for me to finish in the kitchen.

"Sure. That sounds like fun. Stinson?" Our eyes met for a long moment as we both remembered what had happened there.

"Yes, Stinson . . . and Gill, maybe there's something you want to know. There's this girl I live with . . . is that okay?"

5

The revelation that Chris was living with someone had come as something of a shock. The possibility that he was had crossed my mind the first day, but I had shoved the thought away. I didn't want to know. I didn't want him to have anyone else. He said she wasn't terribly important to him. Not to worry. He would work it out. And he had said it all with such ease that I knew he would. I trusted him.

He spent the night at my place and was a good sport about moving from my bed to the couch before Sam got up. I didn't think she ought to know. Not yet. It was too soon.

We left for Stinson Beach at ten after an enormous breakfast of French toast and scrambled eggs and bacon. And we packed a picnic lunch for the beach. It was another glorious day, and this time when we got to the beach I was a little sorry to see that there were people on it. It wasn't just ours. Sam sped off to play with some children down by the water and Chris and I were left alone.

"Does it make a difference to you, Gill?" I knew what he meant the minute he asked.

"About your roommate?" He nodded. "Yes and no. It's sort of a pain in the ass, and I'm jealous. But I'll leave it to you. If she's not all that important to you, I guess it won't make much difference. What are you going to do about her?" That was the key.

"Oh, she'll go. She's just a hippie chick I took in last winter. She was out of money, and she's very young, and I thought I'd give her a hand."

"More than that, I suspect." I was beginning to feel

sour about it. She was taking on flesh. She was a real live girl. And she lived with Chris.

"Hey . . . you really are jealous. Cool it, baby. She'll go. And I'm not in love with her, if that's what you want to know."

"Does she have a nice body?" . . . Oh shit. . . .

"Yes, but so do you, so come off it. There's only one girl who's ever really meant anything to me, and she doesn't anymore, so you're home free."

"Who's she?" I wanted to know everything.

"A Eurasian girl I lived with a long time ago. Marilyn Lee. But she's in Honolulu now. Far, far from here."

"Do you think she'll come back?" I was feeling paranoid.

"Do you think you'll shut up? Besides, I'm in love with your daughter. So get off my back. As a mother-in-law you're tremendous. Type-cast for the role." I slammed him with a fistful of sand aimed at his chest and he pinned me to the sand and kissed me.

"Whatcha doing, Mommy? Is Uncle Crits playing a game with you? I wanna play too." She lay down on the sand and nuzzled her head in with ours.

"It's called artificial respiration and only grownups can play. Go make me a sand horse." Sam thought that was a terrific idea and our game didn't look like much fun to her anyway, so she went back down the beach to her friends while we laughed and watched her go.

"You're good with kids, Chris. It makes me wonder if you have any of your own."

"That's a hell of a left-handed question, Gill. No, I don't. My own would freak me out."

"Why?" It seemed funny. He was so good with Sam.

"Responsibility. I'm allergic to it. Come on, I'll race you to the water." He did, and I beat him by half an inch, which won me an earnest dunking in the chilly surf . . . allergic to responsibility, eh? Okay. Sorry I asked.

"Is anybody interested in Chinese dinner?" We were rounding the hair-raising bends in the road home from

Stinson Beach and everyone was in a good mood. Sam had played all afternoon and Chris and I had talked film. He was crazy about his work, his eyes lit up with passion when he spoke of it. And I envied him that. Being a stylist just doesn't work up the same kind of emotion. All you do is add your own touches to someone else's work. Like his work. He was doing all the creating.

The invitation to Chinese dinner was well-received, and Sam was thrilled at the sights of Chinatown when we got there. Many of the buildings were made to look like pagodas and the streets were lined with shops filled with fascinating junk. The smell of incense was heavy in the air, and there were tiny, tinkling bells over every doorway.

"Do you like Chinese food, Gill?"

"I love it." It seemed funny that he didn't know. I expected him to know everything. It felt as though we had been together for years.

The three of us wrestled over chicken foo yong, sweet and sour pork, shrimp fried in batter, sharks' fin sauté, fried rice, fortune cookies, and tea. And at the end of the meal I felt as though I were going to explode. Chris looked as though he felt about the same, and Sam went to sleep at the table.

"We're some group," he said. I giggled as he looked around and threw up his hands. "I was expecting the last fortune cookie to tell me I'd turn into an egg roll by morning. I feel like one."

"Me too. Let's go home." I saw a funny look in his eyes as I said it, but he didn't say anything, so I didn't speak. The moment passed.

"I want to show you something pretty before we go back. Sam can sleep in the truck. I'll carry her."

We walked slowly to the parking lot where Chris had left the truck and I was sorry Sam couldn't get one last view of the wonders of Chinatown, but there'd be other times.

"Where are we going?" He was driving west up Broadway, and we had just crossed Van Ness Avenue and were entering one of the better residential districts.

"You'll see."

We drove all the way up Broadway to the intersection of Divisadero and then he stopped and made a right turn. We stood on the crest of the hill and looked at the bay and the mountains on the other side, and it was splendid. Everything was terribly quiet and heartbreakingly beautiful. The glory of San Francisco was ours.

He put the truck in low gear and we rolled quietly down the hill toward the bay, past the rows of important-looking, well-kept houses in Pacific Heights, until we reached the cheesy flamboyance of Lombard Street and I was sorry it was over.

We drove into the Marina district and I knew he was taking us home.

"Don't look so sad. It's not over yet."

"It's not?" I was pleased.

He drove along the docks and then parked next to the Yacht Club.

"Let's get out. Sam's sound asleep. We can sit out here for a bit." We walked out into the cool night air and looked across the bay at the view. The water was lapping at the narrow rim of beach and it made a pleasant sound. It was the most peaceful moment of the day and it was lovely. We sat on the low retaining wall, dangling our feet and looking outward, and there was nothing left to say. It was all right there. And I didn't feel alone anymore.

"Gill . . ." He seemed to hesitate as he looked out across the bay.

"Yes?"

"I think I'm in love with you. That's a hell of a way to say it, but I think I am."

"I think I am too. And don't worry how you say it, it's nice to hear."

"You may be sorry that you love me one day." He looked at me earnestly in the dark as he said it.

"I doubt that. I know what I'm doing. And I think I know what you are. I love you, Chris." He leaned over gently and took me in his arms and kissed me, and then we smiled at each other in the dark. All was well with the world.

We drove the few blocks to my house in silence and he lifted Sam gently out of the truck, took her inside, and put her down on her bed. And then he looked at me for a long moment and left the room.

"What's bugging you, Chris?" We were standing in the living room and I could tell he had something on his mind.

"I'm going back to my place tonight. And don't try to make me feel guilty about it. Ever. Do you understand that? Never, Gill, never . . . and besides, you couldn't anyway." I started to answer him, but he was gone. There had been a strange fire in his eyes as he said those words to me . . . and then he was gone.

6

Monday was a horrifically busy day. I got a super job from an advertising agency that had never used me before and I spent the entire day getting accessories for the shooting of some textile ads the following day. It was fun work and I kept busy bouncing in and out of boutiques and department stores looking for jewelry, shoes in the right sizes, handbags, hats, and great odds and ends. All a stylist really needs is taste, imagination, and good, strong legs. You have to run around a lot.

The art director of the agency took me to lunch at Ernie's and it was fun to see the chic people come and go. He was a man of about forty-five, was recently divorced, and had the worst case of the hots I'd seen on anybody yet. He kept trying to talk me into coffee and brandy at his apartment after lunch, on Telegraph Hill where he had a terrific view. . . . Come on, baby, are you kidding? I had work to do. And I had Chris.

My last stop of the day was at I. Magnin's fur shop, and I had a ball picking out sable capes, ermine throws, mink this, and leopard that. They would work well with the textiles, and it was a lovely, luxurious feeling to be picking out furs, practically by the gross.

Sam had been parked with the neighbors again for the afternoon and she was visibly annoyed at me when I swept in in good spirits and a new black wool dress that I'd bought at Magnin's on the way out. I was feeling chic and successful, like the people I'd seen at Ernie's at lunch.

"Is that a new dress, Mommy?"

"Yes, do you like it?"

"No. It's black." Tough, Sam, I like it. But I knew she was mad that I'd been busy all day and hadn't been able to take her to the beach. But this was a big job. Two days for four hundred dollars.

"Come on, Sam. I'll cook dinner and you can tell me about your day."

"Well, it was miberatzil."

"Miserable? As bad as all that?" But suddenly she had taken off towards the house like a shot. And then I saw why. Chris was in front of the house, all cleaned up, the shaggy blond hair immaculately clean, and a fresh pair of jeans, and he was carrying an armful of flowers.

"Wow! How pretty."

"So are you, Gill. Listen . . . I was lousy to you last night and I'm sorry. Really, really sorry. We'll have a nice night tonight, and . . ."

"Relax. I had a nice night last night and the night before. Everything's okay, Chris. I understand. It's okay."

"What are you talking about? I don't understand." I had forgotten that Sam was in our midst and she was looking confused.

"Nothing, Sam. Go wash your hands. I'll cook dinner."

"No, you won't, Gill. I'm taking you out. Get a sitter."

"Now?"

"Now. I'll make the peace with Sam." He pointed at the phone and then left the room to talk to Sam.

He had come through . . . flowers and all. And he was right, he had been kind of lousy. But not very. He had only told me that he was living with someone, which was honest, and he had gone home to sleep, which hurt, but he had to go home sometime. The funny thing was that I really did understand, and I knew he didn't mean to hurt me.

I called the sitter and she agreed to come by in half an hour. But there was still Sam to contend with. I wasn't so sure Chris could snow her. Maybe me, but not her. I put his flowers in a vase and waited for her to emerge. It didn't take long.

"Uncle Crits says you're going out. But I guess it's okay. He said you worked hard all day, and something like that. You can go out, Mommy."

"Thanks, Sam." I wasn't so sure I was pleased with getting permission from a child three feet tall, but it was best that she wasn't mad about it, whatever he'd told her. Then, Chris took charge of me, and it struck me again how nice it was to have a man in the house.

"Now, you go get dressed. Put on something beautiful and sexy and I'm going to show you off. And wear your hair down. And by the way, Mrs. Forrester," he lowered his voice and whispered in my ear as I walked by, "I'm so goddam in love with you I can hardly think straight. You're wrecking me."

"I'm glad to hear it." I planted a kiss on his mouth and practically floated into my room, where I dressed to the sounds of Chris neighing like a horse and Sam playing an ardent cowboy scene. It was nice to hear them, and I felt great.

"Where are we going?"

"Dinner on Clay Street. The competition is giving a party. But I've got something I want to say to you first." What now? He stopped the truck, pulled over to the side of the street, and turned to me with a funny look, then he took me in his arms and kissed me so hard it hurt. "You look fantastic. I said dress sexy, I didn't say make me drool for crissake."

"Flatterer." But I was pleased. I had worn a green and gold Indian shirt a la hippie, and tight black velvet pants with black suede boots. My hair was down, as per his orders, and I had nothing on under the shirt. And it seemed to be effective. Chris looked absolutely lecherous as we drove along.

The party was given by a San Francisco filmmaker who had made a recent hit with a film about drugs, and he was giving a party to celebrate in his brand new house. When we arrived, there were easily two hundred people roaming in the empty house to the sound of a wailing blues singer that was coming at us seemingly from all over the house. That seemed to be the only thing the new tenants had set up. The stereo. There was no furniture, nothing on the walls. The only decorations were the people, and they were exceedingly ornamental, all young, and nice to look at, in the style of Chris. There were girls in hippie shirts and skin-tight jeans with electric-looking hair and Bambi eyes, and long-haired boys in the same kind of clothes. Almost everyone was stoned and the smell of grass hung heavy in the air.

The house itself was a large bastardized Victorian, with a huge, sweeping staircase that seemed to soar toward a skylight miles above. There were people draped all over the banisters in earnest conversation, or necking heavily. It looked just like the parties I'd heard were typical of San Francisco but had never seen.

"Too heavy for you, Gill?" I felt a little bit square in that ambiance and Chris's question made me wonder if I looked it.

"No. It's neat. I think I like it."

"And I think I like you. Come on, I'll take you around to meet some of the troops." He took me by the hand and we drifted through the crowd, occasionally accepting a hit of hash or a puff on a joint as we went, and stopping for refills of red wine from one of the gallon jugs sitting on the floor. There must have been at least fifty of them in key points.

It seemed like a particularly low-key party. And much quieter than the scene at the Art Directors' bash on Friday. I was expecting exciting things to happen at any minute; it looked like the sort of group that would take off its clothes and begin to writhe on the floor in orgiastic glee. But instead, the crowd seemed to be thinning. We had been watching the scene for almost two hours, and then I looked up at Chris, wondering.

"It looks like more ought to be happening. Or am I missing the point?" He looked amused at my question, and seemed to hesitate.

"Like what?"

"I don't know." I felt silly having asked. Maybe this was it.

"Well, little Gillian, you're not too far wrong, but I thought we'd stick with the gang downstairs." We were still on the ground floor of the house. If you can call it that in San Francisco. Ground floor in this case had been two dizzying flights up the side of a hill as we approached the house from the street.

"Is something else happening upstairs?" I was curious.

"Maybe." Chris looked vague. He could have been dodging me, or it could have been the grass and hash.

"I want to see, Chris. Show me."

"We'll see." He introduced me to a few more people, necked with me in a corner for a while, and then we sat down on the floor to talk. But I noticed after a while that the crowds on the main floor seemed to walk up the stairs never to return. The party had moved on, and we were left like pebbles on the shore after the tide goes out. There were only a dozen people left sitting on the floor around us.

"Is the party over, or has the action moved on?"

"Gillian Forrester, you're a pest, but you asked, so . . . here goes . . . get up. We're going upstairs." He made it sound like a major event. "But I'm not sure you're going to like this."

"What lurking evils are you protecting me from, Mr. Matthews? Or should I wait and see?" We were weaving our way through the remaining bodies on the stairs; they were either drugged or drunk, but there seemed to be little life in them. The blues music on the stereo had turned to hard core jazz, and the sounds wailed through the gut as they did through the house, with a kind of strange pull and tug.

At the top of the first flight of stairs, Chris turned and looked at me for a long moment before kissing me longingly with his hand on my breast. The shirt I was wearing was so thin that I felt naked to his touch, and I suddenly longed to go home and make love to him.

"Gill, there are two scenes here . . . in there a bunch of people are dropping acid. It's not much to see, and I don't recommend it, and upstairs they're doing other stuff."

"What other stuff? Heroin?" My eyes were wide and I wasn't happy. I didn't like the idea of that scene at all.

"No, dopey. Not heroin. Other stuff . . . come on, at least I know you can handle that." He grinned to himself as he tucked my hand under his arm and raced up the stairs with me in tow. We were just under the skylight then, and that and two huge candles provided the room with its only light. It took a minute for my eyes to adjust. I knew that there were a lot of people where we were, but I couldn't tell how many, or what they were doing, or what kind of room we were in. It struck me only that there was relatively little noise. And then I saw where we were.

We were in a room the width and length of the house, a kind of loft that lay just beneath the skylight and had few windows, and like the rest of the house no furniture. But it had more action. Lots. In the sea around us were most of the two hundred bodies we'd seen downstairs, their jeans and shirts off, their bodies pretzeled into odd positions, locked into each other in groups of four and five and six, and they were all making love. It was an orgy.

"Gill . . . is this okay?" I saw him watching me in the candlelight.

"I . . . uh . . . yeah . . . sure, Chris . . . but . . ."

"But what, love? We don't have to get into this." A scene behind him had just caught my eye. There were two girls making love to each other while two men stroked their bodies with hungry pleasure and yet another girl wove her tongue between one of the observers' thighs.

"I . . . uh . . . Chris . . . I don't think I want to." I knew I didn't want to, but I was still a little too stunned to speak coherently. I was twenty-eight years old and had been hearing about stuff like this for years. But it was different seeing it . . . and I didn't want to do it.

Chris took my hand and led me slowly back down the stairs, smiling over his shoulder at me, and stopping to kiss me on the way. The kiss was a gentle one and his smile was warm. He didn't seem sorry we had left.

"I'll take you home." . . . And come back here alone? . . . My heart sank and my face must have showed it. "Not like that, dopey. No sweat. I can do without that. Group sex is a bore." I wondered how often he'd tried it until it became a bore, but I didn't say anything. I was grateful for his reaction. And I was glad we were going home, I'd seen enough. My education was complete, without joining in a gangbang. I'd seen it. Basta cosí.

"Thanks, Chris. Am I a horrible stuffed-shirt?"

"Nope. Kind of a nice one." He grinned happily at my transparent shirt, leaned down to kiss one breast, and led me out the door. We were going home.

The ride back to my place was brief and comfortably silent, and I felt even closer to him than I had before. He parked the truck in front of the house and helped me out, and I wondered if he was going to stay.

I paid the sitter and she left. And before she did, she diligently told me there were no messages, which made me smile. I was with the only one I would have wanted anyway.

"Some wine, Chris?" He shook his head and looked at me for a long moment as we stood there. "Are you angry we left?"

"No. I like your style. Come on, Gill, it's late. Let's go to bed. I've got a lot of work to do tomorrow."

"So do I." There was a nice homey feeling as we turned off the lights in the living room and crept past Sam's room to mine. I was glad he was staying and thought it funny that we had so easily slipped into the kind of relationship we had—"let's go to bed, it's late, I've got a lot of work tomorrow." I expected him to peel off his jeans, sit lazily on the edge of the bed as he set the alarm, and then kiss me goodnight before going to sleep. I didn't even mind not being made love to, it was comfortable the way it was.

I was smiling to myself as I brushed my hair and Chris looked surprised.

"What are you doing, Gill?"

"What's it look like? Brushing my hair, you dopey."

"The hell you are. I don't give a shit about gangbangs, but I brought my orgy home. . . . Come here, you, let me do that." He stood up and met me halfway across the room, his hands already stretched toward me to peel off my clothes. I unbuttoned his shirt as he did mine, and then we stood there chest to chest, the smoothness of our skin met and melted into one, as my slacks came off in unison with his, and his whole body seemed to enter mine.

7

"Hey . . . Chris . . . it's getting light outside. And you didn't get any sleep." I felt faintly guilty about that, but not very.

"I'm not complaining. Are you? But I've got to get to work soon. We start at six." It was already five. "Let's get dressed and go outside. I want to see the sun come up."

"So do I." But inside me, it already had. We climbed back into our clothes which still lay in a jumble on the floor and walked outside to sit on the tiny patch of lawn in front of where I lived. It was chilly and the ground was damp, but it felt good as we sat there and watched the sun come up over the East Bay.

"No fog today. That'll be good for my shooting. Want to come watch?"

"I'd love it, but I don't think I can. I've got to get Sam to school, and I've got a shooting at ten. Textile stuff. They're shooting just the fabrics somewhere outside first, and then we do the models at ten. At the Opera House yet. It sounds like fun."

"Of course it does . . . who do you think's doing the camera work?" He looked amused as he grabbed my hair and pulled it back so he could kiss me.

"Hey . . . are you on that job?"

"Who do you think recommended you?" He tried to look pompous.

"Bullshit you did. They told me Joe Tramino gave them my name, you big phoney."

"Well, okay . . . but I told them you were a great stylist."

"After I had the job."

"After you had the job. Boy, the ego of some women."

"Not to mention some men. . . . I'm glad we'll be working together. Think we can ride a horse across the orchestra pit and down Van Ness?"

"We can try . . . baby, we can always try." He rolled his body onto mine on the wet grass and we lay there smiling for a moment in the early morning sun. "I gotta go, Gill. I'll see you at work."

"That's the most unusual morning good-bye this neighborhood has ever seen, Chris Matthews. But I like it."

"Good, because it isn't the last. And this neighborhood can't do a goddam thing about it if they don't like it."

"They could evict me." I was feeling playful and I walked him to the truck.

"We'll talk about that sometime . . . but not just yet." He slammed the door to the truck, put it into gear, and I wondered what he had meant as he drove away. Whatever he had meant, it would be fun to work with him that day, and it was nice to know that the head of the film crew would be at as great a disadvantage as I. I knew exactly what he'd been doing the night before. And neither of us had had a moment's sleep. To hell with the Clay Street orgy. Chris and I had had our own.

I arrived at the Opera House at exactly ten o'clock, stood back to look at its splendor for a moment before going in, and then smiled. It looked like a funny place for Chris.

I went in the stage door, and was told where to go, and arrived somewhere behind the stage to look at the clothes and props I'd picked out the day before, and check in with the agency people who seemed pleased with what I'd dug up. It was going to be a pretty shooting.

They had seven of San Francisco's top models and three they'd imported from Los Angeles for the day. They were beautiful girls and the clothes they were going to wear in the commercial we were filming were superb. Everything from evening clothes to beach wear to show off some new man-made fiber.

I assigned the appropriate clothes and accesssories to each girl and then went off to find Chris. It didn't take long. He and his crew were lying in the string section of the orchestra pit, eating tacos and salami sandwiches and drinking cherry soda.

"Breakfast or lunch? Hi, boys."

"Neither. This is just between the two. Come on down and have a bite." Chris looked wicked for the briefest second, and then looked pleased with his double entendre. It made me wonder how little or how much he wanted his crew to know. I suspected less than more. And I was glad . . . I didn't want Joe Tramino to offer his condolences quite yet. Not till we were sure.

I hopped into the pit, landed on my feet near Chris, and then sat down to guzzle cherry soda and munch on tacos.

"You know what, boys? This stuff is disgusting. Blyergh."

"You know what? She's right." Everyone looked pleased to agree, and we went on eating happily until they told us the models and the scenery were ready to go. We had been allowed the use of some of the opera's stage props for the day, and it was fun to see it all from backstage. As I stood in the wings, checking each girl as she went out, and watching for lack of continuity as girls went out for a second or third time in the same clothes, I looked towards the Boxes, and the Grand Tier, and wondered what it would be like to sing to them . . . or to be in the audience again on the snobby, social nights when everyone would wear white tie and tails. Those days were so far behind me, it was funny to think of them.

"Whatcha thinking about, Gill?"

"Nothing much. What are you doing back here?"

"We're all through."

"Already? It's only . . ." I looked at my watch and gasped. It was four-fifteen.

"That's right. We've been working six hours straight. Let's go pick up Sam and put in some beach time at the Marina."

"Yes, boss." I saluted sharply, and we left hand in hand.

The day of working with him had flown. This time there had been no crazy escapades, just a lot of hard work. And stolen kisses in the pit.

We picked up Sam and wandered over to the beach where she chased sea gulls and we played word games in the sand until the sun began to fade.

"Sam, time to go home!" She was far down the beach and had other things in mind. But Chris changed it for her quickly.

"Come on, podner, I'll give you a ride."

"Okay, Uncle Crits." She galloped down the beach to meet us, hopped on Chris's back, and I watched them hobble home. The child and the man I loved . . . Samantha Forrester and her "horse." My man.

"What are you doing today, Gill? Any work come up?" He had been staying with us every night for a week, and breakfast a trois had become an ordinary thing. It looked routine, but it felt like Christmas to me every day.

"Nope. How about going out to Stinson, Chris? We could take Sam after school."

"Can't. I've got a job today at three. Another cigarette job."

"That's nice. I'll do stuff here. Will you be home for dinner?" That was the first time I had asked him that, and I held my breath.

"Maybe not. We'll see."

I did. He wasn't. He was gone for two days, and when he reappeared on Thursday there was nothing to show that he'd been gone. He looked and sounded the same, but he had left a tiny dent in my heart. Not to mention Sam. I had finally decided that if he didn't show up by the end of the week I was going to use her much dreamt of trick and tie her to a chair and gag her. I couldn't stand the questions anymore.

I wanted to ask him where he'd been but I didn't dare. I made hamburgers and French fries and we all went to Swensen's on Hyde Street after dinner. They had the best ice cream in town.

"Want to take a ride on the cable car, Sam?" She was dripping strawberry, and we were dripping rocky road. We had made the appropriate choice.

"A cable car ride? Wow!" And so it was. We hopped on when it came by and reeled down toward Fisherman's Wharf where Chris bought her a painted turtle. How can you stay mad at a man like that? He ran around us playfully like a big dog, kissed me back into a feeling of almost-security, and further seduced Sam. By the time we got home we were a solid trio again and all was well. Almost.

"Want to go to Bolinas tomorrow, Gill?" We were lying in bed and the lights were out.

"Let's see what the weather's doing." I wasn't sure.

"Don't be a grump, Miss Gillian. I meant for the weekend. I got someone to lend me their shack till Monday."

"You did?" I was pleased. "That would be nice."

"That's what I thought. And now, stop being grumpy. I'm back, and I love you." He kissed my neck and put a hand gently across my lips to silence them, and we lost another night of sleep. But we won each other back.

The weekend in Bolinas was lovely. The shack which someone had lent him was almost that, but not quite. It was a small two-bedroom house buried in the woods. We went to the beach every day, had dinner at the Watson House one night, and the rest of the time spent quiet evenings at home. There was a marvelous aura of peace about the few days we spent there. San Francisco seemed quiet to me after New York, but the time in Bolinas even managed to make San Francisco seem too busy. There was a golden stillness to those days. And I was sorry to leave on Monday.

The week following the Bolinas weekend was busy. I got another job from Carson, but Chris wasn't on it this time; he had other things to do. He came to dinner with us in the evenings though, and most of the time he spent the night. He vanished again that weekend but reappeared Sunday night and never left us for a week after that. It was a bit strange the way he came and went, but I got used to it, and everything was rolling smoothly.

We were unbelievably happy together, and I got to the point where I didn't even mind his disappearances—they gave me some time to myself and I needed that too.

The weeks rolled by and I realized at the end of May that we had spent two months together, which seemed more like two years. I had become a combination wife-mother-girl friend-pal to Chris Matthews and I could no longer imagine a time when I hadn't known him. He was my best friend, and the man I loved. And he was always fun to be with. There was a selfishness about him too—he never did anything he didn't want to do, he couldn't be pressed into anything—but I didn't try. I understood his ways, and I accepted them. In many ways I felt older than he, but I had led a different life. And I had Sam to make me feel grownup. He'd never had anything like that. He only had Chris Matthews to think of and, when he felt like it, me.

We were lying under a tree in the park one Thursday morning, with nothing much to do except enjoy the world and love each other, and I remembered that Memorial Day weekend was that week. Not that it changed things for us a great deal—almost every weekend we had was a long one, unless one of us had a job on Monday, which was never sure for either of us.

"What are you doing this weekend, Chris? It's a holiday."

"Yeah. I guess it is. I'm moving out of town as a matter of fact."

"Very funny. But I get the message. I was just asking." I picked a blade of grass next to where we lay and tickled the side of his face with it, wondering when he'd get rid of the girl he lived with. He hadn't yet.

"I wasn't kidding, Gill. I am moving. Out to Bolinas for the summer. Want to come?"

"Are you kidding or are you for real?" This was the first I'd heard of it, other than vague mention two months back that he usually spent his summers in Bolinas. But with Chris very little was "usual" and nothing ever seemed to be planned.

"I'm for real. I thought I'd move out tomorrow or Saturday. I meant to tell you. Why don't you and Sam come and stay?"

"And after that? She's already so attached to you, Chris, if she gets used to having you around all the time it's going to really hurt when we come back to this. She's already had that once, with her father . . . I don't know. . . ."

"Don't be so stuffy. She'll be happy with us, and you said you were going to send her East to see him anyway,

so that'll wean her off me." . . . But what about me? . . .
"When's she going to see him?"

"Middle of July till the end of August. Roughly six
weeks."

"Okay. So what's the sweat? She'll spend six weeks with
us and six weeks with him. And we can be alone for a
while . . . Gill, please . . I'd really like you to." He turned
to me with the expression of a starving, lonely child, and
my heart melted. I didn't know whether to laugh or jump
at the chance. It would be so nice to live with Chris . . .
but what then?

"We'll see . . . anyway, what would I do about work?"
That was a lame reason not to do it, and we both knew it.

"Don't be a jerk. I work out of Bolinas, so can you.
There's a phone over there. You'll get your calls . . . oh
hell, if you don't want to, screw it." Suddenly I was the
bad guy, and he was hurt. But he hadn't even told me he
was moving. That was so like Chris.

"I want to, I want to, for chrissake . . . okay, I'll come.
I'm just afraid I'll get used to you that's all. Can't you try
and understand that? I love you, Chris, and I want to live
with you, but when we come back to San Francisco at the
end of the summer I go back to my place and you go back
to your roommate." I hadn't mentioned it in a long time.

"As a matter of fact, Gill, you're wrong. She's moving
out next week or something. I gave her notice."

"You did? She is? . . . Hey . . . wow!"

"That's right, little lady. Wow. And I thought that if it
works out this summer you and Sam could move in with
me in September. The house is big enough for all of us."
. . . But what about your heart, Chris? . . . It was a dumb
thing to think. I knew he loved us. And I was thrilled the
girl was leaving . . . at last.

"Chris Matthews, do you know what? . . . I love you.
And Bolinas is going to be super. Take me home, I want
to pack."

"Yes ma'am. At your service."

It dawned on me as we drove back to the Marina that I
had never seen his house in the city. I knew it was on

Sacramento Street, but that was all. I had a sudden urge to see it, to take a long drunken look at the place where we would live in the fall, but that could wait. He had said "if it works out this summer." But why shouldn't it? I couldn't see any reason why it shouldn't. No reason at all.

8

"Chris! . . . Sam! . . . Lunch is ready!" A large red enamel plate was buried under a dozen peanut butter and jelly sandwiches and a pitcher of milk stood next to it. We were going to eat under the big tree behind the tiny house Chris rented every summer, which had become our summer home. It was a gem. He had painted it the year before, and everything was a bright, sunny yellow, and there were splashes of color everywhere. It was simple and rustic, but comfortable, and it was close to the beach, which was all we needed.

"I'm coming, Mommy. Uncle Crits said he'd take me riding this afternoon." Samantha staggered to the lunch table under the weight of the cowboy holster Chris had given her and shoved a sandwich into her mouth with a look of satisfaction.

"You want to come too, Gill?"

"Sure." I looked over Sam's head at Chris for a long moment, and we shared a secret smile. Things were working out. Beautifully. We had been in Bolinas for a month, and it was like something out of a fairy tale. We went riding and swimming, we sat outside at night, and we were so in love with each other we could hardly see straight.

Sam was supposed to leave in two weeks to spend the rest of her vacation with Richard, and for once I felt less badly about Samantha leaving. I was looking forward to being alone with Chris. Even though I couldn't see how things could get any better than they were.

"Hey, Gill . . . what's the matter?" I suddenly felt ill, and it must have showed. My stomach rolled slowly toward my throat and then down again, in a kind of slow-motion roller coaster feeling.

"I don't know . . . must be something I ate."

"Peanut butter? Can't be. Maybe too much sun. Go lie down. I'll keep an eye on Sam." I followed his suggestion, and half an hour later I felt better.

"You still want to ride with us, love?"

"Maybe I'll skip it. I'll go tomorrow."

"Oh shit . . . I forgot to tell you. I'm going into town tonight. I have a job tomorrow."

"Lucky you." I hadn't had a job in almost three weeks. Summer was slowing things down. But it didn't matter much. We were living cheaply in Bolinas. "When will you be back?" It didn't make much difference, we never had any plans, and we were leading a lazy life.

"Tomorrow night, or the day after. It depends how long we take to shoot. This is a documentary for the state." He smiled at me for a moment. "Don't worry, I'll be back."

"I'm glad to hear it."

But he wasn't back the next night, or the night after that. He came back three days later, and I had been worried. I had called the house on Sacramento Street and had gotten no answer.

"Where the hell were you, Chris?"

"I was busy for chrissake. What were you worried about? You knew I'd come back. So what's the big deal?"

"The big deal is that something could have happened to you, that's all."

"You worry about you, and I'll worry about me." And that's the way it was. End of discussion.

"Fine. I'm going into town tomorrow myself. Joe Tramino called me for a job at Carson."

"Great." Yeah . . . great . . . but you were still gone three days and what the hell were you doing? You didn't even call. . . . But I didn't want to ask.

That evening, he acted as though nothing had happened, and I left him in charge of Sam the next morning as I set out to drive across the mountains in his car. I was due in town at nine. And Joe had invited me to lunch if the shooting was over in time. It was. He took me to a late lunch at Enrico's, on lower Broadway, looking down Montgomery Street toward the newly built up financial district. We sat outside, and it was warm and sunny, with a nice cool breeze that rustled through the trees out front.

"You did a nice job today, Gill. How's life been treating you?" He looked concerned. He knew.

"Fine. Everything is really fine."

"You look like you've lost some weight."

"And you sound like my mother." But he was right, I hadn't felt really well since the day the peanut butter sandwich had gone sour on me at lunch. That had been almost a week, but it was probably just worry over Chris's absence.

"Okay. I'll lay off. But I was right. I'm still kicking my ass in for introducing you to that guy . . . and I am crawling my office walls in a jealous frenzy. Haven't you heard?" We both broke into a laugh, and I shook my head.

"You're full of shit, Joe. But you're good for my ego. And just for the record, Chris and I are really happy. You did a nice thing for both of us. All is well." I felt silly having to reassure him, but his concern seemed genuine and I meant what I said. He had done a nice thing for all of us, including Sam.

The lunch was pleasant, we talked about the shooting and a variety of other things, and when we rose to leave I was sorry. He was good company, and it was pleasant to just sit there, watching people come and go, and talking about nothing in particular.

I stopped at my apartment on the way back, picked up my mail, a few odds and ends, like a new kite for Sam, and then I went back. I was a little earlier than planned, but it would be nice to get back into sloppy clothes and go for a swim. The day had gotten hot.

*   *   *

"Hi troops, I'm home." But it appeared that no one else was. It was after five, but they were probably at the beach; they might even have gone to Stinson. "Hello! Anybody here?" But it was obvious that there wasn't or Sam would have come screeching out to meet me.

I kicked off my shoes in the living room, headed toward the kitchen for a glass of something cold, and then noticed that the bedroom door was closed. Closed doors were unusual in our house in Bolinas, and for some reason it suddenly made me wonder if everything were okay. Some maternal instinct spoke up deep within me . . . Sam? . . .

I walked to the bedroom door with three deliberate steps, stopped, took a deep breath, and turned the handle. But what I found was not Sam. It was Chris. Making love to someone else in the bed we shared.

"Ohhh . . . I . . ." I stood rooted to the spot, my mouth frozen into what felt like an iron "O", and my eyes began instantly to blur with tears. Chris turned his head to look at me as I opened the door, and the only thing that struck me was that his face was as expressionless as his buttocks which stared at me from the bed. No dismay, no horror. Nothing. The girl had leapt beneath him as I entered, murmuring a horrified gasp, and looking around the room with terrified eyes, as though she might have wished to escape through the window. I couldn't blame her, I felt precisely the same way. Perhaps that's what we should have done, both left together via the window, leaving Chris alone. But we didn't. She lay there, pinned down by Chris's firm grasp on her arms, and I slammed the door. What could I say? But then it occurred to me that there was something I had to say, and anger welled in me as never before. I spun around on one heel and flung the door open again, addressing Chris.

"I don't give a shit what you're doing or who she is, but where's my daughter?" Another gasp emanated from the bed, and Chris turned to me with a look of fury on his face, but it was no match for my own.

"What the fuck do you think, Gill? That I tied her up

and put her under the bed? The Gillmours picked her up for a picnic hours ago. I said I'd pick her up at six."

"Don't bother." The girl was squirming under Chris' viselike grip, and the ignominy and horror of the entire scene struck me like another blow. "I'll be back to pick up my things in an hour." I slammed the door again, picked up my shoes in the living room, grabbed my handbag, and ran barefoot toward the car. To hell with Christopher Matthews. If this was what it was going to be like, he could take his lousy life and do anything he damn well pleased with it. I didn't want any part of it . . . no, thanks . . . the rotten . . . lousy . . . cheating . . . miserable . . . Tears streamed down my face and sobs choked me as I drove toward the Gillmours' place. All I wanted to do was get Sam and then get the hell out of Chris's house. For good. I was suddenly relieved that I hadn't given up my apartment in the city. Sam and I could go back that night and make believe nothing had ever happened. Chris had never existed . . . Chris was gone. . . .

The tires squealed as I drove into the Gillmours' driveway. I pulled up behind their station wagon, put on the brake, turned off the ignition, and wiped my face. I felt as though the world had just come to an end, and how was I going to face Sam?

Elinor Gillmour came out as I got out of the car and waved as she stood barefoot in the doorway.

"Hi, Gillian. How was your day?" . . . How was my day? Are you kidding?

"Fine. Thanks for taking Sam on the picnic. I bet she loved it." The Gillmours had five children, two of whom were close enough in age to Sam to make an outing with them really fun for her. Visiting them was like going to a playgroup.

"Hi, Mommy, can I stay for dinner?" Sam had come thundering out at the sound of my voice.

"No, sweetheart, we have to go home." You bet . . . home . . . San Francisco, to our place in the Marina.

"Awww . . . Mommy." She wound up for a good long whine and I shook my head.

"I'm not kidding tonight, Sam. We're going home. Thanks, Elinor. Now, let's go." I took her firmly by the hand and led her to the car, as we waved a last wave to the Gillmour brood trickling out of the house. "Did you have a nice time?"

"Yes. Can we do something special for dinner? Like have a picnic with Uncle Crits?"

"No, you just had a picnic, and I have a surprise for you. We have to go back to the city for a few days, so Mommy can do some things." A few days seemed like enough explanation, I had decided. She was going off with her father in a week anyway.

"Why? I don't want to go back to the city. Is Uncle Crits coming too?" She seemed cheerier at the thought.

"No, sweetheart. He has to stay here." You're damned right he does. I was absolutely livid by the time we got back to Chris's house. I didn't even feel hurt anymore. I just wanted to kill him. But I didn't want Sam to know that there was trouble underfoot.

"Gill . . ." He was waiting for us outside the house when we got there.

"Hi, Uncle Crits. It was a nice picnic."

"Hi, Sam. Would you do me a big favor and go water my plants for me again. They look thirsty as a cowboy in the desert. Thanks."

"Sure, Uncle Crits." She looked delighted with the errand, and ran off behind the house to comply.

"Gill. . . ." He followed me into the house as I headed for the bedroom.

"Forget it, Chris. Don't bother saying anything. I'm not interested. I saw what was going on and I don't dig that scene. I'm going back to the city tonight with Sam. I'll see that you get the car back somehow tomorrow."

"Fuck the car."

"That too? My, my . . ." I was yanking drawers open in our room by then, and most of my things were already lying in a heap in my suitcase on the unmade bed. The bed. Where he screwed that girl. The bastard."You could have at least made the goddam bed."

"Look, Gill, please. . . ."

"No. No 'please.' Just nothing. I'm getting the hell out. Now."

"Look, it was no big deal. I don't give a damn about her. It doesn't change anything between us. She's just a girl I picked up in town." He sounded desperate.

"Oh? Is she? I'm thrilled. Just thrilled, to know that she doesn't mean anything to you. But it seems to me that neither do I. The whole time I've known you you've been living with some girl. You come, you go, you arrive for dinner, spend the night, and then disappear for three days. And now you fuck some girl, just for the hell of it. In our bed, and hell . . . it's your goddam bed, but I don't give a shit. We're supposed to be living together. And I don't do stuff like that. That's probably my big mistake."

"No, Gill, it's not your mistake. I love you the way you are. But I'm a man for crissake, and I need to have some fun."

"Then what am I?" My voice seemed to shake the rafters.

"You're not just fun, Gill. You're for real. I love you." His voice had dropped to an almost whisper, and he looked at me earnestly from across the room. "Please don't go, Gill. I need you. I'm sorry this happened."

"Well so am I. But I'm going anyway." But my resolve had been shaken . . . I was for real? But what did that mean? "Chris, it's going to happen again and again, I can smell it. And I just can't take it. I'm sorry." . . . Sorry? . . . Why the hell should I be sorry? . . . But I was.

"Why do you have to turn it into such a goddam major happening? Because it just isn't. It really isn't."

"Maybe not to you. But it is to me. Do you have any idea what it felt like to walk in and see you pumping your prick into her, your ass staring me in the face, and her legs spread fifteen yards apart." The mental image made me sick.

"You make it sound terrific." He had calmed down and he wasn't letting me get to him anymore.

"Well, maybe it was terrific. What the hell do I know? It

sure looked like it from where I stood. Do you know what I feel? I feel stupid and inadequate, and like I'm not enough woman for you. If you're not happy with us, then tell me. But all I know is we ball our asses off, and the minute I turn my back you go off and screw somebody else. Joe Tramino was right." I regretted that the instant it was out of my mouth. I should have left Joe out of it.

"And what did that little dago fart have to say about me?" Chris was suddenly livid.

"Nothing. Forget it. He just said you'd make me unhappy, and it looks like he was right."

"Bullshit. We've been plenty happy. And the fact is if you'd come home when you said you were going to you'd have found me and Sam eating dinner in the kitchen, and nothing would have changed. You wouldn't have known. And if you really cared about me, you'd understand, and nothing would be changed now that you do know." . . . Huh?

"Are you kidding?"

"No, I'm not. It could happen to you too, Gill. And I wouldn't walk out on you. You're right, we live together. And I love you, and I understand how people work, which is something you don't." I was beginning to wonder if he was right, and it shook me. There was something so cool and knowledgeable in his voice. Maybe those things did happen all the time. But why to me? . . . And why did I have to see it? "Gill, will you spend the night, and see how you feel in the morning? This is silly, and you'll get Sam all shook up going back into town now. I have a job in town tomorrow; if you still want to call it quits, I'll drive you in." I didn't want to sleep on it, but he had a point about Sam. I was wavering, and he knew it.

"Well . . . all right. For Sam. But stay out of my way. I'll sleep on the couch. You can have your bedroom back, as of right now." I swung my badly packed suitcase down on the floor and walked out of the room.

"I'll cook dinner, Gill. You take it easy. You look rough."

"I feel rough, thank you. But I'll do the cooking for

Sam. I'm not hungry, and you can take care of yourself." I walked outside to check on Sam before making dinner. She was still devotedly watering Chris's plants and showed no sign that she had heard the fracas. But I was afraid she had.

"Sam, whatcha want to eat, love? How about some cold chicken?"

"That's fine, Mommy." I knew then that she had heard, at least some of it, because she was being inordinately good-natured. But I was grateful.

"You're a good girl."

"Thanks, Mommy. Is Uncle Crits gonna eat with us?"

"No, he's not." My mouth tightened uncontrollably over the words.

"Okay."

She ate the chicken almost soundlessly and then put her pajamas on by herself and told me she was ready for bed. My heart went out to her as I tucked her in. I hated to have her think, yet again, that men wandered through our lives only to go away again. Or have me walk out on them. It didn't seem fair. And I hated Chris for making it all happen again, and myself for letting it. I should never have moved in with him in Bolinas, and I felt nothing but regret as I kissed Sam goodnight and turned off the light.

"See you in the morning, sweetheart. Sweet dreams." A tear crept down my cheek as I walked back to the kitchen for a cup of coffee, and I felt as though all of me were sagging. It had been such a rotten afternoon. And I couldn't see how tomorrow would be much better.

"How are you feeling, Gill?" I hadn't heard him come into the kitchen.

"Fine, thank you. Would you mind listening for Sam? I'd like to go for a walk."

"Yeah, sure. Okay." I felt his eyes on me as I quietly closed the door and walked down the road toward the beach. It was a quiet night and the air was still warm. The fog mustn't have come in. But I had been too busy earlier to notice. I looked up and saw the stars brightly etched in the sky above, but even that didn't make me feel better.

The sea was lapping gently at the beach when I got there, and I lay down on the cool sand, to think. Or not to think. I didn't really care what I did. I just wanted to be alone, and away from Chris. And as far away from the house as I could.

I watched a stray dog amble slowly past and sniff at the water, and then, without thinking, I began to take off my clothes. I slipped into the water, naked, and swam slowly toward the land spit at the end of Stinson Beach, remembering the day Chris and I had crossed that stretch of water with the horse from the Carson shooting. The day we'd met. The first day . . . that had been three months before, and this was such a different day.

Once on the other side, I lay on the sand in the bright moonlight and wondered what would come next, and if I'd ever trust anyone again. It seemed as though I lay there for hours, and then I heard footsteps in the sand behind me and turned in sudden fear.

"Gill?" It was Chris.

"What are you doing here? You said you'd stay with Sam." He could have at least done that much.

"She's fine. She's sound asleep, and I wanted to talk to you."

"There's nothing to say. How did you know I'd be here?"

"I just knew. I would have come to the same place too."

"I didn't think you'd have cared that much." The tears started out of the corners of my eyes again as I said the words.

"I only wish you knew how much I do care, Gill." He sat down on the sand beside me, and I could see his wet flesh glisten in the dark.

"I'd better get back to Sam." I didn't want to wait and be told anything.

"Sit with me for just a minute . . . please." There was something in his voice that caught at my heart, almost the way Sam's quiet good behavior had when she went to bed.

"Why, Chris? What's the point? We've said it all."

"No, we haven't. Or if we have, then let me just be with

you here, quietly, for a few minutes. I can't stand the thought of your leaving me." I shut my eyes hard and squelched a sob before it rose in my throat. "Want to take a walk?" I nodded silently, and we set off down the beach, side by side, but far apart. I still felt terribly alone.

"We'd better go back, Chris. Sam." We had walked halfway to the point at the other end, and we still had to walk back to the inlet, swim back to the Bolinas Beach, and then get back to the house. It would take at least a half hour to accomplish, and I had really begun to worry about Sam being alone in the house. She'd be frightened if she woke up and there was no one there. It wasn't danger-ous, but it still wasn't nice.

"Okay, Gill. I wanted to stop at our cove." His voice sounded like that of a small boy who has just suffered an immense disappointment, but his words were like a slap in the face.

"Chris, how could you? You really don't understand a goddam thing." The peace of the silent walk on the moon-lit beach was totally interrupted, and I began to run to-ward the inlet. When I got there, I dove into the water and swam as hard as I could toward the other side. But he reached the beach even before I did and he swung me into his arms and held me tight when I got out of the water.

"You just shut up, goddam you, Gillian Forrester. I did a lousy thing today. But I love you, and if you don't know that by now you aren't worth a damn." He crushed his mouth down hard onto mine and his kiss touched my very soul.

"Chris. . . ."

"Shut up. We have to go back to Sam." He took my hand firmly in his, walked me over to my pile of clothes, and watched me dress as he slid into his jeans. They were all he'd worn.

When I was dressed, he took me by the hand again, and we walked back to the house without saying another word. The lights were on, and all was quiet when we got in. I checked and was relieved to see that Sam was still asleep. And as I walked away from her room I saw ours. Chris had tidied up, the bed was made with fresh sheets, and there were flowers from the garden in a vase.

"Are you coming to bed?" He was sitting on the edge of it, and smiled a tiny smile.

"You did a nice job." There was no sign to remind me of what had happened that afternoon, except what was already lodged in my head, like an aching splinter.

"You didn't answer my question. Are you coming to bed?" He flicked out the light, and I stood there in the darkness, wondering what to do. I didn't want to get into the bed, but I didn't want to leave him either. I wondered if he had been right when he had said earlier that if I had come home as late as I'd planned I wouldn't have known, and nothing would have changed. Except I hadn't come home as planned.

He turned over on his side in the darkness and I walked slowly into the room and began to take off my clothes. I would sleep with him, but I would not make love. Maybe he didn't want to anyway. He had had his for the day. The memory made me cringe again as I slipped between the sheets, turned my back to him, and fell asleep, exhausted.

I woke up next morning to the smell of bacon frying, and looked at the clock. It was 5 a.m. and it was foggy outside.

"Good morning, sleeping beauty. Breakfast's on the table." I felt more like sleeping ugly than sleeping beauty, and the smell of the bacon made me feel sick. The nausea I felt reminded me again of the day before. My nerves were obviously falling apart.

"Hi, Mommy. We made you waffers."

"Waffles. And you're all dressed. Looks like you two have been up all night." And I felt as though I had, but I had to put a good face on it, for Sam at least.

I got up and brushed my teeth and felt a little better after that, and the waffles were good. I ate two and Sam was thrilled.

"Aren't they delicious, Mommy?"

"Terrific, Sam." I cast a brief glance at Chris, but he

was busy cleaning up the kitchen. "What's everybody doing up so early?"

"I have to be on location at six, and if you still want to go to the city we've got to get moving. I'm already late." He looked at me pointedly across the room.

"Fine. Thanks. I'll get Sam's stuff packed up, and I'll be dressed in ten minutes." Blue jeans and a shirt. I had nothing to do in town anyway. Except congratulate Joe Tramino for his good judgment.

Sam looked downcast as we left, and I tried to get her to sing songs as we wound our way over the mountain road. I was grateful for the fog; I didn't have to see long sweeping views of Stinson and Bolinas stretching behind me as we left. All we could see was a brief patch of road ahead of us, and the fog-crowned hills stretching above us.

The roads were deserted at that hour, and we were in the city in thirty minutes. Chris pulled up in front of my apartment and gave Sam a piggyback ride to the front door.

"I'll be seeing you, podner." She looked as though she were about to cry, and then he leaned down and whispered something in her ear which sparked a smile on her face like a sunburst.

"Okay, Uncle Crits. Good-bye." She ran into the house and slammed the screen door as I turned to Chris.

"What did you tell her?" I wanted to know. I didn't want him telling her any lies about his coming back. "I want to know."

"None of your business. It's just between the two of us. And I have a message for you too. Only that this isn't the end. And don't waste your time thinking this is it, because it just plain isn't. I won't let it be. Do you hear me?" He stared into my eyes for one long moment and then kissed my forehead before he turned his back, walked away, and drove off.

He had made a big mistake. For me, it was all over.

*   *   *

I dropped Sam off at her old playgroup at nine and was pleased to see that she didn't seem to mind being back. And then I went home to unpack.

I also had to call all the advertising agencies I did freelance work for and tell them I'd moved back to town. And then what? Cry, maybe? Yeah, why the hell not?

But as it turned out, I sat around the house drinking coffee until I picked Sam up at school and we went to the zoo. I couldn't face the suitcases or the calls to the agencies, it was too depressing. We ate dinner at the Hippo on the way home, and Sam and I had a minor fight over the menu.

"But I don't like gorillas, Mommy. They're scary."

"It's just a hamburger, Sam. They only call it a gorilla-burger."

She was dubious, but she finally decided to try it, threatening me with an instant walkout if it turned out to be scary. Apparently it wasn't, and the hamburger and French fries disappeared in minutes, while I tried hard to hide a smile.

We went home in the fading light of what had turned out to be a very pleasant summer day, and I gave her her bath and put her to bed. But I knew that sooner or later it would catch up with me. Chris was gone.

"May I come in?" My heart soared as I saw the shaggy blond mane poke through the door. "You should lock your door."

"And you should listen to what people tell you. I told you to stay away." But I was so glad to see him there that I felt like throwing my arms around him. His absence had weighed on me like a hundred-pound backpack all day.

"You're full of shit, Gill. And anyway, I had to come back. I promised Sam." He had already sprawled on the couch and was looking pleased.

"Well, you shouldn't have."

"I'm taking you both back to Bolinas tomorrow. I figured the day in town would do you good."

"It did. And we're staying."

"In that case, so am I. But it's asinine to let the place in Bolinas just sit there empty."

"So don't let it. Go back. I don't care where you stay."

"Oh really?" He had gotten off the couch and was walking slowly to the chair where I was sitting, smoking a cigarette, and shaking inside. "Well, it just so happens that I care plenty where you are, Mrs. Gillian Forrester. And I want you to be with me. Have you gotten that message yet?" He was leaning over my chair, with a hand firmly clenched on each arm of the chair. His face was lowering slowly toward mine and I knew that he was going to kiss me.

"Chris, don't!" I shoved at his chest but he kept right on coming at me anyway, and then he kissed me. "Stop it!"

"No, you stop it. This has gone far enough. I'll eat crow for the next week. But I'm not going to let this thing get out of proportion. So get that into your head." And with that, he swept me out of the chair, carried me into the bedroom, and dumped me on the bed.

"Chris Matthews, get out of this house!" I stood on the bed and shouted at him, but he swung his arm gently in the air and knocked me down on the bed. And then in one swift movement, his body was on mine, and the end was over. We had begun again.

"Are we going back to Bolinas this morning or not? The weather looks lousy, by the way." We were in bed, and we could see from the window that the fog was in again.

"I don't see much point, Chris. I have three jobs next week, and Richard is picking up Sam on Friday anyway. Let's stay in."

"Okay." He was being very amenable.

"But I want to stay here, not Sacramento Street." Chris's place.

"Why?"

"For a number of reasons. For one thing, there's no point feeding Sam stuff that's going to make waves with her father. I'd just as soon she not be able to tell him we've moved out of our place and into yours. It was different in Bolinas. And . . . well, the other stuff's not important." But it was to me. I just didn't want to be someplace where I'd know he had already slept with a hundred different girls. Some of them in the past three months. Even Bolinas still had a faint sour taste. I wanted to stay at my place in the city.

"I think you're silly. But I'll go along with it. I've got a lot of work to do anyway."

So we spent the next week in the city, living at my place, and putting the pieces of the broken dish back together. I was surprised how easy it was, but that was because of Chris. It was impossible to stay mad at him, he had the charm of an irresistible six-year-old boy, and besides, I loved him.

At the end of the following week, I got Sam's bags packed again, shooed Chris out of the house, and we sat down to wait for Richard, Sam's father. He had called to tell me that he had to go to Los Angeles on business and he would fly up to San Francisco to pick her up at noon on July 15. Which meant he planned to get to the house by two o'clock on that date. And when Richard said that, he meant it. He was as irritatingly punctual as ever.

It was then July 15, and he arrived promptly at two-ten, looking painfully neat and well put-together in a dark gray suit, with a navy and white striped tie, white shirt, and highly polished black shoes. It was an odd feeling to watch him come in the door and realize that this had been the man I had been married to and had once gone home to the end of each day. He seemed like someone from another world. And I suppose I did too. I was no longer the Gillian he had known.

"She's all set." I tried to keep my voice firm and wear a cheerful face for Sam's benefit. But I hated to see her leave for six weeks. The days would seem so quiet and empty without her.

"You look well, Gillian. You've been out in the sun?"

"Yes. Across the bay." I kept it deliberately vague, and

was struck again by the inane conversations we had had since the divorce. What did we used to talk about? I really couldn't remember.

"I have a list of where Samantha and I will be for the next six weeks. And if you move around, please send my secretary your itinerary so we can reach you in case of emergency." His face looked like a dry bone.

"Don't worry about it. You'll be hearing from me. I'll be calling Sam." He didn't look overwhelmingly pleased at that, and I stooped to give Sam a giant hug and a big mushy kiss as she stood at the door.

"Good-bye, Mommy. Send me some pretty cards . . . and say good-bye to Uncle Crits!" . . . Whoops . . . I saw Richard's eyes register the name and look toward me.

"Nice to see you, Richard. Have a good trip. Good-bye, sweetheart. Take care."

I waved as the limousine pulled away from the curb and Sam's small face shrank at the rear window as she waved back. It was going to be lonely without her.

The phone was ringing as I came back into the house, and I picked it up, grateful for someone to talk to.

"Can I come home yet? Has the big bad wolf gone?"

"Yes, and so has Sam. I feel lousy."

"I figured you would. I'll be over in ten minutes and we can leave for Bolinas as soon as you want." Suddenly the memory of the girl Chris had slept with didn't bother me as much, and I wanted to go back. The sour taste had faded in the course of the week in town, and I wanted to get out of my apartment. It would be gloomy as all hell without Sam clattering around.

Chris was as good as his word and was standing in the living room ten minutes later with a large bottle of wine in each hand.

"I wasn't sure if you'd want red wine or white. So I brought both. Want a drink?"

"You bet. Several. And then let's go." We each had two glasses of the red wine, and then we were off. Back to Bolinas. Alone this time, and in remarkably good spirits.

9

The next month was once again like something out of a dream. Neither of us got many calls to go into the city and we spent most of our time hanging around the beach, lying in a hammock under the big tree next to the house. And making love.

I had one job in town during the entire month, and Chris had two. Which made finances tight, but we were happy. I pitched in my alimony, and Chris didn't seem to mind the financial assistance.

We had a glorious time. I got into doing some painting, Chris took what seemed like a thousand rolls of film of me in the nude, and the days flew. Brief, frozen letters from Richard told me that Sam was well, and she seemed happy when I spoke to her.

The episode of the girl in Chris's bed never repeated itself, and he was more devoted than I'd ever dreamed. Joe Tramino had been wrong. And Chris and I didn't have a care in the world. Except one small one. I had had what appeared to be sun poisoning twice and food poisoning four times. And in between I had a fair amount of dizzy spells. It didn't seem like anything serious because the rest of the time I felt fine, but Chris wanted me to see a doctor.

"It might be an ulcer, Gill. Why don't you come into town the next time I go in. That's in two days. You could try for an appointment now."

"I just think it's nerves. But if it makes you happy . . . okay, I'll go."

I made the appointment the day before we went in and

tried to forget about it. I didn't want anything to be wrong. Life was so good just then.

"Rise and shine."

"What time is it?" I felt like hell again, but I didn't want to admit it to Chris.

"It's seven-thirty. That's plenty late enough. Get up. I made you some coffee." He was painfully matter-of-fact about the morning, and I tried not to show how I felt as I closed my eyes and attempted not to gag on the coffee fumes.

We left the house at nine. He had been delayed looking for stuff for his shooting, and I was glad. I felt better by the time we left, but I knew the drive over the hairpin turns on the mountain road wouldn't help. They didn't.

"You look lousy, Gill. Do you feel okay?"

"Sure. I feel fine." But I must have looked green. I felt it.

"Well, I'm glad you're going to the doctor anyway. My sister had something like you and she ignored it for a year. The next thing I heard she was in the hospital with a perforated ulcer. And that's no joke."

"I bet it isn't. Is she okay now?"

"Sure. She's fine. So don't worry. But at least you'll know." . . . Yeah . . . at least I'll know. "I want to take you by the house sometime before we go back to the beach. You can see if there's anything you want me to do before you move in. I have Sam's room all picked out too. I hope you like it." He gave me a shy, nervous look that made me smile from deep in my heart. I felt like we were about to be married. There was that funny almost-newlywed feeling about the way he talked about the house.

"I told my landlord I was giving up my place on September 1. He said it's no problem to rent furnished places, so he'll have a new tenant in no time. I'm glad. I felt shitty giving him such short notice." We had waited till the last minute to discuss it, but things had in fact "worked out," as Chris had put it earlier. "I can't wait."

Chris leaned across the seat and kissed me, and we

drove into town making small talk and telling bad jokes. I was feeling fine again and we were having a lovely time.

He dropped me in front of the Fitzhugh Building in Union Square a half an hour early, and I decided to go to I. Magnin's across the square to pass the time.

I noticed a mime on the corner and laughed out loud as I saw him imitate my walk, and then I disappeared into the fairyland delights of the elegant store. I was briefly tempted by the men's department to the right of the entrance, but decided against it. Chris wouldn't wear anything I'd find there anyway. Somehow they didn't look like they'd carry denim shirts. I smiled to myself and walked on until a row of ladies' sweaters caught my eye, and I started to sift through them.

Twenty minutes later, I emerged wearing a new red turtleneck in a thin silk knit, and reeking of a new perfume. I needed something to give me courage. I had the feeling that what I was going to hear wasn't going to be easy to take.

I checked the directory on the ground floor of the Fitzhugh and found the doctor I was looking for. Howard Haas, M.D., Room 312. The Fitzhugh was a medical building, and as I rode up in the elevator I had the funny feeling that I could walk into any door in the building and come out all right. But my appointment was with Dr. Haas. My doctor in New York had recommended him when we came out.

I gave the receptionist my name and took a seat with six or seven other people. The magazines were dull, the air was stuffy, I was starting to get nervous, and the new perfume was beginning to make me feel sick.

"Mrs. Forrester, this way please." It hadn't taken long.

I followed the nurse to a heavy oak door at the rear of the office and followed her as she stepped inside. There was something laboriously old-fashioned about the entire scene, and I expected Dr. Haas to wear horn-rimmed glasses and be bald. He wasn't though. Instead he looked as though he were about forty-five and played a lot of tennis. He had only slightly graying hair and a warm blue-eyed smile as he shook my hand.

"Mrs. Forrester, won't you sit down?" In spite of the winning smile, I was thinking of saying no, but I didn't have much choice.

"Thank you." I felt like a child called in front of the principal in a new school. I didn't know what to say next.

"Let's take down a little of your history first, and then you can tell me your problem. If there is a problem." He smiled at me again, and I reeled off my vital statistics, which seemed hardly worth putting down. A tonsillectomy when I was seven, a lot of earaches as a child, and Sam. That was about it. "That all sounds very healthy. Now, why did you come to see me?"

I told him about the dizziness, the nausea, and the vomiting, and he nodded, without making notes. He didn't seem impressed.

"And when was your last menstrual period?"

"My period?" I had wondered about that, but I think I hadn't wanted to know. "It was a few weeks ago, at least I think it was." I was feeling faint as we sat there.

"You think it was? You're not sure?" He looked at me as though I were very stupid.

"No, I'm sure of when it was, but it only lasted a few hours."

"Is that unusual for you?"

"Yes." I would have been amused by his tone, but I couldn't be. He was speaking to me as though I were a very young, slightly retarded child, and his words came across the desk in slow, painfully deliberated tones like slow-motion tennis balls.

"What about the period before this one?"

"The same thing. But I thought it was from the change in coming out here. Or worry, or whatever." It was a very lame excuse.

"But you have not actually missed a period?"

"No." I wanted to add "sir," but restrained myself. He had me feeling very humble though. And scared.

"Any change in your breasts? Fullness?" I hadn't no-

ticed and told him so. "Well, let's take a look." He flashed
the dazzling smile at me again, and I started to pray, but it
was a little late for that. The entire exercise of coming to
see him had been like checking the list of who passed and
flunked an exam, when you knew you hadn't studied anyway. But you always hope. At least I do.

So Dr. Haas took a look. And he saw. I was two months
pregnant. Maybe two and a half. Sonofabitch.

"Congratulations, Mrs. Forrester. I think the baby is
due in March." Congratulations? "We'll do the A-Z test
just to be formal about it, but there's really no doubt
about it. You're pregnant." He smiled.

"But I'm not . . . that is . . . uh . . . thank you, Doctor."
I had told him about my tonsillectomy, but I had forgotten
to tell him I wasn't married anymore. Congratulations, my
ass.

He told me to make another appointment in a month
and I rode down in the elevator, like a stone going down a
mine shaft. At least that's how I felt. And what would I
tell Chris? He was going to pick me up downstairs, and I
saw by my watch that he had already been waiting ten
minutes. Maybe he wouldn't be there. My spirits lifted at
the thought . . . maybe he had forgotten . . . maybe . . . I
decided to wait and tell him when we got back to Bolinas,
when we'd be sitting under the tree next to the house and
things would be peaceful.

As I stepped outside I saw him waiting for me and my
heart sank again. I wanted to cry.

I opened the door and slid in next to him and tried to
smile. "Hi."

"How was the doctor?"

"I'm pregnant."

"You're what?" The entire exchange was like something
out of a Laurel and Hardy movie as we dodged through the
downtown traffic. It was not at all what I had planned, but
it had just slipped out. I guess I wanted it to. "Wait a minute, Gill. What do you mean, you're pregnant? You use a
thing."

"Yeah, okay, so I use a thing. But I'm pregnant anyway. Congratulations!"

"Are you out of your mind?"

"No. That's what the doctor told me."

"Did you tell him you weren't married?" Chris was looking pale.

"No. I forgot."

"Oh for chrissake." I giggled hysterically and looked up at him and then regretted my mirth. He looked like he was going to explode. "How pregnant are you?"

"Two or two and a half months. Look, Chris . . . I'm sorry . . . I didn't do it on purpose, and I'm wearing it for chrissake."

"Okay, I know. But this comes as a hell of a shock to me. Didn't you know when you didn't get your period? And why the hell didn't you tell me?"

"I did get my period . . . sort of. . . ."

"Sort of? I can't believe this thing."

"Where the hell are you driving me to, by the way?" We had been roaming aimlessly on Market Street for a quarter of an hour.

"What do I know?" He glared in the rearview mirror and then back at me. And then his face lit up. "Come to think of it, I do know. We're going to San Jose."

"San Jose? What for?" Maybe he was going to murder me and dump my body somewhere on the peninsula.

"Because there's a dynamite Planned Parenthood in San Jose and they set up abortions. I have a friend there."

"Bully for you." The drive to San Jose was accomplished in total silence. We stole occasional glances at each other, but neither of us spoke. I guess he didn't want to, and I was afraid to. I felt as though I had committed the most heinous crime of all time.

In San Jose, Chris's friend was very nice, took down all the information, and said he'd call us, and I walked out to the car feeling lonely and nauseous. The drive out had taken an hour and a half, and it would take us longer to get back in rush-hour traffic, and we still had the drive back to Bolinas to contend with. I was exhausted thinking about it, and I didn't want to think of the abortion. Anything but that.

Chris tried to make lighthearted conversation on the way back to San Francisco, but I couldn't stand hearing it. I could tell he was feeling better. The fact that he'd done something to set up getting rid of it gave him a sense of relief. And me a feeling of desperation.

"Chris, pull over." We were just outside South San Francisco when I said it, but I didn't give a damn, I couldn't wait.

"Here? Are you sick?"

"Yes. I mean no, not like that. Look, just pull over." He did, with a worried look, and I faced him as we sat in the car. "Chris, I'm going to have the baby."

"Now?" The word was a squeak, and he looked like his already frayed nerves were going to give out.

"No, not now. In March. I don't want the abortion."

"You what?"

"You heard me. I'll have the baby. I'm not asking you to marry me, but don't ask me to give it up. I won't."

"Why? For chrissake, Gill, why? It'll totally fuck us up, not to mention what it'll do to your life. You've already got a kid, what do you want two for?"

"Because I love you, and I want to have our child. And deep in my heart, I don't believe in doing that if you don't have to. When two people love each other enough to live the way we've been living, then it's a crime not to have the child that results from it. I can't help it, Chris, I have to." My eyes were brimming with tears as I looked at him.

"Are you serious?"

"Yes."

"Jesus. Well, you've got to do it the best way for you. We'll talk about it. But you're taking on a hell of a lot to handle, Gill."

"I know that. But it would do worse things to my mind if I got rid of it. I'm going to have it, whether you stand by me or not." The last words had been sheer bravado, but he didn't respond.

"Okay, little lady. The decision's yours." He slammed the car back into drive and sped off toward the city without another word.

10

We drove back to Bolinas that night, without stopping to see his house on Sacramento Street, without dinner, and without wasting many words. But I was too tired to care. It had been a heavy day and I collapsed into bed and passed out.

I rolled over in bed the next morning and saw Chris staring at the ceiling with an unhappy expression on his face which matched the way I felt.

"Chris . . . I'm really sorry." . . . But in a way, I wasn't. I was too chicken to tell him that though.

"Don't be. And maybe you're right for you. To have the baby, I mean."

"What about for you?" I had to know. And he rolled over on his side and propped himself on one elbow, looking at me, before he spoke.

"No, Gill. Not for me. But you said yesterday that that doesn't matter. Do you still feel that way?"

"Yes." But my voice had shrunk to the barest whisper. He was leaving me. "We split?"

"No. You go back to New York." Which meant the same thing. My heart sank and I wanted to scream, or cry, or die. And I didn't want to go back to New York.

"I won't go back, Chris. You can leave me, but I won't go back."

"You have to go, Gill. If you love me at all. You're doing one thing you want to do. So you owe it to me to do one thing I want." He made it sound so reasonable, but it wasn't. Not to me at least.

"What does my going back to New York have to do with anything? And then what? I never see you again?" . . . Oh Jesus. . . .

"No. I'll come visit. I still love you, Gill. But I just couldn't handle the pressure of your being here. You'll be pregnant, and everyone'll know about it. Hell, Gill, we work in the same business, and don't you think everyone will know? Joe Tramino will see to it. And there would be others." He sounded bitter and sad.

"But who gives a damn? So, okay, we're having a baby. Lots of people do. And we love each other. So what's the big deal? Are you suddenly so establishment that you feel we have to be married? That's pure, total, one hundred percent crap. And you know it."

"No, I don't know it. Besides, it'll make me feel guilty. You see what happens, I come, I go, I disappear sometimes. I won't always do that, but right now I need to. Or at least I need to know I can. And if you're sitting around with a long face and a big stomach, I'll go crazy."

"So I won't wear a long face."

"Yes, you will. And I wouldn't blame you. I think you're nuts. In your shoes, I'd get rid of it. Today."

"Well, we're different, that's all."

"You said it. Look, I told you in the beginning, responsibility blows my mind. What do you think this is? It's like a giant commitment."

"What the hell do you want me to say, Chris?"

"I don't want you to say anything. I want one thing. For you to go home. And you're going to, if I have to carry you there. You've already given notice on your apartment, so you're free and clear. All you have to do is call Bekins, pack up your stuff, and get your ass on a plane. And that's just what you're going to do, if I have to gag you and tie you up. And if you're planning to argue with me, don't bother. You haven't got a chance. You've got two weeks.

You can stretch it a couple of days, and stay at my place while you do, but that's it. Go back to New York and we've got a chance, but if you stay in San Francisco we're through. I'll never forgive you for it. I'd always think you'd stayed to get at me. So do me a favor . . . go."

He left the room as I rolled into my pillow, choked with sobs, and in a few moments I heard him drive away.

He came back that night, but he had made up his mind. I was leaving. And by the end of the week, I knew I was. There was no other way. He had finally made me see that. And his forced cheerfulness during the days before I left was crueler than anything else he could have done to me. He was kinder and more loving than I had ever seen him. And I was more in love with him than ever before. He did some brutal things to my heart in those last weeks, but somehow I loved him anyway. He was Chris. And he was made that way, and you could never blame him for anything. In the end, I felt as though I had first done him wrong making the decision I had, and by getting pregnant in the first place. But I had no choice. Morally, I had to have the child.

He helped me tell Sam we were leaving when her father brought her back, and he packed all my things. He wasn't taking any chances. Chris Matthews may have loved me then, but he made one other thing a great deal clearer. He wanted me to go. And I was going.

After what seemed like a thousand days, we got to that all-time horror, the last day. The last this, and the last that. I couldn't stand it anymore, and the last night was the worst of all.

"Goodnight, Chris."

". . . 'night." And then, "Gill, do you understand at all? I . . . I hate doing this to you, but I can't . . . I just can't. I think maybe I want you to have the baby too, but I don't know. Maybe I'll get it all together. Soon, I mean . . . I feel like such a sonofabitch."

"You're not. I know, everything got kind of screwed up."

"Yeah. It did. And I'm sorry you got pregnant. God, I wish. . . ."

"Don't, Chris. I'm not sorry. I'm kind of glad, even if . . ."

"Why do you want to have it, Gill?"

"I told you. I want to have you near me always. It's sort of a corny thing to say but I . . . I just want to. That's all. I have to." We lay there in the dark, holding hands, and I kept thinking, "This is the last time. The last night. The last time I'll lie here in his bed. Ever. The last . . ." I knew he'd never come to New York, he hated the place, and he had no real interest in seeing his child.

"Gill? Are you crying?"

"N-no." But I choked as I said it.

"Don't cry, oh please don't cry. Gill, I love you. Please." We lay in each other's arms, crying. The last time. The last . . . "Gill, I'm so sorry."

"It's okay, Chris. Everything's going to be okay." He fell asleep in my arms after a while, the boy I loved, the man who loved me and was sorry, hurt me and failed me, and filled me at other times with a kind of joy I'd never known before. Christopher. The giant child. The beautiful man with the soul of a boy. The man who had ridden bareback on the beach with me the day we met. How could I burden him with the weight of my existence? I know I should have. But I didn't quite dare.

I lay awake until the room started to grow light and then curled into his back and fell asleep, too tired to cry anymore. The last night was over. The end had begun.

11

"Look, dammit! Don't look at me like that. It'll do you good to get back to New York. You have lots of friends there and I'll come East in the next couple of months. You'll . . . goddamit, Gill, I'm not going to explain this thing to you again, and I'm not going to stand around here like this, if you're going to wear your crucifixion look." We were standing in the airport, and he was looking crucified himself, guilt was nibbling at him. My fault again?

"Okay, okay, I'm sorry. I can't help it, it's . . ." Oh shit. What's the use? "Did I give you back the key to the house in Bolinas?"

"Yes. Do you have your ski boots? I saw them out in the garden yesterday, and they look pretty shot to me. You shouldn't leave them out there." Good boy, Chris, keep it to the practical.

"I didn't . . . Sam . . . yes. I have them." I looked up and he was giving me one of his encouraging smiles— "there, there, that's better, now you're doing it." We were playing a little game. Nice Uncle Chris sees Auntie Gillian off at the airport, and Auntie Gillian does not have hysterics. There we are. Smile for the birdie. I wondered who we were putting on the show for, the people at the airport, each other, or ourselves. We were acting out all the bad endings I'd ever read about in books; we were really blowing it, no longer reaching each other, just filling the minutes before Sam and I would get on the plane. But filling them with ugly things to remember.

Chris's gentle voice and empty words, punctuated by his little smiles, shrieked at me. "Don't make me feel guilty," they said, and my martyred face shouted back, "I hate you!"

"I put your rain slicker in the back of the car."

"Good."

"Where's Sam?" The general panic of the morning touched everything within me.

"Relax. She's over there, playing with that kid. Don't be so nervous, Gill. Everything's going to be fine."

"Sure." I nodded, looking at my feet, trying not to say something nasty. "I'll call you when we get in tonight."

"Why don't you wait till Sunday; the rates are lower and we can't start this calling every day routine." He was looking at something over my shoulder as he said it.

"Not every day. I just thought you'd want to know we got in okay." Tinges of irritation blazed in my voice.

"If the plane crashes, I'll hear about it. Get settled, then call in a couple of days." I nodded again. I was running out of things to say. "Want a piece of gum?" I shook my head, turning away again, crying toward the lady who stood behind me. She must have thought me very strange, but I couldn't face Chris anymore. I couldn't stand it.

"Will all passengers holding green boarding passes for American Airlines Flight 44 to New York please board the aircraft through Gateway D, at Gate 12. Will all passengers . . ."

"That's you." I nodded, gulping, looking for Sam again.

"I know. We can wait. Too many people . . . no point . . ."

"No point waiting around, Gill. When it's time to go, it's time to go." Thank you, Mr. Matthews, you sonofabitch . . . but I kept nodding, trying not to cry.

"I . . . uh . . . oh God, Chris! . . ." I clung to his jacket and touched the side of his face with my hand, one last time, and turned away blinded by tears. I wanted to scream, and kneel down on the airport floor, to cling to one of the huge chrome airline desks, to stop all the things that were happening without my consent. I wanted to stay, oh God, how I wanted to stay. And I wanted Chris to put his arms around me, but he didn't. He knew I would fall apart if he did.

"Sam, you carry your teddy, and take your mother's hand." Our coats were being lumped into my arms, Sam's hand took mine, and the crowd moved us toward the plane. I could feel Chris angry beside me because I had made a spectacle of myself, but I didn't give a damn. I had never felt so lonely or unhappy in my life. I thought I was losing what I loved and wanted most, I even doubted that I'd ever see him again. And I was positively keening for him, even before we left. Loving and hating him all at once.

"Chris. . . ."

"Good-bye, Gill, have a good flight. Talk to you Sunday." I turned away, squeezing Sam's hand, and started moving through the gate with the rest of the crowd. Half a dozen people already stood between us, and I was looking ahead, not wanting to look back again at what I wouldn't see.

"Gill! . . . Gill!" I stopped in the flow of people, and turned to see him, Sam and I being jostled by the people pushing past us, but I had to see. I just had to. "Gill! . . . I love you!" He said it! He said it! It was always that kind of thing that made me go on loving him, the last-minute contradictions that caught my heart just before it shattered on the bathroom floor.

"Gabye, Uncle Crits! . . . Gabye! . . . Mommy, can I watch the movie on the plane?"

"We'll see." I was looking back at Chris, our eyes saying to each other what we hadn't been able to say that morning. It was easier this way.

"Mommy . . ."

"Later, Sam. Please." Please, please, later, anything, but just later. We were herded into the plane, and then San Francisco was shrinking below us. And then gone. Like Chris.

12

Samantha was angelic on the flight, the plane was full, the food was lousy, and I was numb. Shellshock. I sat back in my seat, nodded to the stewardess at the appropriate times, or shook my head, and did my best to smile at Sam to give her the illusion that I was sharing in her conversation. I wasn't. My brain had died in the San Francisco airport, and somewhere in my chest was something called a heart. But it felt more like a marble watermelon, and I wondered what would happen if I stood up. Maybe it would fall out?

We had spent almost eight months in San Francisco, and now we were going back to New York. Why? That was stupid. I knew why, except I didn't really. I was going back to New York because I was pregnant and Chris didn't want me around. But why didn't he? That's what I didn't want to think about. I just couldn't. It was too much to face. As was the thought of what he'd do now that I was gone. Meet someone else? Fall in love? Have another girl move in? . . . Screw his ass off. . . .

He said he'd come to New York, but would he? I didn't believe he would. In fact, I knew he wouldn't. Which left me where? Nowhere. Alone. Pregnant. And back in New York.

I spent the first three hours of the five-hour flight back to New York pining within myself, the fourth hour asleep, and the fifth hour getting steamed up. To hell with him. To hell with it all.

I was going back to New York and I was going to make it. I would take that town and grab it by the neck until it

gave me what I wanted. Chris Matthews wasn't everything, and then, as the plane circled low over the lights of
Long Island, I knew I was excited to be back. San Francisco may have been beautiful and a place of peace and sunshine, but New York had something else to offer. Excitement. It was alive, it breathed and writhed and made you
want to spring into action, it almost had a musical beat of
its own, heavy, hypnotic, irresistible, and I could already
feel its lure as the landing gear touched the runway.

"Mommy, are we here?" I smiled at the question, and
nodded, taking Sam's small warm hand in mine and looking out the window, into nothingness, only the blue runway lights, but I knew what lay beyond, across the river.
We were back in New York now and we were going to use
it well. Hallelujah. Amen.

We got off the plane and headed toward the baggage
claim area. And suddenly, all I wanted to do was to grab
our stuff and see that skyline as we came over the bridge. I
wanted to see it and hear it and smell it. I wanted to know
that New York was standing there like a naked gypsy,
waiting for me.

"Where are we going to sleep tonight, Mommy?" There
was a faintly worried look in her eyes as she clutched her
teddy bear, and I had a sudden idea.

"You'll see. We're going to stay someplace special." I
stopped at a phone booth on the way to the bags, looked
up a number in the directory, and dialed. Samantha and
Gillian Forrester had just changed their plans.

The apartment we had lived in before had been sublet,
furnished, and I had given my tenants a month's notice
two weeks before. Which left us with two weeks of living
in a hotel, and I had chosen a quiet, inexpensive residential hotel not far from where we'd lived before. But that
was bullshit. This was New York. To hell with "quiet, residential." I had had an idea. And for two weeks, I could
afford it.

"Who did you call, Mommy?"

"The place where we're going to stay. I think you'll like
it. And in two weeks we'll be back in our own apartment."

I realized that she needed to hear that. Maybe I needed something grandiose to drag me out of the dumps, but she needed familiarity. It was all right. We were going to have both. First, two weeks for me. And then she'd be home, safe and sound.

Our bags were revolving aimlessly on the turntable when we got there, and I found a porter to carry them to a cab.

"Where to, lady?" The driver had the standard New York cabdriver look, a dead cigar stuck out of his face which was covered with a two-day beard stubble.

"The Hotel Regency, please. Sixty-first Street and Park Avenue." I settled back with a gleam in my eye, and Sam on my lap, and we drove into town. Our town, Sam's and mine. This one was ours. And it was going to be mine, all mine, in a way it never had before.

13

In typical New York style, we sped toward the city, darting from one lane to another and threatening lives as we went. It didn't seem to impress Sam much but it gave me that heady, hysterical-giggle feeling you get on a roller coaster, everything moving too fast and the view beyond a blur of lights and indistinct forms. I was only aware of the motion and speed, not of the dangers. In New York, you don't learn to live with danger, you thrive on it, you expect it, you come to need it. It's built in.

We raced across the Queensborough Bridge, down 60th Street, and stopped for the light at 60th and Third. And there it was, it was just beginning. Hordes of shaggy-haired young "groovies" sat at Yellowfingers restaurant, eyeing each other, and viewing passersby with a critical air, the sweaters on the girls were tight and transparent, the pants on the men bordered on the obscene, and through it all a look of carefully calculated "laissez aller." In the quick glance I threw at them, I noticed the baubles, the Afro wigs, the painted faces, all the little details you never see in California because nobody dares, not like they do in New York. Across the street, Bloomingdale's Department Store, and in the canyon between the mammoth store and the restaurant, a flood of frantic traffic, horns bleating, fenders dented, Con Edison adding an obstacle course for the entertainment of drivers and pedestrians alike. The entire area seemed to be seething with lights from restaurants, shops, street corners, and movie house marquees, and there was a kind of aura that held me in its spell. We turned right on to Third Avenue, and made our way a few blocks uptown among the other cars, crowding us on either side, tailgating and racing to make the lights. Left toward Park Avenue then, where we circled the island of greenery in the center and came back down the avenue to a screeching halt in front of our hotel. And I was suddenly glad that I had made the call from the airport. That "quiet" hotel would have killed me. I needed this. The Regency.

A liveried doorman helped us out and smiled at Sam, and two bellboys rushed up to take the bags. I paid the cabdriver and doled out tips like Hershey bars on Halloween, but I didn't give a damn. It was worth it.

We whirled through the revolving door, Sam's hand clutching mine, and then we swooped up to the reception desk. It was an immense baroque-looking marble and gilt affair, with a fleet of men standing at attention behind it.

"Good evening, Madame. May I help you?" He wore a dinner jacket and black tie, and the accent was French. Perfect.

"Good evening. I'm Mrs. Forrester. I called for a reservation an hour ago. A double room with twin beds." Sam's eyes peeked over the counter and he smiled at us.

"Yes. Indeed. But I regret, Madame. There has been a

problem. A little misunderstanding." . . . Oh shit. No
rooms. And I suddenly felt like Cinderella, gone from
satin frills to ashes in the flick of an eyelash.

"What sort of misunderstanding? Nothing was said on
the phone." I tried to look commanding and not as disappointed as I was.

"Only that we have no more double rooms tonight, Madame. I was thinking that perhaps you would agree to two
adjoining singles until the morning, but I see that that may
not be suitable with Mademoiselle." His eyes pointed at
Sam and he smiled. "You would surely prefer to sleep
with your Mama." I was about to leap at the proferred
singles, but he burst into speech again. "I have a much
better idea though. We have one unoccupied suite. It will
be a little larger than you wanted," and a lot more expen-
sive. That much I could very definitely not afford to spoil
myself. A suite? No way. "But I will make the appropriate
adjustments on your bill, if you will allow. As you were
promised a double on the phone, we will charge you that
rate. I hope Madame will be pleased with the suite. It's
one of our nicer ones."

"How very kind of you. Thank you." I smiled warmly
at him and noticed with pleasure that he looked quite
overwhelmed. At least I hadn't lost my touch completely.
And I was briefly very glad I'd worn the good black dress
I'd bought at Magnin's that summer. At least I looked the
part. And I felt just right as the elevator rose sedately to
the twenty-seventh floor.

"This way, please." We followed the bellboy and our
bags, turned left twice, and I'm sure I felt quite as lost as
Sam. We walked down what seemed like endless pale
beige halls with rich red carpeting and small Louis XV
marble-topped tables at appropriate distances from each
other. The doors were quietly marked with small gold numerals and had big brass handles.

The boy unlocked a door at the end of the hall, and it
swung open wide. 2709. That was us. Wow! It was a
corner room, with a real New York view. Skyscrapers
twinkled impressively at us, the Empire State stood far in

the distance, and at closer range we had the Pan Am Building and General Motors. Far below us, we could see the elegance of Park Avenue stretched out like a long gray-green ribbon, dotted here and there with stoplights. And at right angles to the panoramic cityscape of skyscrapers was the East River, with all the lovely little town houses of the East Sixties between the water's edge and where we stood. I couldn't have asked for more.

The bellboy retired discreetly from the room after I thanked him and gave out yet another tip, and I looked around the room. It was decorated in yellow and off-white, in thick carpets and rich upholstery fabrics, there were heavy cream satin damask curtains, and an air of opulence throughout. Near the door where we had come in there was a bar and tiny kitchenette, a small dining alcove, and, across from it, a large marble-topped desk. I felt as though I were expected to do something impressive here, like write a $400,000 check.

The bedroom beyond was bright and cheerful; the furniture looked French provincial, the wallpaper and bedspreads were in a tiny floral print, and there was a vast bouquet of fresh flowers. What luxury! And the bathroom! . . . The bathroom! . . . It was a dream. All done in porcelaine de Paris, marble, and bronze. The towels looked seven inches thick, and the tub looked three feet deep. And there was a dressing room which looked like a boudoir in the French court.

"Sam, how do you like it?" I was grinning to myself in self-satisfied greedy glee.

"I don't. I wanna go back to San Francisco." Two huge tears slid down her face, and I felt time stop. Poor Sam.

"Oh, sweetheart . . . I know . . . so do I. But we're back here for a little while now. We'll go back sometime. And this will be nice. You can go to school here, and . . ." My arguments sounded lame and I felt suddenly guilty to be so pleased to be back, and Sam looked as though she felt betrayed.

"Can I sleep in your bed tonight?"

"Sure, sweetheart. Sure. Let's get you to bed. Are you

hungry?" She shook her head and plopped herself down on the edge of the bed, still clutching her teddy bear. She was a portrait of despair. "How about some milk and cookies?" Maybe that would help.

I picked up the streamlined beige phone, consulted the little card beneath it, pushed the right buttons for room service, and ordered milk and cookies for her and a split of champagne for me. I hadn't given up the satin frills yet. Cinderella was still at the ball.

Sam sat on my lap when the enormous pink linen-draped tray arrived from room service, and she sipped milk and munched cookies while I guzzled champagne. It was quite a scene.

"Time for bed, love." She nodded sleepily, let me take off her clothes, and climbed into bed.

"Will we go back soon?"

"We'll see, sweetheart . . . we'll see." Her eyelids already drooped heavily over her eyes and they flickered open only once more to cast a piercing look at me.

"I'm gonna write a letter to Uncle Crits tomorrow . . . first thing!"

"That's a nice idea, Sam. Now get some sleep. Sweet dreams." Her eyes closed for the last time, and I smiled at her as she lay in the bed which dwarfed her small frame. She would "write" to Chris tomorrow, which meant a great, loose, lovely scribble . . . just for him.

I turned off the lights in the bedroom and wandered back into the living room of our suite, the champagne glass still in my hand, the vision of Samantha asleep in the bed still in my head . . . and a vision of Chris too. . . .

The scene at the San Francisco airport seemed a thousand years behind us, and the days in California seemed like a distant dream. And as I looked at the dragon city which lay at my feet, I wondered if we'd ever go back. Or if I'd even want to. In one brief hour, New York had already bewitched me. I had conquered other worlds, but now I wanted to conquer my own. I wanted to enter the contest with New York, and emerge victorious, no matter what the price to pay.

14

"Good morning, Mademoiselle. How did you sleep?" For once I had woken up before Sam.

"Okay." Sam looked at me sleepily; she was a little confused.

"We're in a hotel. Remember?"

"I know. And I'm going to write a letter to Uncle Crits." She had remembered that too.

"Fine. But we have lots of things to do today. So, up you get. And we'll go out in a little while."

I had a few calls to make first. I checked with the tenants at my apartment to be sure they'd be out on time, and called schools for Sam. We were just in time for the beginning of the school year, but by New York standards we were a year late with our application. Too bad. I knew that if I called enough schools one of them would take her, and I was right. It was just down the street from the hotel, and I made an appointment to see it with Sam that afternoon.

I also got a babysitter to come and help with Sam. She was to live out for the two weeks we would be at the hotel and live in after that.

And there was something else to set up too. A job. And I wasn't at all sure it was going to be easy to find one. The economy had tightened up during the year I'd been gone and jobs were scarce. My experience was limited to advertising and magazine work, but according to reports I'd heard they were the two tightest fields to get into just then, and I'd been away for a while. My last job had been at a decorating magazine called *Decor*, but I had little hope of getting a spot there again. Free-lance styling as I had done in California was a possibility too, but I knew that in New York I could never survive on it. The cost of living was too high. So my only hope was *Decor*. At least it was a start, and maybe Angus Aldridge, the senior editor, would have an idea, or know of a job available on some other magazine. It couldn't hurt to try.

"Angus Aldridge, please. This is Mrs. Forrester. Gillian Forrester . . . No . . . F-O-R-R-E-S-T-E-R . . . that's right . . . No. I'll hold."

.He was charming, elegant, and a damned good editor. All Bill Blass suits, and warm smile, and omniscient eyes, showing all those ladies in Wichita "how to." He was thirty-nine years old, his vacations were spent skiing, preferably in Europe, he had been born in Philadelphia, spent his summers in Maine with his family, or in the Greek Islands on his own, and had gone to the school of journalism at Yale. Our Editor. Our God. Our Mr. Aldridge.

Underneath the warm smile, he could be as cold and heartless as an editor should be, yet I liked him; there was very little pretense about him, he was Philadelphia and Yale, and East 64th Street, and he liked being those things. He believed in them. He didn't give a holy damn about Wichita or Bertrand, or the other places like it that he was sending a magazine to once a month. But he put on a good show, and if you played by the rules he was good to work with.

"Yes. I'm still holding."

"Gillian? What a surprise. How are you, dear?"

"Fine, Angus. Great. It's super to talk to you, it feels like years. How's life? And the magazine, of course?"

"Marvelous, dear. Are you back in the city for good? Or just coming back to the watering hole again to revive after San Francisco?"

"I think I might be back for good. We'll see." But I had a sudden twinge for San Francisco again as I said the words.

"Gillian, dear, I'm late for a meeting. Why don't you

stop by sometime. No. How about lunch tod . . . no, tom . . . Thursday? Lunch Thursday. We'll talk then."

"Thursday's fine. That would be wonderful. Nice to talk to you, Angus, see you then. And don't work yourself into the ground before Thursday. I'm dying to hear all the news." Which was a lie, but that's the local dialect.

"Fine, dear. Thursday. At one. Chez Henri? . . . Fine, see you then. Good to have you back." Bullshit, but more of the same dialect.

Chez Henri. Just like old times, when there was something to "discuss" . . . good afternoon, Mr. Aldridge . . . over here, Mr. Aldridge . . . a dry martini, Mr. Aldridge? . . . the expense account, Mr. Aldridge! . . . balls, Mr. Aldridge.

But I wanted a job, and I had always liked Angus for what he was. But why was I sounding so New York all of a sudden? Where was Chris? San Francisco? The new me? Or even the old me . . . where in hell was I? I had become so engrossed in just being back in New York that I felt almost schizophrenic, as though I'd become another person when I stepped off the plane.

I had made up my mind to ask Angus for a job on Thursday, and it was perhaps more easily done over lunch after all. Or maybe harder. We'd see. In any case, it couldn't hurt to ask. All he could do was say no. And it would be a start.

What next? Whom to call? Should I wait till I saw Angus, or call a bunch of people all at once? Well, maybe just one more. John Templeton. Editor of the less elegant, less witty, more earthy *Woman's Life*. The magazine was tougher, straighter, and more diversified. It told you what to feed your child after he had his tonsils out, how to apply Contac paper to bathroom walls, what diet to go on when you were losing your man, and how to sew "at-home" skirts out of remnants of curtain fabric. John Templeton, like his magazine, was a no-fooling-around species, fish or cut bait, produce or you're out, slightly scary individual. But he and I had liked each other, the few times we'd met, and he might remember me. I had done free-lance work for him a few times before I'd gone to *Decor*. So I called.

Once again, the whir of a switchboard, the clicks, staccato, and almost swallowed "Wmm's . . . Lfff."

"Mr. Templeton, please."

And then, "Mr. Templeton's office" cooed by a mildly intimidating, highly poised youngish voice. The executive secretary. Who believed, knew in fact, that she was perhaps not better or smarter than Mr. Templeton, but surely almost as powerful, in her own way. Secretaries invariably intimidate me; they want you to "tell it to them," because of course they too can handle your problem just as capably—except if you had wanted to talk to them, and not the boss, you'd have asked for them in the first place.

"Mr. Templeton, please. This is Gillian Forrester."

"I'm sorry, Miss Forrester. Mr. Templeton is in a meeting. . . . No, I'm afraid he'll be tied up this afternoon, and tomorrow he's going to Chicago for the day. Is there something I can help you with?" There it was. I knew it!

"No, I'm afraid I wanted to speak to Mr. Templeton directly. . . . that is . . . I just got in from California, and I used to free-lance for *Woman's Life* and . . ." Oh shit, why do secretaries do that to me?

"Perhaps you'd like to speak to our personnel office?" Ice in the voice, and comfortable condescension that says, "I have a job. Don't you?"

"No, I really wanted an appointment with Mr. Templeton." Now watch her tell me she can't commit him just now because his schedule is very heavy this week, and next week they're closing the book (i.e., finishing the issue, before it goes to print), and the week after that he'll be in Detroit all week . . . just watch!

"Very well. How is Friday at nine-fifteen? I'm afraid that's all he has open . . . Miss Forrester? . . . Miss Forrester?"

"Sorry, I uh . . . nine-fifteen? I . . . uh . . . ahh . . . yes, yes, nine-fifteen is fine, I mean . . . this Friday? . . . No . . . no . . . that's fine . . . the number where I can be reached? Oh, yes, of course. The Hotel Regency, Room 2709 . . . I

mean 6 . . . no. Sorry. Room 2709. . . . That's it. . . .
That'll be fine. See you on Friday." Well, I'll be damned.

So I was off to a start. And if nothing worked out with
either *Decor* or *Woman's Life,* I could look elsewhere. At
least I had a momentum going.

"Sam? How about a trip to the zoo?"

Sam and I walked out to Park Avenue and then west toward Central Park. She had two pony rides while I stared
at the skyline, and it was a hell of a sight. Fifth Avenue
stretched as far as I could see in either direction, and I
could imagine people living in grand style in penthouses to
my left, and business tycoons making million-dollar deci-
sions in offices to my right. The General Motors building
had sprung up, dwarfing all on its periphery. Everything
seemed new to me again, and enormous.

"Hey, Sam, how about a special lunch?"

"I'm not hungry yet."

"Come on, don't be a drag, love. Do you want to see
some more of the zoo?" But she only shook her head, and
I stooped to kiss her. She was still desperately hanging
onto the world we had just left, the world I was trying so
hard not to think about. Chris. "Let's go, Sam."

"Where are we going?" She was beginning to look intrigued.

"Just across the street. You'll see. Right over there." I
pointed. "That's the Plaza." We stopped to look at the
horses and the hansom cabs and then mounted the steps
into the fairyland magic of the Plaza Hotel. Once inside, it
was like another city in itself, and it had the same independent elegance as an ocean-going liner, totally self-suffi-
cient and reeking of luxury. The carpets felt like mat-
tresses beneath our feet, palm trees hovered above us in
great profusion, and crowds of determined looking people
came and went, some staying at the hotel, others just stopping in for lunch. It had a worldliness about it which
pleased me. It was New York.

"Who's she?" Sam had stopped beneath an enormous
portrait of a chubby little girl, posing next to a pug dog,

wearing drooping knee socks, and a navy pleated skirt. Her expression was one of outrageous devilry, and just by looking at her you could tell that her parents were divorced and that she had a nurse. Miss Park Avenue herself. The painting was somewhat caricatured and I knew who she was meant to be.

"That's Eloise, sweetheart. She's a little girl in a story, and she supposedly lived here, with her nanny and her dog and her turtle."

"Where was her Mommy?"

"I'm not sure. I think she was on a trip."

"Was she real?" Sam's eyes were growing larger. She liked the looks of the girl in the painting that loomed above her.

"No, she was make-believe." And as I mentioned it, a small sign on the table beneath the painting caught my eye. "See Eloise's room. Just ask the elevator man." "Hey, want to see something?"

"What?"

"A surprise. Come on." We found the elevators easily, I asked the elevator man to deliver us to our destination in veiled terms, and we rose slowly toward the floor in question. The elevator was full of overdressed women and overstuffed men, and behind me I heard Spanish, French, and what sounded like Swedish.

"Here we are, young lady. The second door to your right." I thanked him and he winked. And I gently opened the door. Eloise's room was a little girl's dream, and I smiled when I heard Sam gasp.

"This is Eloise's room, Sam."

"Wow! . . . Oh boy!" It was a veritable showcase of pink chintz and gingham, full of every toy imaginable, and cluttered with the kind of mess and disorder that most children dream of leaving in their rooms but can't get away with. A tall spare woman with an English accent was playing "Nanny," and she showed Sam the key points of the shrine with utter seriousness. The visit was an enormous success.

"Can we go back and visit again sometime?" Sam had torn herself away with difficulty.

"Sure. We'll come back. Now, how about some lunch?" She nodded, still dazed from the ecstasy of the visit, and she floated alongside me into the Palm Court, where piano and violins combined their sounds beneath the trees as a myriad of ladies indulged themselves at small tables covered with pink linen tablecloths. It still had the Victorian elegance it had had when I was a child and had been occasionally treated to tea there by my grandmother.

Sam had a hamburger and an enormous strawberry soda, while I dabbled with six dollars worth of spinach salad, and then we started home, satisfied with our morning.

We stopped at the school for Sam on the way and, being pleased with what I saw, I enrolled her starting the next morning. And as we arrived back at our hotel, I was amazed at what we had accomplished. There is so much happening in New York at any given moment, that one seems to do a week's worth of anything in half a day. I had made two appointments to inquire about jobs, had enrolled Sam at school, had had lunch at the Plaza, and had seen to Sam's entertainment as well. Not bad at all.

And now I had a few hours off. The babysitter had arrived and I turned Sam over to her. I wanted to call Peg Richards. I had been itching to all morning and could hardly wait.

Peg Richards and I grew up and went to school together; she is the closest thing I have to a sister. We are totally different, yet we understand each other. Perfectly. And we care about each other. Always. Like some sisters, and some friends.

Peg Richards is rough and tough, uses incredible language, is a no-nonsense sort of girl, stocky and direct, with freckles and immense lively brown eyes. Always the first one to raise hell in school, yet to get things organized too, to tell off the girl who'd done her dirt, and to look out for the girl nobody liked or paid attention to. She'd grown up with a dutchboy haircut, oxfords, and a total lack of interest in clothes and makeup and all the things that most of us were intrigued with. She liked boys less and later than some of us. She was just Peg. Peg. Tomboy. The head of the field hockey team who changed completely while I spent two years in Europe, pretending to study art. When I came back, Peg was at Briarcliff, taking life very seriously. Her language was a little worse, but I thought I could see the glimmer of mascara on her lashes. Three years later, she was a buyer of children's wear at a poshy department store, her language was incredible, and she was definitely wearing mascara, and false eyelashes. She was living with a journalist, playing a lot of tennis, and spending a lot of time knocking the Establishment. She was then twenty-three. And five years later, when I had just come back from California, she was still single, not living with anyone for the moment, and still had the same job.

Peg had done everything for me, mothered me in school, kept me company after I had Samantha and was feeling helpless at home, she'd been around to hold my hand through the divorce, and had seen me through every sort of scrape over the years. Peg is my staunchest friend, strongest ally, and most vehement critic. There is no shame, there are no deceptions, with someone you know that well, and who knows you.

The switchboard answered at the department store where she worked, I asked for her office, and she was on the line in half a minute.

"Peg? It's me." Just as I had reverted to ultra-New Yorker when speaking to Angus, I felt like a schoolgirl again when talking to Peg.

"Holy shit! Gillian! What the hell are you doing in town? How long are you here for?"

"A while. I got in last night."

"Where are you staying?"

"Would you believe at the Regency?" She chuckled and I laughed back.

"Well, la-dee-da to you. What happened? Did you get rich out West? I thought the Gold Rush was all over." Leave it to Peg.

"It is. In more ways than one." She had made me think of Chris and I sobered quickly.

"Oh? Are you okay, Gill?"

"Yeah. Sure, I'm fine. What about you?"

"I'm still alive. When do I get to see you, and my friend Sam? Is she with you?"

"Of course she is. And you can see us whenever you want. I feel like a stranger in this goddam town, and I don't know where to start first. But I'm having a ball."

"At the Regency, who wouldn't? But just a sec, let me get this straight. Are you moving back, or are you here on a visit?"

"Mentally, the latter, but practically . . . we're back."

"Your romance busted up?"

"I don't know, Peg. I think so, but I don't really know. It's a long story, and I had to come back."

"You're confusing the hell out of me. But I wouldn't have been surprised if the love story had ended. That business you told me about the girl in his bed at the beach house didn't sound good." I had forgotten that I had written that to her in my misery.

"We got over that."

"Something else happened? Christ! That would have been enough for me. Good old Gill, you never learn, do you? Anyway, you can tell me whatever you want to tell me when I see you. How about tonight?"

"Tonight? Sure . . . why not?"

"Such enthusiasm. To hell with you. I'll come to the hotel for a drink after work. I want to see your monster daughter. I'm so glad you're back, Gill!"

"Thanks, Peg. See you later."

"Yeah, and by the way, be dressed when I get there. I'm taking you to dinner at Twenty-One."

"You're what?"

"You heard me. We're celebrating your return."

"Why don't we celebrate with room service?"

"Nuts to you." And with that she hung up and I grinned to myself. It was nice to be back. The whole time span with Chris was beginning to seem as though it had never

happened. I was in New York where I had begun, hopefully I'd soon be jobbed, and that night I was having dinner at Twenty-One. It was as though New York was putting on its best face and everything was beginning to go
my way.

15

Peg had reserved a table downstairs near the bar at the il-
lustrious Twenty-One Club, and we were ushered to our
seats by the maitre d' who seemed to know Peg quite well.

"Well, well, at least you've been hanging out in the right
places since I left. Not bad."

"Expense account." She grinned with her pixie look and
ordered a double martini straight up. That was new too.

The reunion between Peg and Samantha at the hotel
had been boisterous and joyful and ours had been scarcely
less so. She looked better than ever, and her tongue was
even sharper than before. She squeezed Sam in a vast hug,
and then called me names while we pushed and shoved
and giggled. It was so good to see her again.

I glanced around the restaurant as she sipped her drink,
and marveled at the clientele. The cream of the cream.
Moneyed New York was out for dinner. And so was I.

In terms of dress, San Francisco alternates between
acute hippiedom and 1950s stock brokerage, with almost
no middle ground. The women are conservative and still
wear pastel wools, sleeveless and knee-length, hats, gloves,
the whole scene. But New York offers a rainbow of looks
that overwhelm the eye. Intense funky, quietly elegant,
outlandish chic, a myriad of looks and colors and styles.
Just as I had noticed as the taxi stopped at Yellowfingers

on the way in from the airport, in New York people dare.
And how.

The table next to us consisted of heavily bejeweled
"Nyew Yawwwk," successful garment center wearing chic
Paris, rich silks and creamy satins, hair fresh out of the
hairdresser, and manicures that made me want to ampu-
tate my arms. At the bar were a slew of fifty-year-old men
with astounding-looking models, statuesque-looking young
women with elaborate eye makeup and closely cropped
hair. It surprised me to see that short hair was "in" again.
In California they were still wearing it long and straight,
but in New York the natural look was dead, it had no
charm at all, and proved only that you weren't trying.

The room itself was dark, and the tablecloths were so
starched they looked as though they could have stood up
on their own. Overhead hung a vast array of toy cars and
airplanes. All you had to do was look at the ceiling and
you knew you were at Twenty-One. The discreet sounds
of good silver, fine china, and paper-thin crystal mingled
with the soft buzzing of conversations, and the entire room
seemed to come to life.

"Whatcha looking at, you hick?" Peg looked amused as
she watched me.

"That's about the size of it. I'd almost forgotten how
New York looks. It's so weird to be back. I feel as though
I have to learn the language all over again, and get myself
together."

"You look like you're doing okay to me. You haven't
lost your touch yet." I was wearing a white wool dress, the
pearls my ex-mother-in-law had given me, and had pulled
my hair into a tight knot at my neck. "That guy on your
right looks as though he's got the worst case of the hots
for you I've ever seen. You're looking good."

"Thanks, but you're full of shit."

"Mrs. Forrester! Such language at Twenty-One.
Gawwd! I can't take you anywhere."

"Oh shut up!" I giggled at her over my Dubonnet.

"Not until I hear what brought you back to New York.
I smell a rat."

"Come on, Peg." I averted my eyes and looked around the room. I didn't want to talk about Chris. I just wanted to enjoy the evening.

"That confirms it. Okay, close-mouth, you want to tell me now or later?"

"There's nothing to tell."

"Oh yeah? Didn't your mother ever tell you the story of Pinocchio, Gill? You should see your nose . . . it's growing longer, and longer, and. . . ."

"Peg Richards, you're a pain in the ass. I just came back, that's all."

"I'm insulted. I thought we were friends."

"We are." My voice got small, and I started on my second Dubonnet.

"Okay, I'll let it go. What do you want to eat?"

"Something light."

"You sick?" Peg eyed me seriously then, and I reached quickly into a metal grab bag of possible excuses, and then gave up.

"Nope. Pregnant."

"What? Holy shit! So you came back for an abortion?"

"No. I moved back."

"What about Chris? Does he know?"

"Yes."

"And?"

"I moved back."

"Did he walk out on you, Gill?" Fire kindled in Peg's eyes; she really was the most loyal friend I had.

"No, we just decided it was best this way."

"We? Or he? It doesn't sound like your style."

"It isn't important, Peg. He doesn't want to get tied down just now, and I can see his point. He's not ready. It's really better this way." But I could see I wasn't convincing Peg. I wasn't even convincing myself.

"You're out of your mind. You're going to have the baby, Gill?"

"Yes."

"Why?"

"Because I love him. And I want to have the baby."

"That's a hell of a big decision. I hope you know what you're doing." Peg looked as though she had just been hit with a bucket of ice water.

"I think I do."

"How about another drink? I don't know about you, but I think I need one." She looked up at me with a rueful smile and I shook my head.

"Look, don't let it put a damper on our evening. Everything's okay, I'm fine, and I know what I'm doing. Honest, Peg. So relax."

"That's easy for you to say. I enjoy worrying. Besides, you're only the mother. I plan to be the godmother, and that's a big responsibility." I laughed and she raised her drink to me in a toast. "To you, you goddam nut. Sonofabitch. I never expected this. What happened to your upbringing for chrissake?" We both laughed at that and then we ordered dinner. The subject never came up again, but I knew Peg was rolling it around in her mind and I'd hear more about it at a later date. She'd let it go by too easily, for Peg, and she wasn't going to feel right about it unless she did what she thought was her duty by me at some point and gave me hell. Maybe she thought I couldn't take it just then. Maybe she was right.

We stayed at Twenty-One until after eleven and were just getting ready to ask for the check when a tall, attractive man stopped at our table.

"Hello, Peg, can I offer you two a drink?" He was speaking to Peg, but smiling straight at me.

"Hi, Matt. What you you doing here?"

"I could ask you the same question, but I won't."

"Oh, I'm sorry. This is Gillian Forrester, Matthew Hinton."

"Good evening." We shook hands over the table and Peg looked pleased about something.

"How about that drink, ladies?" I was about to refuse but Peg gave me a filthy look and accepted.

We sat and chatted with him for half an hour. He was a lawyer, worked on Wall Street, and belonged to the same tennis club as Peg. He looked as though he were in his early thirties and had an easy-going manner but a little too much charm for my taste. I felt as though he were looking me over, like a large hunk of meat he might or might not want to buy, and I resented it.

"How about if I take you two ladies to Raffles for a drink and a little dancing." But this time I beat Peg to it.

"No, really I couldn't. I just got back from California last night, and I haven't caught up on my sleep yet, but thanks anyway."

"She's my best friend, Matt, and the biggest pain in the ass I know. Party pooper."

"Why don't you go, Peg? I'll take a cab home."

"No, I'll pass too. Sorry, Matt." He made a mock tragic face, threw up his hands, and we all paid our various tabs, or rather he and Peg did. I cringed, thinking what she must have paid for the dinner, but it had been a lovely evening.

Matt offered to drop us off at our respective homes in a cab and Peg accepted. And in a few minutes we were at the Regency. And I noticed that Matt seemed to like what he saw. I kissed Peg on the cheek, thanked her for dinner, and tried to stop her from saying anything. Whatever she could have come up with would surely have been mortifying. Matt was patiently waiting on the sidewalk as the doorman stood by.

"You like him?" she whispered in my ear as I disengaged myself from her hug.

"No, goddam you! And don't you dare start any matchmaking! But thanks for dinner." My response was spoken in a hoarse whisper like her own, and I punctuated it with a stern look. But she didn't answer, which is always a bad sign with Peg. I had visions of her setting up a whole scenario for Matt while he took her home.

"Goodnight, Matt. Thanks for dropping me off." I shook his hand coolly as we stood on the sidewalk and started toward the revolving door with a last wave at Peg.

"Gillian!" It was Matt.

"Yes?" He reached my side in two long strides.

"I'll call you tomorrow."

"Oh." But he was already gone, the taxi door slammed, and the cab pulled away and was instantly lost in the city's eternal traffic.

16

The telephone rang while I was struggling with my second cup of coffee the next morning, and I reached for it absentmindedly, holding the paper in my other hand.

"Hello?"

"How did you like him?"

"Peg! You're a bloody nuisance. Will you cool it, please? I told you how I felt about that last night. And I meant it."

"What the hell is wrong with you?" She sounded immensely irritated.

"For one thing, I'm still in love with Chris."

"And that's not going to get you anywhere. He dumped you, remember?

"Okay, Peg, that's enough. Let's just drop it. Last night was really nice."

"I thought so too. And . . . oh hell. Okay, Gill. I'll lay off. I'm sorry. Except I wish you'd go out with him. It would give you a good start back here. He's very social."

"I'm sure he is, but that doesn't turn me on anymore."

"Okay, so I'll find you a hippie, ya nut." She laughed briefly and I felt better. "Well, I just thought I'd put in a good word for Matt. Gotta go to a meeting now. I'll call you."

"Okay, Peg. See you soon."

I no sooner hung up than the phone rang again, and this time I suspected who it would be. And was right.

"Gillian?"

"Yes."

"Good morning. This is Matthew Hinton." So what else is new?

"Good morning." Now what? I really wasn't in the mood.

"I was going to ask you to dinner, Gillian, but something else has come up." It seemed an odd way to start, but I waited for him to go on. "One of the senior partners in the firm just offered me two tickets to the opening of the opera tonight. How does that sound?" I was ashamed of myself for the sudden change of heart, but that sounded too good to miss.

"Wow! That would be lovely, Matthew. I feel very spoiled."

"Don't be silly. The opera starts at eight and we can have a late dinner afterward. I'll pick you up at seven-thirty. Sound all right to you?"

"Sounds fine. I'll see you then. And thank you."

I looked at myself in the mirror and felt briefly guilty for accepting his invitation just because of the opera, but what the hell, it would be a real treat.

Matthew arrived promptly at seven-thirty and gave a long, slow whistle which almost swelled my head. I was wearing a cream satin dress which set off the remainder of my California tan, and I had to admit that I'd been pleased myself when I looked in the mirror before leaving the room.

He was looking very precise and rather handsome in a dinner jacket, with small sapphire studs, and for a moment he reminded me of my ex-husband. I was stepping back into the sedate, establishment world again, even if only for an evening. And it was a million light years from the world I had shared with Chris.

The cab pulled up to Lincoln Center, and the fountain rose in graceful, erratic leaps in the plaza. Little clusters of

well-dressed opera-goers headed in the same direction as
we, and I ignored Matt in favor of the bright dresses and
beautiful people. It was obvious that this was an Event.

Photographers leapt out from oblique angles and invisible corners and flashed lights in the darkness as people
went inside. You could tell who would occupy the boxes
—they were even more elaborately dressed than the others, and the jewels were blinding.

"Mr. Hinton, just a moment please." Matthew turned
his head to the left to see who was calling him, and I followed his gaze, just as a light went off in our faces and a
photographer snapped a picture.

"May I ask who the lady is?" a lithe-looking black girl
at the photographer's side inquired. She was dressed in
brilliant red and was wearing her hair in a natural. She
raised a small notebook and took my name with a smile,
while I looked on in disbelief. It was quite a scene. Pandemonium seemed to reign everywhere, and people were at-
tempting to filter through the assembly of reporters and
photographers.

Matthew shepherded me up the flight of stairs to the
boxes, and an elderly usher smiled at him. "Good evening,
Mr. Hinton." My, my.

"Do you come to the opera often, Matt?"

"Once in a while." But something was beginning to
smell fishy.

The opera was *Lucia di Lammermoor* with Joan Suther-
land, and the performance was breathtaking. During the
intermissions, the champagne flowed like water, and the
photographers continued their field day.

"I ordered dinner at Raffles, since you wouldn't do me
the honor last night. Is that all right with you?"

"Lovely."

And at Raffles we were besieged with "Good evening,
Mr. Hinton's" from every waiter in sight. Peg was right, he
was very social.

But the evening was pleasant, the conversation was
superficial, and he had a nice sense of humor. He had ordered smoked salmon, roast duck, and a souffle au grand

marnier. We drank more champagne, and danced for a while in the muted, gaiety of the club. The decor was done by Cecil Beaton and lacked warmth, but the crowd was obviously New York's elite.

We arrived back at the Regency at one, and I shook his hand in the lobby as the evening came to a close. It had been precisely what I'd expected. The opening of the opera. It meant no more to me than that. Until I saw the papers the next day.

The phone rang once again at nine the next morning, but this time I was asleep.

"I thought you said you didn't want to go out with him."

"Huh?"

"You heard me." It was Peg. "How was the opera?"

"Very nice, thanks." I struggled to wake up and then a question came to mind. "How did you know I went to the opera? Did Matt call you?" The possibility irritated me, like a ninth-grade report to the "gang."

"No. I read it in the papers."

"Bullshit. He called you." I was sitting up in bed by then.

"He did not. I have in hand today's *Women's Wear Daily*, and I quote 'Who is Playboy Matthew Hinton's latest love? Mrs. Gillian Forrester, of course. They attended the opening of the opera last night, which was . . . etc., etc. They occupied his father's box, Q, and were later seen at Raffles, private discotheque where the B. P. congregate. They sipped champagne and danced till dawn.' "

"For chrissake, I was home by one!" I was stunned, "Playboy Matthew Hinton's latest love"? Oh Christ.

"Shut up, I'm not finished. 'Mrs. Forrester wore a gown of cream-colored satin, off the shoulders, and it looked like last year's Dior. But she is a most attractive young woman. Right on, Mat.' "

"Thanks a lot. As a matter of fact, the dress is six-years-ago's nobody. For God's sake, Peg. That's the worst thing I've ever heard. I'm mortified."

"Console yourself. The Times only ran a picture. You looked pretty good. Now . . . do you like him?"

"Of course not. Oh hell, what do I know? I was excited about going to the opening of the opera, and he's about as colorful as papier-mache. He's stereotyped and terribly proper. And frankly, I don't enjoy being smacked all over the newspapers as some playboy's 'latest love.' Jesus!"

"Don't be a bore. Enjoy it."

"Bullshit."

"Well, at least go out with him for a while."

"What? And have all the papers analyzing what we had for dinner. It's not worth it, Peg. But thanks for the introduction."

"You're a creep. But maybe you've got a point. He is a little dull. Anyway, I'll put these in my scrapbook. My friend, Gillian Forrester, latest love of playboy."

"You jerk." And this time I hung up as I broke into a laugh. It really was pretty funny. It would have almost been worth sending the clippings to Chris.

An immense bouquet of roses arrived as I ordered breakfast. The card read, "I'm so sorry about the newspapers. Hope you can weather the storm. Next time dinner at Nedick's." And it was signed "Matt." Weather the storm was right. And that wasn't at all what I had in mind for myself. I put the flowers on a table and answered the phone. Probably Peg again.

"Gillian? Have you forgiven me?" It was Matt.

"Nothing to forgive. That's quite a coming-out party for my second day in New York. It would appear, however, that you're rather notorious, Mr. Hinton."

"Not nearly as much as *Women's Wear* seems to think. How about dinner tonight?"

"And confirm the rumor?"

"Why not?"

"I'm sorry, but I can't make it, Matt. But I had a lovely time last night."

"I'm not sure I believe you, but I'm glad if you did. I'll give you a call at the end of the week and see what else we can think up to tantalize the press. How do you feel about horses?"

"In what sense? As a meal or for transportation?"

"As entertainment. In terms of the horse show. Does that appeal?"

"As a matter of fact, it does, but I'll have to see, Matt. I have a lot of organizing to do." And I had no intention whatsoever of letting myself into a press-inspired romance.

"All right, busy lady, I'll give you a call. Have a nice day."

"Thanks, and the same to you. And thank you for the roses."

Wow! Three days in New York, and I had roses on my table, had had two pictures in the social columns and dinner at Twenty-One and Raffles, and had gone to the opening of the opera. Not bad, Mrs. Forrester. Not bad at all.

17

Thursday arrived, and with it my lunch with Angus. I was anxious about getting a job from him, but not really nervous. It was a glorious, sunny autumn day. I was feeling well and in good spirits.

I arrived at Chez Henri at three minutes after one. Angus was already waiting at the bar, looking more Bill Blass than ever, and perfectly groomed. His hair was a little thinner on top, but it had been exceedingly well-disguised by a loving barber. His smile fixed into place instantly as I stepped through the door.

"Gillian! You look marvelous! Just divine. You're

looking so well, and brown. And wearing your hair differently, aren't you, dear?"

What seemed like 147 "Gillian dear"s later, I got up the nerve to ask him about the chance of finding a job in the hallowed halls of *Decor*, and got turned down, graciously, elegantly, charmingly, the smile broadening just a little more to let me know that he really "cared," and would "love to but". . . . He said all the right things about "just feel terrible about it . . . things so slow . . . but you wouldn't be happy at *Decor* anymore, would you, dear?" He was half right, but I wanted a job and had thought of him first. Actually, I might have liked working there again, but once you left *Decor*, you left forever. Like the convent, or the womb. Never to return.

It was a nice lunch anyway, and I still had the meeting with John Templeton to look forward to the next day. But unlike Thursday, Friday happened with pouring rain and an acute case of nerves which told me just how badly I wanted the job at *Woman's Life*.

I bumped along on the bus, on the way to the magazine, wishing that I had had another cup of coffee to give me that wide-awake, bouncy busy look people get when they're all stimulated by what they're doing. I knew I had the whole thing backward and wanted to cover it up. You have to be put together, in need of nothing, sailing along under full steam, and then jobs fall into your lap like ripe apples. Need a job, for financial or emotional reasons, and it shows. You get that desperate look, that pathetic hungry look, and the tree shakes absolutely nothing into your lap. Need scares people off. Nobody loves the poor little hungry guy sitting in the corner of Riker's. You feel for him, but you don't want to get too close, or give him anything, because maybe proximity and/or recognition will give you his "disease." Maybe his sadness will be contagious, and nobody wants to take that chance.

At nine-ten I arrived at the black marble entrance of *Woman's Life*, with the bronze numerals at the side of the door: 353 Lexington. The slightly tacky chandeliers were being dusted, and as I headed for the second of four banks

of elevators I began to get excited. There was Muzak in
the elevators. And as we rose slowly I was beginning to
hope, to really want to believe that in an hour I'd walk out
of there "jobbed."

Nine-twelve. The third floor . . . the receptionist . . .
"Mrs. Forrester, will you have a seat, please. Mr. Templeton's secretary will be right out." Seven copies of *Life*
Magazine, two issues of *Holiday*, and all the current issues
of *Woman's Life* lay on the low table next to the Nauga-
hyde couch that tried to look like Mies van der Rohe but
didn't quite make it. Seventh cigarette of the day, second
wave of nausea, brief reminder of what was happening inside my body, brief realization that my palms were wet,
and then a smiling girl of about my own age, and looking
as though she might be from Cleveland, appeared to take
me in to see "Mr." Templeton. I suddenly felt younger,
dumber, less competent, and infinitely less useful than she.
After all, she had a job, didn't she? . . . Come on, Gillian,
pull yourself together . . . down three different corridors
whose only apparent purpose was to impress visitors and
make them totally lose their sense of direction, which I ac-
commodatingly did as we reached the second corridor.
Then, a beige on beige anteroom, with a large orange ash-
tray on Miss Cleveland's desk, and another almost-Mies-
van-der-Rohe chair, and a door. The Door. John was
standing in the doorway, smiling at me, looking wiry and
nervous, full of energy, and welcoming. He whisked me in,
shut the door, offered me coffee, lit up his pipe, smiled a
lot, made a lot of small talk, praised all the virtues of San
Francisco, and was "John Templeton: friend" to "Gillian
Forrester: expatriate free-lancer returned." I could handle
that, that was easy. I could be Gillian Forrester. I knew
how to do that. And if he would play Friend, then everything would be okay. I relaxed, looking at the view, inquired about his kids, said the usual things about New
York, and asked how *Woman's Life* was weathering the
publishing crisis. I didn't ask as an interviewee, but as
someone who used to be in publishing. I forgot about the
job.

A capsule report on the business ensued, along with reports on which of the other "books" were threatening to fold, and which ones weren't threatening but were in real trouble, "as we all know."

Seemingly mid-sentence, during my second cup of coffee, John looked up, watched me for a minute, and said, "Gillian, why'd you come back?" Whammmmm. John Templeton was not such a close friend that I could speak truths from the depths of my heart. At least I didn't feel that I could. So? "I had to," "I wanted to," "I missed New York," "I wanted to come to *Woman's Life* to find a job," —the only thing that might have rung true would have been the truth and that was so outlandish that I couldn't begin to offer any part of that as an explanation. What seemed like eight years, and was probably three seconds, passed as I stared into my coffee and listened to my ears buzz and pound: then I looked up and said the most articulate thing I could come up with, "I wanted to leave San Francisco for a while, I thought I should come back here," which made a little sense, and sounded like nothing much, except that maybe I had been wanted in California on a morals charge or something. But he accepted that and only asked me if I thought I was back for good. Which I didn't know. And I said so. I said I was back for at least six months, maybe a year, maybe forever, it depended on what I found in New York, what happened to my life in the next year.

"Have you been looking for a job?" John asked.

"Yes . . . no. That is I called you because, well, because I like *Woman's Life*. I don't want to go back to advertising, and, as you said, publishing is pretty well closed up. I thought it might be worth a try to give you a call."

"What about your old job at *Decor*? Did you talk to Angus Aldridge?"

"Yes. No go." He nodded, and I was pleased with myself for being honest. I had always suspected that there was rivalry between them, but whatever the case, at least I was playing it straight.

". . . Julie Weintraub. . . ." What, Julie Weintraub? How did she get into this? What in hell is he talking about Julie Weintraub for?

"Julie Weintraub?" It seemed the only thing to say to get back into the conversation. Maybe he'd repeat what I'd missed.

"Sure, you remember her. You two worked on a couple of projects together. Christmas, and. . . ." Of course I remembered her, but I still didn't know why John had brought her name up.

"Well, as I said, she broke her pelvis last week, and she's going to be flat on her back for a while, at least eight weeks, maybe ten, maybe even twelve. Jean Edwards and two other girls are trying to take over the mainstream of her work, but we're having some problems. So I'm at the point now where I was thinking that I could get someone in on a short-term basis, maybe even part-time, three, four days a week, and see how that works out. And I was thinking you might want to give it some thought. I warn you, Gillian, slave wages and no by-line, but it wouldn't be a full work week either which would give you more time with your daughter. What do you think?" . . . What do I think? What do I think? I think somebody, somewhere, loves me, that's what I think! Hallelujah! Wait till I tell Chris! "Gillian, stop grinning at me and say something." John was smiling back. He knew the answer from the look on my face.

"I think, dear Mr. Templeton, that the tree shook an apple into my lap after all. I'll take it. I mean, I want it. I mean . . . it sounds great! Like an absolute dream!"

"Can you start Monday?" I nodded, still feeling tongue-tied. "Fine. And you can plan on having the job for at least eight weeks. I want you to talk to Julie about what she's been doing. And we're working on the March issue right now. I guess that's all you need to know for a start. We'll let you have it with both barrels on Monday."

I just grinned and grinned, and silently blessed Julie Weintraub's pelvis.

"That's fine, John. That sounds fine." And still that dumb grin on my face.

John stood up, we shook hands, I picked up my coat, and seemed to float out of his office, as they say. The secretary in the beige anteroom no longer had anything I didn't have, the elevators were playing my song, and the bronze "353" on the front of the building made it look like home. As of the following Monday, I had a job.

When I got back to the hotel, I thought of calling Chris. I hedged about it because I was afraid he'd quell my enthusiasm, be indifferent or nonchalant about it, and I wanted him to be excited too. It's like half the excitement of a new dress you're crazy about is waiting to hear what Prince Charming is going to say about it. You can hardly wait for him to gasp and tell you that you've never looked more beautiful. So, when he tells you it's a great dress but you ought to lose another ten pounds, or that it would be terrific on a girl with bigger bosoms, or it's too bad your legs are too short for that look . . . you die a little, and the glitter falls off your star. I felt that way about the job, I didn't want him to take the glitter off it, but I really wanted to tell him. So I waited. . . . But at four o'clock I couldn't stand it anymore, and I called, sat holding my breath for a minute while the phone rang and rang at Chris's end, disappointment beginning to back up in my throat as I realized he might not be at home.

". . . Yeah? . . ." Whew, he's in . . . and me feeling about fourteen years old at the other end.

"Chris? It's me. I've got a job. Stylist at *Woman's Life*. I start Monday for eight or ten weeks, taking over for one of the editors who's in the hospital. I just got the job. Isn't that super?" All of it pouring out in one breath. Why couldn't I make it sound more grownup, or professional, or something? My excitement and something like embarrassment at talking to Chris made it sound so small and kind of foolish. Or maybe that was just me, feeling small, and sounding foolish.

"That's nice, Gill. It'll keep you busy for a while. Why didn't you look for something longer term? You'll just be out looking again in two months this way." He would think of that . . . i.e., "too bad the dress has that hemline, with your legs" . . . oh well, nice try.

"Look, Gill, I don't think you ought to call here any-more. Now don't get all excited and mad, it's no big deal. Just temporary. I've got a roommate. She's going to pay half the rent, and it really helps."

"A roommate? She? Since when? And who the hell is she that all of a sudden I can't call you anymore?? What the hell do you mean?" Oh God, why am I doing this, it's none of my business. Why am I dying and shaking all over? Third cigarette . . . who cares about John Temple-ton's old job anyway? It's over, everything is finished with me and Chris, the Queen is dead, Long Live the Queen. . . .

"Look, it's really not important, Gill, you don't even know her, and it's just for a while." You rotten bastard, you big son of a bitch. . . .

"I do too know her. I can hear it in your voice. Who is it? It's no big deal, you said so yourself, so tell me, just out of curiosity. Who is she?" A slightly hysterical pitch get-ting into my voice.

"Marilyn Lee." Sonofabitch, I knew it. She was the one he had told me about at the beach one day. The only girl he had ever really cared about. But it was supposed to be over. And now it wasn't over at all. She was back. "Hey, Gill, come on, cool it. It's just for a while. She called yes-terday and she's in town for a couple of weeks, so she's staying here, maybe for a month, no big thing."

"Stop telling me it's no big thing, will you please!" That hysterical note again. "And if it's no big thing, how come I can't call? Afraid you might upset her, Chris? Would it bother her to know that I'm calling? Is she just a little teeny, tiny bit jealous? Why should she be, baby? she's been getting you for years, she's not losing anything."

"Will you take it easy, it's not good for the baby if you get upset." The baby? The baby? Since when is he so interested in the baby?

"Look, forget it, Chris. It's your life. I just wanted to tell you about the job. Got to get off the phone now anyway. Take it easy. Oh, and Chris . . . I won't call anymore. Have a nice life." Stupid, stupid, sophomoric thing to say. Why can't you be glib and cool? He can hear you crying, you big ass.

"Gillian . . . I love you, baby, you know that."

"Try telling that to Marilyn. Chris. . . ." And there I was, sobbing. Humiliating myself, begging him to love me. Why did I have to be that way? Why? I hated myself, but I couldn't stop.

"Gill, I'll call you next week."

"Don't bother. Just don't bother. Marilyn might not like it. For once in your life, Chris, just this once, do something all the way, not half-assed. If you want to be with her, be with her. If you want to be with me, come to New York. But don't shit up her life, or mine, or your own, by double-timing everyone you ever spend an hour with. Try being honest with yourself for a change."

"If you're going to behave like an ass about this, I won't call you."

"Fine. Tell it all to Marilyn."

"You're supposed to understand me, Gill. You're the only one who ever knows how I feel. What do you want me to do? Be something I'm not? Well, I can't. This is how I am." Christ, now he's making me feel sorry for him. The little boy kicking dirt around with his toes, being misunderstood by the world. Poor sweet Chris, and big bad Marilyn, and mean old me. Shit. "Let's talk about it another time. I love you, Gill."

So Chris was living with someone else. The excitement of the morning was dispelled and forgotten. The hour I had spent in John Templeton's office felt as though it had been a month before. Who cared about goddam *Woman's Life?*

18

But Monday was a day of bliss. I was busy. I had a job. And I lost myself in it all day long.

I shot out of the hotel at twenty minutes to nine and headed downtown with the crowds. It was a heady feeling. I took the bus to work, and by the time those bronze numerals announcing "353" loomed into view I felt as though I owned them. I exchanged a smile and good morning with the maintenance men who were once again polishing the bronze and dusting the chandelier, and I felt as though I belonged. At that precise moment I belonged to New York and had been born under the sign of those bronze numerals. The Muzak was blaring fuzzily in the elevator, and the coffee wagon was ringing its bell and doing a sizable business on the third floor when I stepped off. Welcome home.

I looked for John Templeton's office and, after a few wrong turns, found it, with his secretary still sitting in the same place, wearing beige-on-beige to match the anteroom.

"Mr. Templeton is in a meeting, Mrs. Forrester. He said you were to go in and see Jean, Mrs. Edwards, and then he'll see you and the whole decorating group at eleven." Another exchange of smiles and . . . "Oh, Mrs. Forrester, Mrs. Edwards will show you the office you'll be using. And please see Mr. Porcelli about your social security number. Payroll is on four." Magic words. It was real.

Further down the maze lay Jean Edwards' office, tucked in between two larger ones. Hers was tiny, disorderly, littered with fabric samples, needlepoint kits, bright posters, dirty coffee cups, and scraps of paper with eight or nine messages scrawled on them in different directions. Her office was bright and friendly and full of potted plants. An arrow with "Up" painted on it in red letters pointed down, and a huge poster that said "Smile" showed a photograph of a little girl in tears, looking at her ice cream cone lying on the pavement at her feet.

I waited for Jean while people came and went, looked in, rushed by, and had the air of very busy people. I felt like a guest.

I remained alone, nervous, and itching to get to work. Where was Jean? Where was everybody in fact? It seemed like everyone had something to do except me; it was like a giant game, and I wanted to play too. Faces continued to appear in the doorway and then go away again, and the minutes ticked by as I glanced through the three most recent issues of the magazine.

"Waiting for Jean?" I looked up when I heard the voice, and a tall man in his mid-forties met my gaze. He had black hair, bright blue eyes, and was sporting a well-trimmed beard.

"Yes. I am."

"Friend or foe?" The eyes twinkled as he asked.

"I'm not sure, but I think I work here."

"Oh, the new secretary. Right." His face lost interest, and he sped away down the hall before I could respond, with irritation mounting in my throat. Secretary indeed!

I continued to wait, and just after ten o'clock Jean raced in with an arm full of folders, fabric samples, and contact sheets. Her smile brought the morning back into perspective, and the long wait in her office seemed like only a moment.

"Hi. I hear I have a new secretary waiting in my office." Her dark eyes flashed in amusement as she looked up at me, and then I had to laugh. "Don't let him get to you, that's just his style. He's a little brusque. When I told him you were the new wife of the French Ambassador, and you had agreed to come here to discuss our photographing your house, he almost died."

"Good. Who is he. Anyone important?" I suspected he was. There had been an air of officialdom about him when he walked into the room.

"More or less. He's Gordon Harte. Senior Art Director and Assistant Managing Editor."

"That sounds like 'more' rather than 'less.' Hard to deal with?"

"Sometimes. but mostly just standoffish. And we all get bitchy when we're getting ready to close an issue. You'll see."

"I remember that much."

"Good. Look, I haven't got time to brief you now. We have a decorating department meeting in Templeton's office in five minutes, and I've got to get this crap off my desk. There's a list on Julie's desk of the stuff you'll be doing for the next week at least. You've got to find me a very unusual dining room for a shooting, and we're doing children's bedrooms, and . . . what the hell was that other thing? . . . Christ! . . . Oh! Right! You're supposed to talk to the food editor about something tomorrow morning, and John has an interview for you to do next week. It'll get a little saner in a week or two, before that though you'll mostly be shoveling your driveway, so to speak. Okay? Ready? Off to our meeting. I have to stop and look at the slides from last Friday's shooting on the way. Lamps. We'll talk later, and Julie's office, yours, is two doors left of mine." The entire time she had been speaking to me she had been sorting through papers on her desk, shoving things into files, stacking photographs, and making notes, but the stream of conversation never lagged for a second. She was one of those wiry, dynamic women in her late thirties who lives for her career. She was tough, competent, and nice, which was a rare combination. And I guessed correctly as I watched her that she was also divorced.

The meeting in John Templeton's office was brief and to the point. Mimeoed sheets were handed out listing future features in the magazine, and I listened intently, feeling as though I had somehow missed the first two weeks of school and already needed to catch up.

By noon, I was following Jean back down the hall. She zipped into her office, and I proceeded two doors down to mine.

I gingerly opened the door, wondering what I would find, and then stood and looked around for a moment, liking what I saw. Two walls were blue, one was orange, and the fourth was brick, there was thick brown carpeting on the floor, and the walls were covered with photographs, posters, and funny little plaques. "Too much of a good thing is wonderful" was attributed to Mae West, two others said "Mierda" and "Courage," and behind the desk was one that said "Not Today, Johnny Boy." There were two plants on the desk, and in the corner an immense array of multicolored paper flowers. It was a small room, but it looked like a pleasant place to work and I plopped myself down in the chair that said Madame Director and momentarily felt like the winner on "Queen for a Day." I felt every bit the part, and the first day at school feeling began to wear off.

"I hear I owe you an apology. And how is the Ambassador, by the way?" It was Gordon Harte, standing in the doorway, with a solemn expression, watching me try my office on for size.

"I trust he's well, Mr. Harte. And how are you?"

"Busy, thank you. Why aren't you?" I wondered for an instant if he were serious, and groped for an icy retort, but then I saw his face relax.

"I feel like I've taken a job in a factory all of a sudden."

"Don't kid yourself, you have. And don't ever let Eloise catch you sitting around with empty hands. Even a spoon will do. You can tell her it's a prop for a photograph you're checking out."

"That bad, huh? I hear the Art Director's pretty bad too." I raised an eyebrow and tried not to smile as I gave him back a little of his own. But I knew he was right about Eloise. Eloise Franck, Managing Editor, and resident terror. I still remembered her from the days I had free-lanced at *Woman's Life*. She was an ex-newspaperwoman who was at least sixty, and looked forty, and had a heart of ground glass and cement. But she was a pro. From head to foot, a pro, hated by her underlings, feared by her colleagues, and valued only by John Templeton, who knew her worth. She knew how to run a magazine, never lost control, and had an infallible sense for what was right for *Woman's Life*.

"By the way, Mrs. Forrester, there's a general staff meeting at nine sharp tomorrow morning. You're expected to be there." I had almost forgotten Gordon's presence while I remembered the terrors of Eloise Franck.

"Fine. I'll be there, Mr. Harte."

"You'd better be. Now get to work." And then he vanished, still something of an enigma. It was hard to tell when he was serious and when he was joking, or if he joked at all. There was an edge of sarcasm to everything he said. Those eyes would look at you, and take hold . . . turn you around . . . squeeze you for a moment, and then drop you when you least expected it. As though life were a game. His height and slimness exaggerated the leanness of his face, which somehow reminded me of an El Greco portrait . . . what was it? I wondered to myself that day. Perhaps that despite the glint of humor in the eyes there was something else there, a quality of hurt, something that made him seem just out of reach.

"Oh well, Mr. Harte, you do your thing and I'll do mine, and hopefully we won't get on each other's nerves." I mumbled to myself as I began to ferret through the stack of notes on my desk. It looked as though I had a lot to do. And a lot to catch up on.

I was so totally engrossed in sorting out what lay ahead that I didn't pick my head up until almost five, having forgotten everything but my work, including Gordon Harte.

I poured myself a cup of coffee from the machine across the hall and returned to my desk as the phone began to ring.

"How's it going?" It was Jean Edwards.

"Okay. But I feel swamped. I've just spent the entire day going through the stuff on Julie's desk. But I think I'm catching up."

"In one day? Not bad. Have you been notified of the staff meeting tomorrow?"

"Yes, thanks. Gordon Harte came by to tell me."

"That's quite an honor. As a rule, he speaks only to John Templeton and God. And I'm not even sure he speaks to God."

"That doesn't surprise me. He looks like he could be a real. . . ."

"Don't say it, Gillian. But you're right. Just don't step on his toes and you'll be all right. He's a perfectionist, but you can't quibble with it; he drives himself even harder than he drives the rest of us. He's had some kind of a chip on his shoulder for years."

"Sounds like someone to stay away from."

"That, my dear, is up to you. And now I've got to run. I'm having people in tonight."

"Okay, Jean. See you tomorrow, and thanks for the help." I hung up slowly and wondered about Jean's last remark about Gordon. One thing was for sure, chip on his shoulder or no, he was a very attractive man.

I looked at my watch then and decided it was time to pack up and go home. I had promised Sam a pizza, and it would be nice to have a few hours together before she went to bed.

As I left my office I took a last look over my shoulder and smiled. It had been a lovely day. I felt useful again, and busy, and pleased with the job I had found.

I walked slowly down the corridor and turned right into the maze. One more right and a left, and I was at the elevator bank. And so was Gordon Harte, looking preoccupied, and carrying a large manila envelope in one hand and a huge portfolio in the other.

"Homework?" I asked him.

"Yes, in the left hand. No, in the right. I teach a life drawing class on Monday nights. The portfolio has some of my old nude studies in it, to show the class."

The elevator arrived then, and we moved into the Muzak-infested aura of people from other floors. Gordon saw someone he knew and was busy talking, so I thought I'd walk out quietly without saying anything more. But when I reached the revolving door he was just behind me, and we hit Lexington Avenue one after the other, like gum balls out of a nickel machine.

"Which way are you headed, Mrs. Forrester? I'm walking uptown to pick up my bike. Would you care to join me?" I wasn't sure, but I acquiesced, and we walked slowly through the crowds on Lexington.

"Do you ride the bike to work?"

"Sometimes. But it's not the kind I think you mean. It's a motorcycle. I picked it up in Spain last summer."

"Sounds terrifying in this traffic."

"Not really. There is very little that terrifies me. I just don't think about it much." . . . Or maybe you don't care? . . .

"Do you have children?" It was something to talk about as we walked along.

"A son. He's studying architecture at Yale. And you?"

"A daughter, she's five, and she's still at the stage where she enjoys taking houses apart more than putting them together." He laughed and I noticed as he did that he had a nice smile, and he looked more human when he forgot to look fierce. I had noticed too something odd in his eyes when I asked about his son.

We talked about New York on our way uptown, and I mentioned how strange it seemed to be back, how different it was from California. I liked it but I didn't feel at home anymore. It was like watching animals at a zoo.

"How long have you been back?"

"About a week."

"You'll get used to it again, and you'll probably never leave. You'll just go on talking about how weird it all is. That's what we all do."

"Maybe I'll go back to California one of these days." It made me feel better just to say it.

"I used to say that about Spain. But those things never happen. One never goes back."

"Why not?" I felt naive as I asked the question, but it just slipped out as I looked up at him.

"Because you leave when you have to, or when you're meant to. And part of you dies when you go. You leave it there, it stays there. And what's left of you moves on to someplace else." It sounded pretty heavy but I knew myself how true it was. Part of me had died when I had left San Francisco, and part of me had stayed with Chris.

"I hate to admit it, Mr. Harte, but your analysis sounds apt. What made you go to Spain in the first place?"

"It was a moment of madness, as they say. My marriage had just broken up, I was bored and frustrated with my job, and I was thirty-two years old. I figured that if I didn't get going right then and there I never would, and I think I was right. I've never regretted going there. I spent ten years in a tiny town near Malaga, and in retrospect they were the best years of my life. The people in our business call them 'wasted years' but I don't. I cherish them."

"Have you ever thought of going back?"

"Yes, but at thirty-two, not forty-nine. I'm too old for grandiose gestures like that now. That's behind me. This is it"—his right hand swept across the skyline"—for better or worse, until death do us part." It struck me that he was a little morbid.

"But that's absurd. You could go back anytime you want to." Somehow it bothered me that he should be so loath to run after his dream. It was as if he didn't even care anymore.

"Thank you for your concern, my dear, but I assure you I'm far too old to cherish delusions about living on bread crusts in Spain, or being an artist." He punctuated his words with a dry little laugh and I saw then that we were standing on the corner of Sixtieth. I was almost home. He shook my hand while I noticed that the spark of amusement hadn't died in his eyes. For some reason he had apparently enjoyed our conversation and I had to admit that, despite his penchant for sarcasm, away from the office he was almost an agreeable man.

I turned right toward Park Avenue as he walked away, and reached the Regency thinking of Sam. Gordon Harte had already vanished from my mind.

"Hi, sweetheart. What did you do today?"

"Nothing. I don't like Jane. And I want to go back to Uncle Crits. I don't like it here." Sam looked unhappy, tear-stained, and rumpled. Jane was the baby-sitter, and neither one looked too smitten with the other. Sam could be tough when she worked at it.

"Hey, wait a minute. This is home, you know. We'll go back to our apartment soon. And it's going to be nice, and Uncle Chris will come and visit us in a while, and you're going to make new friends in school, and . . ."

"I don't want to. And there was a big, bad dog in the park." God, she looked so cute, those big eyes looking up at me. "Where were you all day? I needed you." Whamm. The nightmare of the working mother all rolled up in that "Where were you all day?" and the clincher, "I needed you." . . . Wow! . . . But Sam sweetheart, I have to work . . . we can use the money and I . . . I have to, Sam, I just have to, that's all. . . .

"I needed you too. But I was working. I told you all about that. I thought we agreed. Hey, how about our pizza? Mushroom or sausage?"

"Ummmmm . . . mushroom and sausage?" She had brightened at the mention of the pizza.

"Now come on. Pick one." I was smiling at her, she was so nice to come home to.

"Okay. Mushroom." And then I saw her look up at me, and I could tell she had something on her mind. "Mommy . . ."

"What, love?"

"When is Uncle Crits coming?"

"I don't know. We'll see." And let's not get into that dammit . . . please. . . .

The pizza arrived half an hour later, and Sam and I lunged into it, seemingly free of our problems. I didn't know when or even if Chris was coming, and maybe I didn't even care. I didn't want to care. Sam and I had all we needed. We had each other, and a great big, drooling, cheese and mushroom pizza spread all over the Regency's best Louis XV. What more can you ask of life? On some days, not much. Not much more at all. I looked at Sam and wanted to laugh I felt so good, it had been a beautiful day, and she looked up at me and smiled back. She could feel the good vibes too.

"Mommy?"

"Uh huh?" My mouth was full of food.

"Can I ask you for something?"

"Sure. What? . . . but not another pizza." I felt like I was going to explode.

"No, not a pizza, Mom." She looked at me with disgust at my simplemindedness.

"Then what?"

"How about a baby sister sometime soon?"

19

The second day at work was even better than the first. I felt as though I belonged. The staff meeting was no different than any other, but it gave me a chance to take a look at the other faces I'd be working with, and what was going on.

John Templeton conducted it like a board chairman in an early fifties movie, and Gordon Harte stood at the back of the room watching the show while I sat with Jean. I half expected Gordon to say something when we walked past him on our way out, but he didn't. He was involved with briefing one of the junior editors on some project John had discussed. He didn't even try to catch my eye.

The only thing directly pertaining to me during the two-hour session had been that Milt Howley, the black singer, had agreed to give *Woman's Life* an interview, and John Templeton had assigned me to do the job. It sounded like the proverbial plum.

When I got back to my office, Matthew Hinton called, and I succumbed to the lure of the opening of the horse show the following night. Once again, I couldn't resist.

And before lunch, I called Hilary Price. I had tried her a few days before and had been told by her secretary that she was in Paris for the collections.

I had met Hilary Price during my early years of work. We worked on the same magazine briefly, and she had since risen to rather impressive heights on one of the more important fashion magazines. A far cry from *Woman's Life,* it was one of those super fashion books that paint women's faces green and then paste peacock feathers on them.

We took a liking to each other when we first met. It's not a deliciously noisy, rude, obvious friendship like the one with Peg, but, though more polite, relaxed in its own way. I always feel I have to rise somewhat to Hilary's level though, which in a way is good for me. But the effort is never overwhelming. I can still let my hair down and kick off my shoes. In a way she's kind of mind expanding. . . . Hilary. Always calm, always unruffled, discreet, elegant, witty. Obviously strong, but basically kind. Very chic, very "New York," an intelligent woman whose mind appeals to me immensely. She looks amazingly flamboyant because she has a lot of style and a look that classifies easily as "sophisticated." But in spite of the looks, she's actually quiet. About thirty-five, or thereabouts, her age is permanently veiled by an aura of mystery. . . . She never tells . . .

or gives herself away. Divorced also, she has lived in
Milan, Paris, and Tokyo. Her first husband was an aging
Italian Count, whom she refers to once in a while as
"Cecco," short for Francesco, I gather. He had been on
the verge of death when she married him, or so she had
thought, but he managed to revive long enough to marry a
seventeen-year-old girl three weeks after their divorce.

The phone rang in Hilary's office and on the second
ring she picked it up herself.

"Hello?"

"Hilary? It's Gillian."

"Welcome back, my dear. Felicia gave me your message. And what brings the little bird of peace back to the
Mecca?" She was laughing in her funny way.

"Who knows? God, it's good to hear your voice. How
was Paris?"

"Exquisite. And rainy. The collections were abhorrent.
Rome was much better. I ran into my ex-husband Cecco.
He has a new mistress. Delightful girl, she looks rather
like a palomino colt."

"How was he?"

"Alive, which is in itself remarkable. I cringe to think of
how old he must be. . . . It must be costing him a fortune
to keep having the dates changed on his passport. . . . The
paper was wearing thin years ago . . . ," and we both giggled, she was so bad sometimes. I had never met Cecco,
but I had these terrible visions of him. "And you, Gillian
. . . how are you, dear? You didn't answer my last letter. I
was a little worried."

She sounded throaty and sarcastic and the same as ever.
There was a warmth beneath the sarcasm, and a tone
which suggested that she cared about the person she was
speaking to. It was a knack she had, which might have
been cultivated, but I thought it was sincere. Hilary
sounded great, and asked for a brief résumé of "all the
news, please"—"in other words, Gillian, the bare essen-
tials: when did you get back? how long are you here for?
and what are you doing?" I answered the first two briefly,
and then told her about the job at *Woman's Life,* about

John Templeton and the miracle of an eight-week job that was made to measure, about Julie Weintraub's broken pelvis, and even about my dining room search. I thought she might have an idea.

Hilary's laugh came back at me again, and an order to "slow down, there, what's all this about Julie Weintraub and a dining room? If I understand you correctly, you are looking for a broken pelvis, and just bought Julie Weintraub's dining room, or you bought Julie's pelvis, and broke your dining room . . . and do I have a what? A pelvis or a dining room? I have both, but you are welcome to neither, my dear, and it is quite clear that New York is too much for you."

By then I was laughing harder than Hilary, and trying to unsnarl the whole thing which I knew she understood perfectly well anyway.

"Actually, Gillian, I've never met Julie Weintraub, but I'm delighted you have the job; it sounds like just your cup of tea. By the way, I have a very old friend who works on the magazine, fellow by the name of Gordon Harte. Have you met him yet? Though I suppose one could hardly expect you would have in two days."

"Actually, we did meet. He seems nice enough. Kind of a sarcastic bastard though. I didn't know he was a friend of yours; you've never said anything about him."

"Oh, not that kind of friend. I knew his wife years ago, when she was a model and I had just arrived in New York. They were getting divorced, and he was on his way to Spain to make like the Ernest Hemingway of the art world, or some such. Then I bumped into him myself in Spain years later, and afterward we began meeting at official functions for the magazine types. He's one of the few redeeming features of those events. He's a very capable man. And a nice one; the sarcasm is . . . well, something he uses to keep the world at bay. . . . There's a wall around him a mile high. . . . In any case, Gillian dear, how's your Christopher, the Big Romance?" Like Peg, I had written to her from California.

Silence at my end, and brief paralysis of the mouth, or

was it my heart? "Hilary, I don't know for the time being. Can't talk about it."

"Good enough. The less said the better for now. But if you need me, you know where to find me. Why don't you come up for drinks on Thursday night, after work, and we'll have a good long chat about anything you do want to talk about, and I'll see who I can get for dinner. Maybe Gordon, and four or five others. It's awfully short notice though. Anyone special you'd like me to ask?"

"No, I'll leave it to you. It sounds marvelous. But will you think about a dining room for me too, please, genius lady? Hilary, you really are super. And thanks. What time on Thursday?"

"Six?"

"Fine. I'll be there."

Now that would be an invitation worth accepting. Hilary gave the best goddam dinner parties in New York. And she was also a marvelous scavenger. She called me back that afternoon to say that she had remembered "just the dining room!" It belonged to a couple who were both actors, and in the course of taking a class on scenery design the wife had attacked their dining room with brush and paint. She called it an environment; Hilary's description was more specific: ". . . looks like the whole goddam jungle looking over your shoulder while you eat." But she convinced me it was worth a try. So I called and made an appointment to see the place on my way home.

It was a wow. It looked like a movie set for a jungle scene: trees and fruit and flowers were painted everywhere, clouds hung overhead, the floor was a lake, and animals peered out from behind the painted shrubbery. The furniture was like the kind you'd use on safari, with the exception of a handsome glass table and an immense network of candles. It was really something else.

After that, I called it a day. At least there was one mission accomplished for the magazine. I headed for the Regency with the intention of having a nice, cold glass of white wine and a nap before Sam came home from the park.

As I unlocked the door to our suite the phone was ringing, and for once I didn't even think about it being Chris. Which was just as well, because it wasn't. It was Gordon Harte.

"Hello. I understand from Hilary that we're to be dinner partners tomorrow night. Can I give you a lift?" His voice sounded mellower than it did at the office, and more like it had during our walk the day before.

"That would be nice, but I'm going over early for a drink. I haven't seen Hilary since I left New York."

"Then I won't intrude. How are you finding the job?"

"Great fun, and a wee bit hectic. I'm out of practice."

"I'm sure you're doing fine. I was going to ask you to lunch today, but you vanished. We'll make up for it another time."

"I'd like to do that."

"Then consider it done. Have a good evening, Gillian. See you tomorrow."

"Good-bye." Strange call, strange man, it was as though there was an enormous gulf between him and the rest of the world. He seemed cold even when his words were friendly, and it was a little bit confusing. But at least there seemed to be more to him than to Matthew Hinton. Gordon Harte had spirit and texture and soul. And you could tell that somehow, somewhere, at some time in his life, he had suffered. But over what? Or whom? I fell asleep on my bed as I mulled it over.

I woke up to the sound of the phone ringing again and reached out groggily, not quite aware of what I was doing, and far from awake. This time it was Chris. And all I could think of were warm thoughts, and kind things, and how much I loved him. I smiled sleepily, blew kisses, listened to the sound of his voice. And then rolled over and looked at the clock to see what time it was . . . four-fifteen . . . that's one-fifteen in San Francisco . . . and then, for some reason, I remembered Marilyn, and before I could stop it I had let loose with a bitchy sounding "And where's Marilyn? Doesn't she come home for lunch?" . . . Ouch. I

blew it. I could feel Chris bounce back as though I had
slapped him. After that, we talked about my job, the
weather, Chris's projects, his films, and we pointedly
stayed off the subject of Marilyn, or anything else of any
importance. It was a lousy conversation. We played our
little games, and Marilyn was as much with us as though
she had been listening on the extension. We were ill at
ease, I was angry and hurt, and Christopher felt awkward.
He should have. He should have felt much worse than
that. But he didn't know how.

20

On Wednesday, the opening of the horse show was similar
to the opening of the opera, from a social standpoint. It
was something to see, and someplace to be seen. Matt was
as charming as ever, but I thought the polish was beginning to wear a bit thin. I was already bored with his scene.
Afterward, we dined at La Caravelle, where again everyone bowed and scraped to "Monsieur Eeentone." And the
newspapers were kinder this time than they had been the
first, though they didn't ignore us entirely. They merely
made note of our existence by publishing a photograph of
our attendance. But this time Peg didn't call.

On Thursday, I appeared for my interview with Milt
Howley. He was living in a penthouse at the United Na-
tions Plaza and for a brief moment, as I braced myself for
the interview, I stood on the sidewalk and gazed upward,
impressed once again with the towering heights of New
York. Everything was up, everything was big. There was a
breathless, overwhelming bitchiness to it, and every min-

ute of every day you knew that you were "there." It was
the Mecca. It was Sodom, it was Hell and the Garden of
Eden, and, like any other human being with a thrill for
life, I was enthralled. And I knew then that even if I left
the city the next day, never to return, for one brief moment I had looked at a building fifty stories high, and New
York and I had come to terms. It was just what I had said
I would do as our plane had landed in New York. I had
the city by the balls. But it had me by the throat.

I was let into Milt Howley's apartment by a tiny, blonde
girl who was Howley's current "old lady," as he put it. His
mistress. And from that point on, a whirlwind day began.
He ran from Rockefeller Center for a meeting to Double-
day's to autograph records, to his agent's office to sign
contracts, to a three o'clock lunch at Mama Leone's,
where between the salad and the spumoni I managed to
squeeze in some interview time. He was an interesting
man. He had started singing blues in Chattanooga, Ten-
nessee, ten years before and had made a minor hit in Hollywood before being lured into the protest scene which
landed him in jail thirty-seven times and kept him so busy
he let his career slip. But now he was up, Mr. Superstar,
three albums in one year that had sold over a million copies each, two movie contracts, and appearances in Las
Vegas, Hollywood, and New York. The whole bit.

After lunch, I rode to the airport with him in a rented
limousine. He was going to the White House for dinner. It
was exhausting and exhilarating and I liked him. He was
all man, and he had been good to interview. He was direct
and human and had a raucous sense of humor which made
the pressure of his schedule more bearable.

His valet had put his suitcase in the car during the afternoon, and as we drove to the airport he calmly answered
my questions as he checked its contents and took care of a
double bourbon, seeming totally unflustered by the fact
that he was in a moving car, having a drink, being inter-
viewed, and on his way to have dinner with the President.
He had a lot of style.

The last I saw of him was as he went through the gate

to his plane and stooped to kiss my cheek while he purred in my ear. "You're one all right woman, Gillian . . . for a honky chick."

I laughed and waved as he got on the plane. I had exactly seventy-one minutes to get to Hilary's.

When Hilary opened the door, she looked wonderful. A mixture of Henri Bendel and Paris and Hilary. Put together to perfection, the kind of woman other women envy but that make men feel a little uncomfortable—they wouldn't want to get her hair messed up. She is the kind of woman who spends a lot of time with homosexuals, other women, and old friends. All her lovers are temporary, some of them indecently young, but very attractive, and most become friends eventually. Hilary must be hard to love. I would have felt sorry for her, except I wouldn't have dared. Pity was something you did not dare to think about in the company of Hilary Price. Respect was more like it. In fact, a feeling akin to what my grandmother had inspired. Tough, ballsy women like that make you stand taller, command their due. These are the women whom friends put on pedestals, the same women who would do anything for those friends with one hand while castrating their men and their sons with the other.

Hilary has an incredible amount of style. Everything she touches is done to perfection: her manicure, her home, the dinners she prepares, her work, and her friendships. There is another side of Hilary which is cold, and could be very cruel, but she reserves that for the people who cross her. I have never had the occasion to incur her wrath, and for that I'm grateful. I have seen her take people apart verbally, and it is formidable and terrifying to watch. Perhaps it is that that men sense, which makes them keep their distance, or move on quickly.

Hilary and I have never had the sloppy ease with each other that I share with Peg or some of my other friends. I wouldn't pick my teeth, use all the curse words I might otherwise, or show up at her house in blue jeans and a ragged sweat shirt. But I share something else with Hilary which I do not share with the others. The others have known me as a child, and there is still much of the schoolgirl in all of us when we meet—we still look upon our relationships with each other in the same spirit that they began. The friendship with Hilary, however, began when we were both grown up, so perhaps we expect more of each other. Besides, Hilary as a schoolgirl is unthinkable, unless she went to school in Chanel suits, with perfectly arranged hair. I just can't imagine Hilary playing hockey. In the drawing room of Mme. de Sevigne surely, but not on the hockey field looking the way we had.

We had an hour and a half to talk before the first guest arrived, and we covered most of what we wanted to know and say. Hilary mentioned briefly and without much passion that she had a new beau. A young German boy named Rolfe. He was a poet, younger than she, and a "beautiful child," according to Hilary. He was expected for dinner. She continued to live alone because it suited her better. And I envied her that. That sort of thing would never suit me better. Hilary's dream princes were all dead and gone, if they had ever existed. Mine was still waiting in the wings of my dreams. For however much I may have loved Chris, he was a far cry from a dream prince, even to me.

I had planned not to talk about Chris, but Hilary brought it up while she was making her second drink. "Gillian, if it's going to work out, it will. And better yet, if it works out on your terms. And if not, hard as it is for you to think that way, try and believe that you haven't lost a great deal. I'm sure Chris is a charming boy, but I don't think he's for you. Frankly, I think you deserve better. And you need the kind of things Chris will never be able to give you. He's too much like me, he doesn't believe in the kind of things you believe in, and I don't think you're ready to stop believing in them either. But whichever way you go, I want you to know I'm around to help, or to listen. I can't tell you much more than that."

Hilary's words touched me, but it disturbed me that she should think Chris wasn't good enough for me. He was, he was. . . I wanted him to be, no matter how much I had to swallow, or bend over backward. I still wanted it to work.

Hilary then walked over to her library, looked for something for a few minutes while I gathered my thoughts, and came back with a book in her hands. Leather bound and very old, it looked like something Hilary, or my grandmother, would have. "Here, this may sound trite to you, but there's a great deal of truth in that," and she held it out, open to the fly leaf, where a strong hand had written in brown ink:

> He who bends to himself a joy,
> Doth the winged life destroy;
> But he who kisses the joy as it flies,
> Lives in Eternity's sunrise.

and it was signed with the initial L., and a date.

"That was the first man I ever slept with, Gillian. He was thirty years older than I, I was seventeen at the time. He was the greatest concert violinist in Europe, and I loved him so much I thought I'd die when he told me that I was 'a big girl now' and he felt I didn't need him anymore. I wanted to die, but I didn't. One never does, and I have learned that there's a great deal of truth in those words. I live by them."

I was moved, and was still holding the book in my hands when the doorbell rang. Hilary got up to answer it, and in walked a tall good-looking boy about three years younger than I, with blond hair and big green eyes. He had the grace of a very young boy, with none of the awkwardness. It was a totally sensual pleasure to watch him, and a little embarrassing to watch him stare adoringly at Hilary. This was Rolfe. He kissed my hand, called me "Madame," and made me feel a thousand years old. Except this was what Hilary expected, what she liked. It put no strain on her. And in a brief flashback, I realized that she had become her concert violinist, the man she had loved twenty years before. She sent all these little boys on their way when she felt they didn't need her anymore, like a dancing mistress at a finishing school. It was an odd re-alization, and I wondered if she gave them each a bronze plaque inscribed with the lines I had just read as their grad-uation present. It was a funny thought, and I giggled, which snapped Hilary's attention toward me and made Rolfe look confused, as though he might have said something he shouldn't have. Poor Rolfe.

The rest of the guests arrived shortly thereafter. Anoth-er editor from Hilary's office, an extremely elegant Italian girl, Paola di San Fraschino, the daughter of some noble-man or other. She spoke charming English and was ob-viously very well-bred. After her, a lively girl who looked very horsey, had a rather odd laugh, but a kind face. She had just published her second book and didn't look at all the type. She had a very definite sense of humor and livened up the group considerably. Her husband was a music critic for an English paper, and they had the air of country squires about them. She wore some kind of caftan with Moroccan jewelry, had none of the super chic of ei-ther Paola or Hilary, but nevertheless a certain style. And her husband had none of the ethereal qualities of Rolfe, which was refreshing. I was beginning to find the golden poet a little hard to talk to. The doorbell rang twice more after that, once for a terribly pompous but good-looking Frenchman who owned an art gallery on Madison Ave-nue, and the last time for Gordon Harte, who seemed to know Paola and Rolfe. He and Hilary embraced, and he then proceeded to the bar to make his own drink, looking very much at home. Much more so than Rolfe, who looked as though he was not allowed to touch anything without Hilary's permission. Before doing anything, or opening his mouth to speak, Rolfe seemed to check with Hilary first, and it made me nervous. It reminded me of the way I had been when I got married, and it was embar-rassing to watch someone else doing it.

The evening passed delightfully. It was like flying back and forth on a trapeze, being part of an acrobatic act. We rushed from Japanese literature to French tapestries, to the new rages in Paris, to Russell Baker's latest editorials, to the political implications of American literature vs Russian literature at the turn of the century, on to homosexuality in Italy, and speculation as to the demise of the Church and organized religion in our society . . . on to Oriental cults, yoga philosophy, and the *I Ching*. It was exhausting and exhilarating, the kind of evening you can only stand about once every six months. It takes you that long to get all your faculties refurbished afterward. It was a typical evening chez Hilary, with people from the arts, and publishing, and a smattering of literati.

The lady writer and Gordon impressed me the most. They seemed knowledgeable, and informed, but more down to earth than the others. Infinitely more aware of "reality," something which had become important to me since my days with Chris. My days of enjoying the purely theoretical were over. And I had come to have a healthy respect for the real.

Gordon took me back to the hotel, and we spoke of nothing in particular, the excessive intellectualism of the evening having been dispelled when the group disbanded to go home. As we reached the hotel I expected him to invite me for a drink. But he didn't. Instead, he looked down at me and said, "How about dinner tomorrow?" He looked suddenly vulnerable, and kind. And I wanted to have dinner with him.

"I'd love to."

"Good. I'll give you a call in the morning and let you know what time. I have a meeting with John at five, so I doubt if it will be much before eight."

"Suits me. Thank you, Gordon. And thanks for the lift home. Goodnight."

I could hardly wait till dinner the next evening, and as I rode up in the elevator I made a mental note to buy a new dress.

21

"Where are you going, Mommy?"

"Out to dinner, love."

"Again?" Ouch. Oh, Sam. . . .

"Yes. But I promise to be home this weekend." Meager compromise.

"Is that a new dress?"

"What is this? The inquisition?"

"What does that mean?"

"It means you're asking a lot of questions, Sam."

"Well, is it a new dress?"

"Yes."

"I like it."

"Well, that's a relief. Thank you." She was sprawled on the couch and checking me out with a critical eye.

"You know, you're getting fatter in the middle, Mom. You don't look skinny like you used to."

"What do you mean fatter?" My heart sank. I didn't think I showed yet.

"Just a little. Don't worry." The phone rang then and I kissed Sam on the top of her head.

"I won't. Now you go take your bath and I'll answer the phone. Scram." She took off, and for a sad instant I thought it might be Gordon calling off our plans. He would be held over at the office, or had been poisoned at lunch, or had broken an ankle, something . . . like cold feet maybe, or another date . . . That's okay, Gordon . . . I understand . . . but what about my new dress?

"Hello? . . . Yes, Operator, this is she. . . . Hello, Chris. . . . Yes. . . . What's up? . . No, I am not uptight . . . no

145

. . . no . . . I'm alone. . . . Okay, okay. . . . I was just getting ready to go out to dinner. . . . What the hell do you
mean 'it didn't take me long'? . . . Just dinner with a friend
of Hilary's (why did I have to put it that way?) . . . No,
he is not a greasy Italian count, he works at the magazine.
Woman's Life. . . . You know, I think you could really
hold off on those remarks. For someone who's living with
a girl, you're awfully touchy, dearest. . . . Oh really? . . .
And why is that so different? . . . Would you like me to tell
you why? . . . Hardly. I'm still pregnant, or have you forgotten that little detail? . . . It's not too late for what? . . .
Forget it, that's out of the question. . . . How's Marilyn?
Okay, I don't want to hear about it. . . . Don't explain,
Christopher. It's very clear as it is. . . . Leaving? . . .
When? . . . I'll believe it when I see it. . . . Look, Chris,
will you please get off my back about tonight. . . . I'm here
because you wanted me here, it wasn't my idea. . . . All
right we'll talk about something else. . . . Wouldn't want to
get Uncle Chris upset, would we? . . . She's fine. . . . Yes,
she still asks for you. . . . Concerned with our little family
tonight aren't we? . . . Why? . . . Marilyn giving you a
rough time???? . . . Look, Chris, I think it'd be better if
you didn't call for a while. I can't take it. It just makes
things worse. You've got Marilyn, you don't need me, and
I can't handle it. I'll call you. . . . Oh, I see, fine. . . . Look,
go to hell, you've got her, so just get off my back, please.
. . . Write to me then. . . . No, I'm seeing the doctor next
week. I guess everything's okay, I don't know. . . . A little
tired, but okay. . . . Chris, how are you really? . . . I miss
you so goddam much I can't stand it. . . . No, that is not
why I'm going out with Hilary's friend. . . ." The doorbell
rang then, and I panicked. "Look, Chris, I've got to go.
I'll call you . . . Okay, okay, fine. . . . No, don't call . . . all
right then, call. . . . Not till Monday? . . . Oh that's right,
the weekend . . . I forgot. . . . Look, I have to get off the
goddam phone. I love you. . . . Chris? . . . Yeah, baby, I
know. . . ." It was quite a phone call, with Gordon waiting
at the door.

*   *   *

Gordon and I had a wonderful evening. He took me to a tiny Italian restaurant somewhere in the east twenties and then we went uptown to a penthouse restaurant on Central Park South for a drink. The restaurant was housed in a faceless little office building and the moment we stepped off the elevator it was like entering another world. The decor was East Indian. A girl in a gold sari greeted us and parted richly embroidered curtains to lead us into the rooms beyond. There was a heavy aroma of incense in the air, the tables were long and low, and the room seemed to pulsate with a music I didn't understand but couldn't help but respond to. It made me want to sway and close my eyes, in rhythm to the sensual sounds of the East. There was a single rose on each table, and the waiters were tall and dark, many of them had beards, and some wore turbans.

We drank exotic drinks and I looked at the view in silence. It seemed as though everywhere one went in New York there was a new vista to be seen. This one from yet another angle, facing north, Central Park lying below like a child's toy bedecked with Christmas lights, and framed by the buildings on three sides of the park. I felt a million miles from anywhere I'd ever been, and the scenery beyond the windows was merely a skillfully achieved decor, meant to remind one of New York, and nothing more.

Gordon ordered a delicate white wine and rose cakes, and after the waiter served us and proceeded to disappear Gordon held my eyes for what seemed an interminable time. It was as though he were asking questions without using words, and perhaps finding his own answers.

"Why didn't you stay out West, Gillian?" He looked as though he already knew, but his gaze continued to hold mine as he waited for me to answer.

"I wanted to come back."

"That is not the truth. All right then, did you run away? I imagine that you'd be capable of that."

"I'm not sure I know what you mean. But, no, I didn't run away. I just came back."

"Because of a man?" I hesitated for a long moment and then nodded.

"And you? Why did you leave Spain?" Tit for tat.

"I was hungry."

"Now you're not telling the truth." I smiled at him and pulled the rose from its vase to finger the petals.

"Well, let's just say that the time for me to be there was past."

"Did you run away? Or did she?" It seemed the right question to ask in view of what he had asked me.

"Neither and both. She committed suicide, and after that I ran away." His face held a quiet sadness, but none of the shock I felt. He was the most incredibly direct man I'd ever met.

"I'm sorry, Gordon." I looked away, sorry we had begun the questioning. It was a dangerous game to play. We both had our painful pasts.

He looked away, a sad, serious look on his face. And I couldn't see his eyes. "That's all right, it was a long time ago. Her name was Juanita. She was the most beautiful girl I've ever known. Good and pure. Like a child. I found out that she had been a prostitute in Malaga. So she killed herself. The funny thing is that I wouldn't have cared. I didn't care, it didn't change anything, and I had suspected something like that anyway. But she never knew that. The man who told me, told her, and before I got home she was dead. And after that I left. I couldn't handle it there anymore. I never really belonged in the first place, but I had loved it." I nodded again, There seemed to be nothing to add to what he had said. "And your man, Gillian, who was he?"

"Just a man." I didn't want to talk about Chris because I couldn't give Gordon the kind of honesty he was giving me. Chris was not as far back for me as Juanita was for him, I hadn't come to terms with it yet, and whereas his story was narrative, mine was more likely to sound like true confessions.

"Is it still a going thing?"

"No . . . well, not really. We still talk. But I think it's

over." I knew deep in my heart that I was lying, because I didn't think it was over. I thought it might be, but I didn't really believe that.

"What was he like?"

"My father."

"And what was your father like?"

"In a word . . . a bastard." I looked up with a grin. There was a nice feeling of relief in saying it.

"And what does that tell you, Gillian?"

"Bad things. But I didn't see the similarity until just recently."

"Were you happy with this man?"

"For a while. Yes, very happy. He has some good points after all, or I wouldn't have stayed around as long as I did. But I think, underneath it all, he's a bastard just like my father. Not a nice man. I don't think so anyway. He's incapable of a lot of things I need. I knew that, but I didn't want to know it." It felt so strange to be talking about Chris as though he were a thing of the past.

"Why did you stay with him then, since you can't tell me why you left, because the fact that he was a 'bastard' doesn't explain anything. You liked him that way." Ouch. Gordon was right, I think I did.

"All right. I left because he forced me to. I stayed because . . . because I loved him, I needed him, I wanted it to work. As long as I stayed on his terms, it was okay. Oh, and I stayed because there were other things. It's sort of a complicated story."

"And not over yet, is it, Gillian?"

"Yes, and no. Oh hell, Gordon. There's a lot to this thing." I looked up and let my eyes take hold of his. "It's over because I don't believe he loves me, and it's not over because I'm having his child. In that sense, it'll never be over." And then panic at what I'd just said.

"Does anyone know?" He looked perfectly unruffled.

"Only one friend. And he knows, of course. But it doesn't seem to make much difference."

"Have you thought of having an abortion? I suppose you have."

"Yes. I've thought of it. But I want to have the child. I'm going to bring an awful lot down on my head, but this is how I want to do it. I'm sure."

"Then you're doing the right thing. But I wouldn't tell anyone, Gillian. However much I admire your determination, it isn't the accepted lifestyle for someone like you, after all."

"I know. And I had planned to keep it to myself. I don't know what happened tonight. It just slipped out." I tried to smile without looking at him, and felt him take my hand in his.

"Don't look so sad, Gillian. You're going to make it through."

"Thanks for the vote of confidence. . . . Once in a while I need it." I tried to smile at him. And it was strange. It was almost as though we were on a carrousel of revelations. In less than an hour we were covering every inch of each others' scars and markings. As though we both felt we had to know what had come before. And then, almost unconsciously, I hurled the ball into his court again.

"What about your marriage?"

"In a sense it never existed, Gillian."

"But you said. . . ." I was puzzled. He seemed too honest to lie about something like that.

"For Heaven's sake, don't look at me like that, child! I was married. What I meant was that it might as well not have existed. It was brief, painful, and devoid of all emotion."

"How in hell did you ever get married then?" It seemed so unlike him.

"Easy. I had to. Or felt I had to. That was twenty-five years ago, and I had seen a young lady briefly, and . . . well . . ."

"She got pregnant."

"Right. She refused to have an abortion, so I decided to do the noble thing. I married her. But it was untenable. As soon as Greg was born we got a divorce, and that was it."

"Well, at least you got Greg out of it. Are you two

close?" His eyes hardened at the question and took on a strange kind of bitterness.

"Hardly, my dear. Greg is a charming young man. Intelligent, witty, independent. And a stranger. When I left, I cut him out of my mind and tried to forget he existed. I never saw him as a small child, and you forget, I was in Spain for ten years. When I came back he was fifteen. It's difficult to become a father to a fifteen-year-old boy you don't even know."

"Perhaps one day you will."

"Perhaps. But unlikely. He thinks me a dreadful materialist. And he's quite right, I am. To earn his respect, I'd have to do something grandiose. Like become an artist for a cause in Afghanistan, or something of the sort. And that's not in my plans. And now, young lady, we have both talked long enough about our grisly pasts. Let's get you home, it's late." He signaled to the turbaned waiter, and it was clear that the confidences had come to a close. Gordon Harte had the evening well in control. And then he looked at me and the brief tenseness left his face.

"You must have a strange power over me, my dear. I haven't talked like this in years." It was a nice compliment, and he reached for my hand as we rose from the cushions we had been sitting on. His hold was gentle but firm, and he kept my hand in his as we rode down in the elevator and stepped outside. It was a lovely night, the air was warm and there was a slight breeze, and the horses tethered to the hansom cabs neighed softly from across the street.

"This city looks like a movie set to me. So unreal." I looked around again and saw Gordon watching me.

"Come, Gillian. Let's walk back to the hotel." It was only three blocks to the Regency and his arm around my shoulders felt just right. We said nothing on the brief walk, and at the hotel he stood outside the revolving door and looked down at me with a small smile.

"How about lunch in the country tomorrow? I'm going to see friends in Bedford. The country air would do you good." Not "I'd like you to be with me," but "the country

air will do you good." I would have liked him to say the
words, but I could see that he meant them anyway as he
waited for an answer.

"I'd like to, Gordon."

"Would you like to bring your daughter?"

"She has other plans. But thank you. She's spending the
day with a friend from school."

"Fine, I'll pick you up at eleven then. And don't be
sorry about tonight, little one. You needed to talk . . . and
so did I." He made no move to kiss me then, but only
touched my shoulder gently before he walked away.

We waved at each other one last time as I went in, and I
floated past the desk, wondering what lay in store, and
fearing that the magic would be gone by the next day.

"Would you mind getting the map out of the glove
compartment for me, Gillian?" We were racing along the
East River Drive with the top of his car down, and he had
been cool when he picked me up. There was no reference
to the confidences of the night before, and very little
warmth.

"Sure." I snapped open the little door on the dash-
board, pulled out the map, and handed it to him.

"Open it, please." I was a little surprised by his tone,
but dutifully unfolded the map, and then laughed. There
was a cartoon, showing a much caricatured portrait of myself and Mr. Gordon Harte, eating hot dogs under a
lamppost outside the building that housed *Woman's Life,* a
Chihuahua and a St. Bernard were dutifully lifting their
legs on the lamp post, and what looked like the entire
magazine staff was leaning from the windows of the building. The caption read "Let's get away from it all," and
when I looked up, Gordon was looking pleased by my obvious delight.

"That means you owe me lunch this week."

"You've got a deal. This is super, Gordon."

"So are you."

The lunch in Bedford was pleasant, I liked his friends,
and the afternoon sped by.

By five o'clock I was back at the hotel, in time to meet Samantha.

On Sunday, Sam and I moved back to our old apartment with Peg's help, and the absence of the Regency was sorely felt, by me at least. As for Sam, she was ecstatic to be home. I was less so. Sunday night was spent scrubbing floors and scouring closets, and it seemed as though I hardly had time to go to bed before another work week began.

"Samantha! . . . Breakfast! . . . Hurry up, you'll be late for school!" And I for work. It was quite a major feat of organization to get the show on the road, Sam ready for school, and myself for work. I had lost the knack, and getting it all together at eight o'clock in the morning was like climbing an iceberg wearing roller skates. It had been easier to be up and dressed at six in San Francisco. Maybe it was the clothes.

"Sam! Come on! . . . Where are you?"

"Here I come, Mommy!" and she arrived in a burst of cowboy gear Chris had given her. "Here I am!"

"Okay, love, eat the cornflakes. We're in sort of a hurry."

"Cowboys don't eat cornflakes." She looked insulted.

"Oh yes they do. Now come on, Sam. Eat!" I was trying to juggle coffee and the paper, while wondering if my shoes needed a shine.

There were the usual thousand phone calls to make at work, shooting of the children's rooms to be set up, the dining room assignment to be finalized, and John Templeton had a horde of minor things for me to attend to.

Gordon and I had our promised lunch on Tuesday, and he invited me to a black tie press party at the Museum of Modern Art on Wednesday night.

On Wednesday afternoon, I rushed home from the office, got out a black velvet dress and raspberry satin evening coat, and waited for him to pick me up at seven. I realized as I waited for him to arrive that mixed with the elation of going out with him again was a sagging feeling. Chris hadn't called all week. And as usual, it hurt. I ached for Chris Matthews, for his arms around me, for his quiet voice, even for his indifference, anything.

"Mommy! The doorbell is ringing!" Sam's voice rang through the apartment.

"Okay. I'll get it." I hadn't even heard it. It was Gordon.

"All set? My! Don't you look smashing! You look just lovely, Gillian." He studied me appreciatively and gave me a peck on the forehead.

"Thank you, sir. How was your day?"

"As per usual. Gillian, is there anything wrong?"

"No. Why?"

"You look as though you've had a rough day, as though something hurt." Very perceptive, Mr. Harte.

"No. Really. Maybe a little tired, but that's all. Would you like a drink before we go?"

"No, I think we'd better get started."

"Who are you?" Samantha was suddenly in the doorway, studying the scene.

"Gordon, this is Samantha. This is Mr. Harte, Sam."

"Who's he?"

"Someone I work with and a friend of Aunt Hilary's." I watched them carefully, afraid she'd set his back up by saying something rude. I knew he wasn't used to children.

"Can I touch your beard? Is it real?" Samantha approached carefully and Gordon stooped down to talk to her.

"Yes, and it is real. Hello, Samantha." I watched with trepidation to see if she would give it a yank, but instead she just patted it and I stopped holding my breath.

"Feels kinda like a horse. You know?"

"That's a compliment," I interpreted.

"Do you like horses, Samantha?"

"Yeah! A lot!" A lengthy discussion followed, and I was surprised to hear how much Gordon seemed to know about them, and even more surprised when he reached for a pad on my desk and did a few quick sketches for Sam, which delighted her. Gordon and Samantha were discovering each other.

"Gillian, we'd better go now. Samantha, I hope to see you again sometime."

"Sure. Come back and visit, Mr. Gordon."

"Mr. Harte, Sam. Goodnight, sweetheart. Be a good girl with Jane." We exchanged great big hugs and a series of watery kisses, and then Gordon rang for the elevator.

"That was nice of you, Gordon. Thanks." We were waiting for a cab downstairs and my spirits were restored. It was nice to see Samantha enjoying him.

"I like her. She's bright and very direct."

"That's for sure!" I laughed and shook my head as a cab pulled up and we sped off toward the museum.

The evening was wonderful, it was delightful to be swept along in his wake, being introduced to everyone and having a fuss made over us. Gordon was on the board of the museum, something he had neglected to tell me when he had invited me. Hilary was there, sans Rolfe, looking smashing in a long skinny black knit dress and an equally long skinny white coat. Gordon asked her to join us for dinner afterward, which I thought was nice, but she refused.

This time Gordon took me to Lutece for dinner, where he was received as though he owned the place or, at the very least, paid the rent.

We had run into Matthew Hinton at the museum, accompanied by a striking redhead who clung to his arm as though in desperate gratitude. We greeted each other, but coolly, and it was apparent that he had as little interest in what *Women's Wear* had called "his latest love" a week before as I had in him. He was nice, but there just wasn't much to him.

And I may not have been making the social columns with Gordon Harte, but I was having a beautiful time.

22

Friday was pandemonium. The actors who owned the eccentric dining room stood amidst a bevy of people, ready to begin the shooting. And four hours later we were still only beginning. They managed to get loaded during the shooting, kept the setting constantly rumpled and disorderly, and drove the photographer crazy. At midnight it was over, and I wondered if we had a single usable shot. And we weren't through yet; we had promised everyone dinner in compensation for their "patience." At 2 A.M. I finally crawled home, exhausted and feeling as though I were about to die.

An hour after I went to bed, I got up, vomited, had chills, cramps, and panicked, thinking I was losing the baby. I should have called Peg, or the doctor, or even Gordon. Someone sensible. But I wasn't feeling sensible. I had that wild animal feeling one gets when surprised at feeling suddenly sick. So I operated on reflex and emotion, and dialed Chris.

"Hello?"

"Chris? . . . I think I'm losing the baby, I feel so awful. We worked until one o'clock . . . No, for God's sake, I mean it. No, I'm not drunk . . . I'm sick . . . what am I going to do?"

"For Chrissake, Gillian, stop crying. Why did you call me? I can't do anything about it, and you know what I told you. Call the doctor. . . . Look, I can't talk to you now. I'll call you Monday."

Monday? Monday? What the hell does he mean, "Monday"? Sonofabitch . . . I put on some clothes and went to the emergency room at Lenox Hill Hospital where I spent the night and was treated for exhaustion and hysteria.

I was sent home at noon, feeling sheepish, and still very tired. Gordon called almost as soon as I got home.

"And where have you been so bright and early this morning? I called you at nine. I hear the shooting was a madhouse last night."

"Yes, it was." And then I told him about the night at the hospital, omitting the part about my call to Chris.

Gordon was sympathetic, and said he'd check on me on Sunday, and why didn't I take Monday off?

I slept all day and when I woke up there were flowers from him, a small basket that looked like a nest, filled with tiny blue and orange flowers. The card read, "Work is the opiate of the masses, but it sounds like you had a bad trip. Have a good rest. Apologies from your Senior Art Director, Gordon Harte." Funny and thoughtful and nice, because it wasn't pushy and signed "G." or something equally irritating.

He called again on Sunday, and I was feeling better, but still pretty tired, so he agreed not to drop by, but instead invited me to dinner on Thursday.

As I lay in bed on Sunday afternoon, pleased with the easiness of the Gordon situation, and maybe feeling a little supercilious about it, as though for once I had "control," the doorbell rang. Who the hell is that? I got up to answer it. It was Gordon.

"Changed my mind. Besides, Hilary says you love having people drop in on you on Sundays. We just had lunch and she sends her love. May I come in?"

"Of course," but I was angry, really mad. I looked a mess, he had agreed not to come by, I didn't feel well, and unannounced visits from him constituted an "act of pressure" in my book.

"You don't look too pleased to see me, Mrs. Forrester."

"Just surprised. Would you like a cup of tea?"

"Yes. But I'll make it, you go back to bed."

"No, that's all right, I'll stay up. I'm really fine." . . . I wasn't about to get into one of those "now tell me, doctor," scenes with him on the edge of my bed. . . .

"You look fine to me, but I don't know much about these things. I'll make the tea."

He returned from the kitchen after much scraping and banging, and he sat there looking unaffected by it all, making easy conversation and looking around pleasantly. Samantha was out and the apartment seemed horribly quiet.

I was in the midst of making stiff, pompous remarks about nothing, and looking into my cup of tea to cover the fact that I was uncomfortable, when Gordon got up, came around the coffee table, sat down, and kissed me. His beard felt scratchy, and his mouth felt soft, and I was too embarrassed not to kiss him back. He kissed me, and then leaned back a little, looked down at me, and hugged me.

He hugged me. A nice hug. The kind I had longed for when I was eight years old, and still longed for twenty years later. And there was Gordon Harte, hugging me, while I sat in the circle of his arms and was suddenly in tears.

I tried to make light of it after that, for fear that he was going to try to take it too many steps further, and I didn't want to get into a scene like that with him yet.

"You want to be wooed, don't you?"

"What?" It sounded so ridiculous, it made me laugh.

"Mrs. Forrester, we could spend the next few weeks eating dinner together twice a week and enjoying preambles, I could 'woo' you, and we could say agreeable things to each other, and in three weeks you would probably agree to go to bed with me, or we could go to bed now, and enjoy the three weeks more. What do you say?"

"I can't. I'm sorry, but I just can't. I know I'd get upset, and I couldn't handle it. I know myself." I was almost whispering when I said it, and looking down at my hands clenched in my lap.

"All right." . . . I was a teensy bit sorry that he agreed so readily, but for the most part I was relieved.

We sat talking in low voices, and listening to the rain,

kissing on the couch in my living room for a while, and each time we kissed I wanted him more, and we held each other for longer, until he kissed my breast, and my whole body surged upwards toward his, and we were suddenly hand in hand, heading for my bedroom, still kissing and touching and holding along the way, almost knocking over a lamp, and in a great hurry to get to bed. He took off his clothes, and I noticed with a shock that he didn't wear any underwear. . . . "Why Gordon Harte, you look so goddam serious all the time, and there you are walking around that magazine all day with no underpants on! What if your zipper breaks?" I was laughing, it really struck me funny.

"It never has."

"What if you get in an accident? My grandmother always said. . . ."

And he roared with laughter, and walked over to help me take off the rest of what I had on. . . . "Gillian, you're beautiful." He sounded as though he meant it, and for the rest of time our bodies rolled together, merged into each other, touched and fell away, and joined again. We made love, and lay together feeling close, and familiar, easy with each other. We had become friends. We had fallen in like. It was the first time in my life that I didn't feel I had to shout "I love you" to justify doing something that I had been told all my life was not a nice thing to do. Instead, we hugged and laughed, and I felt right with the world.

It was better with Gordon than it had ever been with Chris, which seemed odd to me because I didn't love Gordon. But that afternoon I stopped being angry with Chris. I didn't make love with Gordon to wreak vengeance on Chris for Marilyn. I made love with Gordon because I wanted to, and I liked him. Nothing more than that.

And I lay in Gordon's arms, smiling, while he drew figure eights around my breasts with his finger, and I thought of the poem on the flyleaf of Hilary's book . . . "he who kisses the joy as it flies, lives in Eternity's sunrise. . . ."

23

In every possible way, October was a good month, a warm month full of people and things to do. Samantha was happy at school and, while I hadn't come to love New York, I had done a little better than just resign myself to it. New York was being good to me, it was looking its best, and was on its best behavior. There is a time of year in New York, in the fall, which comes suddenly, and doesn't last long, but is enough to make you love it for the rest of the year. If you go away then, you will always think of New York in golden hues, but if you stay you see the filth, the soot, the slush, and, later, live in the stench and torrid heat of a New York summer. But in the fall, it becomes beautiful, it is red and gold and brown, it's clear and windy and crisp, the streets look cleaner, people step as though walking to a march, the smell of hot chestnuts is everywhere, young people are in the city on weekends, making it look as though there are some nice young people who live there after all, because summer weekends are over and it's too early for skiing. It's the time of year I love best, and if there is a warm spot in my heart for New York it is for that city at precisely that time of year. And the spell it weaves for two, or three, or four weeks in the late autumn.

And as though the city itself had planned it that way, on my last year in New York, those magical weeks happened, and were crisper and livelier and more beautiful than ever before. To me, New York is like a bitch of a woman, she's too much to handle, and I don't admire her lifestyle, but, in deference to what she is and what she stands for, I have to admit it when she moves out in style. And in October she does.

Gordon and I were seeing each other two or three times a week, went some place really "nice" about once a week, met some place after work sometimes, or one of us cooked dinner at his place or mine. Halfway into the month, we pooled our resources and address books and threw a party. It was crazy and fun, crowded and full of amusing stereotypes, like most parties in New York.

Gordon had a full schedule, and I had enough to do, so that it never became an everyday thing.

There were no assumptions made about each other's time, but everything just seemed to fall into place, like the weather. And life moved on.

Halloween came and went leaving Samantha richer and happier with the loot she had collected from our building and Gordon's. He had taken her over to his place to test his neighbors' mettle, and she was delighted. By then, she and Gordon were fast friends.

We decided to spend Thanksgiving together, quietly, at my place, and I was just leaving the office to pick up our turkey when the phone rang. It was Julie Weintraub.

"Hi. I just spoke to my doctor, and it looks like you've got the job for another month. How's that for a bitch? Actually, I'm enjoying the rest, and there are a couple of interns worth staying around for. Who needs John Templeton with a setup like this?" Her words sounded funny, but she sounded disappointed. Lying on your back with pins in you, and traction pulling at you, just isn't a whole lot of fun, interns or no. Given a choice, I'd even take Eloise Franck. Poor Julie.

"Have you told John yet, Julie?"

"Yeah, I just called him. He ought to be barreling down the hall any minute with the good news."

"Come on, you know everybody here wants you back. All anybody ever says to me around here is 'when's Julie coming back?' " which wasn't entirely true, but I thought it might help.

"Bullshit. But that was a nice try. I saw stats of your

last issue by the way. Looks good to me. Maybe I won't have a job anymore when I get out of this place." . . . And that was something I knew was worrying her.

"Bullshit to you, lady. I'm just making like a Kelly girl here. Purely temporary. I'll start wearing white gloves if it'll make you feel any better," and she broke into a more Julie-like laugh. . . . "Listen, seriously, what did the doctor say? How's it mending?"

"I don't know, nobody tells me much of anything. All I know is that they want to reshift something, which means yet another orthopedic surgeon, and the operating room again, which is not exactly my favorite scene. It also means another four weeks. Kinda depressing," and that's just how she sounded.

"Well, keep the chin up. Might as well get it all done now rather than have to go back in six months. That's nothing to mess around with. Besides, you don't think I'm going to break my ass for you here every six months, do you?" and I heard Julie chuckle again. "I'll come up and see you this weekend and give you all the news . . . which reminds me, you remember that little love seat in John's office?"

"Yeah."

"Well, I hear Lucius Barclay humped Eloise on it yesterday afternoon," Lucius being the faggy beauty editor. Even women's lib couldn't get upset about our having a male beauty editor. There was absolutely nothing male about Lucius. Nothing.

But the crack had served its purpose, and Julie was in hoots at the other end of the phone.

"Hey, listen, don't do that to me . . . it hurts," and then more chortles and chuckles. . . . "Anyway, you got it wrong. I heard that story this morning: Eloise humped Lucius," and we both laughed.

"Okay, Julie, gotta go, but I'll come by this weekend. Anything I can bring you?"

'Yeah. Sex."

"What about all those interns? Listen, save one for me. Hang in there, Julie, we miss you. I can't wait to give you this job back anyway. I want to start collecting unemployment."

"Screw you, you don't qualify. Gotta work six months and then get fired. And if you think I'm gonna lie here for six months, you gotta be nuts. So just take damned good care of my job. . . . See you soon. Hey, and Gillian? . . . Thanks."

"Don't be an ass. The thanks go to you, now get off the goddam horn before we get sentimental, or I get fired. See you . . . take care." Poor Julie, it didn't sound good, and I wondered what the score really was, as the phone rang and I was told that "Mr. Templeton would like to see you in five minutes, Mrs. Forrester."

Half an hour later, when I came out of John's office, I was not feeling like laughing anymore.

John had spoken to Julie, as she had said, but he had spoken to her doctor too. Julie was not healing at all, and her hemoglobin was low. They suspected bad news. They weren't sure, but they "suspected" it, and they were going to operate to find out. They thought she might have bone cancer. Julie didn't know.

When John had finished talking, I felt weak, and rotten, and sick. He told me not to tell anyone. And thank God he had the good taste not to mention the possibilities of extending my job into a permanent one. I would have thrown up at that point, or burst into tears.

As it was, I walked straight back to my office, shut the door, and leaned back against it with tears pouring down my face, wondering how in hell I was going to face Julie on Thanksgiving Day. It was one of those horrible soap opera ironies that happen all the time, sometimes even to people you know.

The following day, Sam, Gordon and I had Thanksgiving dinner. It was lovely and comfortable, and I tried not to think about Julie.

At that point, I was five months pregnant, and hadn't seen Christopher in over ten weeks. I still missed him but I had settled in. I was happy with my job, enjoying Gordon, and rolling along nicely. The baby was more mine than Chris's, and men on the street didn't look quite so much like Chris anymore. They were beginning to look a little more like Gordon, and a lot more like themselves.

So when Gordon left my apartment shortly after midnight on Thanksgiving night and the phone rang at two, I almost fainted when I heard Chris on the line.

"Gill, I'm at the airport now. I've got a film to do in New York for the next month. The plane gets there about six hours from now. American Airlines. Meet me."

24

The plane came to a stop just in front of the window, and rumpled looking passengers began to disembark. Mostly men, carrying suits on hangers covered by plastic bags, and attaché cases. And a few women. One woman with two small children. People. And more people. And no Chris. Where was he? Had he missed the flight? Had I heard the wrong airline? Would he be on the next flight? . . . And then there he was, smiling, looking a little sleepy, and more beautiful than I remembered him. Had he stopped walking, I would have thrown myself into his arms, but he just walked up to me, and we kept right on walking, never breaking stride.

"Hi, Gillie, how's it going?" . . . How's it going? . . . After almost three months? . . . You big shit. . . .

"Fine."

"Don't I get a kiss?" and he held out a cheek for a peck as we neared the baggage claim area.

"Wait till we get home."

"Oh is the young lady playing it cool now?" and he looked amused.

Everything amused him, mostly me, and I felt silly, in my fur hat, looking for something to say that would pass for conversation.

He was totally engrossed in collecting his bags. The flight had been fairly full. I stood watching him, wondering what it really was that held me close to this man. Why did I still feel the way I did, how could I still feel as though the world stood still for him, how could I still believe in dream princes when I looked at Chris? But I did.

I was frowning as I looked over at him. He seemed taller and wider than I had remembered. And he looked so brown and healthy. So different from the pale, city-looking people you see in New York.

He picked up the last of his bags and we headed for the exit to look for a cab. The ride into the city was a little uncomfortable because it seemed odd not to have a phone resting between us. I had grown accustomed to dealing with a disembodied voice, not to looking into the eyes of this big, suntanned man. He noticed my hat and liked it, and commented briefly on the fact that I didn't look pregnant.

"What'd you do, get rid of it?"

"It's the coat, Chris. My clothes still hide it pretty well."

"Yeah, I'll bet you're not even pregnant." I knew he didn't mean it, but it was a typical Chris remark, which annoyed the hell out of me, but somehow I managed not to snap back.

When we got home, Chris walked in, dumped his bags in the hall, and headed for the kitchen where we could hear Samantha expounding on the virtues of her teacher.

"UNCLE CRITS!" Screams, and yells, and hugs, and much tossing around, and more yelling. It was so nice to watch them together. The two people I loved most in the whole world crawling all over each other, and hugging, and laughing. It made me laugh too, and brought back all our days in California. It was sunshine and beaches and love.

"Uncle Crits, I'm going to show you my room, and you can't come in, Mommy."

"Okay, I'll make breakfast." They disappeared down the hall, hand in hand, with Samantha telling him all about school and Chris asking if she'd been a good girl, and had she been putting honey on her corn flakes like he'd shown her?

Poor Sam, she needed Chris almost as much as I did. He had been the closest thing she'd ever known to a full-time father, and our days in California had been the closest thing she'd had to a normal home life.

"Breakfast! Come and get it!"

'Okayyyy. . . ." came back, muffled, from down the hall. And then Chris appeared with a jumprope tied around his head and Samantha shouting "Giddyap horsey" as she skipped behind him.

"Horses don't eat at my breakfast table, Mr. Matthews."

"Since when? Things must have changed a lot in the last two months," and we all laughed and ate eggs and waffles, and toast, and bacon. We ate and talked and joked with each other, and I knew how terribly I had missed Chris. Just as much as I had thought, and then multiplied by twenty.

My mother's helper appeared when breakfast was over, to help clear up and take Samantha to the park. . . .

"I don't wanna go, I wanna stay with Uncle Crits." She looked as though she were going to cry.

"Come on, podner. Your mother and I are going to talk. You go to the park and see if you can't find some hay for the horses. I'll be here when you get back, now giddyap, there. . . ."

She looked dubious, but she went, waving back over her shoulder, "Gabye, Uncle Crits, see you later. Bye, Mommy."

"Bye, sweetheart."

"You've still got her spoiled rotten, Gillian. Nothing's changed."

"Look, she needs a lot of love."

"She's got a lot of love, she needs a lot of time. And spoiling isn't going to make up for that. If you didn't have your goddam alimony you wouldn't have that girl taking her to the park and you'd both be better off."

"I have to work for crissake."

"That's not the point. . . . I'm going to take a bath. Which way's our room?"

"I'll show you," and as I walked down the hall I was annoyed at Chris. What did he know about children?

"Run my bath, will you, Gill? I'm going to open the bags."

I turned on the taps full blast, and felt a little balkish about taking orders again. . . . Yessir, Mr. Chris, sir. Yo baff is fillin up dere, yo honor, sir. . . . Run your own goddam bath. . . .

He walked back into the bathroom, stark naked, and I noticed the bathing suit marks which hadn't quite faded since last summer.

"You're peeking."

"Don't be ridiculous."

"Come on, take your clothes off, and let's take a bath."

"I had a bath before I went to the airport. I'll unpack for you."

"No, I'll unpack for me. Take your clothes off and get into the bath. I want to see that belly of yours."

"Chris, I don't want to take a bath."

"You're taking a bath. Now, move your ass, girl. . . ." He was stretched out in the tub, looking up at me, with that look of his. . . . "You can take your hat off now, too. I said I liked it, but I think you could take it off now."

"Thanks. Yeah, okay," and I was pulling my clothes off, feeling silly about it, as Chris watched.

I was standing naked next to the tub, and Chris held out a hand to help me in. "Yep, you're pregnant."

"Who told you?"

"Wash my back, will you Gill?"

"Sure," and there I was, lathering his back, with my gardenia soap, smiling at the moles and freckles. I could have drawn a diagram of where every spot was on his body. I knew him, his soul and his body, every inch of him. It was a happy thing to be doing. . . . If anyone had told me that week that I would be washing Chris Matthews' back the day after Thanksgiving, I'd have laughed in their face. But there we were, and I was grinning from ear to ear.

"Watcha smiling at, little fat girl?"

"What do you mean, 'little fat girl'?"

"I mean little fat girl, now what are you smiling at?"

"Nothing. Us. You. It's so nice to have you back, Chris. It's just not the same on the phone, it's no good. I get hung up on the words, I forget the looks that go with things, and you can't squeeze them into a telephone. I've missed you so terribly."

"Yeah, I know." And for some reason, there was Marilyn again. I could see him thinking of her too, and she was there, blowing bubbles up to the surface of our bath water, like a fart.

"Okay, now wash my chest."

"Come on, Chris, you can do that yourself."

"No, I can't, I want you to do it. Wash my chest. And listen, will you do me a favor on Monday? Get some decent soap, will you please. Get rid of this orchid crap."

"It's not orchids, it's gardenias. From Magnin's."

"Well get rid of it, try something from the grocery store."

"You plebe."

"I may be a plebe, but I am not a fag, and I don't want to go around smelling like a goddam gardenia. Now wash my chest."

So I soaped up his chest and leaned over to kiss him . . . he was smiling again.

"Come here, little fat girl . . . come here, you," and there we were slathering soap all over each other, like some ridiculous French movie, and trying to make love, slipping around, slapping water all over the floor, and laughing hysterically, like two kids.

"Come on . . . ," and Chris pulled me out of the tub, still

half-covered with soap, and we lay down on the bathroom floor and made love.

Afterward, we lay there and grinned at each other. . . .

"Chris?"

"Yeah, baby?"

"I love you."

"I know. I love you too," and then he squeezed me a little and stood up. "I'm going to take a shower to get this soap off. Get me a glass of milk, will you?"

"Sure," and life was back to normal again, Chris was singing his lungs out in the shower, and there I was with soap drying on me, my pregnant belly, standing naked in the kitchen, pouring him a glass of milk. As I stood there I thought of Gordon. This was a far cry from what I had with him. He was my old side, this was my young side. This was the side of me that still had all the dreams left in it, and they just wouldn't quit.

I left the glass of milk on the bathroom sink and walked back into the bedroom while Chris continued to steam up the bathroom, when the phone rang.

"Gillian? How about some lunch?" It was Gordon . . . oh, Jesus . . . what could I say? At least Chris was in the shower, so he couldn't hear.

"I can't. Something has come up, the weekend is kind of screwed up."

"Anything wrong?"

"No, but I really can't go into it now. Let's have lunch Monday."

"You're sure nothing's wrong?"

"No, really, I'm sure. Don't worry. And Gordon . . . I'm really sorry."

"That's all right. I have some work to do anyway. See you Monday. But I'll give you a call later. Good-bye."

"Who was that?" Chris's voice, between gulps of milk. I hadn't heard the shower stop.

"A friend from the office."

"Oooohhh . . . does little fat girl have a lover boy?"

"No. And stop calling me little fat girl."

"Okay," and he blew me a kiss.

It struck me that he seemed to feel totally at home, which was a quality Chris had. And I headed for the tub to rinse off the soap and wash again. I was thinking of Gordon, and what I had said to him, and to Chris. No, Gordon was not a "lover boy." And no, "nothing was wrong." Except that I had lied to both of them, and I didn't like doing it. Chris's stay was going to be an interesting month.

Chris slapped my ass as I walked back to the bedroom. . . . "Put on your grubbies, Gill. I want to go for a walk."

"Okay, love," . . . and the door slammed and Samantha's shrieks of "Uncle Crits" reverberated through the apartment. "Uncle Crits! Uncle Crits! . . . Hi, Mommy. Guess who I saw on the way home? Gorrrdon," She rolled it around her mouth like a marble. "I told him Uncle Crits is here, and he said that was very nice. He said to say hello."

Oh shit. Happy Thanksgiving . . . and at that point in time I felt an overwhelming kinship with the turkey.

25

I stood before the door to Gordon's office, and hesitated for a moment. What in hell was I going to say?

"May I help you with something, Mrs. Forrester?" His secretary eyed me curiously as I stood there, and I no longer had any choice. I had to go in. I turned the knob carefully in my right hand, as I knocked with my left, and then stopped with one foot in the room. He was in the middle of a meeting. As he saw me, the look he gave me chilled me to the bone.

"Yes, Gillian?" His eyes were cold and blank, and his face looked taut beneath the beard.

"I'm sorry, I didn't know you were busy. I'll come back later."

"I'll call you when the meeting is over." His eyes moved away from me then, and I felt unwelcome in the room. I closed the door softly behind me and walked slowly back toward my office, wondering what lay in store.

Distractedly, I bought a cup of coffee and a Danish from the coffee wagon and sat down at my desk. Whatever was coming, I could tell it wasn't going to be pleasant. And I couldn't blame him. I know how I'd have felt in his shoes. Rotten. And pissed.

The phone rang almost an hour later, when I was absentmindedly trying to get into my work, without much success.

"Gillian, meet me downstairs in ten minutes."

"Gordon, I . . ."

"I don't want to talk about it, we'll discuss it downstairs."

"Fine." But the word went unheard, he had already hung up. I closed my eyes and tried to clear my head, and then got up to go. It would have been ironic had we met in the elevator on the way down, but we didn't. He was waiting on the street when I got there, and as soon as I reached his side he started walking uptown on Lexington Avenue at a pace I could hardly keep up with.

"Why didn't you tell me he was coming? Did you think I couldn't take it?"

"Of course not. I didn't know he was coming. He called right after you left, and a few hours later he was here."

"By what right?" That was a tough one to answer. And we were crossing streets against the lights, taunting traffic and moving along at breakneck speed. It was obvious that Gordon was livid.

"It's not a question of rights, Gordon. He's making a film here and he doesn't realize how things stand."

"And precisely how do they stand? I'm not sure I understand myself. Is he your lover or am I?"

"He's the father of my child. I lived with him. And we left each other under difficult circumstances."

"How terribly tragic. And if I recall, the difficult circumstances you just mentioned were that he threw you out? Have you forgotten that? Or doesn't it matter? All he has to do is get on a plane and arrive and everything's fine. I imagine he's staying with you." My "yes" caught in my throat, and Gordon grabbed my arm and spun me around. "Isn't he?"

"Yes! He is! So what for chrissake?"

"So plenty. I don't want that sonofabitch near you, Gillian! Not for an instant!" People were beginning to stare at us in the street, and the grip Gordon had on my arm brought tears to my eyes.

"Gordon, I've got to get this thing sorted out. Please."

"Grow up for God's sake, and be honest with yourself. There is nothing to sort out. The man doesn't want you. Don't you understand that?"

"Maybe he does." And then I was horrified at what I'd said.

"So that's it, is it? Well at least now I understand. I make a good fill-in when he's not around. You bitch!" He pulled back his arm and for a moment I thought he would hit me, but he restrained himself. "Well, I'll tell you something. Do you want to know why the men in your life have treated you badly? Because you want them to. You wouldn't know what to do with them if they didn't. You eat it up. I'm the first man who's ever been decent with you, and look at what you're doing. Take a good long look, because it's the last look you'll take." He stared at me with fire leaping from his eyes and a sense of horror grew within me as I realized what he was saying.

"Gordon, there's nothing I can say. I don't want to be dishonest with you. I loved the man. But you mean so much to me too. I love you. I need you."

"You want to use me. And I'm not up for that. It's too goddam late for that. I'm too old for that bullshit. I haven't gotten this far to play games with some hippie filmmaker and his fucked up girl friend. Because that's just what you are. Fucked up!" He had a grip on both arms then and was shaking me until my teeth rattled, and with sudden shock I saw a policeman approaching us from across the street.

"Gordon! Let's talk about this someplace else . . . there's . . ."

"There's nothing to talk about." He gave me one last shake and then pushed me away. "To hell with you!" And then he walked away and turned the corner, just as the police officer reached me.

"Lady, are you all right?"

"Yes, Officer, I'm fine thank you."

"Looked like that guy was giving you a bad time. I thought I'd check it out."

"Just a little misunderstanding." And feeling shaken, I started back toward the office. The whole scene with Gordon had been awful, I had lost him, it was over. And for what? In a few weeks Chris would be gone again. Maybe this time for good. What in hell was I doing?

The prospect of returning to the office was dismal. I had no desire to face the tasks of the business day anymore. I just wanted to go home and hide. But I didn't want to see Chris, so I was better off at work.

The day crawled by, and my heart felt like it was sitting on my feet. And suddenly I couldn't stand it anymore. I put my head down on my arms and sobbed. The phone rang and I didn't answer it, I didn't give a damn who it was, it could wait, and the tears just wouldn't stop. Goddam Chris Matthews, all he ever did was screw up my life.

"Gillian?" I heard a voice, but before I could look up to see who had come in his arms were around me. "Darling . . . I'm sorry." He pulled me gently to my feet and I went on crying in his arms.

"Oh Gordon . . . I . . . I . . ." I couldn't find the words.

"Sshh. . . ."

"I'll tell him to go away, I'll tell him that . . ."

"Quiet. You won't tell him anything. We'll wait till he goes and see how you feel." I looked up at him, stunned.

"You can't do that!"

"I can do anything I want. And I think you're right, you've got to get it out of your system. So if you can put up with an occasional fit of the glooms on my part, let's just let it ride. How does that sound?" He kissed me tenderly above each eye, and the tears began to flow again. He was so incredibly good to me. Always.

"That sounds beautiful if you're sure."

"I'm sure."

He held me tightly in his arms, and half an hour later he walked me home.

And as I turned the key in the lock, I dreaded seeing Chris.

When I walked in, Chris and Samantha were roughhousing, her toys spread all over the living room floor.

"Hi, Sam. Hi, Chris, how'd it go?"

"Okay. They're a funny bunch though. Very 'Nyeww Yawwk.' And they're still trying to get their heads straight and figure out what they're making a movie about. It's all fucked up."

"Watch the 'forks and spoons' with the little people around please!"

"Yes, ma'am. How was your day?"

"Okay. Nothing special. Looks like I'll be pretty busy for the next few weeks though. I might have to work late." Which meant I wanted time with Gordon.

"No sweat. Once this thing gets started I probably won't be home till eleven or twelve most nights."

"That's okay."

"Maybe it's okay with you. But it's not my idea of a swell time, but bread is bread, and in this case the money's good." I noticed that he wasn't offering to pay the grocery bills with it.

"Hey, listen, you didn't unpack the small suitcase, Chris. Want me to do it?" It was cluttering up the room.

"Okay, just dump it all in a drawer." As though I had twelve empty ones just sitting around, waiting for Chris. He really was incredible, in New York for three days and I was beginning to feel as though I were visiting him.

I went into my bedroom with the package of soap I'd

bought at the drugstore and unwrapped it, waving a mental farewell to my gardenias from Magnin. I stooped down to open Chris's suitcase and fiddled with the catch for a minute before it opened. When it did, I saw that the bag was full of sweaters, and some extra underwear, and his ski clothes, and little yellow slips of paper—"i love you, m." . . . "who's kissing you now? m." . . . "more than yesterday and less than tomorrow, m." . . . "come home soon, m."—I gathered them up and put them in a pile on Chris's bedtable. There she was again. Marilyn in my bedroom, in my bathtub, in my kitchen, ramming herself down my throat incessantly. Chris walked in and said, 'What're those?"

"Take a look. Messages from your lady." It was almost as if Chris had left that bag for me to find them.

"Hey, you don't think . . .?" His voice trailed off.

"No, I don't think . . . but I don't enjoy them anyway. There are about a dozen of them. I only read four or five. Sorry."

He didn't say anything but read them, tore them up, and threw them in the toilet. He had to read them first though. Each and every goddam one.

The time I spent with Chris that first week was odd. We alternated between heading straight into the subject of Marilyn, and rather delicately trying to stay off it. Either way she was right in the forefront of our consciousness most of the time, or mine at least. I realized too that I had changed, that I had in fact gotten a little more independent. I had depended on the idea of Chris, but had stopped leaning on the reality of him. The flesh and blood reality of him was a little harder to live with than I had remembered. I saw him in a different light, a light which was not always flattering. I also realized that Gordon had spoiled me in a number of ways. He was easy to be with, he was thoughtful, took care of me, spent a good deal of time smoothing over rough spots rather than creating them. But in spite of it all, I still continued to glow and grin and love Chris, and feel foolish, falling all over myself, loving the fact that I was able to reach out and touch him again. In spite of how I felt about Gordon. Chris was Chris.

On Thursday of that week, Julie was operated on again, and the hospital would only say that her condition was satisfactory and that she was in the Intensive Care Unit and could have no visitors. My knowledge of hospital language was meager but nevertheless adequate enough to make a reasonable translation of what they were saying. Satisfactory didn't mean a whole hell of a lot, but the Intensive Care Unit meant plenty. You didn't go there for a broken toe, you went there with a good chance of not coming out again, and you weren't liable to enjoy your stay while you were there, if you even remembered it. It was a highly specialized unit, for very, very sick people, with monitors that told the staff exactly what your body was doing and what the chances were that your body would go on doing it. They didn't relay that kind of information to anyone except each other, so there was no way of knowing how Julie really was, other than "Satisfactory."

On Friday, John Templeton called me into his office, with Jean, Gordon, Eloise Franck, and three other people who looked familiar but whom I didn't know. I realized once we were seated and John started to talk about Julie that we were the select elite who knew the truth about Julie. And we were about to get the next bulletin.

"Julie was operated on yesterday, as you all know. They did a biopsy of the bone tissue. She has . . . (pause; count on John for a little drama) . . . bone cancer. The prognosis is a little vague. It could be a year, or even two years, or it could be a matter of weeks. They just don't know. A lot depends on how she rallies from the shock of the operation. She's very weak, and we're keeping close tabs to see how she's doing. She can't have visitors, but as soon as we know something I'll let you know. In the meantime, all we can do is pray, and once again I'd like to ask you not to share this information with the rest of the

staff. There will be time enough for that later. And if she
rallies in the next few weeks, then she'll enjoy as many visitors as possible. Until then, I don't think there's much
point in talking about it. Thank you, and I'm very sorry. I
feel just as rotten about this as you do."

With that, there were murmurs of "Thanks, John," and
a shuffling of chairs, there were a lot of cigarettes lit, and
we all walked out of the office, without speaking to each
other, looking somber, feeling alone.

Gordon walked me back to my office, and walked in
with me, closing the door behind him. He took me in his
arms, and we rocked back and forth together. We were
both crying. Gordon Harte, the man who had seen everything, who had lost Juanita, the girl that he hadn't minded
finding out had been a prostitute, was crying for Julie
Weintraub, and we stood in each other's arms, crying also
for each other.

26

Surprisingly, the relationship with Gordon suffered little
from Chris's sudden appearance. Thanks to Gordon. He
was making a tremendous effort not to change the pace.
There were no mercurial ascents, or descents, no pressure,
despite the fact that we saw each other less. And, inevita-
bly, slept with each other less.

In contrast to things with Gordon, life with Chris was
stormy, up and down, subject to hourly changes, as always. There were beautiful moments, followed by anger,
and tears, and bitterness on my part about the recurring
theme of Marilyn. We spent increasing amounts of time
discussing our problems, and it was apparent that the situation needed action, either repair or commitment to one

alternative or another. It had stood too long in one place and, whereas Chris was willing to let it stay there, I was not.

As for Julie, she stayed in a coma for two weeks following the operation and then proceeded to rally behond everyone's hopes and prayers. She looked thin and wan but sounded wonderful. Her sense of humor was the same as ever, her interest in the magazine continued, she gave us some very good suggestions for the next issue, and she ran a sort of Rest & Recreation Club, cum bar, for everyone at the magazine. People were in and out of her room all day long, and at any given time you could find at least five or six editors sitting by her bed. And, to be honest, Eloise Franck was unbelievable. She was there every day, not hanging on like the hospital ghouls who come to sniff the ether-flavored air and watch the dying, but she was there being herself: tough, cheerful, efficient, and bitchy. She organized a blood donors' committee at the magazine, and at other magazines where she knew the editors, to minimize the cost of the constant transfusions they were giving Julie. Eloise may have been a tough number, but I respected her, and there was a heart somewhere beneath it all. She surprised me, and so did some others. It's amazing who crawls out of the woodwork when the chips are down. The people you expect to surface first sometimes let you down, and the guys way out in left field come in and knock you off your seat with a whole lot of loving. It was nice to watch. Eloise became human, and so did the rest of us. We all stood around in a magic circle, trying to keep Julie buoyed up, giving blood, and trying to give her something more, that magical life serum which makes you want to keep going.

I had asked Chris to come up and see Julie with me, but he wouldn't.

"What's the point, Gill? It's not going to do anything for either of us, and she doesn't even know me. Besides hospitals and funerals are against my principles. It would be hypocritical, like going to church, which you know I don't believe in either."

"It's called humanity, Chris. Or don't you believe in that either?" . . . And there was one more thing to bitch at each other about.

Nothing is ever cut and dried, however, and neither was the situation with Chris. Had it been all bad, had he really appeared as the Villain from the Far West, it would have been simple. But it wasn't. He was good and bad, lovable and hateful, beautiful and ugly. It was all very gray, and even if it had been black, the fact was that I loved him.

As our month together drew to a close, I hadn't come to any further conclusions about it, and neither had he, but he hadn't come East for me to come to conclusions anyway. It would just have been nice if I had.

The last few days had a kind of tenderness to them, because we didn't know when we'd see each other again and once again I was trying to drink it all in to hold onto it in memory. It was like twilight, like a beautiful summer night when the fireflies begin to come out once again. I loved Chris as much as I had in California, and the bitterness about Marilyn was momentarily forgotten. I was resigned to the fact that he was going back to her; there was nothing I could do.

Gordon seemed to sense what was happening and didn't ask me to see him the last five or six days before Chris was to leave. He steered a wide berth, and I was grateful. I just wanted to be alone with Chris. I took an extra day off from work and we took Samantha to the country after the first snow, had snowball fights and walked in the snow, kissed and laughed and sang Christmas carols.

Christmas was the following Wednesday, and I had hoped to spend it with Chris, but he seemed to want to go back. His job was over and he had no reason to stay on, except for me. That never played much on Chris. Whenever had decided to go, he went.

I expected him to leave that weekend, though he hadn't said it, and I was bracing myself for the impact. I had Christmas shopping to do but was putting it off until after he left. I didn't want to waste a second of our time together.

On Friday, I woke up and Chris was already dressed.

He had that "I've got something to tell you" look on his face, and I braced myself to hear that he was leaving that afternoon.

"I've decided when I'm going."

"Okay, hit me with it quick."

"Christ, Gill, will you please not look like that. You make me feel like such a bastard. You almost make me think I should leave now, just to get it over with."

"I'm sorry. It's just that . . . well, you know how I feel."

"How could I help it? I was going to tell you, you big worrier, that I'm going to leave the day after Christmas, Thursday, the twenty-sixth. Sound okay? Hope I'm not messing up any plans."

"What plans? Christopher Matthews, I love you!!! Hurrah!!!! Hallelujah! Let's go Christmas shopping today."

"Oh Christ . . . I'm leaving . . . in New York? Do you know what the stores look like? And you shouldn't be in crowds like that."

"Come on, don't be such a drip, we don't have to stay long. Anyway, I want to take Sam to see Santa Claus."

"Why does she have to see Santa Claus? Don't you know it's not healthy to fill kids' heads with all that bullshit?"

"Come on, Chris, be a sport. Please???"

"Okay, okay, but after that we get to do what I want."

"Deal . . . Chris? . . . What about Marilyn?"

"What about Marilyn?"

"Well, I mean, with Christmas and all?"

"Look, you seem to forget that I'm not married to her. And it's my problem, and Gillian I'm just not going to discuss it with you anymore. I mean it. The subject is closed."

"Okay, get me a cup of coffee will you. I'll be dressed in half an hour."

I bought Chris a Patek-Phillippe watch, which was insanity on my part, but I knew he'd love it. He loved fine things, and the watch was beautiful. Like a Salvador Dali painting, it was as flat as they could make it, and had a beautiful simple face, and a black suede watchband. For my mother I got a dressing gown, for my father a humi-

dor, which I knew he'd have twelve of, but I couldn't think
of anything else. For Hilary and Peg I got small, silly
things. For Julie, the sexiest bed jacket I could find and
three dirty books. And for Gordon, I bought an old
leather-bound volume of Don Quixote. I had ordered a
rather spectacular doll house for Samantha a few days before. I knew Chris would disapprove of it and she would
love it.

I had decided to send John Templeton some Scotch,
unimaginative, but it seemed okay and for Jean Edwards
and the girls at the magazine I had gotten funny hats in a
thrift shop weeks before, thinking we'd have some good
laughs out of them.

On the twenty-third, Gordon and I went up to see Julie
at the hospital, and she didn't look well at all. She had that
bright, glittering look that people get with a fever. We
brought her a bottle of champagne, and our presents, and
there was something so unbearably sad about the whole
scene that I had to turn away once or twice to pull myself
together.

Afterward, I gave Gordon his present and he gave me a
lovely hand-wrought leather box, "a magic box for your
treasures, Gillian . . . and old love letters." In it was a card
with a poem, signed "Love, G." . . . and I was touched. It
was an odd gift, not personal and yet terribly personal . . .
very much like Gordon. . . . I had always wanted a box
like that, something to put eucalyptus nuts in, and dried
flowers, and buttons from shirts, and things like that,
things which mean nothing to anyone because they're so
ordinary, except they mean everything because of what
they stand for. Gordon was going to be with his sister in
Maryland for Christmas, which made things easier for me.

On Christmas Eve, Chris and I stayed home and made
popcorn in the fireplace and chased Samantha back to bed
every ten minutes. We decorated the tree and kissed, and
he did the top while I did the bottom, because ladders
were off limits to me.

"Well, little fat girl, want your present now?" He had a
gleam in his eye.

"Yup. How about you?"

"Sure."

I brought out the Cartier box and began to worry. Maybe it was the wrong gift for him after all, the wrapping looked so pompous next to the little box wrapped in cheap paper that he put in my hand.

"You first," I said. Chris agreed, and began to tear off the paper, while guessing what might be in the box. He sat there with it in his hand, unwrapped, and the box still closed, while I held my breath and wished I had bought him something for his stereo, or a ski sweater, or new ski boots. . . .

He opened the box and his wide little-boy grin appeared and he just chortled. I felt like Santa Claus. He liked it! He liked it! Hip! Hip! Hooray! He had it on his wrist and was winding and checking, polishing, and looking at it, and he almost squeezed me to death he was so pleased.

"Your turn. . . ."

"Okay, here goes." I began tearing the blue foil paper off the little box. Underneath the paper was a silver and red cardboard box, the kind you get at the dime store. I pried open the lid and there was a midnight blue velvet box that snapped open on a stiff hinge to reveal bold letters saying "Tiffany & Co.," and an unbelievable flash of blue-white diamond lying on the velvet. It lay there staring at me, attached to a thin gold chain. It was a pendant. I could hardly breathe, I was so stunned, and it made me want to cry.

"You sneak. You big fraud, you phony shit. I love you so much, how could you give me something like this?" and I hugged him and squeezed him and gulped. "It's so beautiful, darling . . . wow!"

"I don't know. I might take it back and sell it some time." Typical Chris remark.

"You will not. Put it on for me. My hands are shaking too hard."

And I headed for the mirror and saw it staring back at me, like a headlight. Wow!

We turned off the lights and looked at the Christmas tree for a while, and then went to bed and made love, and lay there, holding hands, almost asleep.

"Hey, Gill. . . ."

"Yes, love?"

"Let's get married sometime before the baby's born."

"You mean marry you?"

"Uh huh. That's what I said, isn't it?"

"I accept!" I didn't ask about Marilyn, but I thought it. I didn't think he meant what he'd said. But I hoped to hell he did. As I hugged him closer, I saw that he was wearing his watch, and I smiled and touched the diamond around my neck before I fell asleep.

27

The next morning was Christmas, and it was chaotic, and full of squeals from Samantha. As predicted, the doll house got rave reviews from Sam and a disapproving look from Chris.

At the end of the day, we went for another long walk in Central Park. There was more snow on the ground, and the park was empty. Everyone was busy with family and friends. It was nice to have the park to ourselves.

"Chris?"

"Hmmmm . . .?"

"Did you mean what you said last night?"

"Yeah. Why not? You only live once, and it'd be too bad to have the kid be a bastard."

"Is that why you're doing it?"

"No, you ass. What do you think? I'm not made that

way. I just figure maybe I better keep you off the streets before that guy, Gordon, decides to marry you from his wheel chair."

"Chris! He's not that old, and what makes you think he'd marry me anyway?"

"I may be good-natured, but don't think I'm stupid. Besides, I can read."

"Oh, the poem."

"Yeah, that. And some other things. Besides I had a feeling. . . . How soon do you think you could come out? I think you ought to give me about two weeks . . . ahhh . . . 'to get my house in order.' "

"Yes. I'd think you'd need that. I can't leave before that anyway. I can't leave them in the lurch at the magazine. Chris? How're you going to handle that . . . I mean out there?" What I meant was Marilyn.

"You let me worry about that. You just keep your ass in line, and come on out when you get squared away."

"You know, it'll take me a little time to rent the apartment again and get everything settled here. Besides, the magazine . . ."

"You and that goddam magazine, woman. I need you more than they do."

"Since when? . . . Do you Chris?"

"What do you think?" We kisssed again and walked home hand in hand.

In bed that night, I lay there looking at his stuff all piled in a corner and the impact of his departure began to hit me. And I began to cry, because I was sorry to see him go, but there was more.

"Chris, it's not that simple. There are a lot of problems. Like Marilyn, and the other Marilyns; maybe there'll always be a Marilyn. I couldn't stand it. And we're so different, and I irritate you so much sometimes, and . . . oh hell, I don't know. I really worry about us sometimes."

"Are you trying to tell me you don't want to marry me? Give me my diamond back."

"Nuts to you. No, I'm serious. I'm not telling you I won't marry you, but I'm telling you I'm scared."

"Of me?"

"Well, no . . . yes. In a way."

"So don't marry me."

"But I want to marry you . . . oh, you don't understand. . . ."

"I understand. Now just shut up and go to sleep. Jesus, if you were in Heaven you'd find something to worry about. Stop bitching and go to sleep."

"I'm not bitching. . . ."

"Yes you are. Now go to sleep. I have to get up early tomorrow." . . . That was so like Chris. I wanted to talk.

"How soon do you want to get married, darling?"

"Are you still at it? As soon as you're ready. In the delivery room, if it makes you happy. Okay?"

"Okay. Goodnight. Hey, Chris?"

"Now what?"

"Merry Christmas."

"G'night." He was already half-asleep.

The next morning I watched him go with the proverbial heavy heart. Departures always make me sad, and I felt so alone after he was gone.

Strangely, when I got back to the apartment I had a desperate urge to call Gordon and cling to him, but it seemed like a dirty trick, and I hadn't yet decided what to say to him. Basically, it was simple. "Gordon, I'm leaving. Chris and I are getting married." But how do you say that to someone? How do you even start?

I gave John Templeton notice on Monday and managed to avoid Gordon for the entire day, berating myself for being a monster and a coward. The rest of the week I spent at home with a bad cold, hovering between bed and the living room, where the packing cases for our move were rapidly filling up. I was going to leave right after New Year's, come hell or high water.

I hadn't heard from Gordon all week, but I had decided that somehow I'd tell him at Hilary's on New Year's Eve.

Maybe the champagne would make it easier for both of us.

She had another of her quiet, but stimulating gatherings. And at midnight, Hilary made a lovely toast, and held her glass up in honor of her guests. We rose and drank to her, and then everyone sat down again in small groups. The conversation was carried on in low voices, the room was bright with candlelight, and the magical sad/tender aura of New Year's Eve surrounded us all.

And then Gordon looked up and saw me watching him, smiled a tiny smile, and spoke softly so the others couldn't hear.

"To you, Gillian. May the new year bring you wisdom and peace. May your child bring you joy, and may Chris be good to you. Vaya con Dios." Tears sprang to my eyes as he lifted his glass and his eyes reached into mine. He knew.

The next time I saw John Templeton in the hall, he looked at me with a harried air of fatigue.

"Why is it that I always lose the best people I've got?"

"Thanks for the compliment, John, but you'll do fine without me. You did before." He only shook his head and moved on down the hall, and that was the last I saw of him until the farewell party they gave me on Friday. Gordon and I went together and we said little to each other. He had been kind but remote since the party at Hilary's and he seemed to have a lot on his mind. And then I caught the gist of what was happening as I said good-bye to the staff. Gordon was leaving too. As he took me home, I wondered why he hadn't told me. He must have been thinking about it for a while.

"When did you decide?"

"Oh, I've been thinking of it for some time." But he avoided my eyes and sounded vague.

"Are you taking another job?"

"No. I'm going back to Europe."

"Spain?"

"No. Eze. It's a little town in the South of France. It may have gone to hell by now, full of pizza parlors and tourists. But it was beautiful ten years ago and I thought I'd go back and take a look. I want to spend the rest of my life painting somewhere like that, not wasting the years in this bullshit jungle."

"I'm glad you're going, Gordon. I think it's the right thing."

He nodded, smiled, and kissed me on the forehead as he left me at the hotel.

"See you tomorrow."

"Fine, I'll give you a call." But he didn't look as though his heart was in it. We had agreed to spend my last day in New York together, Saturday. I was leaving on Sunday morning.

That night, I went up to see Julie at the hospital, and it was the hardest thing I did before I left. What do you say? "Thanks for the job"? "Good luck"? "See you soon"? No, you just try not to cry.

We made small talk, but Julie's mind was wandering, and before I left she fell asleep. Her mind was greatly affected by the Demerol and whatever else they were giving her. She had shrunken, and faded, she looked old and gray, so tiny and frail in that bed.

I watched her sleep, and patted her arm, and she opened one eye and smiled. I kissed her cheek, and mumbled something without thinking, probably just "Thanks, Julie," and she closed her eyes again and drifted off. As I looked at her one last time, I heard myself murmur, "Vaya con Dios." The same thing Gordon had said to me.

28

Sam and I were staying at the Regency again for our last two days in New York. And through some miracle we had ended up with the same suite. We were going to leave as we had arrived. In style. Except that so much had happened in the four months we'd been in New York that it was hard to believe we hadn't been back for years.

The phone rang as we were finishing breakfast. It was Gordon.

"This is your tour leader and social director, Mrs. Forrester. We have your schedule all planned for you," and I giggled, wondering what was coming next. "First, you will be picked up by the tour leader, and you will proceed to point one on the day's itinerary: 59th Street and Fifth Avenue, where you will be drawn by an ancient horse around Central Park. The horse may or may not die en route, and in case he does, your tour leader will place you on his shoulders and continue the journey. Please do not wear shoes with spurs, as your tour leader has very sensitive ribs. Thank you for your consideration, Mrs. Forrester. Next, you will go to the Hotel Plaza for lunch in the Edwardian Room, and after that you have a choice between (a) a quick stop at Parke-Bernet Auction Galleries, (b) a tour of the Museum of Modern Art, (c) a shopping tour, or (d) you may tell your tour guide to fuck off, and you may go home and rest. After that, you will be taken to the Sherry-Netherland Bar for one and one half drinks, please present your coupon to the bartender. And then you will be taken to La Caravelle for dinner, check your camera at the cloak room, and be sure to wear gold shoes, a sweater with a mink collar, or fox will do fine. After dinner at La Caravelle, you will then go to Raffles, where you will dance with your tour leader. Again please do not wear spurs; your tour leader also has sensitive arches. And after that you will go to one of New York's most charming hide-aways, for our mystery surprise. And that, Mrs. Forrester, is the day we have planned for you. Welcome to New York." And it struck me again what a good man he was and what a hell of a good sport.

"Gordon Harte, you are something else. What time do we start?"

"How about eleven?"

"Well. . . ."

"Make it eleven-thirty. I'll meet you in the lobby."

"Oh, listen, Gordon?"

"Yes?"

"I promised Sam I'd take her to the zoo 'one last time.' "

"No problem. When?"

"I have a sitter for her now.

"After her nap? Say around four?"

"That's fine. Ask her if I can come too."

"I think that can be arranged. See you soon, and thanks."

Gordon appeared in the lobby at eleven-thirty sharp, looking terribly pleased with himself.

"Well, Mr. Tour Leader, what's next?"

"The hansom cab, but first your chariot awaits," and as we pushed through the revolving doors of the hotel I looked for his car, and wondered who belonged to the outlandish fire engine red Rolls Royce parked smack in front of the hotel. It had license plates with a "Z" at the end, which meant it was rented, probably for some Texan, or at least someone with a sense of humor.

"Madame," and there was Gordon holding open the door of the red Rolls, with a sweep of his arm, and a huge grin. The chauffeur stood by in a liveried uniform, looking as though he took the whole scene seriously. It was absolutely absurd, and I stood there and whooped. I laughed so hard I felt like doubling over. I looked at Gordon, and back at the car, and then laughed until tears ran down my face.

"Oh, Gordon, really."

"Come on, get in. I thought your last day in New York should be memorable," and so it was. Once inside the Rolls, there was a bar, a television, a stereo, a telephone, and a vase with a red rose. It was definitely something from a Rock Hudson-Doris Day movie.

We did all the things Gordon had planned, except that after lunch we went for a walk instead of choices (a), (b), (c), or (d), and then we went to pick up Sam at the hotel. She was thrilled with the red car, and the first thing she said was, "Is it a present? Can we keep it?" with wide eyes. Gordon and I started to laugh again.

"No, sweetheart, it's just for today, kind of a joke. It's a present from Gordon, just for today."

"I don't think it's a joke. I like it."

"Samantha, you remember that when you're a big girl," Gordon said with a serious expression and I added the suspicion that she probably would.

When we got to 64th Street and Fifth Avenue, the chauffeur stopped the car and whipped around to my side to let us out, and we headed for the zoo. Gordon was carrying a camera I hadn't noticed before.

"I want to take some pictures. Do you mind? I won't if you'd rather not."

"No, it's okay. I'd like to have some myself. But be sure you take one of the car," I said grinning over my shoulder, trying to keep track of Sam.

"I don't have any pictures of you, Gillian, and I'd like to have some. . . . Who knows, we may not meet again. . . ."

"Oh, Gordon, don't be silly. Of course we will," but I wondered too.

"Eze and San Francisco are not exactly next door to each other, my dear. And when you leave someone, you never know what will happen. When I say good-bye, I always believe that it will be forever."

"That's funny, when I say good-bye I always tell myself that we'll be seeing each other again."

"Do you believe it?"

"No, I guess not. Not deep in my heart," and I felt sad then. I looked up at Gordon, but he looked away.

So for an hour Gordon took photographs of Samantha with balloons, Cracker Jacks, on the pony ride, watching the seals, and of me. They were quick photographs. He kept catching us with our mouths full of Cracker Jacks, and our eyes closed, or a hand up, or laughing. He shot, and he shot, and he ran around the other way and took more pictures . . . click, click, click, click, click, click . . . the last day in the life of Gordon and Gillian . . . "sing me no songs, tell me no tales, cry me no tears" . . . but remember me kindly.

The last photograph on the roll of film was taken by the chauffeur of all three of us as we stood in front of the open door of the red Rolls, Samantha holding a bright red balloon, and I realized as we stepped into the car that it would be the only photograph that would include Gordon.

The rest of the day went according to the "tour leader's" plan, and at midnight we were ready to leave Raffles and head for the big "mystery surprise." The Rolls was still with us, and we headed uptown and East, toward what I assumed correctly would be Gordon's apartment.

We arrived and went upstairs. He opened the door, stepped in ahead on me, flipped some switches, lit candles, and then came back to help me with my coat. The room looked lovely—it was full of flowers, and there was champagne in an ice bucket on the coffee table, in front of the couch. He lit the fire and turned on some music, and it all looked perfect. Kind of a funny scene for a lady about to go off and get married to someone else three thousand miles away, and expecting that man's child. But it was lovely. I knew that life with Chris would have its own kind of beauty, many tender moments, and many problems too. But life with Chris was of another texture; it would not be of candlelight and champagne. Sadly enough, one rarely marries the candlelight and champagne. One marries instead the blue jeans and rumpled T-shirts, the Coca Cola and burnt toast, and one puts away the candlelight and champagne in a magic box. In the long run, I guess Coca Cola and burnt toast are easier to live with.

As though he had read my thoughts, Gordon handed me the champagne cork and said "for your magic box." I took it and smiled back at him, and then he took the cork back for a moment and wrote something on it. When he returned it, it had the date, only that, nothing more.

"I don't want to confuse your children in fifty years with a lot of initials they won't know." It was kind of a sad thing to say, because I knew he meant it.

"When are you leaving for Europe?"

"Oh, I'd say in about a month."

"How does Greg feel about it? Have you told him yet?"

"Yes, I called him yesterday, as a matter of fact. You know something, Gillian, I think he's impressed. I think I've finally gone and done something that my son approves of. I'm 'abandoning' all the materialistic things he holds me in contempt for, and doing something he thinks he understands. He said he'd come over and see me next summer. I think he means it."

"I'm sure he does. I can't blame him. I wouldn't mind a summer in the south of France myself."

"What, and leave sunny California?"

I tried to smile and then looked at him for an interminable moment. "Gordon, will you write to me?"

"Maybe. I'm not very good about that though. And I don't think Chris would think it such a great idea. But I'll let you know where I am." He had already taken his distance, and it showed.

"Chris won't mind." . . . And I want to hear from you . . . please. . . .

"Don't be so sure. He's no fool, and he doesn't like me. That much I know. And I don't blame him. I wouldn't like me either, in his shoes. Gillian, don't leave yourself open to where he has an excuse to hurt you." I nodded silently and he poured two more glasses which emptied the bottle.

Louis Roederer 1956, the champagne of Charles de Gaulle. And Gordon Harte.

We emptied our glasses and then sat looking silently into the fire, each with our own thoughts. We had been so very civilized, so controlled, and had said so much with the way we looked at each other, and so little with our words. And I knew that leaving Gordon was going to be one of the most difficult moments of my life . . . that last instant . . . that very last look. I had already been through that once, with Chris, and in its own way this would be no easier.

I turned toward his profile next to me on the couch. The splendid head was turned slightly away from me, the beard jutting out, the eyes closed, and then his hand made a brutal gesture, and there was the sound of tinkling glass as his glass crumbled in the fireplace. I knew what he had meant by the gesture. Perhaps by hurling the glass away and watching it smash it was easier to understand that what we had had was over too.

Gordon stood up without speaking, got my coat, and we walked slowly toward the door.

All the way back to the hotel, we sat without speaking, holding hands, and looking out at the city rolling by. Leftovers of the last snow still lay in the gutter, freezing one more time, getting a little grayer.

The car stopped at the hotel, and Gordon moved to get out as the driver held open the door on my side of the car.

"No, don't get out. Please." My voice sounded hoarse. Gordon took me tightly in his arms and kissed the top of my head. I moved my face up to his and we kissed, my eyes squeezed tightly shut, tears oozing slowly out of the corners toward my hair. I opened my eyes then and saw that Gordon was crying too. . . .

"I love you, Gordon. . . ."

"Good-bye, my darling. Know always how much I care."

I stepped out of the car and ran toward the revolving door, never looking back . . . good-bye . . . good-bye . . . au revoir, not adieu. . . .

But there was no point thinking of what I might have had with Gordon. I had chosen Chris. I loved Chris. And I went up the elevator, with my eyes tightly closed, whispering to myself . . . I love Chris . . . I love Chris . . . I love . . . .

29

The flight to California was peaceful and a little strange. I felt as though I were suspended in a cocoon between two worlds, a special place in which to hide and think. I had five hours to totally abandon Gordon's world and reenter Chris's, and I was grateful for the few hours I had to belong to no one but myself. It was eerie how the metamorphosis took place.

As I soared high over the skyscrapers of New York, my heart tugged painfully as I looked down to the rapidly shrinking places which had meant something in the past few months. And as though I were sliding down to the other side of my rainbow, I began to feel excitement grow within me as we circled low over the peninsula, nearing San Francisco. I was going back to Chris. . . . to Chris . . . to Chris!

I looked at Sam and squeezed her hand. I had the feeling that we had finally made it home. Hallelujah, baby!

We arrived exactly on time, and when we emerged into the terminal building, there was Chris. And I lit up inside. He smiled that little boy smile of his just for me. We looked into each other's eyes, and all was right with the world. New York, Gordon, Julie Weintraub, they were all a million miles away, on another planet.

"You look tired. Bad flight?"

"No, good flight. Bad week in New York. It was one hell of a lot of work," not just work, but easier to put it down to that.

We collected our bags and piled into the Volkswagen bus Chris had borrowed from a friend. I waited for Samantha to tell him about the Rolls the day before, and kind of held my breath. I didn't want to have to get into explanations just then. But she didn't say a thing. I figured it would come out instead one day when it was least expected, maybe two months later. And by then it wouldn't matter anymore.

We drove into town and I looked around with this incredible feeling of, "My God, here it is . . . wow!" San Francisco does that to me, it takes my breath away, and scoops me up, and I feel like I'm going to fly away. I wanted to drive all over the city and see everything I loved, but that was not Chris's style. It would never have occurred to him that that was what I wanted to do. We drove straight home, where we dumped the bags in the living room, and I went to see what there was in the refrigerator. Nothing. Welcome home. Two half-full bottles of club soda, three cokes, a moldy lemon, and a jar of peanut butter that had probably been untouched since last July.

"There's nothing to eat in here, Chris."

"I know. It's still early though. We can go to the store. You drive my car while I take the bus back."

"What about Sam?"

"We'll take her with us."

"Okay, but I want to get her to bed early. It'll be late for her with the time difference and she's tired from the trip."

"She doesn't look tired to me." She was racing through the place and had taken possession of "her" room.

Well, I knew I was back. The refrigerator was empty and we were going to the store. No roses or champagne in sight. That had been yesterday. But I had known that. I had chosen moldy lemons and flat club soda over roses and champagne. I knew I could have had the roses and champagne, but I didn't really want them. I wanted to go to the store with Chris, and ride around in a borrowed Volkswagen bus.

"Whatcha thinking, Gill?"

"That I love you," and I meant every word of it. I was home, and it felt great. I put on my jeans, with a safety pin to cover where the zipper wouldn't close, and a sweater of Chris's, with my raincoat, and we went out to return the bus and buy food. We looked like a family, and Chris looked beautiful. I was so happy I felt as though I were about to burst.

As we walked out of the house I thought of something, "Chris? Where are we going to put the baby?"

"Cool it, will you. You've been here one hour and you're already bitching at me. We'll put it somewhere. Don't worry about it now for chrissake."

"I'm not worrying. I just thought of it."

"Well, stop thinking. I'll meet you at the Safeway in ten minutes." He gave me a peck on the cheek and drove off with a wave. Then he shot back in reverse, almost hitting the car, as I got ready to start it.

"Watch the choke!"

"Okay. . . . Hey! . . . And stop bitching at me!" I was giving some of his own back.

"Fuck you." He grinned and drove off.

"Same to you, fella." . . . God, it was so nice to be back. It wasn't elegant, or anything like a fairy tale, but it was my fairy tale, and at the same time it was real. Beautiful and real. Like Chris.

30

Chris lived in a ramshackle Victorian-style house on Sacramento Street, just near enough to the elegant Pacific Heights district to make the neighborhood pleasant, but not so close as to be actually in it. We were up at the west end of the city, and the fog would stay up in that section till almost noon on mornings when the sun would be shining downtown. At five o'clock the fog would roll back in, and at night you could hear the fog horns, very faintly in the distance.

To me, San Francisco has always been an enchanted city, something of a dream place. It has all the physical beauty that the postcards suggest, and an easy lifestyle that reminds me of Europe. People are friendly, not in the put-on way of Los Angeles, but in the way of smaller towns in the West. It is a city, and a noncity. Within minutes you can be in the country or at the beach, and the mountains are only a couple of hours away. The air is still fresh, and we had a tiny garden where Samantha used to dig for worms and look for snails.

The house itself was something of a bomb shelter. It could have been really super if Chris had wanted to spend any time fixing it up, but there was always something else he wanted to do, so it got a little shabbier and a little more weather-beaten all the time. Victorian houses are fairly common in San Francisco. The exteriors have a lot of charm, and inside the floors slope, the ceilings are arched, and the windows are often bayed.

The morning after our arrival I turned over in bed and looked up at the ceiling, and out the window, at the trees that reached up from the garden. It was quiet and I felt as though I were in the country. I looked over at Chris, still asleep, and grinned. I thought that even without Christopher I would have loved San Francisco. After all I had fallen in love with the city before I had fallen in love with the man. I heard Samantha walking around and got up to make her breakfast. No more mother's helper. That had been part of the deal with Chris. Sam and I came out alone.

Chris rolled over as I got out of bed and opened an eye. ". . . time is it? Come on back to bed. . . ."

"Got to feed Sam," and I kissed him. "Good morning. It's so nice to be back, Chris."

"Sure, honey. Bring me a glass of orange juice, will you?"

"Better than that. You stay in bed, I'll call you when breakfast is ready."

"Okay." And he turned over again and went back to sleep, looking like a boy, his hair all rumpled up and his head tucked under his arms, the covers almost over his head.

Breakfast was long and noisy, and we decided what to do for the day. Chris had some things to do and Sam wanted to "go see Julius," i.e., the Julius Kahn playground in the Presidio.

"You can see Julius tomorrow, Sam. We're going to stay home and unpack and clean up the house a little. How about helping Mommy today?"

"I don't want to," and the whining started.

"Well then, how about looking for worms in the garden." Yech, me suggesting that?

"That's a good idea, Mommy. I'll see if I can find some for you." Wonderful.

I wanted to unpack, but what I really wanted to do was get the house in order. Before, it had been Chris's place, but if we were going to get married the house was going to undergo some changes. The mechanical stuff Chris would have to do, but I was going to attack it with a lot of soap and water, and at least put up new curtains, and get a bedspread . . . and the bathrooms! . . .

I dug around for some cleaning equipment as Chris headed out the door shouting, "See you later, gang!" I was busy thinking that, whatever else Marilyn may have been good at, she had been one hell of a lousy housekeeper. That had probably been part of the charm.

By two o'clock the place looked a lot better, and Sam and I went to buy some flowers, "How about woses, Mommy?"

"How about daisies, Samantha, and corn flowers, and maybe some nice red flowers?"

"Wed woses."

"No, wed something else. Roses cost too much money."

"Are we poor now? Are we gonne staaaarve?" Her big eyes looked up at me, half-filled with fear, and half-seeming to enjoy the prospect.

"No, we are certainly not going to 'staaaarve.' We just don't want to spend too much money, that's all."

"Oh." She seemed disappointed. "When do we pick up the baby?"

"Not for a while yet. Almost two whole months. That's still a long way off."

"Oh . . . why not today?"

"The house isn't ready yet," which reminded me that I had discovered the right place for the baby that morning and wanted to tell Chris. It was kind of a walk-in closet with a window, just about the right size for a crib and a chair and a little chest. It was right next to our room and had two doors, one leading to the hall, the other to our room. We didn't need the closet and, fixed up, it could be really cute. That way the baby would be right next to us, without actually being in the room. It wouldn't work forever, but for six months or so it would be just right. After that, we could put the baby in Sam's room.

Chris's house was roomy, though small. It had a living room, a tiny dining room and kitchen downstairs, two bedrooms on the second floor, and above that a bright studio room which Chris used as his office. That was sacred

territory, and there was absolutely no question of putting
the baby up there. Besides, it was drafty, and the heating
didn't reach up there. It had a great fireplace, though,
which Chris had going most of the time.

When Chris came home I told him about my idea for
the baby's room and he promised to get some paint and to
get to work on it.

"Hey, Gillian, it smells funny in here. What is it?"

"That, my love, is an unfamiliar odor called clean. I
scrubbed the place all morning."

"Should you do that? Don't go around being an ass now.
Did you pick anything up?"

"No, I did not pick anything up," and I kissed him and
smiled over his head. He was beginning to sound as
though he cared about the baby, or about me. It was new
and made me feel kind of tingly.

Chris leaned over and whispered in my ear, "Get rid of
Sam."

"What do you mean?"

"I mean, get rid of Sam . . . want to make love to
you. . . ."

"Oh . . . Sam, sweetheart, how were the worms this
morning? Find any?"

"Nope, they musta been sleeping."

"How 'bout taking another look before it gets too
cold?"

"Okay. You want some too, Uncle Crits? Mommy loves
worms."

"Sure, you bring me some too," and she banged out the
back door and marched off to the garden with two old
spoons, a toothpick, and a paper cup.

Chris grabbed my hand and we started running upstairs.
"Hey, wait a minute, you nut."

"Wait nothing. I've been horny all day. Come on,
woman!" And we ran up the stairs, laughing and giggling,
and I almost tripped on the top step, which kind of sobered us a little, but not for long.

*   *   *

"I found 'em. Three of them," and there was Sam. The door burst open and she had a whole handful of dirt and something that was squirming. "Hey, you all sick? What's everybody sleeping for?"

"We're just having a nap. Your mother's tired."

"Oh, well, here they are. I'll give 'em to you," and she placed the whole revolting mess in Chris's hand and walked out singing to herself.

"Oh Jesus, Gillian, I think I'm going to throw up."

"Me first," and we both rushed for the bathroom, laughing.

Chris got there first and threw them into the toilet and flushed. "Bllyyyyeeeeerrrgggggghhh. Who said all that shit about girls being sugar and spice? Hasn't anyone told Sam yet?"

"Come on, Chris, be a sport."

"Be a sport? I didn't see you holding out a hand for that little handful of delicious." And we started laughing again, while I ran the tub.

"Let's go for a drive before dinner. I haven't gotten a good look at the place yet. We worked in the house all day. I want to take a look around."

"What d'you want to do that for, Gill?"

"Come on, Chris, please. As a special favor to me?"

"Okay, okay, but a short one. There's a game I want to watch on television."

"Yessir."

"Say, Mrs. Forrester, by the way, when are we getting married? Or haven't you made up your mind yet?" He said it facetiously, but I knew he meant it. I had made up my mind, so it was all right.

"Well, I'll have to check my appointment calendar. How about Saturday?"

"Why not tomorrow?"

"Do you have a license?"

"No." He looked crestfallen.

"That's why not tomorrow. Today's Monday, we can go and get the license tomorrow, which leaves Wednesday,

Thursday, Friday . . . we can get married Friday, if you want."

"No, I've got a job to do Friday. Saturday'll be okay. . . . Gill? . . . Are you sure this is what you want? I mean, do you really know? I'm not the best husband material in the world."

"Sounds like you're changing your mind, Mr. Matthews."

"It's not for me to change my mind. You're the one who's got to be sure."

"Boy, talk about a switch! I'm sure, now just shut up and get in the tub, or I won't get to go for my drive."

Chris took us down Broadway past the big old mansions, and then left on Divisadero down the steep hill where Steve McQueen had filmed the chase scene in *Bullitt,* and the house where they filmed *Pal Joey,* and as we came down the hill there was the bay, and Sausalito on the other side, with the mountains behind it. As I came down that hill, I felt the way the pioneers must have as they came across the mountains and saw the Pacific. The roads had changed, but I was willing to bet the feeling hadn't. It took my breath away, and always gave me that same feeling. We drove all the way down to the Marina, and sat in the parked car at the waterfront, looking at the water, and watching the fog roll in slowly, coming through the Golden Gate Bridge, as though it was being held together by the structure of the bridge. It headed toward Alcatraz, and the fog horns started up. After a while, Chris said, "Had enough?"

"No, but you can take us home now."

"No, no, I wanna see Onion Square!" Sam squealed from the back seat. "And the Hare Krishna people with the orange sheets and the bells."

"They're probably home by now, Samantha, but we can go to Union Square if you want."

Chris was really being a good sport about it.

"What about your game?" I didn't want to push a point. . . .

"We've got time," and he smiled over at us. I think he was enjoying it too.

We drove down Lombard, and down the part where it gets all crooked just before you get to Leavenworth Street. Sam squealed all the way down and loved every minute of it. We could see the Bay Bridge and Oakland as we were coming down. Up Powell, behind a cable car, waving at the people, mostly tourists, and they waved back. Union Square looked the same as always, and that is one part of the city that doesn't excite me a whole lot, but Sam loved it, even though she was disappointed that the Hare Kirshnas had gone home. On the way home, Chris drove through Chinatown, which was another treat for Sam.

"Hey, want to have Chinese dinner?"

"No, come on, you want to watch the game. This has been plenty. But you're a love to ask."

"No, I mean it. Let's stop and have an early dinner."

"No, Chris, come on, let's go home."

"Quiet. . . . Sam, what do you think?"

"I want to eat dinner here. Can we, Uncle Crits, can we????"

"Yes, ma'am," and we drove into the St. Mary's garage and walked toward the milling people on Grant Avenue.

Dinner was delicious, and as usual I ate too much. Chris and Samantha worked it out with chopsticks or at least Chris did. Sam ate most of it with her fingers, and poked with the chopsticks. I ate with a fork, which got me a lot of scornful comments from both of them. But I was hungry and never could manage chopsticks.

Driving home we went through the Broadway tunnel, and that completed an evening of Heaven for Sam. A tunnel!! And it was an evening of Heaven for me too. Chris and I looked at each other over her head, and I blew him a kiss and mouthed, "Thanks, I love you." He mouthed back, "Me too," and by God we did. Whatever the last months had been, whatever Chris had done, or Marilyn, or I, or whomever, it was all buried by that look. Bad times may come again, but a prophecy had been fulfilled. "The good times are coming," the song said. And they had. They really, really, finally had.

31

On Tuesday, I put Sam back in her old playgroup in the morning, and then Chris and I went downtown to get the marriage license. The place was crawling with Mexicans, and little kids, and odd-looking people who either looked too old to get married or as though they didn't really want to. I guess most of the young people weren't getting married anymore, because we were about the only people our age that I saw. But then again, we didn't look so typical either—I was seven months pregnant and had suddenly blossomed. I stood there in my jeans and Chris's sweater, leading with my belly, and the clerk looked over and shook his head. "I hope you make it, lady." And then he shot a nasty glance at Chris, which made him squirm, and cracked me up.

"Did you see that old bastard, I mean did you see him?"

"Yeah, so what? What do you care?" Look who was getting sensitive. Poor Chris.

We picked up Sam and he dropped us off at the house. "Got some stuff to do, see you later."

"What stuff?"

"Just stuff, now come on, get out of the car." He'd been in a bad mood since the marriage license bureau. Stupid to let something like that bother you, but he was really upset.

"Okay, see you later," and as Sam and I walked into

the house I wondered if Chris were going to see Marilyn. It was just a thought, there was no reason why I should think of it, and the last couple of days had been perfect, but the thought crept up on me and took hold. I wondered if I'd always worry about that, or distrust him. He had learned one thing, and that was that his old openness had cost him something. I doubted if he'd be as honest about it next time he pulled a stunt like that. So I worried all afternoon, and started getting mad, and then worried again, and by the time he came home I was so relieved to have him back I didn't care where he'd been. I purposely didn't ask him what he'd done because I was still pretty much convinced he'd been up to something I didn't want to know about.

"Aren't you going to ask me where I've been?"

"No. Should I?"

"What's with you?"

"Nothing. Why?"

"You look funny. Feel okay?"

"Yeah, I'm okay," but I was thinking about Marilyn again.

"Come over here, you big dope. Do you think . . . ?" And I squirmed away because I knew what he was thinking, and I was thinking it, but I was ashamed of it. "Hey, Gillian, Jesus . . . don't cry, there's nothing to cry about, everything's okay . . . hey . . . baby . . . ," and there I was like a big fool, crying in his arms, admitting what I'd been thinking all afternoon.

"I told you. It's over. You don't have to worry about it anymore. Now, come on out to the car." He took my hand, led me down the steps, opened the car door, and started ripping newspapers off something in the back seat. It was a cradle, a beautiful, beautiful antique cradle, in dark burnished wood, with delicate carvings on it.

"Oh Chris. . . ."

"There was an auction in Stockton today. I wanted to surprise you. D'you like it?"

"Oh Chris! . . ." and I was crying again.

"Now what are you crying about?"

"Oh Chris. . . ."

"You've already said that, now come on you silly girl. Give us a smile. There. Much better."

"I'll help you get it out of the car."

"No, ma'am. As long as you're still carrying what goes in the cradle, I'll carry the cradle. Just hold the doors open," and he struggled up the steps holding the cradle.

"Don't hurt it," and I held the doors open as wide as I could.

"You're too much," and he grinned at me over his shoulder as he set it down in the hall.

"Chris? . . . You know something? You've changed."

"So have you," and we looked at each other for a long moment, and knew it was true.

32

The next couple of days were quiet. Sam was in school in the morning, and Chris was up in his studio most of the time, working on projects, busy with whatever it was he did up there. He'd come down for lunch and we'd have a quiet half-hour together before I picked Sam up at the playgroup. We were settling into a nice routine, and I felt as though I had never left, except for the fact that everything was better.

On Thursday, I looked up at Chris at lunch and told him I wanted to go downtown, shopping.

"What for?"

"A wedding dress."

"You're kidding. Gillian, you don't mean it."

"Yes I do. I want to get something new to wear. You know, something old, something new. . . ."

"You've got something new: the baby. Does the maternity department carry wedding dresses these days?"

"Come on, Chris, be nice. I want to get something."

"Have you thought of a color? Like red maybe?"

"Chris! I shouldn't have told you."

"No. You can do it. It's your business. It's your wedding, after all."

"Well, it's yours too. But I want to look nice, and I don't have anything to wear."

"What do you want to look nice for? Have you invited someone?"

"No, but I was going to talk to you about that too. . . ."

"Oh no, Gillian, no way. You and I are going down to the justice of the peace, and we're getting married. No tourists. You can wear anything you goddam please, but you're not going to invite anybody. And I mean that." And he looked as though he did.

"Okay, love. Okay. Don't get excited about it."

"I'm not excited," but he looked irritated and went back up to his garret while I cleaned up the lunch dishes.

After Sam was down for her nap in the afternoon I got dressed to go downtown and went up to the studio to tell Chris I was leaving.

"What's wrong with that?"

"What?"

"What you're wearing now?"

"Chris, I can't wear black to our wedding. It'd look like a bloody funeral for chrissake. Now come on . . . you said."

"I know, I know. Go ahead and get yourself a veil while you're at it . . . with plastic cherries on it," and I saw then that his good mood was back. He seemed to be finding the whole thing very funny. And as I closed the door behind me he started singing, "Here comes the bride," at the top of his lungs.

"Bug-off, Christopher," but he just got louder.

I decided to make a real trip of it, parked the car in the

Union Square Garage, and then headed for I. Magnin's. They were showing cruise clothes in all the windows, and once inside it felt more like New York than San Francisco. Everyone was all dressed up. It seemed a long way from Sacramento Street.

I went up in the elevator looking for the card that said "Maternity" in the long line of descriptions of the different departments above the elevator doors. The elevator operator looked over at me, smiled, and said "Sixth." I couldn't resist, so I looked back and smiled at her, and said, "Bridal?" and her face froze. I laughed and said sixth would be fine.

"For a minute, there, I thought you meant it."

I just laughed again as I stepped out. . . . Oh lady, I do mean it. Yes I do.

The maternity department had as little charm as those places do, and I went through the racks finding nothing. The fabrics looked crummy, the colors were awful, everything had a bow just over the belly, or a high belt, or something that made me dislike it.

"May I help you?"

"I'm looking for something for my sister's wedding. It's an afternoon wedding, and it will be very small, so I don't want anything too formal." That just about told her all she needed to know.

We looked and looked and came up with nothing. Black was out, white was out, red was out, and I was pretty much out by the time we'd tried everything else on. "How about a coat and dress? We got something in yesterday that would look very well on you. It's very tailored and light gray."

Gray? For a wedding? And I really didn't need another coat.

But out came a marvelous soft gray dress with long sleeves and a perfectly straight shape, with buttons down the front, and a soft pointed collar, and wide cuffs; no belt, no bow over the belly, just two very large pockets set at a slant on either side. The buttons were covered in the same gray fabric, and the coat was perfectly plain and had the same straight, simple line, with a tiny gold chain belt in the back. It looked divine . . . with my grandmother's pearls, and black shoes . . . and . . . .

"How much?"

"One forty-five." Ouch, but what the hell, it was my wedding, and I could always use it again. I was getting a coat out of it after all.

"I'll take it."

"Good. It looks wonderful on you. Your husband will like it."

"Yes, he will." He might. But a hundred and forty-five? I still had quite a lot of money saved up, so I explained it to myself all the way home as being a reasonable thing to do.

When I got home Chris and Sam were eating ice cream in the kitchen.

"What'd you buy, Mommy?"

"A new dress."

"Let me see it."

"Not till Saturday. That's in two days." And Chris started humming "Here comes the bride" again. I went upstairs and hung it in the back of my closet, feeling very pleased with myself. It was beautiful. The same kind of luminous gray as the fog. My wedding dress.

Early Friday morning, Chris jumped out of bed, gave me a shove and told me to get him some orange juice.

"Now?"

"Yes. Now! I have to be in Oakland by eight. We're shooting a film and I have to be there on time. Come on, lady, move it!"

"Okay," and I rolled out of bed, not too pleased by the hour.

Chris left with his arms full of all sorts of boxes, and notes, and odds and ends that didn't look like much to me. He gave me a quick kiss and said he'd be home late and not to wait dinner for him. "Now go back to bed."

I hung out the door as he started the car, waved, and

shouted a hearty "Love you!" wondering if the whole neighborhood was being awakened by my shouting, or his car coughing and gagging as it got started. Or his "Love you too," as he drove away. I went back to bed then for a little bit before getting up to feed Sam and get her to school.

The house seemed quiet without Chris when we left and Sam was in a grouchy mood. I thought she might be catching a cold, and decided to ask Chris to check on the heater in her bedroom. I didn't think it was working too well.

On the way back, I stopped off at the hardware store up the street from the house and decided to buy the paint for the baby's room. A lovely bright yellow. I figured that if I didn't buy it Chris would never get around to it. So I loaded it into the car and headed home.

When I got there the phone was ringing but it stopped before I opened the door. Probably a wrong number. Chris' calls usually went through his answering service and nobody knew I was back yet.

The house was in order, so I went back upstairs to our room, opened my closet, and looked at the dress again. It looked so perfect, and as I stood there looking at it I decided to try it on again.

I whirled around in front of the mirror, wearing black shoes, my grandmother's pearls, and my alligator bag. I pulled my hair up off my neck and felt just like a bride. It was a far cry from my first wedding . . . a far cry. And I giggled at myself in the mirror. "Gillian Forrester, my how you've changed!"

The phone rang again as I was preening in front of the mirror, and this time I got there in time to answer it.

"Mrs. Matthews?" I didn't recognize the voice. Maybe someone from one of the shops looking for new customers. So I wound up my "sorry, we don't need any" voice . . . "this is the cleaning lady," etc.

"Not till tomorrow. Yes?" I didn't see any point in volunteering my name. It couldn't be anyone we knew anyway.

"This is Tom Bardi. I'm a friend of Chris."

"Yes?" I remembered hearing the name, but only vaguely.

"Mrs. . . . uh . . . we were working on the same film over in Oakland this morning and. . . ."

"Yes?" My God, was something wrong? "Yes? Is anything wrong?"

"Chris fell off a rig, trying to get a shot, and, I'm so sorry to tell you this, like this, but . . . he's dead. He broke his neck when he hit. I'm calling you from St. Mary's Hospital in Oakland. . . . Are you all right? . . . Are you there?"

"Yes . . . I'm here." I was leaden. There just wasn't anything else for me to say.

"What's your name?"

"Gillian."

"Gillian, are you all right? Are you sure? Look, can you come over here now?"

"No. Chris has the car."

"All right, don't move. You just sit there and have a cup of coffee. I'll be over right away and I'll drive you back here."

"Why?"

"Well, they want to know what to do with the . . . body." The body? The body? The body! Chris, not "the body." Chris, Chris, and I started to whimper.

"Now, you just hang on. I'll be right over."

I just sat there, on my bed, not moving, not even able to move my head or turn around. I just sat there in my new gray dress, looking down at my shoes, whimpering. And then I heard footsteps coming up the stairs, strong man's footsteps, taking the stairs two at a time. . . . Chris! . . . It was a lie, it was a crank call, and he'd hold me and tell me it was a bad joke. . . . Chris . . . and I looked up and there was a strange man in our room, looking down at me with a look of tenderness and embarrassment.

"I'm Tom," and I just nodded my head.

"Are you all right?" and I nodded again, but I didn't mean it.

"Can I make you a cup of coffee?" I shook my head. I stood up, not remembering where I was supposed to go, or what I was supposed to do, but knowing this man was here for something.

"My God, you're pregnant. . . . Jesus. . . . Oh, I'm sorry." I knew he was, he sounded as though he meant it, but I really didn't give a damn. I stood up and saw myself in the mirror, with Tom Bardi standing behind me. I was still wearing my new dress, with all the tickets on it.

"I've got to change. I'll be ready in a minute," and I started whimpering again. "It's my wedding dress." He looked at me for a minute as though he thought I was hysterical. He had a nervous, doubtful look about him like that was something he really couldn't handle.

"No, it's all right, I mean it. We were going to get married tomorrow." I had to pull myself together to explain.

"Oh, I thought you were. I mean Chris said something about his wife . . . and a little boy named Sam. . . . He never said anything about the baby though."

"A little girl. Sam, I mean. Samantha. . . . Gee, what am I going to do? I have to pick her up at school in a little while."

"What school?"

"The Thomas Ellis School."

"Okay, you get dressed and I'll call the school, tell them to hold on to her for a while. We won't be long. . . . I mean . . ." and he turned around to walk downstairs. "Where's the phone?" he shouted back.

"In the kitchen, behind the door."

I put on my jeans and Chris's sweater again, grabbed my bag, and the dress lay on the unmade bed, half inside out, next to the T-shirt Chris had slept in. . . . Jesus, oh good God, sweet Jesus . . . what have You done?

I clattered down the stairs in my wooden sandals and heard Tom hang up the phone.

"It's all set, they can keep her till four thirty. We'll be back before that." He looked uncomfortable again. "Do you know what you want to do? I mean they want to know over there. What're you going to do with him?"

I hadn't thought of that. "I don't know. Maybe I should call his mother. . . ." Where the hell did she live . . . ? Let me think a minute. . . . Chicago . . . ? No. . . . Detroit . . . ? No. . . . Denver. That was it. I had met her once when she came to see Chris on her way some place else. They weren't very close, and his father was dead.

I dialed long-distance. "Denver Information, please.

"I'm sorry, you can dial that yourself. Dial 303, then 5, 5, 5. . . ."

"Look, goddamit, will you please do it for me. My husband was just killed in an accident."

"Oh . . . yes. . . . Oh, I'm sorry. Just a moment, please."

"Directory. What city please? May I help you?"

"Yes. Denver. Helen Matthews. I don't know the address.'"

After a pause, she came back on the line. "That's 663-7015." I repeated it back to her. Why did I sound so calm, why did I sound so much like me? 663-7015 . . . 663-7015. . . . Now dial it, tell the nice lady, go ahead tell her, Chris Is Dead. That's right, Mrs. Matthews, he's dead. . . . Oh my God. . . . I flicked the button on the phone up and down a few times. "Operator? . . . Operator? . . ."

"Yes, ma'am. Do you want me to get that number for you now?"

"Yes. Please."

"Station? Or person to person?"

"Station. No, person . . . no, oh anything . . . I don't care."

"I'm sorry, but I have to know which."

"Oh shit . . . make it person to person then. Helen Matthews, Mrs."

She dialed, and the phone rang twice.

"Hello?"

"Hello. We have a person to person call for Mrs. Helen Matthews."

"'This is she." She sounded a little like Chris.

"Go ahead please."

"Hello . . . Jane?"

"No, Mrs. Matthews. This is Gillian Forrester. I'm a friend of Chris's. I don't know if you remember me. I met you last summer when you were here . . . I . . ."

"Yes, I remember. How are you?" She sounded a little puzzled.

"Fine, thank you. How are you?" Oh Christ, I couldn't get it out. And I looked over at Tom Bardi and knew how he had felt when he called me. I squeezed my eyes shut and sat down, holding the receiver with both hands to keep it from shaking.

"If you're looking for Chris, he isn't here. He's in San Francisco. Where are you? I'm afraid this is a very poor connection." It was, and it wasn't going to get any better in a few minutes.

"I'm in San Francisco, too . . . that is . . . Mrs. Matthews, Chris just had an accident. He's . . . dead. . . . I'm sorry. I'm really sorry. . . ." Oh Christ, don't go falling apart now, don't do that to her. "Mrs. Matthews, I'm sorry to do this to you, but the hospital wants to know what to do with, well . . . I thought I'd call and ask you what. . . ." Oh God, she was crying. The nice old lady I met last summer was crying. "Mrs. Matthews? Are you all right?" Dumb question, and I looked up at Tom again. He was looking out the window, with his back to me, seeming to sag.

"Yes, I'm all right," and she pulled herself together. "I don't know what to tell you. His father is buried in New Mexico, where we used to live, and his brother is buried in Washington. He was killed in Viet Nam." Oh God, why did this have to happen to her? I had heard about the brother from Chris.

"Do you want me to bring him to Denver, Mrs. Matthews?"

"No, I don't see any point in that. My daughter lives in Fresno. I think you'd better handle it in San Francisco. I'll fly down today. I have to call his sister first."

"You can stay here with me. At the house" . . . his house . . . our house . . . oh Jesus, what would she think of us living together? It was a little late to worry about that.

"No, I'll stay at a hotel with Jane, my daughter."

"I'll pick you up at the airport. Call and tell me when you're getting in."

"You don't have to, dear."

"I want to . . . Mrs. Matthews . . . I'm so awfully sorry," and my voice broke again.

"I know you are, dear," and there were tears in her voice again too.

I nodded, and we hung up.

Tom Bardi was watching me as I hung up and handed me a cup of coffee. "Want something stronger?" I shook my head and took a swallow of the coffee. It was cold. "We better get going." I nodded and started toward the door.

"Oh, I want to make one more phone call. Please. . . ." Peg. I had to tell Peg. Who else could I turn to? Who else had seen me cry and throw up and die over the years? Peg.

I dialed her direct, at her office.

"Miss Richards, please."

"One moment please. . . . Miss Richards' office."

"I'd like to speak to her."

"I'm sorry, Miss Richards is in a meeting."

"Get her. Tell her it's Gillian Forrester. She'll take it."

"Well, I'll have to see. Please hold." Hold your ass, lady. Peg would come. And she did.

"Gillian? What's up? I'm in a meeting."

"I know. Peg . . . he's dead." And I broke down all over again.

"When?"

"This morning . . . accident . . . broken neck . . . goddam crane. . . ." I could hardly get the words out.

"I'll take the eight o'clock plane tonight. At least I can spend the weekend with you. You okay?"

"No."

"That's okay, you just hang in there till Aunt Peg gets there, then you can let go. I'll be there tonight." Let's see, eight and five makes one a.m., minus the three-hour time difference. Peg would be there at ten. "And listen, don't pick me up. I'll take a cab. Same address?"

"Yes."

"Do you need anything else?"

"Just you. Oh Peg, thanks; thanks forever on this one."

"Gotta go now, take it easy. Listen, do you have any Librium or something?"

"Yeah, but I don't want to."

"Take it. You listen to Aunt Peg and take it," but I knew I wasn't going to.

"Okay, thanks again . . . g'bye."

"G'bye," and we hung up.

I looked up at Tom Bardi still standing in the kitchen but beginning to fidget. "Okay, let's go," and he looked relieved. Maybe he thought I was going to call everyone I knew, and make him stand there, listening.

33

We drove to Oakland in silence. I had nothing to say. And I was grateful that Tom didn't try to talk. He just drove. Very fast. And I stared out the window, not crying, not thinking, not even feeling anything. I was just driving along in Chris's car, with a man named Tom Bardi, whom I'd never seen before today. It was strange, really strange, so I didn't think about it. I just sat.

The car veered suddenly, and I realized that we had swooped into the parking lot of St. Mary's Hospital in Oakland. We stepped out of the car and Tom led the way into the emergency room.

Once inside, there was a little group of people, long-haired and blue-jeaned. They looked stunned, and huddled together as though to keep warm. The camera crew.

Tom led me up to a desk and said something to the nurse

in charge. She looked up, the only expression on her face
a question, "Mrs. Matthews?"

"Yes," I lied, because I didn't think she could handle
the truth, and I knew I couldn't handle an explanation.
What difference did it make anyway?

"Would you step this way, please?" and she led me into
a little room with a red light lit up over the door, and a
sign on the door that said "Do Not Enter." And there was
Chris, dressed as he had been that morning, lying
stretched out on a gurney, looking peaceful, one side of his
face sandy, but no visible part of him bruised. They were
wrong. He wasn't dead, he was just sleeping. I brushed the
sand off his face and smoothed his hair. I leaned down to
kiss him and great horrible gulps of air got caught in my
throat and made odd gurgling sounds. I leaned my face
down to his and held him. But he felt strange, and his skin
felt funny. The body of Christopher Caldwell Matthews.
No longer Chris.

The nurse had been standing in the corner, watching,
and I didn't give a damn. I forgot she was there. She
walked up to me slowly, and held my elbow, propelling me
very professionally toward the door. I kept looking back
over my shoulder at Chris, watching to see if he'd move,
or get up, or open an eye and wink. This was just one of
those really ugly jokes, like Tom Bardi's phone call. . . .
Look, really, Nurse, I know he's just putting you on. . . .

She kept holding onto my elbow, and moved me down
the hall, back to the main desk again. "Would you sign
this, please? . . . And this?" She held out a ball-point pen.
I signed Gillian Forrester twice, and turned around, not
knowing where to go next. I looked up at her and asked
what had to be done after that.

"Have you called a funeral home?"

"No, not yet." He wasn't even cold yet.

"Well, there's a phone booth across the hall. If you look
in the yellow pages, it might give you some idea." That's
it, find it in the yellow pages, let your fingers do . . . oh
God.

Hobson's . . . Hobson's . . . that's the one . . . George

Hobson's . . . "put your loved ones in our hands.". . . I knew the guy who had done their ad campaign.

I looked their number up in the book in the phone booth and called.

"Hobson's Home," in a mellow voice . . . oh Christ.

"This is Mrs. Forrester. I'd like to speak to someone about. . . ."

"Certainly, one moment please."

"Yes?" A deep muted voice hit my ears. He had to be a fag. And I found out later that he was, when he minced across the lobby of Hobson's with a plastic grin, and a very tight black suit.

I told him the story. He said there was no problem. One of their cars would pick up Mr. Matthews at three. Would that be all right? I said yes, it would be.

"And will you meet us here at three-thirty, Mrs. Forrester, to make the arrangements?"

"Yes, that'll be fine."

"Are you the sister of the deceased?"

"No, I'm his wife."

"Oh, I'm so sorry, I understood 'Forrester,' " and he was all unctuous apologies.

"That's right, Forrester. I'll tell the hospital you'll pick up Mr. Matthews at three." I didn't give one holy damn what he thought. I was Chris's wife, wedding or no wedding.

I told the nurse at the desk that a car from Hobson's would pick Chris up at three and then went back to tell Tom.

"Do you want to go back to the city now? I'll drive you in; someone else can take my car."

"No. I'll wait. But you can go back now, if you want. There's no point in your waiting here too."

"I'll stay." It sounded very final. I was grateful, so I didn't protest.

"Do you want to lie down or something?"

"No, I'm okay."

"Sure?"

"Sure. Thanks." And I tried a smile for his benefit. He

didn't smile back but walked over to the group of people who had seen Chris last and talked to them in a low voice. They all stood up, one by one, looked over at me, and then away again, quickly, and shook hands with Tom. I saw him hand his keys to someone, and then they were gone. The silent mourners, gone.

"Tom, I can ride back in the car from Hobson's. I'd sort of like to do that."

"No you can't. How do you think Chris would feel about that?" That was a hit below the belt, and I flinched.

"Okay."

"Come on, there's a place to eat across the street. I'll take you over for a hamburger."

"I couldn't. . . ." I got nauseous just thinking about it.

"Then you can drink a cup of coffee. Come on."

We sat, and drank coffee, and smoked, and the time passed, and we never said more than ten words to each other. This friend of Chris's whom I had never seen before was sitting there with me, the closest friend I had at that time. I needed him there, I clung to him, and barely even spoke to him.

The car from Hobson's finally came, a long maroon car with a man driving who looked like a chauffeur. It was a hearse. A hearse for Chris.

Chris came out on a narrow metal stretcher, covered with what looked like a green tarpaulin, and strapped onto the stretcher. They slid him into the back of the hearse and snapped the door shut, and the driver looked at me and said, "Okay, want to follow me, or meet me there?"

"We'll follow," I said before looking at Tom. I wanted to follow Chris.

I looked up at Tom and realized that I had been squeezing his hand the whole time we watched Chris being put in the car. My nails had dug into his hand and he had never said a thing. I don't think he noticed.

We got into Chris's car, and Tom started the motor. . . . "Watch the choke," I told him, Chris's words . . . "watch the choke" . . . the first day we'd been back . . . watch the

choke, and I threw my arms around Tom Bardi, and cried
and sobbed and choked.

"Ready to go?" The driver of the hearse wanted to
know. Tom looked at me and I nodded. I lay back in the
seat and wished I had taken the Librium Peg had suggested. But no, I wanted to "handle" this on my own, no Librium. But thank God for Tom Bardi.

34

At Hobson's, I was led into a small office with elegant,
pseudo-Louis XV furniture. Tom waited outside. The
man who belonged to the voice on the phone came in. I
had already seen him in the lobby. "I'm Mr. Ferrari. Mrs.
Forrester, isn't it?"

"Yes."

"Now . . . when is the funeral?"

"I don't know yet."

"Of course. We are going to put Mr. Matthews in our
Georgian Slumber Room, which I will show you after you
look over these papers. Then I will introduce you to our
cosmetician and we'll go downstairs to look at a casket.
And after that there will be nothing left for you to do. Let's
see, today is Friday, so I would imagine that the funeral
will be on Sunday, or perhaps Monday?" Sympathetic alligator smile, and a pat on my hand. . . . oh Christ, get your
fucking hands off me. He sounded like a goddam social
director on a Caribbean Cruise, "and now . . ." shit.

"Oh yes, and Mrs. Forrester, will you bring us a full suit
of Mr. Matthews' clothes some time this evening? Including shoes." A suit? I wasn't even sure Chris had one.

"What for?" I had obviously shocked the man beyond
all possibility heretofore known feasible.

"To lay him out." And that smile again, coupled with an
expression that sympathized with my stupidity.

"Lay him out? Oh, in the coff . . . no, that won't be nec-
essary. I want it closed. He can wear what he has on."

"Is he wearing a suit?"

"No, Mr. Ferrari, he is not wearing a suit. He does not
own a suit, and I like what he's wearing." I began to snap
back, and it made me feel better. "I'll have to check with
his mother about some of the details. She's coming in tonight."

"From the East?"

"No, from Denver." But don't worry, we can pay for it,
Mr. Ferrari. You'll get your money. That's what the
papers were all about.

And he smiled at me, sure that Mr. Matthews' mother
would agree with him about the suit. Maybe she would.
She was his mother after all.

"Now, shall we go downstairs and look at the caskets?"

We stepped out of the cloistered little office and I saw
Tom, still sitting there. It was reassuring to see him still
there.

"We won't be long," I said, and Tom nodded. Mr. Ferrari looked shocked. He was obviously prepared to give
me the full show.

For some reason, in the elevator it dawned on me how I
must look, in my jeans and sandals and Chris's old
sweater. Poor Mr. Ferrari. What one had to deal with
these days, but I thought it was just as well. Maybe the bill
wouldn't be so high. I didn't know how well Mrs. Matthews stood financially and, while I could have paid for it
with my savings, it would have left me pretty flat afterward. Funerals could run into thousands.

Mr. Ferrari opened a door and revealed a room full of
caskets, displayed like cars in a showroom, on platforms,
circled around the room, with crucifixes and without, with
all sorts of adornments and hardware, lined with satin,

velvet, and moire. And I saw Mr. Ferrari winding up to give me the full speech. An Automobile Salesman at His Best.

"I'll take that one."

"That one?"

"That one."

"Very well, but wouldn't you like me to show you. . . ."

"No. How much is it?"

He consulted a list and said, "Three hundred and twenty-five dollars."

"Fine," and I turned and walked out of the room, pressing the elevator button before Mr. Ferrari had either caught his breath or rejoined me.

Upstairs, I shook hands with Mr. Ferrari and prepared to leave.

"Mr. Matthews will be ready at seven this evening. You haven't seen the room yet."

"I'm sure it'll be fine, Mr. Ferrari." I was exhausted and wanted to get out of the place.

"You're sure about the suit?"

"I'm sure. Thank you," and with all my dignity, headed for the door, with Tom following me.

Once we got outside, he looked at me again. "You okay?"

"Much better. Let's go pick up Sam," and I gave him the address of the school. It was almost four-thirty and she'd be wondering what had happened.

At the school, Sam was drawing pictures in the office of one of the admissions people and looked perfectly happy.

"Where were you?"

"Busy. Let's go, sweetheart, it's time to go home."

And she picked up her jacket and headed for the door, with her pictures all rolled up in one hand. After she was well out of the room, the admissions lady came around the desk to me and shook my hand. "I'm so very sorry, Mrs. Forrester."

"Thank you." I was going to have to get used to that. There would be a lot of "I'm sorry's" in the next few days.

Tom was waiting in the car when Samantha and I came out.

"Who's that?"

"A friend of Uncle Chris."

"Oh." That was okay then, in her book.

Tom and she chatted all the way back to the house, which left my mind free to wander as we drove home. I was so tired I was numb.

"Tom, I want to stop at the florist on the way home. There's one just up the street from us. Do you have time?"

"Sure."

"What do you want flowers for, Mommy? We've got enough at home."

"I want to send some to somebody." Oh God. It began to dawn on me that I'd have to tell her, what and how I didn't know. But I'd have to tell her something.

At the florist, I ordered two hundred dollars worth of wild flowers in varied colors to be delivered to Hobson's by seven o'clock. I couldn't stand the thought of all white or salmon-colored gladiola, not for Chris.

Outside, Sam and Tom were tickling each other in the car, and I gave a tired smile when I saw them. Tom had been unbelievable.

He drove us home and asked me if I wanted him to come in.

"You don't have to. I'm okay. But I could make you some dinner."

"No. I'll go home."

"Want me to drive you?"

"No. I live about six blocks away. I'll walk. I'll park the car for you."

Sam and I stood in front of the house while he did, and he walked back toward us, looking as tired as I felt. He stopped for a moment in front of us, not knowing what to say.

"Tom . . . I don't know how to say it, but . . . thanks. . . . You've been unbelievable . . . wonderful," and tears started welling up in my throat again.

"So have you, Gillian, so have you." He bent down and
kissed my cheek, rumpled Sam's hair, and walked up the
street with his head down. I think he was crying, but I
wasn't sure because I was crying too.

"What are you crying for, Mommy? Do you hurt?"

"Yes, sort of."

"Well, I'll take care of it, and you'll feel all better."

"Thanks, sweetheart," and we walked up the stairs to
the empty house, hand in hand, the two of us alone again.

Mrs. Matthews called while Sam was eating dinner. She
said she'd get in at nine, but I didn't have to go to the airport. I told her I would and then set about finding a sitter
for Sam. I called the only one of our neighbors whom I
knew, and she said she'd be glad to. And, "Oh, Gillian, I
heard it on the news, and I'm so sorry," so sorry, so sorry,
there it was again.

"Thanks, Mrs. Jaeger, thanks." On the news? Christ.

Sam was as good as gold, took her bath, ate her dinner,
and went to bed without any problems. She asked for
Chris once and I put her off. I didn't want her to associate
his going with the tears and unhappiness she'd see in the
next few days. Better to tell her when I could handle it.
When would that be? Anyway, not just then.

Mrs. Jaeger came at eight and I drove to the airport for
Mrs. Matthews. I had remembered to change my clothes
before going and wore something plain and black. My
blue jeans and Chris's sweater lay piled on our still unmade bed, along with the gray dress.

35

I stood in the airport, waiting for the plane to come in. I looked around, wondering which of the people standing around might be Jane. Nobody looked the way I expected her to, so I stopped thinking about it, and stared out instead at the lights on the airfield. Half a dozen planes were lining up for takeoff, and there were others coming in.

"United Airlines, Flight 402, from Denver, has arrived. Passengers will arrive at Gate 3. . . . Flight 402. . . ." She was one of the first people off and I recognized her right off, a smallish lady who must have been pretty once, with gray hair and a neat-looking black suit. She looked around, and past me. I don't think she recognized me at first.

"Mrs. Matthews?"

"Gillian?"

"Yes."

"Thank you for coming, dear. You needn't have," and she looked around me, and over my shoulder as I was telling her it was quite all right, and all the things one is supposed to say.

"I don't see Jane. She said she'd meet me." And then, as I looked around with her, she waved, and I saw a tall girl walking toward us. . . . It was Chris transformed into a woman. It was the oddest feeling to look at that girl and see Chris, his walk, his shape, and, as she came closer, his eyes. It made me want to shudder, but I was fascinated, mesmerized by the apparition coming toward us. I couldn't take my eyes off her. She walked straight up to her mother and put her arms around her in a silent hug. And I was sorry I had come. I had no place with them. They needed each other, and I was a stranger there. I turned away, feeling awkward, and tried to think of what to say to Jane. "I'm sorry"? No, not from me. Not me too. As I looked back at her, staring at the resemblance again, she let go of her mother and took a step toward me. And hugged me too.

"I know, Gillian. I know. I won't tell you I'm sorry. I know how you feel. Chris wrote to me last week."

"He did? He didn't tell me a thing." I was so surprised I didn't know what to say.

"He wouldn't have. Mom, why don't we get your bags," and the three of us walked slowly toward the escalator to the baggage claim area.

We collected Mrs. Matthews' things and I went to the parking lot to get the car.

"I'm sorry, it's not very roomy. Chris . . . I . . . well, we like it," and there was an embarrassed silence.

Driving into the city there was very little said. There was very little to say. And then, as though all at once all three of us felt we should be talking, we all started to talk at once, and then laughed nervously. We talked about San Francisco, the weather in Denver, flying, anything except Chris, and the accident.

"When is the baby due, Gillian?" Wow, talk about openers. That from Jane.

"Not for another two months. You have three, don't you?" She nodded, and while I tried not to look at Mrs. Matthews, I hoped she hadn't noticed. Because, what we all forget, with our free-thinking friends, is that they have parents, and the great, liberated Christopher Caldwell Matthews had a mother who might not think illegitimate children were so cool. Chris hadn't thought so either, so I expected nothing short of horror from his mother. I could feel her looking at me than and chanced a quick glance and nervous smile in her direction. After all, I had only met her once.

She looked back at me, just as nervously, with a tiny smile, and her big sad eyes. "I hope you won't mind me saying, this, but I'm glad. My other son wasn't married either, and well, Chris, . . ." and she trailed off. I wanted to kiss her, but couldn't while I was driving, so I looked back at her again, with a real smile this time.

"Do you want to stop . . . there . . . on the way in?"

"No, Mother, why don't you wait till tomorrow? Let's go straight to the hotel."

"No. I want to go tonight, Jane. I want to see him . . . ," and the last part of her words trailed off again.

"Ummmm . . . Mrs. Matthews, I had the . . . uh . . . I had it closed. . . . But it can be done the other way, if you like. . . ." The other way . . . the other way . . . with Chris lying there, so still . . . for all to see, until we buried him.

"Oh." It was such a small sound. "Does he . . . ? Was he very . . . ?"

I cut her off; I didn't want to hear the words. "No, he looks . . . fine." I wanted to say "beautiful," but I couldn't. He did look beautiful, the sleeping boy I had watched so often late at night, or early in the morning. All peaceful, the soul of a boy in the body of a man.

"I think Gillian was right, Mom. Let's leave it like that," and Mrs. Matthews just nodded.

After that the conversation lagged. There was nothing left to say, and we all sat deep in our own thoughts until we got to Hobson's. I pulled into their parking lot and parked the car. We all got out and I led the way in.

There was a pale—ghostly?—looking girl at the desk in the lobby, and Mr. Ferrari was talking to a small group of people in a corner. He looked up as we walked in, nodded briefly, and looked as though he approved of my change of clothes. Schmuck.

I stepped up to the girl at the desk and my voice sounded hoarse again. "Mr. Matthews, the Georgian Room. Which way?"

"This way, please," and she headed down the long hall, past other rooms, and I was afraid to look toward the open doors for fear that I'd see a body, and I didn't want to see that. She stopped at the last door on the left and we went in. And there it was, the dark wooden box I had picked out a few hours ago, and the flowers I had bought on Sacramento Street. They looked beautiful. They were red, yellow, and blue, with baby's breath spread through them. They looked so fresh and pretty, not heavy and dead. They were like Mozart, or Debussy. That was just what I had wanted.

There were two huge candles in bronze candelabra at either end of the casket, and a small prie-dieu just in front of it. Two settees and a few chairs against the wall. The lighting was dim; it looked so solemn, like a church. It seemed like the wrong place for Chris. I could just hear him saying something like, "Oh fuck off, Gill, what the hell is this?" But it had to be, and his mother looked as though she thought it was right.

"The flowers are lovely, Gillian. Did you do that?" And I nodded. She walked forward toward the casket then, and Jane squeezed my arm as Mrs. Matthews knelt at the prie-dieu, and we stood back watching her, this woman who had lost two sons and a husband, all her men.

She got up after a moment and Jane took her place while Mrs. Matthews sat on one of the settees and looked at her feet. I didn't have the courage to look at her anymore, I just couldn't.

Jane rose and came toward me, leading her mother gently off the settee on the way. "Come on, Mom, it's been a long day, and I told the hotel we'd be there by ten."

As we walked down the hall I asked Jane where they were staying. "The Sir Francis Drake."

"I'll drop you there."

In the car on the way over, Jane continued a normal conversation, while patting her mother's shoulder and occasionally giving her a squeeze.

"Mrs. Matthews, I hate to bring this up now, but when do you think we should have the . . . funeral?" There. I'd gotten it out.

"Is Sunday too soon?"

"No. I don't think so. I think it might be better that way. Do you want to do it in church? I'm sorry to bring it up like this . . . so soon . . . but they want to know . . . at Hobson's, I mean. . . ."

"Bastards." It was Jane, sounding so much like Chris.

"Jane! They have a job to do just like everyone else."

Jane and I didn't add anything to that, but our sentiments ran in the same vein, and bastards was a nice word for it.

"Did Chris still go to church much?" Ouch.

"Not too often." Better to lie a little than to say "never."

"I'm a Presbyterian, and his father was a Methodist. I don't think Christopher felt much one way or the other. He never leaned particularly to one side." That was one way of putting it. In a way, it was the truth.

"There's a nice little Presbyterian church near our house. I could speak to the minister in the morning."

"May I come with you?"

"Of course, I'm sorry. I didn't mean to take over, I just thought. . . ."

"Gillian, you've been wonderful. Don't you worry about that."

"I'll come and get you in the morning and we'll all go and see him together."

Jane sounded as though she were grinding her teeth in the back seat. She really was like Chris. A church funeral for Chris. But it wasn't for Chris. It was for his mother, and for us. That's who funerals are for, a dirge for the living, not a celebration of the dead.

In front of the hotel we all hugged again, and they disappeared into the lobby, the tall fair girl who walked like Chris and the small lady in the black suit. She was only a little smaller than I, but she looked tiny to me, somehow, maybe because she was Chris's mother. I looked at my watch and decided to go back to Hobson's. Just for a minute. To be alone with Chris. Mrs. Jaeger wouldn't mind waiting just a little bit longer. She'd understand.

I parked in the lot again and went in, relieved to see that Mr. Ferrari was gone. The pale-looking girl was still at the desk, drinking coffee out of a styrofoam cup. It reminded me of the coffee at *Woman's Life,* and I walked down the hall thinking "to her, this is just a job," and I couldn't help wondering what kind of person would want a job like that. The magazine had been throbbing with life, and people, and color, and noise. Working in a place like this was as good as being dead yourself.

I reached Chris's room and walked in slowly. I sat in one of the chairs and thought for a while, leaning back and closing my eyes, resting, and thinking. Of little bits and pieces, short moments, and tiny words. . . . Fifteen hours ago, Chris went clattering down the steps of the house, and now here I was in this quiet room filled with bright flowers, with Chris lying there. . . . Maybe, maybe if I hold my breath and close my eyes, and count to 712, it will all go away, and I'll wake up. But I didn't. I gasped and opened my eyes, and it was all there, just the same except that I was out of breath, and the baby was kicking harder, infuriated by the momentary lack of oxygen.

I walked slowly toward the prie-dieu then, and knelt looking toward where Chris's head rested, though I couldn't see it. Tears ran down my face slowly, making plopping noises as they hit the velvet on the top of the prie-dieu. I think I prayed, but I'm not sure, and then I got up and left. Slowly, alone, wishing that I could feel that Chris was with me, near me. That's what you're supposed to feel, but I didn't. I felt as though Chris was shut up in that box. He was gone, and I was alone.

Chris's car was the only one left in Hobson's parking lot, and I started it, remembering about the choke. I drove home through the fog and got to Sacramento Street just before midnight, a little worried about Mrs. Jaeger. I opened the door with my key and walked in, leaving my coat on the chair in the hall and heading toward the kitchen where I supposed she would be. The kitchen light was the only one that was on.

"Mrs. Jaeger? . . . Mrs. Jaeger?" Maybe Sam had woken up and I went upstairs to see. When I reached the top of the stairs I saw that the light was on in our room, and I could see Peg through the open doorway, making my bed.

"Oh, Peg, you're a saint," and I sagged in the doorway and just looked at her.

"No talk. Just get into bed. Here, sit down. I'll help."

"Oh, Peg, you must be exhausted. It's three o'clock in the morning your time."

"It's worse, your time, so no arguments. This is what I came out here for."

"God, Peg, what am I ever going to do if I grow up one day and you're not around anymore?"

"Oh shut up. None of that stuff."

"What about Mrs. Jaeger?"

"She left just before you got here. I didn't think she was going to trust me, but I talked so much, and so fast, and kept ushering her out the door at the same time, so she went. Where have you been?"

"I picked up Mrs. Matthews at the airport, and then took them to Hobson's, and after that I dropped them off at the hotel, and then I . . . went back to Hobson's."

"Went back to Hobson's? Hobson's being the local Frank Campbell's, I take it. What are you trying to do? Kill yourself and the baby?"

"Yes, I mean no. I mean yes, Hobson's is the local Campbell's, and no I'm not trying to kill myself or the baby. Peg, someone had to be there to pick her up."

"There was no one else?"

"Chris's sister, but. . . . Hell, I wanted to."

"Good enough. Now, how about some hot chocolate, or something. And I brought you some pills from New York."

"What kind of pills?"

"Cool-it pills. I called your obstetrician and he gave me a prescription for you."

"Christ, Peg. . . ."

"Did you take any Librium today?"

"Well, actually. . . ." I shook my head.

"I figured."

And I started looking around the room. Everything

looked the way I had left it, except neater, and the stuff was cleared off the bed. The new gray dress was hanging on a hanger on the closet door.

"Peg . . . would you put that away, please? I don't want to see it."

"Sure," and it vanished into the closet.

"The funeral's Sunday, so you'll be able to get back to the office on Monday."

"You giving me the bum's rush or something? I told them I'd be gone a week."

Peg . . . Peg . . . unbelievable Peg who had held my head the first time I got drunk, who had always, always been there. And here she was, a few hours after I called, having traveled three thousand miles to be with me, and making my bed within five minutes of walking in the door. She was treating me like a patient, and she was the night nurse, flown out direct from New York. Just for me. It was the kind of friendship Chris couldn't understand, but thank God for Peg. There were one in ten million people like her, and I had been lucky enough to go to school with her.

She gave me the pill, and the hot chocolate, and I sat there thinking about Chris at Hobson's. "Peg. . . ."

"Try not to talk. Just tell me where you want me to sleep. Can I sleep in Sam's room?"

"Peg, you sleep here. I'll sleep in Sam's room."

"No way. If you so much as put a foot on the floor, I'll give you one of my world-famous left hooks!"

"You mean the one that almost got you kicked out of school?"

"The same," and we giggled.

"Peg?"

"Yes?"

"You know . . . I . . . um . . ."

"I know . . . ," and she turned out the light and I began to fall asleep as she was picking up the empty chocolate cup. She just seemed to fade away, and for a minute I tried to keep awake thinking that that looked like Peg

Richards standing over me. But no, it couldn't be. Peg was in New York. . . . Must be Chris. . . . I'd have to re-member to tell him in the morning. He'd think it was funny. . . .

36

The sun was streaming into the room and I could hear voices downstairs. . . . My God . . . what time is it? Eleven-forty-five. I jumped out of bed and went to the top of the stairs.

"Chris? . . . Sam? . . . Why'd you let me sleep this late? Today is . . . ," Oh no, oh God no. . . . I dropped back onto the top step and sat there with my face buried in my hands. Peg rushed up the steps, with Sam behind her, and she pulled me gently off the step and led me back to the bedroom.

"Whatsa matter with Mommy, Aunt Peg?"

"She's just very tired, Sam. Why don't you go back down and be a big girl and put the dishes in the sink? That's a good girl," and Sam clattered back downstairs. Peg sat me on the edge of the bed. And sat next to me, with an arm around my shoulders, while I started to sob and shake. "Ohhhh Peg . . . ohhh." We sat like that until Sam came back, looking puzzled and a little worried. I looked over at her and tried to smile a little for her, which made me cry more.

"Oh, Peg . . . I can't stop . . . I can't. . . ."

"That's all right, Gill. You'll be okay. Why don't you go wash your face?"

"I was supposed to call Mrs. Matthews. We have to go see the minister."

"Jane called. She and her mother are coming by at one."

"I'll pick them up."

"No, they can take a taxi. Stop being a hero. You're being selfish, Gill. Think of the baby. You loved him, so take good care of his child." It was kind of a harsh thing to say, but it was like a splash of cold water. Peg was right.

"Peg . . . no more pills, please . . . huh?"

"We'll see. Listen, you've had a lot of calls. A guy named Tom Bardi, He wanted to know if there was anything he could do. I said we'd let him know. And Hilary Price, and Gordon Harte . . . and . . . let's see, oh, John Templeton . . . and . . ."

"How do they know?" I looked at Peg and knew. "You called them?"

"Just Gordon and John Templeton. Before I left. And your mother called. I think Gordon must have called her."

"I don't want to talk to any of them . . . please." I saw Peg watching me. "I've got to call the minister. Where the hell is the phone book?" and I started scrambling around under the bed while the phone rang. I gave a horrible start as it rang next to me. "You get it."

Peg answered it and paused for a moment, listening. "I'll have to see if she's in, Operator," and she looked over at me as I shook my head frantically from side to side and waved a hand . . . no . . . no . . . I can't. . . . She put her hand over the mouthpiece and whispered, "It's Gordon. Do you want to talk to him?" I started to shake my head and then looked up at Peg for a long two seconds and reached for the phone. She handed it to me and ushered Sam out of the room again, closing the door behind them.

"Hello. . . . Yes, this is she. . . . Gordon? . . . Hello. . . . Thanks for calling. . . . Peg told me that. . . . What?"

"I said I'd like to come out for a couple of days, if I can help."

"No . . . no . . . Gordon, thanks, but I'd rather you didn't. It wouldn't. . . . well, I don't think it's such a good idea."

"How are you feeling, Gillian?"

"I don't know. . . . I don't know. Today was going to be our . . . ," and I started to cry all over again while Gordon tried to talk.

"I don't know what to say. I'm so sorry, Gill." There it was, from Gordon this time—"I'm so sorry."

"I know you are."

"Gillian, I know it's too soon for you to have thought about it, but why don't you come back to New York with Peg? There's nobody to take care of you out there."

"No. I'm staying." It was the most forceful thing I'd said in two days, except for my quick bout with Mr. Ferrari, and this was one hell of a lot more important to me than whether or not Chris was wearing a suit. Nobody was going to tear me away from here. Not now. Not ever. NO!

"Well, don't put it out of your mind yet. Are you sure I can't do anything?"

"No . . . yes . . . I'll let you know if there is anything. There's nothing left to do. It's . . . ," and I just went on crying. "I can't talk anymore. . . . Thanks for the call. . . . Thanks for everything."

"Gillian, we're all with you. Please know that." I nodded again and choked on another "thanks" and hung up while he was still on the line.

I called the minister, and when Jane and Mrs. Matthews arrived we went over and set it up with him. We'd have to do it at two-thirty. They couldn't do it sooner because of Sunday services. And I guess he had to eat lunch or something. We had missed our own lunch by the time we'd spoken to him, and we stood in a small group just outside the church wondering what to do next.

"Let's go back to the house."

"Well, I'd like to go back to Hobson's for a while, Gillian." It was Mrs. Matthews speaking. Jane and Peg said nothing, and I offered to go back for the car. We walked slowly toward the house, Jane and Peg falling behind and talking in soft voices, Mrs. Matthews and I discussing

Bible passages for the funeral. We had sorrow as our bond, and our plans to hold us together. After this? Maybe the baby. He would be her grandchild, and maybe she would love him. Maybe he would look like Chris.

At the house, Sam saw us from the window and she and Mrs. Jaeger waved. I could see Sam discussing something heatedly with Mrs. Jaeger and suspected she wanted to come out.

"Let's get into the car, everybody, or Sam will get upset and want to come too."

Everyone waved, and we got in as quickly as one pregnant woman and one older, less agile, woman possibly could.

On the way to Hobson's, no one spoke, and I parked once again in the same spot in their lot. We walked inside, still silent, and headed down the now familiar path toward the room where Chris was lying. I expected to find it empty and just as I had left it the night before, but we walked in to find Tom Bardi and the whole camera crew there, standing around, looking solemn, and in the process of signing the white and gold leaflet that Hobson's left out for guests to sign, to show that they had done their "duty."

Introductions were made, and there was a lot of shifting from one foot to the other, with no one knowing what to say. After a little bit they filed out, looking back at me again, and I saw that one of the girls was crying, and a boy had his arm around her, leading her out. Had she known Chris well? Had she been in love with him too? Had she slept with him? Did she feel sorry for me? I was curious, and felt guilty about it.

Tom stayed back for a few minutes, to talk to me.

"It was in the paper this morning."

"What did it say?" I wanted it to say something nice.

"It was just a small news item, page eleven, not an obit, or anything like that."

"I heard that it was on the news last night too."

"Yeah . . . ," and he nodded, and then he left.

I walked over to the little guest register to see what their names were, wondering which one was the girl. Just

a lot of names. There were so many I didn't know. I was
sorry I hadn't been there earlier. And then my eyes
stopped halfway down the list. . . . There it was. The tenth
one down. Marilyn Lee, in a slanting, elaborate script.
Marilyn Lee. She must be feeling like this too. Poor Marilyn. I hoped that she had had a few minutes alone in here.
The rivalry was over now. The two widows standing side
by side.

"Who are all the flowers from, Gillian?"

"Flowers?" What flowers? And I looked around, realizing that there were more than wild flowers in the room, at
least a dozen more arrangements, some of them pretty,
some funeralish and grotesque. I was surprised. I saw a little pile of invoice slips and cards on the table, and realized
that this was one of Hobson's services. Yellow invoices
describing each arrangement, and saying who it was from,
with the sympathy card stapled on the back. White spider
mums from some film company whose name I didn't recognize. White and yellow roses: Hilary Price. Mixed flowers on stand: John Templeton and the Staff. Spray of lilies
of the valley: G. Harte . . . Gordon . . . and more, whose
names I didn't know. Our friends, mostly my friends, and
I reached out for Peg and started to cry again. Poor Mrs.
Matthews, that didn't make it any easier for her.

We sat for a couple of hours, and a few people drifted
in and out, nodding to us, and one or two shook Mrs.
Matthews' hand and murmured the same "I'm sorry" to
her over and over again. How often had she heard that?
For her husband, her other boy, and now for Chris.

Toward the end of the day, a neatly put together man in
a dark suit stepped in, and for a moment I thought he
might work for Hobson's. He looked so serious, so proper,
but Mrs. Matthews rose and said, "Gillian, this is my son-
in-law, Don Lindquist." We shook hands and he put his
arm around Jane after kissing Mrs. Matthews.

How do you do's were exchanged, I introduced Peg,
and then he stepped away from us and bowed his head
near where Chris lay.

When he came back to our little group, he suggested he

take us all home, and then out for dinner later. I declined and Peg shot me a look, but I just couldn't face that scene.

"I drove up so I have the car."

"Oh." I would no longer be chauffeuring Jane and her mother around, which upset me a little. One of my jobs had been taken away from me, one of the things that was keeping me busy, helping me to keep my sanity. . . . Oh.

After they left, Peg looked at me and stood up. "Okay, kid, you're going home."

"No, I'm not," and I felt defiant. I was *not* leaving. "You go home to Sam. It's late and the last two days have confused the hell out of her. Tell her I'll be home later."

"That's just the point, Gillian. My going home to Sam is not going to unconfuse her. You come home too. You can come back later if you want." Good old Peg, giving it the old honest heave-ho. Wham. She was right. I got up, put on my coat, and left with her, looking back at Chris's casket, "just one more time."

"Where've you been all day? Nobody plays with me. Just fat old Mrs. Jaeger. I don't like Mrs. Jaeger." Sam was mad, she was feeling left out. "And where's Uncle Crits?" She was mad at him too. We had all deserted her. And she started to cry. I took her in my arms and rocked her back and forth, taking as much comfort as I was giving.

"How about taking your bath with me?" and she cheered visibly, momentarily forgetting Chris, and she started up the stairs in a rush.

Peg said she'd cook dinner, so I headed upstairs, feeling relieved that I hadn't had to say more about Chris, and thinking that the hot bath would do me good too. I was feeling leaden again, and had had small cramps in my back all day. The baby was beginning to feel very low, and I felt heavy as I walked up the stairs.

Sam was in high spirits at dinner, and the three of us laughed and giggled and told silly jokes to entertain Sam. And each other. I laughed too hard at everything, everything seemed so funny. It was a relief to be away from Hobson's, to be away from that dark wooden box, away from the yellow invoices with the sympathy cards, and the stuffy floral smell, and from Mrs. Matthews and Jane and . . . it all went together. And the joke about the 400-pound canary was suddenly hysterical to me again, Sam and Peg and I each laughing till the tears ran down our faces.

We put Sam to bed and then walked out into the hall. "Peg. . . ."

"No," and we looked defiantly at each other for an instant, and I came close to hating her briefly. She was not going to keep me from going back there. "You're not going back, Gillian, you're not."

"I am," and she stood there between me and the stairs, and I wondered if one of her famous left hooks was going to come at me after all. And then we both looked so silly standing there I started to laugh again, and we both stood there, doubling over with giggles, like the time we unhooked the toilet seat in Miss MacFarlan's john and she fell in and we could hear her screaming as we ran all the way down the hall, then stopped breathless on the back stairs, laughing, and doubling over just like this.

"What's so funny?" Sam was back in our midst.

"Back to bed, young lady." Peg shooed her back in while I got my coat and ran down the stairs. When Peg came out I was already at the front door, the car keys in my hand. "See you later, Peg."

"Okay, but if you're not back by eleven I'll call the police."

"I'll be back by then," and I blew her a kiss as I closed the door and went back out in the fog. I could hear the fog horns, and I sat in the car for a few minutes just listening.

37

At Hobson's, the same pale girl was there, in the same dress, drinking the same coffee, reading the paper. At least she could read, and then I remembered something. "Can I see that for a second?" and she looked up with a surprised rabbit look. No one ever asked her for anything except "Which way to Mrs. Jones?" or "Where is the Greek Grotto Room?" She handed me the paper, and I turned to page eleven. Where the hell is it? Then there it was, in a small box, at the bottom of the page: "In Safford Field, in Oakland, yesterday, Christopher Caldwell Matthews, age thirty-three, of 2629 Sacramento Street fell to his death from a crane while filming a documentary movie. He was rushed to St. Mary's Hospital in Oakland, but had died on impact, of a broken neck." That was all. They'd gotten it all in there, hadn't they? And people would read it and think, "Gee, too bad," or "Crazy hippies," or "You never know about those movie people," or . . . oh shit. "Thanks," and I gave her back her paper while she still looked surprised. I smiled at her, but that was too much for her. It wasn't in her Hobson's manual.

I walked back toward Chris's room, feeling as though I had been doing this all my life, like visiting a very old aunt in a nursing home. I felt as though Chris had always been there and I had always been coming to Hobson's to see him. It gave me a place to go to. But it was the dead Chris. The live Chris lived on his side of our rumpled bed, in the slippers that stood in opposite corners of the room, in the frazzled toothbrush that was still lying on the sink, in

the studio I couldn't bring myself to go up to now . . . There
was something sick about holding on to this dead Chris,
but it seemed more alive to me than the live Chris just then.
The live Chris would come back to me later in shooting
moments, in flashes while I was doing dishes, or thought I
heard him closing a door upstairs. That Chris would be
with me always, but he was temporarily eclipsed by the
Chris who was supposed to be lying in that box, being vis-
ited by people who signed the register.

Back in the Georgian Slumber Room, I looked at the
register to see who had been there. There were two more
names on the list, and I wondered if Marilyn had been
back. I took off my coat and started picking up the flower
petals that had fallen in the last few hours. I didn't want
the room to look messy. We wouldn't want that. And I
suddenly jumped, realizing that there was someone else in
the room. I wheeled around, feeling as though a ghost
were behind me. It was Tom Bardi, sitting quietly in a
corner, smoking a cigarette.

"Hi."

"Hi," and we sank back into our comfortable silence. I
wanted to be alone with Chris. But it was better to have
Tom there. With him in the room, I just sat, and looked,
and fought off the constant desire to walk up to the box
and look at it, wondering if Chris were really inside.

We sat and we sat, and smoked endlessly. No one came,
no one walked by, nothing stirred.

"It's eleven-thirty. Don't you want to go home, Gill?"

"No . . . I'm . . . going to stay here tonight. It probably
sounds crazy to you, but it's a tradition . . . my family . . .
I want to."

"Peg said she thought you would."

"Peg? When? Did she call you?" And it began to be
clear.

He said "no" too fast, shook his head too hard. I knew
he was lying. Peg had called, that was why Tom Bardi had
been sitting there when I arrived. He must have jumped in
his car and driven straight down, in time to be sitting in
the corner when I got there. Peg had done it again. And so

had Tom. What in hell would I do without them? I would
have resented their high-handedness, except I needed it. I
really needed it. . . . Two o'clock . . . three o'clock . . . five
o'clock. . . .

"Tom?" He was asleep, leaning over in a corner of the
settee. I had wanted to tell him that I was going to do
something, that he could leave if he wanted to, but I had
to do it. I was going to open the box. I wanted to make
sure it was really Chris, that he was wearing his work
clothes, that they hadn't snuck a suit on him after all.

I tiptoed up to the dark wood box, lifted off the "spray"
of roses his mother had ordered, and stepped back,
holding my breath. It was a hell of a thing to do, but I had
to do it. Now or never. Tomorrow would be too late. The
Matthews would be back, they would be horrified, and
after that he'd belong to all of them, and to the minister,
and to the people in the church. Tonight he was still mine.
Still Chris. Not "Christopher Caldwell Matthews, age
thirty-three of 2629." . . . And I was still Gill. Not "dearly
beloved we are gathered here." Why do they only use that
for weddings and funerals? Dearly beloved . . . by whom?
God? If he loved me so much why had he done this to me?
I remembered Gordon's "Vaya con Dios." And Dios must
have taken the wrong turnoff somewhere. Back about Friday.

I stood there and looked back at Tom, still asleep . . .
okay, here goes. There was an ornate-looking key in a
lock, halfway down the side of the casket. It turned easily
and I tried to lift the lid. It was a heavy goddam thing. But
I got it up, and it rested upward, with its gray velvet. I
looked down, and there was Chris . . . Chris . . . looking
just as he had in the hospital on Friday, except they'd
taken the sand off his face. And there was something
wrong, something else . . . his hair! They'd combed his
hair all wrong. I went to my bag, took out my comb, and
combed it the way he wore it, falling over his ears, a little
scrambled in the front. I leaned over and kissed the hair

above his forehead, the way I do to Sam after I do her hair. I tried to hold his hand but it was stiff. Like a wax doll. He looked so pale. I knelt at the prie-dieu and just watched, sure that I had seen him move, or breathe. I sat and watched, and then finally got up and put my arms around him. It felt so odd, it didn't give, his body didn't bend anymore, that supple body, with the soft skin. The light began to stream in and touch his face, and it was the same Chris who had lain in bed next to me, the sleeping boy-man I had watched so many mornings before, as the night turned pale gray. My tears fell onto his hands, and onto his shirt, and ran down my neck. Good tears. Not the broken sobs of the past two days. I was crying for Chris, not for me. I kissed him on the cheeks and on the eyes, and on his hands, folded so strangely over his chest. I put a tiny white flower next to him, and took the thin gold chain from his neck. Maybe that was against the law or something. But he always wore it, and I knew he would not mind my having it. It was the same as a wedding band . . . forever, until death do you part. I looked away as I lowered the lid. I didn't want to see his face disappearing as I closed it.

I looked over at Tom still asleep on the settee, and sat in one of the chairs. Morning continued to come, still gray, and we sat there, the three of us, Tom and Chris and I. I was glad I'd done it, because I had faced death, I had touched it, and kissed it. I had buried the dead Chris in that box, I had said goodbye to the dead Chris, and the live Chris began to come to life again. I would never see the body again, or touch that face, but I would see the smile, and hear the laugh, remember the shouts, and see his face when I got up in the morning and heard a familiar sound. Chris had come back to me, and would stay with me always, and I leaned my head back and fell asleep.

Something was shaking me, and I looked up into Tom Bardi's face, surprised, forgetting where I was.

"Want some coffee?"

"Yes, what time is it?"

"Eight-thirty. You must have been sleeping a long time. I sacked out hours ago myself." Yes, a long time. He came back with two cups of steaming coffee in those styrofoam cups. We drank them and made small talk. The room was not so formidable in the daylight with sun beginning to stream in through the windows.

We finished the coffee, and Mrs. Matthews arrived with Jane and Don, all of them looking very neat and dressed up, Mrs. Matthews in another black suit, Jane in a navy blue coat dress, and Don in the same dark suit.

Tom said he'd drive me home, but we both had our cars, so we followed each other up toward the west end of the city, through the empty streets. It was still too early for any traffic on a Sunday. Mrs. Matthews had told me to meet them in church, so there was no need for me to go back, and I was grateful to have a few hours at home. I had said good-bye to Chris and to Hobson's and I wondered who would be in the Georgian room tomorrow. I would never forget it. I would walk by years later and look down that hall, visible from the street, and wonder who was in the Georgian Slumber Room now.

Tom waved as I stopped in front of our house and he drove on. I meant to ask him in for a cup of coffee, but it was just as well. Peg and Sam were eating breakfast, and I stopped for a cup of coffee, feeling more tired than I had since Friday, but more peaceful, much quieter. After breakfast I went upstairs and lay on our bed, not sleeping, just lying there, grateful that Peg and Sam were in the garden and away from me. Today was a day I wanted to be left alone.

At one-thirty, Peg came up to see how I was doing, and poked her head in the door. "You've got about half an hour," and I was reminded of when Peg had been the maid of honor at my wedding. She grumbled and bitched, and complained about wearing "that jackass veil you picked out, Gill, you bitch," but she had ended up being the ringleader, and had been very bridesmaidish about the

whole thing, except when she burned her veil straight up
the front, smoking a cigarette before we went up the aisle.
Peg.

I did my hair, and got all ready, except for the dress. I
hadn't really decided what to wear. The black dress that I
had worn in New York looked so worn out, and my coat
was a tweed which wasn't dark enough. My dark blue
dress was too tight, my charcoal dress had a huge egg stain
down the front, courtesy of Samantha, and I had forgotten
to send it to the cleaners after I got out to San Francisco,
which left the "wedding dress," the pale gray dress Chris
hadn't even seen, hanging in the back of the closet where
Peg had put it at my request on the night she arrived.

Twenty minutes later I stood in front of the mirror
wearing the dress and coat, the black shoes, my grandmother's pearls, and my hair rolled into a neat bun at the
base of my neck, looking just as I would have on my wedding day with Chris. It was a day and a lifetime too late
for the wedding. And I reached into the collar of my dress
to touch the gold chain I had taken from Chris's neck that
morning . . . too late . . . much, much too late.

38

Mrs. Matthews and the Lindquists were waiting in the
minister's office behind the church. We met there, looking
somber, all of us dressed up, and each one engrossed in his
or her own thoughts. We spoke to the minister for a few
moments, and then he left and we heard the music start,
softly, in the background. I had forgotten all about talking
to the organist, and I didn't recognize what he was playing. It just sounded very sweet and sad. We walked into

the church then, and I slipped into the first pew with
Chris's family, Peg and Tom Bardi sat just behind us, and
I looked around to see Peg, just once more. I reached
back and she squeezed my hand, and then I noticed that
there must have been seventy or eighty people scattered
through the church. Not a great many, I guess, nothing
like the huge pompous funeral we had had for my grandmother, but a lot of people for Chris, for a man who really
didn't see many people. A girl in a black dress and veil
caught my eye, over to the left, and I looked again, knowing who I'd see. It was Marilyn. Our eyes met and held, no
real kinship, no bond as there was with Chris's family. But
we understood each other better than Chris's family would
have understood either of us. Both of us stood alone now.
Chris had moved on. And I turned back to look at the
minister.

Chris lay in his casket, the flowers around it, front and
center.

"Dearly beloved . . . that he may rest in peace. Amen,"
and we stood in silent prayer, as the organ played something that sounded like Bach, while I wished I had remembered to ask for Ravel. The pallbearers from Hobson's
wheeled the casket down the aisle, and Mrs. Matthews
stepped out on Don's arm and walked behind it, slowly,
looking still smaller than she had seemed before. Jane followed, and I fell into step behind her, wondering if Marilyn was going to follow me. I felt everyone watching us as
we walked out, following us with their eyes, and heard a
few sniffs, and a couple of loud sobs. They could do that;
we couldn't. I knew Marilyn wasn't sobbing. It's always
the people who knew the "deceased" the least who can cry
like that.

Outside, we climbed into Hobson's long maroon limousine, behind the hearse. I saw Peg get into Tom Bardi's
car, and the procession began, down Sacramento to
Gough, and then out on the highway to Daly City, which
specializes in used car lots and cemeteries.

Jane and Don talked on the way out; Mrs. Matthews
and I said nothing. We sat next to each other, she looking

down, while I looked out the window, realizing that this was the same strip of road we'd traveled coming in from the airport a week ago, when Sam and I had come in from New York. A borrowed Volkswagen bus, and a maroon limousine. A thousand worlds apart, and only one short week.

At the cemetery, the minister reappeared, and we stepped forward toward the grave site, the four of us, and Peg and Tom, and five people I didn't know . . . and Marilyn. At first, I hadn't seen Marilyn. She stood a little apart, looking beautiful and tragic, the veil putting a soft gray cloud over her face, making her eyes look even larger than they were, the black dress beautifully cut. She had a wonderful grace about her, a certain style I guess. There was pride too in the way she stood. Dignity. She stood so alone, and yet she had come there for Chris, in spite of us. She looked straight at me, not showing any sign of emotion, but there. With Chris. Like us. I admired her for coming, and for the way she stood there. I guess, in her shoes, I would have done the same, but I would have looked embarrassed, or nervous. There was none of that about Marilyn.

The minister said the Lord's Prayer while we bowed our heads. And then silence. I jumped as his voice boomed out, "Christopher Caldwell Matthews, we commit you to the earth, and into the hands of God," and I added silently, "Vaya con Dios."

We returned to our various cars, and as we drove away I looked back and saw Marilyn, still standing there, straight and proud and alone, a widow, in a black veil.

39

The Lindquists left San Francisco right after the funeral, taking Mrs. Matthews with them. She was going to stay in Fresno for a while. I promised to call when the baby was born, and then they were gone. When they dropped me off at home. I saw Tom Bardi's car out front. Inside, he, Peg, and Sam were talking, and they stopped when I came in.

"Hi, Mommy. Where's Uncle Crits?" It was a sad wail, and those two big eyes looked up at me, wanting an answer this time. Now or never. I took a deep breath.

"Sam, let's sit down for a minute."

"Has he gone away like my real Daddy?"

"No. He hasn't." I didn't want her to think that life was a series of men who went away, and came back to visit once in a while. Maybe it was, but not Chris, not this time. "Sam, do you remember when Grandma Jean went to Heaven?"

"You mean Daddy's Mommy?"

"Yes," and I saw Peg and Tom get up quietly and leave, and go into the kitchen, closing the door soundlessly behind them. I thought Peg was crying, but I wasn't sure. I was looking at Sam. I had to see this child, really see her, and tell her something that she could carry with her always, something of Chris.

"Well, darling . . . sometimes God loves people, specially much, and he feels they have done everything they had to do, and then he takes them up to Heaven with Him."

"Does he love everybody that much?"

"Yes, he loves everybody, but he lets some people stay

here for a very long time. And other people, he takes up with him a little sooner."

"Mommy . . . does he love you that much?" Her chin was beginning to quiver.

"Sam darling, nothing is going to happen to me." I could see where her reasoning was leading. "But he needed Uncle Chris to help with some things now. So now, Uncle Chris is in Heaven, with God, and Grandma Jean."

"Will he ever come back to visit us?"

"Not the way you mean, Sam. But every time you think of Uncle Chris, that'll be like a visit. When you think of Uncle Chris, he'll always be with you. We can talk about him, and think about him, and go right on loving him. That's what forever means."

"But I want him with us here." That look. . . . Oh God . . . that look. . . .

"So do I, but this is how God wants it. We're going to miss him very much, but we have each other. And I love you very, very much." She threw herself into my arms, and we were both crying. "Sam, please don't be sad. Uncle Chris wouldn't want you to be sad. He isn't sad, and he doesn't hurt, and he still loves us. . . ." We sat there rocking back and forth, her tears mingling with mine, and her tiny fingers squeezing the back of my neck, holding on for dear life. We rocked and rocked, and when she stopped, I looked down and saw that she had fallen asleep. My tiny wild Indian girl who had put three worms into the hands of Chris Matthews last week, who would have to live with the fact that he was gone. I sat looking at her in the darkening room, and lay her against the cushions on the couch, her face still streaked with tears.

I stood up and went to look down at the garden, took another deep breath, and went to find Tom and Peg. When I found them, they were still sitting in the kitchen, and looking a little red-eyed. They looked up at me, embarrassed, and Peg said, "How about a drink?"

"I don't think it would help."

"Where is she?"

"Asleep on the couch. I'm not going to wake her up for

dinner. It's been a rough couple of days for her too. I hope she sleeps through."

"Want me to carry her up to bed?"

"Thanks, Tom, that's a good idea. I think I'll go to bed too. I've had it." I could hardly get up the stairs. Tom was walking ahead with Sam in his arms, hanging limp like a rag doll. And Peg walked behind me. I almost wanted to ask her to push, the top of the stairs looked too far away.

I lay back on my bed, still wearing the gray dress, and Peg came in to help me get undressed. "I just can't, Peg."

"I know. Just take off the dress. You just lie there for a while."

I took off the new gray dress and lay down while she closed the shades and turned off the lights, and I was asleep as suddenly and as soundly as Sam had been.

I was being stabbed, someone was trying to murder me, or pummel me, they were tearing at my back, and slashing open my stomach, ripping at every muscle. . . . My God, help me, somebody help me, please. . . . I fought to wake up to get rid of the pain, to escape from the bad dream. I woke up limp, and exhausted, and turned to look at the clock next to the bed. I lifted my head to see, and the same pain seized me again, tearing through my back and reaching across my belly like hands tearing through my guts. It made me cry out, and Peg came in as I was trying to catch my breath, while the pain went away again.

"Gill? Something wrong? I heard you. . . . Christ, you look awful."

"I don't feel so great." I tried to sit up and the pain ripped through me again, making me clutch at the sheet and squirm so as not to cry out.

"Don't move. I'll call the doctor. What's his name?"

"Morse. Number's on the pad in the kitchen. . . . Tell him . . . I think I'm in labor. . . . Tell him . . . ," and another pain tore through me. I lay in bed fighting the panic and trying to ride with the pain, waiting for Peg to come back.

"He said to bring you to the hospital right away. Can you walk to the car?"

I tried to stand up but couldn't even sit up, and as I tried to roll over toward the side of the bed we saw that there was blood where I had been lying.

"Oh my God . . . Oh Jesus, Peg. . . ."

"Now just take it easy, Gill. I called Tom, he's coming to stay with Sam. He can carry you down to the car."

I lay back, hurting too much to talk anymore. Peg blurred and faded away and came back again, and the pain kept hitting at me, and grabbing me and lifting me up and throwing me against what felt like sharp rocks. I wanted to hold Peg's hand but couldn't lie still enough. And then I saw Tom Bardi in the doorway. He was standing over me after that, and soon I was lifted out of bed, with the blanket, and set down again in Chris's car. I saw Tom and Peg exchange looks, and I think I must have fainted then because the next time I opened my eyes there were a thousand lights above me, a lot of noise, and people, and metallic sounds, and I felt woozy, as though I were floating just under the lights, and above the people, suspended between two worlds. I floated for a while and then . . . oh God . . . oh my God . . . they're tearing me apart . . . they're killing me . . . oh God . . . Chris . . . Peg . . . please stop them . . . I can't stand it, I can't, I can't . . . I can't . . . and everything went black.

I woke up in a strange room, feeling as though I were going to vomit. I looked over and saw Peg, and then it all faded again. It kept coming and going. I'd wake up and see Peg, and then she'd go away again. It kept coming and going. Somewhere in another world there was someone in a bed, with transfusions and tubes and all sorts of things happening to her. I could see it clearly, but I didn't know who she was. I wondered, but not enough to ask. I was too tired . . . too tired. . . .

Oh Jesus, do my guts hurt. "Peg? . . . what happened?" And I turned toward her to talk to her . . . my stomach . . .

it's flat . . . the baby . . . "Peg . . . Peg . . . the baby?" But I already knew. I knew what had happened. The baby was dead.

"Lie back, Gillian, you've been out of it for a long time."

"I don't care." Sobs shook me and made everything hurt worse.

After a while I asked what time it was. "Two o'clock."

"In the afternoon? . . . Jesus. . . ."

"Yeah, Gill . . . and . . . it's Tuesday. . . ."

"Tuesday? . . . My God!"

Nurses came and went, Peg came and went, and time passed. There was nothing left to rush for, or to think about. Sam was at home with Peg, and Mrs. Jaeger, and Chris and the baby were gone. Nothing mattered anymore. Nothing and no one. Not Chris, not the baby, not Sam, not me. Not anything.

Peg must have made her phone calls again, because there were flowers from Hilary again, and Gordon, and "John Templeton and the Staff." It looked like an instant replay of the funeral. Only this time, I wasn't touched. I just didn't give a damn anymore.

I also discovered that it's hospital practice to put a woman who has just lost a baby in the maternity wing along with everyone else. It's one of the most psychologically inhuman facts of modern medicine, but there it is. And there you are, hearing the babies being rolled down the hall, listening to them cry. And wishing you were dead.

I was informed of how much the baby had weighed, how long he had been, what his blood type was, and how long he had lived. Seven hours and twenty-three minutes. And I'd never even gotten to see him. It was a boy.

By the end of the week I was feeling stronger and they decided to let me go home on Sunday. I had to get back anyway. Peg had to leave.

"I'm staying another week."

"No you're not. You've been out here long enough, taking care of me and my recurring disasters."

"Stop being dramatic. I'm staying."

"Look, Peg, I'll call an agency and get another mother's helper. I'm supposed to sit on my ass for three weeks. You don't expect to stay out for that long, do you?" Peg wavered then, and we agreed to compromise. She'd stay until the following Wednesday.

On Sunday, I went home. I was evicted along with a half dozen starry-eyed girls holding their babies wrapped in pastel-colored blankets. Peg picked me up with the car, and I grabbed my little overnight case from the nurse, got into the car, and all I could say was, "Come on, Peg, let's get the hell out of here." She stepped on the gas and we were off, toward Sacramento Street.

At home, everything was in perfect order. The superwoman efficiency of Peg Richards was visible everywhere. Sam was waiting for me at the door with a little bunch of flowers she'd picked in the garden. And it was so good to be back with her. I felt guilty because I had given her so little thought while I was in the hospital. I had almost stopped caring about her too. But there she was, sweet Sam.

Peg shooed me upstairs, put me to bed, brought me a cup of tea, and I felt like a queen. A sick queen, but nevertheless, *a queen*. There was absolutely nothing for me to do except lie there and be waited on.

I was still feeling very weak, and it was nice having Peg to run interference for me. The phone rang twice after I got home. Once it was Mrs. Matthews, and the second time it was Gordon. Peg looked over at me both times, and I shook my head. Not yet. Everyone knew. That was good enough. I had nothing left to add. Mrs. Matthews would only tell me how sorry she was, and I was sorry enough on my own, and also felt badly to have added to her grief. Gordon would only want to come out, or for me to go back to New York, and I didn't want to hear about it. I had chosen blue jeans and daisies . . . and I still wanted them. I didn't want to hear about New York, or the magazine, or anything else. It was all behind me, however things had turned out.

I looked through my mail and saw that Gordon had sent the picture of the three of us standing in front of the Rolls. I looked at it once and tossed it on the table next to my bed while Peg looked on. "That was such a long time ago, Peg." She nodded and put the picture back in the envelope.

The only good thing the hospital had done for me was that it had put a little more time between me and the brutal realities that had hit me so suddenly. For a while, I didn't have to wander around the house, touching things, looking at things, being reminded. Not right away. And now I had to rest, and there would be more time.

The next few days slid by, and on Wednesday Peg left with hugs and good-byes and the kind of thanks you can't even begin to say, and promises to call and write. She even said she'd come out for a week in the spring. Tom Bardi took her to the airport, and I began to wonder if there was more to that than just helping me. Their week and a half together had created the same kind of bond that happens on sea voyages. They had been isolated from their own worlds, and thrown together constantly, not on a pleasure trip, but by a series of disasters, and they had formed a circle around me, becoming enmeshed in it themselves. Maybe like after a sea voyage they would find nothing in common when they met again, if they met again. Peg didn't say anything before she left, so I was left to wonder.

Tom was of Chris's world, very much like him in his directness and no bullshit ways, yet he was simpler than Chris, and he seemed kinder; he didn't have Chris's ruthless honesty. Or his sparkle either, for that matter. But I suspected that he might have been easier to live with because of it. He was also less adept with words. And I noticed before Peg left that he looked at her with a kind of awe. It was something for me to think about anyway.

I had a mother's helper again by then. She was sleeping in Sam's room, and the entire routine rolled along, while I got my strength back, and some of the emotional pain began to dim. As I had told Sam, Chris was always with us. We talked about him, the memory of his face lit up my days, and the sound of his voice filled my dreams. I found myself sleeping most of the time, too much of the time. It was an easy escape, and in sleep there was always Chris. He was always waiting for me to fall asleep, ready to stretch out a hand and pull me to his side, away from the empty house . . . and the truth.

40

In March, I learned in a letter from John Templeton that Julie Weintraub had been in a coma for almost three weeks, and had then died quietly, never regaining consciousness. It was merciful, as her last days of lucidity had been filled with excruciating pain. To me, that seemed to close a whole volume of my life. Chris, the baby, Julie. All gone. My life was beginning to fill with ghosts. I was back on my feet by then, and spending a lot of time around the house, painting a little, being with Samantha, and letting time move on, without actually filling it. There seemed to be nothing to fill it with. I had gained back some of the weight I had lost, and was looking healthy from the long walks I took with Sam.

Tom Bardi dropped by a lot, brought small presents for Sam, and had dinner with us occasionally. He hadn't a great deal to say, but he was a nice presence, and Sam and I enjoyed him. He almost never mentioned Peg, but whenever I did he seemed to shoot up straight in his chair and listen to hear everything I said. It was sweet to watch, and I wondered if Peg knew about it or if they both did, and I was just the last one to know for certain.

One day, I couldn't resist. "Do you ever hear from Peg, Tom?"

"No," and he blushed.

"Why don't you call her sometime?"

"Call her?" He looked so shocked that I dropped the subject. They were grownups; Peg was one of the most straightforward people I'd ever known, and Tom looked like he could take care of himself, so I decided to shut my big mouth and mind my own business.

I had heard from Gordon twice before he left for France, empassioned pleas begging me to think of myself, and of him, and join him. But I didn't want to leave San Francisco. Or Chris.

I still hadn't done anything about clearing out Chris's things, and when I got too lonely I'd open his closet and look at the boots, and the jeans and sweaters, and his smell would put its arms around me and Chris would only be out for a little while. His studio remained untouched. I had been up there once to look for some papers, but not again. Everyone in the house knew that it was off limits. It was becoming a kind of shrine.

I wrote to Peg regularly and told her what we were doing, and she answered sporadically. I knew that she was getting tired of her job, and once she mentioned that she might come out. But she never brought it up again. She knew that my doors were always open to her, and I hoped she would come.

She began to prod me in her letters: ". . . You have to see some men. . . . You should get a job. . . . You should take a trip. . . ." She never suggested going back to New York though. She knew better.

Sam's school year ended at the very end of May, and I sat with her at breakfast one morning, thinking that it had been five months since Chris had died. In a way, it seemed as though Sam and I had lived that way forever, and in another way, it seemed as though he had walked through the

room that morning. I was keeping it that way, keeping
Chris alive, to keep myself alive, to hang on.

It was lonely, but not the kind of lonely that I had suffered through in New York when I'd gone back. That had
been a fierce, biting, rolling kind of thing; it was full of
worry and alternatives, and constant frustration, though I
may not have seen it that way at the time. It was a time
full of anger. But the spring after Chris's death had no
anger to it, nothing in common with those days, except for
the fact that I was alone. There was an irrevocability to it,
a quiet acceptance. My ship lay at anchor and I had nowhere to go. There was nowhere I wanted to go, except
where I was. I was painting more, reading a lot, and becoming increasingly introspective. It was like becoming a
nun. It was also a little bit like a dark tunnel; I was pass-
ing through it, and when I got to the end of it . . . if I got
to the end of it . . . then I'd see.

Sam was due to visit her father in June, and I was
thinking of going up to the mountains around Lake
Tahoe, just to get away a little, but I hesitated. I was
happy at home, with Chris's things all around me. Happy
sleeping in his bed, happy in his sweaters and workshirts. I
had finally married Chris. But I had married a dead man,
and was drifting along with him. I was almost as dead as
he.

"Sam, the doorbell. Be a big girl and answer it for me.
I'm upstairs, but ask who it is first," and then Tom Bardi
was racing up the stairs, two at a time, and he burst into
the room.

"Peg is coming!"

"When?"

"Tomorrow." He was grinning from ear to ear.

"She is? Are you sure? How do you know?" It seemed
funny that I wouldn't have heard anything about it.

"She just called me," and he looked irritated with me
for doubting it. As though I could make it not true by my
questions.

I hadn't heard anything, other than the vague hint in her last letter. That's funny.

"She's coming in tomorrow morning. Early. I'm going to pick her up." I was tempted to ask if I could go too. After all I had known Peg all my life, and here was a stranger going out to get her. But I didn't say anything. Maybe Peg would like it better this way. She had called him, not me.

The phone rang then, and it was Peg.

"I'm coming out tomorrow."

"I know."

"Oh."

"Tom's standing right here."

"Say hi for me. Can I stay with you again?" And all my suspicions went down the drain. Or almost.

"Sure. I'd love it. How long do you think you'll be here?"

"Week, maybe two, maybe three. I'll see. I've got three, but really should go see Mother on the way back."

"Great. Tom said he'd pick you up. Why don't you come over afterward? Or . . . just see how it goes. See you tomorrow. Peg, I can't wait!" We said good-bye and hung up.

"Did she want to talk to me?"

"She had to run. She'll be here tomorrow, Tom." He looked like a little boy, that same look Chris had had, the same look Samantha got.

Then Tom clattered back down the stairs and vanished, and the next time I saw him he was at my front door, standing behind Peg, and he looked as though he had found the pot of gold at the end of the rainbow. Peg threw herself into my arms, and we laughed and squealed and hugged, and Sam got into the act. It was a genuine homecoming.

"Welcome back. We've missed you."

"Well, I see the place hasn't changed. Boy, it's nice to be back." Tom took her things up to Sam's room and reappeared. We had lunch together, and sat around for a while, and then they went out for a walk and said they'd go to a movie. I went to bed early and didn't hear Peg, come in.

Next morning she came down to breakfast, and she had that serious look on her face that meant she was going "to talk to me." Mother Peg. Lecture time. I braced myself with a cup of coffee and a grin. I really had missed Peg.

"Gillian." She sounded very firm.

"Yes, Peg? Or should I call you 'Margaret?' You sound like a Margaret this morning," but she didn't smile back.

"Where's Sam?"

"Out with some friends. Why?"

"Because I want to talk to you, and I don't want Sam to hear this. Gill, when I said that the place looked the same yesterday, I didn't know how true that was. Jesus, Gill, his stuff is still all over the place, his papers, his clothes, his shirts, his toothbrush. What the fuck are you trying to do to yourself? You're twenty-nine years old. He's dead. You're not. I bet you haven't even touched his studio. Have you? Well, have you?" Christ, she had hit low. It was true, but how could she understand? How could she begin to understand? Peg had a warm heart and a full life of her own making, but she'd never been married, never had children, never lost the man she loved, or his child. She couldn't understand.

"Peg, you don't understand."

"I do understand. I understand much better than you think, much better than you do even. I see it better than you do. And Tom says it too. He says you wear his clothes, talk about him as though he were still here. You don't do anything, you don't go out. Jesus, Gill, it's goddam creepy."

"It is not creepy. It's how I want to live. And you make it sound as though I go around in drag in his clothes, goddammit. Get off my fucking back, will you?" I was getting mad because I didn't like the truth of what she was saying. She had no right.

"I have no right to talk to you like this . . . except I do. Because I love you, Gill. I can't stand to see you doing this to yourself. You've done some crazy things and I've always stood by you. You came back to New York, to have his baby, and I didn't say anything because I thought maybe you were right. I wouldn't have done it, but I could at least understand it. But this . . . this is different, this is sick. Please see that, oh please, Gill, see what you're doing to yourself . . . and to Sam. What the hell do you think this is doing to her?" And again I knew it was true, and I wound up to fight back, without looking up at Peg.

When at last I did look up, I saw that she was crying. For me, and for Samantha, and maybe even for Chris.

When I saw her crying, tears welled in my own eyes, and I laid my head down on the table, and cried, all those months of peace and adjustment, blown to hell in ten minutes. Because I had never adjusted. I had known peace because I had lived in a dream, and had never come face to face with the truth. Maybe I could have faced losing Chris if I had had the baby, but when I lost the baby there was nothing left. Nothing real. So I created my own dream world, and hung on to Chris. In those ten minutes the whole shell I had built around myself cracked wide open, and I sat there naked and raw, and bleeding, exposed to all the things I had hidden from in all those months, exposed to the truth. Chris was dead.

Peg let me sit there and cry it out, moving quietly around the kitchen. Just once she put her hand on my shoulder and said, "I'm sorry, Gill," and I managed to choke out, "Don't be." Because she was right, and she was right to say it. I had been wrong. Terribly, terribly wrong, and I had been doing something awful to Samantha in the bargain.

"Peg, will you help me?"
"How, baby?"
"Help me go through his stuff."
She nodded. "When?"
"Now."
"Now?"

"Now. If I don't do it now, maybe I'll never do it. Maybe then I'd just live forever in this spider web I've spun for myself."

"Okay. Let's go," and for hours we sat there and sorted and made piles and divided up. It was just as though we had done it the day after the funeral; it wouldn't have made any difference. The pain was all there. Intact.

I made a small pile for Mrs. Matthews of things I thought she'd want to have. And another small pile for Jane. And I kept a few things out for myself, things I wasn't ready to give up, things that were Chris. But this time I put them in a box. I'd have them; I didn't have to hold them and smell them every night. I'd just know they were there.

The rest of the stuff we put in big piles in the downstairs closet, ready to go to Goodwill.

At the end of the day I thought Sam might be coming home, so we stopped. There was nothing left to do on the first two floors anyway. We'd cleaned it out.

"Tomorrow, the studio."

"You want Tom to help?"

"Yes."

The next day the three of us went through the place, dividing and sorting. I gave a lot of things to Tom; they were the tools of his trade and he could use them. We worked like demons through the day, and at 6:07 p.m. the studio was no more. The earthly goods of Christopher Caldwell Matthews had been divided up and disposed of. End of an era.

41

After Peg's second week with me I was beginning to wonder. She made no mention of leaving, and I didn't want to bring it up and make her think I was pushing her out. She was spending a lot of time with Tom, and I wasn't seeing too much of her, but she looked happy, and San Francisco seemed to agree with her.

Sam and I were enjoying our last days together before she went off to be with her father for a month. And I was thinking about getting a job. As usual, Peg's visit had had an effect.

I was mulling over the want ads one morning when Peg came in and stood in the doorway with that "I've got to talk to you" look again.

"Come on, stop looking so official. Come and sit down. And don't give me hell about anything. I've been a good girl. I'm even looking at the want ads in the paper."

"Christ . . . do I look like that?" and she laughed.

"Yes you do. What's up?"

"Well . . . Tom and I are getting married," and she sat there, looking as though she were holding her breath.

"Peg! . . . Wow!" I jumped up and hugged her. "When?"

"Tomorrow."

"Do you have a license?" The same words I had asked Chris not so very long ago.

"Yes."

"Well, for chrissake! Couldn't you have said something?"

"I didn't know. Honest, Gill, I wasn't sure. I had this feeling after I went back to New York, but I never heard from Tom and I didn't know if he felt it too . . . and . . . oh shit."

"Jesus, Peg, I can't believe it. Fairy tales do exist . . . for some people," and we both looked away, both of us knowing that her dream had started with my nightmare.

Tom rang the doorbell then and I kissed him and said, "Congratulations!" and he blushed furiously.

"She told you?"

"Told me what?" and he blushed even more, while Peg and I burst into whoops.

"She's putting you on, love. I told her." He looked relieved.

Thomas Hugo Bardi and Margaret Allison Richards were married the next day, at City Hall, along with what looked like all the same funny old people who had been there the day Chris and I had gone down for our license, which I still have.

Samantha and I stood by to watch the whole thing happen, along with a friend of Tom's, and we all went out to lunch in Sausalito after that.

After lunch, Tom picked up Peg's things at my house and they went off to his place for their honeymoon. After they left, I couldn't help thinking what a far cry it was from the little girl dreams we had all had in school. Peg had always sworn she'd elope with a professional cowboy or something of the sort. But none of our dreams had looked very much like this. Better this way, I thought. She has a better chance. They're going to be okay. I wondered if Peg's mother knew yet. The formidable Mrs. Richards who was as unlike Peg as mustard is to caviar. She was going to have a few things to say.

By noon the next day they were back at my place for lunch, chatting with Sam, sitting at my kitchen table as though they had been married for the last seven years.

"What are you going to do about your stuff in New York?"

"Oh one of the girls at the office said she'd pack it up and send it. I don't really have a whole lot. And she can keep some of it, she's taking over my apartment," which reminded me that the lease on Chris's house was up next month, and I had to sign the renewal paper. "They were really nice at the office though. They said they figured that something like this would come up sooner or later. And they offered me a job in the Oakland buying office as a wedding present."

"You're going to commute?"

"For that price, you better believe it!"

"What'd your mother say? I forgot to ask you the other day."

"Nothing I'd care to repeat, but she'll get over it."

We sat around talking about nothing much for a while, and I thought about how nice it was to see them together. But it made me miss Chris again. It was all so closely linked. It was painful to see them, though I would never have admitted it to Peg. But I think she knew.

"Gillian?"

"Yes?"

"Why don't you go on a trip or something? And you know, I was thinking, it might do you good to move into a smaller place."

"Hey, now wait a minute, Peg. Cool it. I cleaned out my house, and followed all your advice, but don't let it go to your head. It stops there. You just cool it. Why don't you start picking on Tom, henpeck him a little, show him how a wife behaves."

"Now don't go getting all huffy. I mean it. At least you could go on a trip. You don't have a job yet, and Sam will be gone. Why don't you go to Hawaii, or something?"

"Because I don't like Hawaii. Richard and I went there before Sam was born and it rained the whole goddam time."

"Well, go someplace else then."

"I'll think about it," but I really didn't mean it. Cleaning out the house was one thing, leaving it was another.

Tom and Peg got up to leave, and they said they'd be back sometime tomorrow or the next day.

"Listen, you guys, you're on your honeymoon. You don't have to baby-sit with me."

"No. We just like the coffee," that from Tom, who patted my shoulder again as they left. I think they felt they had to take care of me. It was a nice thing to do. Maybe they felt they owed me a debt for bringing them together. Whatever it was, it was nice to have them around, they were nice to watch, but they kept giving me this lonely feeling as I'd watch them leave or look at each other in a funny way or hold hands when they didn't think I was looking. Chris had been gone a long time.

42

I had had a letter from Gordon telling me how well things were going for him and how much he liked Eze. He was thinking of having a show in Paris in the late fall, if all went well, and if his work kept up at the pace he was keeping. He was settled, had rented a tiny house with an incredible view, and a skylight, and he was learning to play boule.

He suggested that I might like to come and visit for a few days if I was in Europe for the summer, or I might want to spend a month with him, "if that appeals," but I gathered from the tone of the invitation that he knew I wouldn't accept. I hadn't seen him in months, and it might as well have been years. I felt so much older, and different. Not wiser, just a little more tired, and yes, different.

I was in the midst of packing Sam's things for her visit with Richard, and was thinking that it was going to be nice to have Tom and Peg around. It wouldn't be quite so lonely. The house would be so empty without Sam, but it was better than having her commute on weekends or getting confused by constant visits had her father lived nearby. I wondered if she'd grow up with the same sense of unfamiliarity with her father that I had had with mine. Maybe that's the price you pay. Or just the price some fathers pay.

The phone was ringing . . . probably Peg.

"Hello?"

"Allo? Allo? Oui? . . . Allo?"

"Yes, I'm here. . . . Hello". Terrible connection; it sounded like little gnomes grinding rocks in a coal mine.

"Madame Foe-ress-taire, s'il vous plait. Nous avons un appel de la part de Monsieur Ahrte," and the aahhrte rolled in the operator's throat, reminding me of French teachers in school.

"C'est elle-même." This is she.

"Gillian?"

"Yes. Gordon, what the hell are you doing calling me all this distance? You must be getting rich over there."

"I'm sitting in front of the most exquisite sunset I've ever seen. I had to call you. I want you to come over."

"For a sunset? I think I might miss it. You're too much. It's a long way off, Gordon. I want to stay here for a while."

"Why don't you come over? And bring Sam. It would be marvelous for her."

"Her father is picking her up in two days. She's all set for the summer, or one month at least. So I'm going to stay home and keep house."

"For whom?"

"Me."

"Gillian, please. Don't answer me now, think about it, please."

"All right, I'll think about it."

"No you won't, I can tell." He was right.

"Really, I will. I'll write and let you know what I decide." I'll write and tell you no.

"No. If you write, that means you're not coming. I'll

call you in a few days. There's a flight out of Los Angeles that goes direct to Nice. I could pick you up there."

"Christ, I haven't been there since I was a kid."

"Well, it's time you came back . . . please." There was that pleading tone in his voice again.

"Well, I'll think it over. How's everything else?"

"Wonderful. I'm happy here. You were right." At least I had been right for someone. But that wasn't fair. It wasn't anyone's fault that Chris had fallen off a crane.

"How's Greg?"

"He was over here during spring vacation. Loved it, said he's coming back in July," and there was something new in Gordon's voice. I could hear it in spite of the little gnomes hacking away at our transatlantic connection.

"Look, this is costing you a fortune. I'll talk to you soon."

"Think about it, Gill. . . . I need you."

"Good-bye."

"Bye . . . I'll call you at the end of the week."

. . . I need you. . . . I need you. . . . How long had it been since a man had said that to me? Months? Longer? Had Chris ever really needed me, or just wanted me? And Gordon hadn't needed me before either. Not until the very end. How long since a man had needed me? Ever? . . . I need you. . . .

I called Peg and told her, and her reaction was instantaneous. "Go!" It was a command. But I had known she would say that. Why did I call her? To hear her tell me that? To hear her say "Go!"?

"Don't be an ass. All I need is to go to the south of France and get all messed up with Gordon."

"Messed up? What's messed up? He was good enough for you before. Do you have something better I don't know about? Shit, Gillian, I'd jump at the chance."

"Don't let Tom hear you say that."

"All right, all right, but if you don't go . . . baby, you're out of your mind," and we hung up, equally irritated with each other. I was annoyed with Peg, and with myself for calling her. Now, I'd have to listen to her push and harp for the next few days, and then bitch at me all summer about not going.

Sam left with Richard and they flew to London. Before he left, he looked at me and I think he felt sorry for me. "I'm sorry this has happened to you, Gill," and he only knew the half of it.

"Thanks. So am I. But we're doing fine. Sam likes San Francisco." Anything to get off the subject.

"You never go to Europe anymore. Why don't you come over this summer, to pick up Sam? It would give you a chance to roam around again."

"And recapture my youth?"

"I didn't say that."

"No, but you thought it. I'll see." Everyone was pushing Europe this season.

I told Sam I'd call her, and she looked tearful as they left. I remembered that same feeling from when I was a child, and it tore at my heart as they drove away while I stood on the steps waving.

I sat in the house, listening to the emptiness, looking at the toys she'd left in the living room, wondering how people survive without children.

The phone rang again. I hoped it was Peg. It would be nice to have them over to put some life and voices back in the place.

"Allo?" Oh Christ. Gordon again. And I hadn't really given it any thought. Not yet. I needed time. Please, some time. Not yet . . . always not yet.

"Gillian? What's the word? But before you tell me, I want you to know that I'll understand if you don't come. I want you here, but I understand. I have no right. . . ."

"I'm coming," and I almost fell off my seat I was so surprised at myself.

"You are?" I wasn't the only one who was surprised.

"Yes. I just made up my mind. This minute, in fact." I was still stunned.

"When are you coming?"

"I don't know. I really hadn't thought about it till this second. When's the next plane over?"

"Tomorrow."

"Too soon."

"All right. There's another one a week from tomorrow. That ought to give you time to get yourself together. When's Sam leaving?"

"She just left, about eight minutes ago."

"All right, I'll meet you in Nice, a week from tomorrow. I'll be at the airport. And Gillian . . . darling . . . thank you. You'll love it here, you really will. . . . Thank you."

I murmured something in response and we hung up. What the hell had I done? I had given myself a vacation, nothing more. Oh, yes, much more. I had held out a hand and allowed myself to be needed again, because I needed Gordon too. It was a beautiful feeling. Chris . . . Chris . . . darling, I'm sorry . . . but as I walked upstairs I remembered Chris. And Marilyn. The real Chris. He'd understand. He really would have.

"Peg? I'm going. I just talked to Gordon. I'm leaving a week from tomorrow."

"Hallelujah! We'll be right over." And they were, with a bottle of Spanish wine, which we finished in an hour, amidst great giggles and back pounding. They were "proud" of me. Too proud. I felt as though I had betrayed Chris, and in a quiet moment I went out to the kitchen to get more ice. And get away from them.

Tom was right behind me and he was looking down at me as I fiddled with the ice tray. I was trying not to cry, and not to look back at him, when he grabbed my arm and pulled me out of my hiding place in the refrigerator.

"Gillian. He would have wanted it. He wouldn't have liked you like this."

"I know. But I can't help it. I have to . . . I had to."

"I know that. But now you have to stop. Love him, Gillian, remember him, remember what he was. But don't turn him into a ghost. He wasn't that kind of man. And you're not that kind of woman. Hang on to him. We all will. And maybe you'll never love anybody as much as you loved him, but I'll bet you never loved him alive as much as you love him dead." It was true, it was true. I had had doubts and bad moments. But I did love him, and I looked up at Tom with tears running down my cheeks again, and feeling defiant. "I did love him."

"I know you did. But be brave, Gill. Don't settle for halfway. You never have before and he never did," and I hung onto Tom and cried. It was almost over . . . don't settle for halfway . . . step out, walk ahead, move on, reach out . . . to love again . . . be brave enough . . . to go to Eze . . . brave enough for Gordon. Brave enough for Chris.

When we walked out of the kitchen, Peg looked up at us and said, "Kissing in the kitchen, huh? Listen, Gill, I hate to ask you this, but . . . can we borrow the house while you're gone? We have to give up Tom's place. It's too small and it's driving me nuts. The lease is up this month and we should be able to find something else pretty soon."

"Sure! You don't even have to ask. You can move in tomorrow."

"Well, I think we can wait a week." It was a nice feeling to know that there would be people living in the house while I was gone. Living people. Happy people. Our friends in Chris's house.

A week later, Tom and Peg drove me down to Los Angeles. I had insisted that I could fly down and just change planes, but they wanted to go down and see Tom's parents, and they wanted to see me off.

"How do I know you won't sit in Disneyland all summer and tell us you've been to France?"

"Don't you trust me?"

"No," and she looked as though she might mean it. It was a nice trip down; we took turns driving, and the trip went quickly.

"Pan American Flight 115, departing from Gate 43 . . . final call for all passengers departing to Nice, France, on Pan American Flight. . . ."

"That's it."

"Yeah." We stood around looking nervous, not knowing what to say. That same feeling we had had at Hobson's. God, how I hate good-byes.

"Peg, take care . . . I'll write . . . Tom . . . ," and he squeezed me in a big bear hug and passed me on to Peg who hugged me too and looked shaken.

"Now get on that goddam plane before I fall apart, willyouforchrissake." That was the old Peg.

"Good-bye, you two."

Tom gave me one of his boy-man grins. "We'll take good care of the house. And let us know when you're coming back so we can sweep up the dirt." I nodded, and they waved, and I walked through the gate to Flight 115. I looked back and they were still there, watching, and holding hands.

43

It wasn't quite tourist season yet, so the flight was less than half full. It was a long flight, and most people prefer to break it up by stopping in New York. Most of the people looked European, and I sat alone, with three seats to myself, across the aisle from a man who was also traveling alone and who looked definitely American. He looked over at me a few times, and I thought he might try to start a conversation so I looked away.

I slept for most of the trip, and looked down at the clouds, thinking about Peg and how far we'd come together. Tom too. He had become one hell of a good friend, and it seemed fitting that he and Peg should end up together. Who would have believed all this a year ago? Who would believe anything the year before it happens?

"Excuse me, but aren't you Lillian Forrest? I think I met you in New York." It was the man from across the aisle. I was tempted to say, "No, the name's Jane Jones."

"Gillian Forrester. You were close," and I looked away again, hoping he'd be satisfied with having established who I was. I didn't ask him to reciprocate the information, for fear it would lead him into further conversation.

"You won't believe this, but I met you at a party you gave, oh way back in October it must have been, last year. In New York. Great party!"

"Thanks."

"I was working for a bank in New York, and this chick says, 'I've been invited to the greatest party, I mean this girl really knows how to give them.' And she was right. Great party! Would you believe, after that she got married, and I got transferred to Los Angeles, and my sister had twins? I mean, all that since last fall," and he looked at me, as though I really shouldn't believe it.

"Thanks, about the party, I mean. Sounds like you've had a busy year," and I cringed, thinking I had encouraged him to expound further.

"Yeah. Sometimes I just sit back and think, 'whoda believed it a year ago, here I am in Los Angeles.' I mean it's a whole new world. A whole new life."

"Mmm . . . I know what you mean. Who would believe?" and I turned away again, to look out the window, down at the clouds.

"You know something, Lillian, you look different. I almost didn't recognize you, except I never forget a face." He stared at me for a moment. "Yeah, you've changed.

Something about the way you look. Not older, just different." That's right, brother, "different," but older; it's okay, you could have said it, because, baby, I earned it.

I turned away then, for the last time, and slept the rest of the way to Nice.

"Veuillez attacher votre ceinture de sûreté, et ne pas . . ."—please fasten . . . "We will be arriving in Nice in approximately fifteen minutes; the local time is three-thirty-five and the temperature is 78 degrees Fahrenheit. Thank you for flying Pan American. We hope you have enjoyed your flight, and wish you a pleasant stay in Nice. If you wish to make reservations for the trip home, please see our ticket agent in the main lobby of the terminal building. Thank you and good-bye. . . . Mesdames et messieurs, nous allons atterrir à Nice dans. . . . Merci et au revoir."

The plane came to a bumpy stop on the runway and taxied in toward the terminal building, stopping just far enough away to allow a gangway to be rolled up next to the aircraft. I came down the stairs and looked around. No sign of Gordon. And then I remembered customs. La douane. He would be waiting on the other side. I felt surprisingly calm, only a little irritated that I hadn't at least had time to comb my hair properly before landing. I had slept till the last minute and had had to do all possible repairs from my seat. I felt rumpled; it had been a long trip.

The douanier looked North African, and stamped my passport and bags without a second glance. American passport. Abracadabra, like magic. They hate your guts, but at least they don't rip your luggage apart. Not like in the States.

"So long, Lillian . . . see you 'round." My friend from across the aisle. Still no Gordon. Maybe he had been delayed by traffic, maybe. But what if? . . . Oh not something else. Oh please, Lord, don't do this to me. You can't hate me this much. . . . No, oh no . . . and as I began to panic I looked up and there he was. Taller than I had remembered, thinner, his beard looked fuller, his eyes bluer in the tanned face. He stood looking uncertain, as though he wasn't sure he ought to come and get me after all. All the last months stood between us, the story of it in his eyes, just as I knew it was in mine. We just went on standing there.

"Watch your step, madame, it's a very big step. Watch your step, sir." There were two steep steps down from the customs area, and a guard was warning arriving tourists. You're right, it's a very big step monsieur. And Tom's words rang in my ears: "Be brave, Gill. Don't settle for halfway. . . ." I stepped down, slowly, carefully, deliberately, looking down at the steps to be sure of my footing. Always look to be sure of your footing. Look at those steps . . . one . . . two . . . and I was at his side.

He continued to look down at me for an endless moment, doubtful, as though he didn't dare believe. He pulled me to him, slowly, holding me gently in his arms.

"I'm back," I whispered into his shoulder.

He closed his eyes then and pulled me closer. "Now I know. I thought I'd lost you too." After a moment we faced each other again, all our years reflected in our eyes, the people we had been, the people we had loved, the people we had lost in different ways . . . his wife . . . my husband . . . Juanita . . . Greg . . . Chris . . . they stood around us, and watched us go, hand in hand, going home.